ARCHWAY OF
TEARS

David Conroy

Brewin Books

First published by Brewin Books Ltd
Studley, Warwickshire B80 7LG
in 2001

ISBN 1-85858-184-2

British Library Cataloguing in Publication Data
A Catalogue record for this book is available from the British Library.

Printed and Bound by
Heron Press, Kings Norton,
Birmingham

To Fred and all those less known,
who shone through the darkness.

About The Author

David Conroy was brought up in London and Essex. He left
home in 1961 and worked as an apprentice mine surveyor
at collieries in South Yorkshire until 1965, when he became
an M.P.'s constituency agent. In 1972 he left politics to run
his own businesses; first a partnership in a window
business, and then his own fibreglass moulding business.
The business was sold in 1987, and he has since worked as
a management / sales consultant.

His interest in the social history of Birmingham was
triggered by the discovery and tracing of a half-brother who
was born in Dudley Road Infirmary.

He is married with one daughter and lives in Fareham,
Hampshire.

Part One

Devon

1

He sat alone at the small circular table, a slightly shabby, hunched, greying figure. He cleaned his old clay pipe noisily in the ashtray, attracting a few glances from the several other regulars in the bar. He studiously judged the level of the beer in his tankard, then slowly read again the now dog-eared reply he had received from the Salvation Army.

"Our unit in Birmingham has contacted all known associates of Winifred Norah Pow, but they have obtained no knowledge of her whereabouts after September 28th 1922. On that date, in the company of two other women, one unknown, and one Dora Coote, who also left the Birmingham area shortly afterwards, she without authority removed her son from the care of the local authority. As both Winifred Norah Pow and her son were a charge on the parish rates, the city authorities are most unlikely to pursue them."

He looked up at the North Devon Journal calendar by the bar. March 18th, 1923. Exactly five years to the day since his wife Bessie had been laid to rest in Trinity churchyard.

Since that day he had become a prisoner of the past in his own home. All its other occupants, Maria, George, Barbara and now Winnie's child had arrived there after events that he had never wished upon himself or those around him.

It was as though the ground had never healed over Bessie's grave.

Some malign spirit seemed to drive up the never-ending family feuds that sent him into the "Rose and Crown" most evenings.

The warmth from the fire combined with the congenial hum in the bar to turn his eyes into pebbles. Two regulars on bar stools nudged each other as they saw his head roll to one side, as it often did at this time of night.

"Old Philosopher Pow's off in his dreams again, then," commented Peter Ridd.

In his mind Frederick could see them all there those five years ago. They were waiting for the vicar to lead them to her graveside.

The soft, steady rain ceased as they emerged from Trinity Church and followed the bearers the short distance to the plot in the Sanders family's area of the graveyard which was to be the last resting place of Bessie Pow, beloved wife of Frederick, and mother of Eva, Fred, Elizabeth, Kate, Jack, Lorna, Winnie and Leah.

As the vicar, Mr Every, began the final rites, Frederick's veined and reddened eyes gazed blankly at those around him.

He caught sight of the gaunt, spectral figure of Frank Sanders, Bessie's older brother who had tried so hard to prevent their wedding those thirty-five long years ago. The years between had not been kind to Frank. He held slightly back, like a bird of prey, his eyes searing into Frederick's as they met for a second, his tight, slightly trembling blue lips uttering an unspoken accusation.

Frederick's mind would not accept blame for his wife Bessie's early death. People in the Borough - mostly the Sanders' and their cronies, had put it around Barnstaple that her passing at only fifty-four was the result of the almost endless child-rearing, plus the strain of living with his uncertain income and temper. This, it was said, had caused her strength to finally drain and lose its fight with the consumption that had hovered for so long.

But then the Sanders' would say that. In his mind, his marriage to Bessie Sanders had been a step towards restoring him and his family to his appropriate social position. This, so the family lore said, had been lost by his father being born in the wrong order to inherit the share of the family fortune. Careful research would have led to the uncomfortable discovery that his grandfather, "Gentleman John" Pow had managed to spend most of his allocation of the modest family wealth on his extravagant lifestyle. Not that the Sanders themselves were nobility; they were 'trade", as Frederick would teasingly point out to his wife in their early courting days. Bessie would invariably retort with her family's claim that the Pows were descendants of Scots mercenaries who had become horse thieves on the moors. Frederick could not deny that the Sanders were well respected in Barnstaple as hard businessmen. Owning all the boats on the River Taw was not a feat achieved entirely by kindness. Added to this were their many other business interests in the Borough and their record of civic service. This made them influential and dangerous people to cross.

Quarrelsome as they were as a family, they had all been aghast when they learned of shy young Bessie's affection for the ambitious young man that she had encountered whilst helping her cantankerous father collect the rents from tumbledown Sanders Row. Right to the time of their wedding the young couple had received nothing but outright hostility from the Sanders family.

Over the intervening years the Sanders' malice had become a kind of acrid residue. It was not served regularly, but was available for use at every opportunity to take the sweetness from the happiness of this stubborn young woman and surplus son of a rakish family who earned his living as a plumber.

His five surviving daughters were all there, fanned around the wound in the earth. Eva, her dark coat slightly shabby, looking older than her thirty-two years. She had been their firstborn in 1885. An ember of warmth smouldered in his grieving heart as he recalled the day of her christening, all those years ago. The church at Combe Martin had been full. His status as plumber, *master* plumber, in their adopted village, had been established by the time of Eva's birth. His education at the public school at West Buckland had given him the ability to converse with his social superiors in a way given to few of his fellow tradesmen. Many of his fellow villagers had been present to celebrate Eva's christening. He had smiled graciously at them, particularly those who had taken advantage of his greater learning to ask his advice and help. It was only later, after the fiasco of his purchase of the house at Sunnyside, that he had discovered their true feelings about him. Any one of them could have told him that the house was built over one of the tunnels from the old silver mines, and was bound to subside. The sting of their treachery had been too much for his pride. The grins, the averted gazes, the guffaws. Yes, they had shown him that he was no cleverer than they. They were unworthy of him, and as soon as the opportunity presented itself, he, Bessie, and their two sons and six daughters had left the ungrateful village in 1904 to go to Fremington and work for the Bourchier Wreys on their estate.

By that time Eva was a comely, if heavy-featured teenager. He had been flattered to learn that she was the subject of attention by the younger son of one of the Bourchier Wreys' aristocratic neighbours, the Chichesters. When Eva fell pregnant, his initial horror had turned to a sly hope that young Chichester might feel obligated to make an honest woman of Eva. However, his dreams of continuing the restoration of the Pow family to their status as members of the county set had been dealt a mortal blow by the interview with Sir Bouchier's agent that had followed. Langhorn had actually laughed in his nervous, horsy way when Frederick had made a tenuous enquiry about a betrothal. It was *inconceivable* that a marriage could be considered. Frederick and his family were most fortunate that the Chichesters felt a responsibility to help Eva. Frederick had nodded sagely as Langhorn reminded him that it was *always* the girl's responsibility to refuse. Young bucks could not be blamed, he agreed without persuasion. Langhorn had then laid out Frederick and Eva's future in the form of a series of factual statements.

Eva must stay indoors until her time came closer. She must then go away from the area to have the child. If it lived, the child would be brought up by Pow and Bessie, as she was still of child-bearing age. Chichester would pay for the upbringing of the child until she left school at the earliest legal age of twelve and could earn her keep. Sir Bourchier's brother, the rector, would arrange for the payments to be forwarded. As soon as Eva recovered from the birth, she would go to Taunton, where Sir Bourchier had arranged employment for her in the station refreshment rooms through his friendship with a director of the Great Western Railway. Eva would still be close enough to Barnstaple to visit the child from time to time should she choose to do so, but never at any time was she to try to contact the Chichesters. Should she do so, the payments would at once stop. These arrangements would continue for the time that Pow was employed on the estate. He was sure that Pow would realise that what Sir Bourchier had arranged was the best solution, and generous in the unfortunate circumstances.

Frederick had controlled his stirring temper as this upstart of an agent had described his own future as a tied employee, and the exile of his first-born daughter as the actions of a benefactor. He had confined himself to requesting Langhorn to pass on his sincere thanks to Sir Bourchier. He had derived malicious satisfaction from the agent's obvious attempts to decide whether Frederick's ingratiating tone meant that he was indulging in the sarcasm for which he had a reputation.

Frederick had bided his time. He had no real choice. He had a wife and family to keep.

After Eva, Bessie had crowned their marriage the following year by producing Fred, his eldest son. Two years later, Elizabeth had followed, then two years on again, Kate had arrived in 1890. The two girls had been chalk and cheese.

Elizabeth was fine-boned with a skin like marble. You knew when she was displeased, but when she smiled, which was frequently, she seemed to light up the whole of the room that she was in. She had a natural grace and sweetness of nature. Her only handicap was a weakness to minor ailments, which her doting parents indulged. She was growing into one of the beauties of the area, and knew it.

Kate, however, was not one of the area's outstanding beauties, either in looks or temper.

"You're all arms and legs, Kate," her parents would joke, while Elizabeth grinned demurely.

Unnoticed and unvalued by her parents, Kate had grown up in the half-light of Elizabeth's shadow. She had discovered quite early that contrived bad behaviour made it impossible for them to ignore her, however much they wanted to. Over the years this had developed into an irresistible compulsion to mischief and spitefulness.

Where Elizabeth had settled well in her modest position in the drapery shop, Kate had gone from place to place, losing jobs when either her temper or her trouble-making caused her dismissal. Then the War had come along, and her parents had literally marched her down to the recruiting office.

Frederick blinked as the watery sun pushed some frail rays through the clearing filter of cloud, flickering on Eva's daughter, Vera. She was sixteen now. Stiff chinned, eyes staring through him. She was conspicuously standing with the younger girls, as far as possible from her mother; both victims of Eva's sister Kate's mischief.

His gaze turned to Kate herself. Even in her army uniform, she looked ungainly. At least the War had given them the opportunity to get her out of the house. They could thank the Kaiser for that. An RSM. God help them all. Still, with all their children, they were bound to make one mistake, he ruminated.

His younger son Jack was standing straight-backed, immaculate as always in his naval uniform. His fiancée, Alice Cowler, stood by his side, arm in arm with her narrow-eyed mother. He wished Jack and Alice all God's gifts, but did not relish the prospect of Ethel Cowler as a sister-in-law.

Bessie had wept as he had never seen her when she had fallen pregnant for Jack, six years after Kate's difficult birth. Frederick reddened as he recalled again her sobbing voice, berating him as though he had been guilty of some crime. He had told her. It hadn't been his fault if the bloody doctor had been wrong when he had told her that she would not conceive again. He had told her, all right. He had his rights as a husband. She had got over it. Women always did. Got over it four times to produce first Jack, then Lorna, Winnie and Leah.

Jack was their star. He had more than fulfilled their faith in him since he had won his scholarship to West Buckland school. Studious, conscientious and compliant, he would go far in his chosen Navy career. Officer material, they said. The investment in Jack's education and necessary uniforms and extras had proved well worth the not inconsiderable cost. This was greater than Frederick knew, and Bessie had prayed every time that she found the money requested by the school bursar that time would allow her to repay the unknowing lender.

Jack's letters home were immaculate. Beautifully written, they were composed like musical pieces. Jack came home during his leaves and proved a helpful and obedient young chap. He wasn't overgood with his three younger sisters and was uncomfortable with their teasing. But Frederick could sympathise with that. Girls weren't much use, anyway.

Lorna, Winnie and even Leah would have taken exception to those uncharitable thoughts.

Lorna was now nineteen, and was a strangely serious girl for her age. She had a calm assertiveness, even authority, in her manner. Whilst at home, she had realised without being told that her mother needed additional help. Apart from her own efforts, she also organised her less responsible younger sisters.

He remembered the day the previous year when Lorna had announced to her astonished parents that she had decided to leave her job at Uncle Art's dairy, and go to Birmingham to work in the munitions business. It was pointless to argue. Lorna never acted without careful consideration. She explained that she had spoken to several other respectable girls locally who were in Birmingham, or had sisters already up there, before deciding on this course. The pay was excellent - quite out of scale with the local Devon rural economy. The only concession to her parents, which she had not fought, was that she would live at St. Brigid's Hostel for Catholic Working Girls in the Deritend district of the city. This was run by Father John Lopes, who was known to Frederick's friend, Father Le Haye. The priest had been insistent that in a city awash with all manner of itinerant war workers and recovering soldiers, including some from the Empire, this hostel was one of the few places where moral welfare was guaranteed. The priest lowered his voice to repeat to Frederick and his wife his Midlands colleague's opinion that the earnings of the girls gave them dangerous notions of independence.

These warnings had been unnecessary in Lorna's case. Lorna had had a daily reminder of the perils of men at the tea table at home every day when Vera sat down. She needed no convincing of her moral responsibilities. It would have been a brave man, war or no war, who would have considered trying to storm Lorna's defences.

The younger girls, Winnie and Leah, stood reverently together with Vera. Winnie was holding tiny Barbara's hand, his late daughter Elizabeth's child. He looked again at little Barbara, with her heart-shaped face. Her widowed father, John Beer, was standing, shoulders sloped, in his typical slovenly posture. Something about Beer's appearance always made Frederick uncharacteristically aggressive. Beer was a man he could have hit, and not regretted it. Frederick could forgive Beer the failure of his marriage with Elizabeth. He knew in his heart that Elizabeth had always been too pretty for her own good. What he could not take was that Beer showed no concern for Barbara's upbringing. He would not stand idly by while a member of his family was passed round Beer's feckless family like a surplus farm animal. His chin stiffened as he raised his eyes to salute the mythical Pow family banner.

His gaze caught the plump form of his youngest, Leah. She was an unenthusiastic girl, and had not reacted well to her work at the dairy as she was junior to Vera, who had been there a year longer. Still, at least it had got her out from under Bessie's feet during the day.

Vera plainly considered the dairy a temporary sojourn before her marriage to an appropriate member of the gentry. Kate had received quite a slapping from her enraged mother some months before for telling Vera the details of her parentage. In fact, Kate had failed to cause Vera the distress she intended, as Vera was quite flattered. She certainly wasn't surprised to learn that her father was "gentry". Her mother Eva, however, had become an object of contempt to Vera, which caused her great pain.

Winnie was his greatest problem. She had grown up strong-minded and wilful, constantly seeking her parents attention, like a plant struggling for the daylight. Behind Winnie's insubordination lay the inner unhappiness of being the "middle" girl. For all that she could recall of her seventeen years her mother had been busy with another distraction, usually the simpering Leah. Her father paid no more attention to her than the other girls, and Lorna bossed her about. Always, she was being extolled to be more like Lorna. Lorna the responsible, Lorna the help to her ailing mother, Lorna the bloody great.

Her confrontational attitude had spilled over into her schoolwork. Throughout her later school life, the reports were consistent. Academic she was not, but she had a naturally outgoing personality. She would organise the children's games, and the teachers admired her energy, noisy and overenthusiastic though her efforts could sometimes become. When things went her way, she was a charming girl. The trouble started when things went wrong. The usual punishments did not seem to have the desired effect on her. She would go into black moods of sullen wilfulness. Considerable determination was required by the exasperated teacher to make her conform. More often than not, the teacher would grow weary of the conflict and Winnie would celebrate a triumph.

The one person who exercised any real influence over Winnie was his eldest son, Fred. If Jack's letters were like classical music, Fred's were more like a very loud, happy, slightly out-of-tune brass band. His letters came from ports all over the earth. The strange stamps on the envelopes were the signal for the excitement to start. The girls would pester their father until he opened the letter and read it to them at the table. They all loved Fred, but no-one loved him as much as Winnie. She would wait until the formal letter reading was finished. Then she would retrieve the letter and go to her room with it, reading it over and over again. She kept all Fred's letters. During grey afternoons she would retire to the bedroom that she shared with Leah. Leah would often try to follow, but Winnie would shoo her out and lay on the bed trying to imagine the fantastic places and exciting events that Fred described.

It was even worse when he came home on leave. His parents kept the dates from his young sisters to avoid the build up of hysteria in the house.

When Winnie went to sleep, her last thoughts would often go out far across the oceans to her adored brother, protector and confidante.

Fred was the only one of their children who was absent. He was away again on the "Valiant". He worried about Fred sometimes. During his last leave he had seemed more moody and quick-tempered. He had also complained about headaches. His father presumed that it was the after effects of the Battle of Jutland, where Fred had been a gunner. Perhaps he needed a wife now. He was coming up to thirty-two.

His cousins Art and Carrie had closed their dairy for the day to attend.

Fat Jack, his brother from Anchor Woods, stood reverently with his bony wife Lena. He remembered the first time that he had taken his new bride to meet them. They had served cream tea in their garden. It always seemed like summer when he thought of Jack and Lena's tidy little farm.

His neighbour and brother-in-law John Goss was standing, head bowed. It was through him that he had finally been able to leave the Bourchier Wrey estate to establish his present business as a plumber in Barnstaple. He had been lucky that John Goss had heard that the adjacent semi-detached cottage, 2 Laurel Cottages, was available for rent. The house was spacious, with three good-sized bedrooms and a large attic room. When he had met Mrs. Bowman of Croyde, who owned the house, he had shrewdly also rented a small building, formerly a hay store, down the alley at the side of the cottages. From this unpromising location he had built up his local trade during the five years since the move from the estate cottage at Fremington. As news of his skill spread, he had become comfortably busy. In addition to the undoubted quality and ingenuity of his work, his customers enjoyed his educated conversation, and dry humour.

John Goss and his toothy wife had brought their son William with them. William looked very smart in his new naval uniform. He noticed Winnie eyeing William, and frowned.

Nurse Newcombe, who had been such a comfort to them in the final, uneven contest with the consumption, was, surprisingly, sobbing.

Consumption was on the certificate, but everyone present knew that Bessie had lost the will to fight after the death of their beloved daughter Elizabeth the previous autumn.

The vicar finished the short service and looked expectantly at Frederick. For an instant Frederick hesitated, uttering a silent goodbye to his wife. Just for that private moment they were holding hands together as they swayed along on the top of the old stage coach that had taken them on their way to their honeymoon at Lynton. Bessie's laughter rang down the years to him as the wind blew through her lush copper hair.

The vicar pursed his lips into a half-smile as he gently touched Frederick's arm. Bessie's laughter faded as the capricious wind flicked his moist eyes. He returned to the matter in hand, and, after a final glance downwards, turned and led the party off. The gathering breeze chased them on the short walk past the church and the little school. The gravel crunched quietly under their feet as they moved in a body down the path. Behind them a single bell tolled forlornly from the stern tower of Trinity Church. He paused as he passed through the outer gate into Trinity Street, causing the throng behind him to bunch. He stared back a challenge at the dark church. The tired bell lumbered a muffled final peal, then sank into echoing silence. "Gone" rang heavily through his heart, sinking and fading to the edges of his mind. Now he knew. He would see Bessie no more in his world.

The hissing of the kettles gave up the contest with the murmurs of the arriving mourners. The overcoats and hats were shed and left on the worn hallstand.

The mourners made their way into the front room where the fire greeted them, and settled in the motley array of chairs. The awkward whispers ceased as Frederick entered the room. As he thanked them, contrived conversations began again, vainly trying to cut into the unspoken grief in the heavy air.

Lorna now took centre stage. The sturdy young woman skillfully took them away from the scene of sorrow with a description of the munitions factory in Birmingham where she was now working. She lowered her commanding voice to reveal that amongst the thousands of products manufactured, some were so secret that management had forbidden all staff to discuss them with anybody outside the business - even family. If she disobeyed, she could be charged with treason, she confided in her impressed listeners. Her eyes caught Winnie's bored and supercilious expression, and her cheeks coloured.

The effects of the family schisms could be seen in the room, where Eva and her daughter Vera passed amongst the guests with tea and cakes, studiously avoiding any contact other than the absolutely necessary. Leah appeared from time to time, as usual trailing after someone and requiring constant direction. She offered the little cakes that Eva had made to Winnie, who balanced one on her knee as she sat on the stool next to young William Goss's chair. She looked quite comical, holding her tea cup so delicately in an action she felt was very sophisticated for her seventeen years.

She was a really attractive girl now. Not quite her sister Elizabeth's delicate bonework, lacking in Elizabeth's natural grace of movement, but a face full of character. The deeply emotional eyes set in the well-sculpted face, the rosebud lips, the firm chin, betraying that edge of stubbornness identified at the school in past times. Loveable, flirtatious, infuriating; even during his late wife's last fight, when she had been gasping for breath, Bessie had made him promise not under any circumstances to allow Winnie to go to Birmingham like Lorna. He could hear her now, and felt her squeeze his hand with her weakening grip.

As he surveyed the slowly emptying room, it occurred to him that the truce which had been in force during the last stages of Bessie's illness would now dissolve. The making of the necessary arrangements for Bessie's funeral had concealed the future from him. Without Bessie, or Lorna to exercise control as her mother's proxy, he had no real idea how he would cope with the running of the house.

2

The daffodils on Bessie's grave faded, and the spring of 1918, warm but wet, gave way to the longer days of the summer.

The momentous national events, the regular exhortations by the local great and good in promotion of the war effort, now met with a stony-eyed response from most of the inhabitants of Barnstaple. It was not that they were unpatriotic. Far from it. They were just tired.

Many homes had received the dreaded telegram. It was like a kind of silent, wasting disease that stretched its white, bony hands across the whole community. At first, the pain was acute. The first few families affected received much sympathy and press coverage. But as the war progressed, it was only when a rash of casualties occurred that comment was aroused. To the parents and loved ones of those serving, although few would ever have admitted it, there was an element of the lifeboat about it. If all could not be saved then, pray God, save mine.

Bessie had been particularly enthusiastic about the War, and this zeal was evident in the photograph that Frederick now gazed at from his fireside chair. She looked unflinchingly at the camera, her resolution outlined in the firm set of her chin and mouth.

His own, slightly more questioning expression, formed the features of the seated figure on the left of the photograph. Between them were their uniformed sons, Jack, handsome and intelligent, seated by his father, and the standing Fred, straight as ever, hand an hip, eyes plum at the camera. A family at war.

As the War had dragged on, Jack had become quieter and more maudlin each time he returned on leave. On his last leave Jack had seemed so depressed that his father had enquired aggressively what the matter was with him. Eventually Jack had blurted out the secret nightmare that had been eating him from inside for the past two years or more.

He was back in the cave with the Anzac. On the rocks, a little above their sheltered position, was the crudely fashioned gallows. Hanging upside down from two ropes, his splayed legs slowly rotating, was the British soldier. His head gyrated helplessly. Before they had time to consider any other movement, their eyes became transfixed by the blade of a large axe raised by a Turkish woman. Beneath her ragged headscarf and above her yashmak they caught sight of her eyes as she brought the axe crashing down between Joe's legs and split his body completely in two with one sweep. The eyes did not even display hatred; just indifference. The other women standing in the semicircle let out shrieks of pleasure. Realising at once that this momentary relaxation gave them a split second to escape, the Anzac had roughly pulled Jack away down the hill as he crudely exhorted him to run for his life. Jack still heard the jeers and wails of derision from the hill. At the time he had hardly noticed the shots that were fired behind them more in contempt than intention. They had stumbled, fallen, got up and run on. They had cursed the sheeting rain as they had run into it on the way up. Now they blessed it as they vanished into it's curtain.

He had returned, a trembling wreck, to the Anzac's tent. Stunned and frozen, he had agreed the more acceptable report of the events suggested by the Anzac. As the Anzac had told him, leaving a man hanging and running away from a bunch of women wouldn't sound too good; could even be a court martial job.

He had then returned to his ship. Jack's report was accepted without reservation by the officer. He would be considered for commendation. A commendation! For running away.

All these months the horror had remained sealed up until these last weeks when, like some river rising ever higher against its banks, it had poured forth in the form of these nightly dreams.

Frederick had looked into his son's face with genuine compassion. He realised, as he had never before, that he had regarded Jack as little more than a flag-bearer for the Pow family pride. Everyone knew that Jack was naturally conscientious and dutiful. What no-one had taken into account was that he was also intelligent and sensitive. The sharp edge of war had pierced his mind.

Whilst Jack would always remain a loyal and obedient servant of the Royal Navy, his experience that day on the icy hillside in Gallipoli took away for the rest of his life any romantic notions of war that he had read of in boys books or been told at school. Just the retelling of the story had had the same effect on Frederick. He suspected that many other homes in the Borough had experienced the same transition. Rather like bright fireworks going out one by one, leaving only a stunted glow.

The trains of casualties; the men who had come home from the front but nobody ever saw, and who were kept in the old Isolation Hospital. Those who could no longer speak, or, worst of all, those poisoned and blinded by that infernal gas.

Sometimes his work took him into the Infirmary, part of which was now used for war casualties. He hadn't noticed much enthusiasm amongst the inmates there.

On the other hand, Lorna had written in one of her recent letters that the Dudley Road Infirmary in Birmingham was being used for the treatment of British and Empire casualties from as far afield as New Zealand, Canada, Australia and South Africa. She said how cheerful and uncomplaining the men were when she visited them with Father Lopes from the hostel. Well, there it was.

Maybe he was just reflecting a general fatigue with the War.

Fred's leaves were altogether different affairs from Jack's. They were waiting for Fred now. The girls were cooking the evening meal. The squabbling and cackling was even worse than usual as they waited for the knock on the door.

Fred surprised them by undoing the catch on the front door and appearing under the arch leading into the living room.

The girls reacted in their different, predictable ways. Vera, delicate, offered her hand, almost haughty in her manner. Leah, looking even stumpier than he remembered, reluctantly broke into the preparations for the food that she obviously looked forward to, to give him a sloppy kiss on the cheek. Winnie, her face alight with joy unseen since her mother's passing, threw herself at him, and engulfed him in a passionate embrace.

The meal followed the same pattern. Winnie, excited and garrulous, dominated the conversation. On and on she went, louder and louder. The dramas at Maples, where she worked, the fortune teller at the "Push for Victory" fete last month who had told her that she would travel far and have many adventures, a pig that had got loose, all the world was reflected in the excitement in her glowing eyes. She was just waiting now for Welsh cousin Ivy to arrive from Uncle Jack and Aunt Lena's, where she was staying. Even Frederick gave up trying to enter the conversation in the end.

The meal was over. Fred had made no arrangements for the evening; it always seemed strange to have options available, instead of the ordered life of the navy. His father was anxious to continue giving Fred his opinions of the world's worries, but Fred was becoming a little tired of this excess of philosophy. Strangely for a man who spent most of his life in cramped ships or shore accommodation, he began to feel claustrophobic.

Winnie had been studying him, and sensed an opportunity.

She asked her father with untypical politeness whether she could take Fred for a walk. Her father and the other girls saw this as a device to avoid her share of the clearing up, but decided that there would be no peace if the request was refused, and wearily Frederick agreed.

Winnie pulled Fred to the front door by her hand, and led him triumphantly into the street. Although the sun had set it was fairly light, and he could not help being carried along by her infectious enthusiasm. She swung his hand or skipped ahead of him, pointing out various landmarks, and giving him vivid descriptions of some of the more colourful local characters.

The nearby pottery and its adjacent cottages were taken in. She interrupted the tour to supervise a game of skipping that wasn't in her opinion being carried out properly. She lowered her voice as they passed Ceramic Terrace to warn him to beware of "Woodbine Winnie", who was definitely a witch. He nodded solemnly as she gripped his hand tighter.

She introduced him proudly to the smiling shopkeeper's wife in the sweetshop. Fortified by her favourite humbugs she took him through to the Rock Park, where she seemed to know a lot of the other young people. She glared menacingly at the several older females who seemed to take an interest in *her* Fred.

Partly to save him from the attention of these sirens, she took him back through Trinity Churchyard. She reverently pointed out the area nearest the church entrance. This was where the Sanders family had their plots reserved. There was a plan somewhere that would unite them in their last resting places as firmly as when they had been alive. The blackbirds sang their evensong as brother and sister stared silently together at their mother's grave, still raw and unhealed in the earth.

"You will always love me, Fred, won't you?" she asked him without warning.

"Gracious me, of course, Wyn. You know you're my favourite."

"But will I always be, Fred? On mother's grave."

"No-one will ever replace you. Now stop being so serious."

They passed the tiny schoolroom where she had finished the last few weeks of her largely wasted education, and then, turning left out of the church path, they were back at the head of Trinity Street again. The darkness had closed in now, and most of the children had gone in. Fred had had a long day. He never understood why travelling tired you out like it did.

He persuaded Winnie that he did not want any more tours just now, and they went back into the house. Winnie tugged his hand through the dimly lit hall of the cottage to the kitchen, unwilling to relinquish her grasp on him until the last possible moment.

In her excitement, she had forgotten that Ivy was coming over for the evening.

Ivy wished her a slightly abrupt "Good evening" in her lilting Welsh accent. She tilted her head slightly to indicate that she had been less than thrilled with the entertainment provided by Leah and Vera while she waited. Winnie ignored these asides and proudly introduced Fred.

"Hello, Fred, nice to meet you," said Ivy, with a lot more enthusiasm than she had shown greeting Winnie.

"Oh, hello, Ivy," Fred stumbled out, to Winnie's amusement. But she saw something else, something she didn't expect. Fred was smiling, and a blush was spreading across Ivy's cheeks.

"Time for us to go for our walk, then, Ivy," said Winnie crisply to her cousin.

Frederick seemed to be asleep by the fire. Fred motioned Winnie not to awaken him. He whispered goodnight to Vera, who was quietly sewing, and Leah, who barely returned his salutation as she had just been told by Winnie that she could not tag along with Ivy and herself.

Winnie kissed Fred goodnight with all the vigour of the screen heroines, but a certain lack of technique, he noticed. She made certain that Ivy had a good view.

Fred retreated upstairs to his room. He took off his shoes and felt the relief. When he turned in, he found himself thinking that he might fancy a run over to Anchor Woods to see Fat Jack and Aunt Lena the next day. Perhaps he would see Ivy, too. Just perhaps.

His father was not actually fast asleep. He was in a strange half-world that had developed in the weeks since Bessie's passing. He was physically tired most nights. The loss of his wife had led him to concentrate more on his work. Not just because Bessie's small private income had gone with her. He now realised as never in her lifetime how dependant he had been on her to run their home.

Winnie was still the main source of his problems. Vera could irritate with her assumed airs and graces; Leah could try his patience with her simpering, but Winnie indulged in deliberate provocation. She seemed to hate to see him recovering from his grief. She would goad him with hints about her evening activities. She would return far into the night, taking care that he heard her arrival and exaggerated behaviour. She did little housework. If he complained, she had more than once accused him of killing her mother with work, and informed him that she did not intend to follow. He had shouted at her, even threatened her with the flat of his hand. Now he just ignored her; that didn't work either. Worse, if anything. Bloody girl. Probably just her age.

He spent more time away from the house, usually adjourning to the "Rose and Crown," to avoid the mental fatigue of Laurel Cottages, and Winnie in particular.

He had had enough of it.

He had hesitated for long enough, but a man could only take so much. He would now put into action his plan to resolve his difficulties at Laurel Cottages.

* * * * * *

The Rose & Crown was a well run house.

The landlord, John England, had been beyond the reach of the various extensions of conscription, and, anyway, he had done his service in the earlier South African conflict. He was a good listener and the sanguine expression beneath his full, if greying, head of hair concealed an observant nature and alert mind. He tended to keep to the smoking room end of the long bar, leaving his wife and the barmaid to deal with the public bar. His well-built and still straight body would gravitate that way if he heard the noise level rising. Trouble was unusual and normally the miscreants would be visitors who would be dealt with by the locals without his involvement. His one real concern was to retire with "clean sheet".

He enjoyed his banter and general conversation with the regulars in the smoking room. He didn't dislike the occupants of the public; they just bored him with their repetitive conversation subjects. The smoking room contained a more varied section of the local men. They included small tradesmen, and some foremen who sought to emphasise the sometimes slight difference in status between themselves and the occupants of the public. Before the recent restrictions in pub opening hours, children had frequently come in with their fathers, especially at week-ends. If a skittles match was on, they might earn themselves enough for a ginger beer by retrieving the balls or re-setting the skittles. Women were not numerous during the week, but appeared in their finery on Saturday nights, accompanied by their husbands, of course. The only single female visitors were the few widows. The opening restrictions, combined with the debilitating effect of the conflict, had changed people. The carefree days had gone. A weight was on everyone.

As he ruminated on these thoughts, his eyes focused amiably on one of his favourite regulars, Frederick Pow, the philosopher plumber.

Sitting in his usual place by the window, his back against the dark-stained wood of the bench seat, Pow had been coming to the Rose and Crown for several years. His little plumbing business seemed to prosper. Pow had become more regular in his visits during the three months or so since his wife's death. Until recently, he had entertained his friends with his strongly-held and well expressed views on the war, local history and religion. Within the past few weeks, though, an extraordinary development had taken place. He was seldom to be seen out of the company of Maria Woolway.

As a widower, Pow was of course a free man. The pub regulars had indulged in some light-hearted conjecture on where this ageing but still handsome man in his fifties might cast his net. But nobody would have bet on Maria. She looked nearer sixty than fifty, did not look overclean, and dressed as though she was a walking advert for jumble sales. Despite judicious enquiries, nobody seemed to know much about her background. Her clipped, musical voice revealed her Welsh origins. She was apparently a widow. She liked to drink her gin, usually keeping her own company. She had been part of the furniture until her new role as the chosen escort of Philosopher Pow. The bar speculated on what they could talk about during the long evenings that they spent together. If the eavesdropping became too obvious, Pow and Maria played their trump card. They conversed in Welsh.

John England eyed them speculatively as he casually sorted the glasses behind the bar. He wondered why Maria, normally smiling and jovial, looked so serious as Frederick spoke earnestly to her.

Maria was looking serious because she was considering Frederick's offer. During the six weeks or so of her relationship with Pow, Maria had enjoyed being the object of mystery and speculation. But she had not expected this.

He had been quite honest with her. His plan was to "rescue" his grand-daughter Barbara Beer, and he knew he could not cope with bringing her up by himself. That would be Maria's job, as well as the general housekeeping. In return, she and her adopted son George got a roof over their heads. If she wished it, he would marry her.

Her hand was not a strong one, given her age, prospects for work and the dire state of her finances. He had not enquired, and she had thought it unnecessary to enlighten him on the detail of all that.

Her mind blinked frantically through the gin-haze. She nibbled her bottom lip as she sought to grasp the words to gain the time she craved.

The setting sun painted up the colour in Pow's animated face, heightening the tension-raised lines and furrows. Frederick had plainly worked out his scheme carefully, and she could not fault the logic of it. Her compliance was plainly not just a necessary practical requirement. It was now a matter of pride. Men could always be depended upon to do two things, in her long experience. Firstly, to be guided by their physical needs, and secondly, to be almost totally oblivious to the effects of their self-motivated actions on those around them, especially where their pride was threatened.

She broached the subject thoughtfully. If she asked the right questions, surely he would realise that she needed time to decide such a serious matter.

Her mind raced as she attempted to sound calm.

"Do your daughters know about this?" she enquired.

From this enquiry Frederick immediately concluded that she had decided to come. Her hopes evaporated as she saw his facial muscles relax.

"No, not a clue, but if I make a decision, they'll just have to accept it."

That's just great, she thought. Three months after your mother dies, in walks a stranger and you have to accept her because your father tells you to.

"They'll just bloody well have to. I pay the rent and I won't stand any nonsense from them. That's for sure." he confidently continued.

A wave of sympathy washed over her as she pictured his three girls in her mind's eye, sitting in their home. They would have noticed the changes in their father's behaviour - "not a clue!" like Hell. She wondered what was missing from men's brains - and this was one of the better men.

She had to raise the stakes.

"Look, Frederick" she carefully commenced, "I can't just turn up one day. These girls are at a difficult age. Prepare the ground a bit. Tell them that you cannot manage without a live-in housekeeper or explain about Barbara or..."

She stopped abruptly in mid-sentence. Whether it was the effects of the several drinks that he had consumed, the tension caused by the seriousness of the proposition, a perceived sense of rejection or just his naturally quick temper she was not sure. But when he spoke, it was in an ill-controlled hiss.

"I know my family, Maria," he erroneously but dogmatically asserted. "They need firmness. They were used to discipline from their mother. That's what's lacking now. They will do what I tell them. If you want to come, bloody well say so, or else forget it."

So there it was. Further reasoning was plainly impossible. Like a fairground whirligig, round her mind raced George, the hovel where she lived, the comfortable looking house in Trinity Street and looking after this seven-year old Barbara. It was no contest really. She didn't know why she was hesitating. She turned to him and smiled.

"All right, Frederick, I'll come tomorrow."

He returned her smile, and placed his palm over her high-veined hand. It just proved once again that you only had to be firm with women to get them to do what you wanted.

Maria clumsily sucked at her empty gin glass. Frederick's face resumed it's genial expression as he politely enquired whether she would like a refill.

It was almost as though nothing had happened.

A lead-filled fear gathered deep in her stomach. She screwed her eyes up and sought guidance from the barometer on the nicotine-stained wall above Pow's vacant seat.

"Change," she read.

3

Winnie gazed round the room with that expression that she knew her father hated so much; a carefully contrived mixture of malice and resentment. Her facial expression hardened as she surveyed the panorama of overflowing ashtrays, children's toys and plates of unfinished food that had invaded the living room during the two months since Maria, George and Barbara had descended on 2 Laurel Cottages. Amongst the wreckage her mother stared sternly out from the sepia photograph on the mantlepiece. Winnie's lip trembled as she felt the gnawing inside her. She averted her gaze.

Vera had gone, too - a loss much easier to bear. She could go and pretend to be royalty with her mother now. It must have been a difficult choice for Vera to decide between the stepmother she hated and the mother she hated.

A malevolent smile crept across Winnie's face as she thought about this, and her cupidic lips widened. Her father detected this facial movement and glanced suspiciously in her direction. She widened the smile into a grotesque grin and then gave him one of her stony stares, like those she had seen the heroines give the Sir Jaspers in the movies at the Picture House. And, to her, her father was Sir Jasper, with his greying moustache and recently grown sideburns.

They had never really been close to each other. From her earliest days she had realised that his interests lay with his sons, and that the girls were only judged and tolerated for their usefulness and obedience. It had to be said that she did not score well on either count. She had genuinely tried to help in the running of the house after her mother's death. But she was not the natural organiser that Lorna was, and she had not that air of authority that Lorna achieved without apparent effort. The age gap between her and Vera and Leah was too small for her to be able to control them, and after an initial attempt she had given up.

Instead of bringing them closer, the sense of loss and grief that both Winnie and her father felt in their different ways sharpened the hostility between them. In his mind Frederick sometimes harboured a feeling that Bessie's illness and early death had resulted from some lack of support and worry caused by her daughters. Winnie stood proxy for them all. In her mind, she held him responsible for her mother's death, and blamed him for surviving her.

At seventeen she was unable to rationalise these thoughts, and Frederick could not be bothered to. The unperceived opportunity for mutual love, support and kindness quickly festered into suspicion, blame, indifference and now, in the person of Maria, outright focused hatred on Winnie's part.

She remembered getting home from Maples that July day to find that Maria, George and Barbara had arrived.

It had been a warm, pleasant evening and she had felt quite happy as she had crossed into Litchdon Street. She sang as she passed the almshouses and waved to the three inhabitants taking the sun in the yard. Their old, lined faces had brightened as they returned her cheerful, infectious smile.

She had realised that something was wrong before she got to the front door of the cottage. Her father had been waiting for her, and opened the door for her, almost a first. She had heard young voices, and frowned as she walked purposefully through the hall and into the large living room. She had almost fainted when she had seen the outlandish figure sitting in her mother's chair. It wore a greasy-looking bonnet, a large ragged black shawl and beneath it, and worst of all, her mother's pinafore.

She looked into the puffed, overblown face beneath the bonnet. She saw the surprisingly alert brown eyes returning her scorn with a mixture of apprehension, determination and defiance.

She looked suddenly downwards to where a grubby looking boy of about three was proferring his hand, his pale face looking up trustingly and hopefully at her. It flashed across her mind to hit him squarely across the face, but the figure in the chair instinctively straightened slightly from the slumped posture in a clear act of warning. She had next caught sight of Leah nursing a petite girl of about seven. She frowned as she recognised Barbara. Leah's face had been stained with tears, and contrasted to the tight expression on Vera's face next to her on the sofa, which Winnie had referred to rudely but accurately as Vera's "trying to fart" look.

It had been like something out of a bad dream. She presumed that her dumbstruck father was responsible, and turned to glare at him. His face showed a mixture of tension and surprise at the strong emotional reactions that the execution of his plan had created. Fleetingly, an appeal for understanding, help even, crossed his face, but it aroused only her contempt. She ran past him into the passageway, up the stairs and into the room that she shared with Leah. She slammed the bedroom door and threw herself theatrically onto the bed.

She had lain there for nearly two hours before Leah had clumped up the stairs to join her. Winnie had refused her tea and a further request from her father to join them. Leah had eaten her tea, of course. Nothing kept Leah from her food. But she had had to ignore Leah's treason in order to obtain from her the information that she so desperately desired.

Leah had told her in her stumbling, matter of fact way that the old woman in the chair was called Maria. Father had told them that she was their new mother. She had come to live with them to keep the house and look after Barbara, who father had collected from the Beers that morning. The little boy was George, who Maria had saved from going into an orphanage.

Winnie had felt a burning hostility flicker through her numbed senses. She stared briefly at the hapless messenger before sobbing herself to sleep.

For a short time after their arrival, she had entertained hopes that if she and Leah were obnoxious enough, they might drive Maria and her brat away. This had not lasted long as Leah could not be persuaded to take part in a long campaign of dumb insolence. Also, they could not direct hatred at Barbara, who was a very sweet-natured child, and plainly as bewildered as they were about the events.

Eva had heard about the arrivals the following day. She had gone to Laurel Cottages straight after work the same evening. Father had, unusually, shown Eva into the front parlour. Winnie could hear the tone of her father's voice. He was animated at times, but mostly he used the lowered patronising speaking voice that was normally enough to deal with the placid Eva. As the discussion progressed his voice was raised more often. She sensed with satisfaction that Eva was showing unusual resistance. Vera had joined Eva and her father in the hallowed front parlour and the discussions had become quieter. A little later Vera had rejoined them in the living room and announced to Leah and Winnie triumphantly that she was leaving that very night, as her mother had stated that she would not allow her to stay one more night in such a house where a man and a woman shared the same room and were not legally married.

The words had hit Winnie like arrowshafts. Naively she had assumed that Maria and the children were in Kate's old room, which she herself had had designs on. Now, the full truth lay before her, stark and ugly. She felt like having a bath.

Her bitter feelings for her father deepened and widened, and became a vengeful crusade. Anxious as she was to get away, she now felt another emotion. She felt a deep, burning desire to heap revenge and humiliation on her father. But how?

Immature as she was in some ways, she was not without a maturing guile. As she lay in bed that night listening to the rhythmic beat of Leah's sleep-laden breaths, she turned over several ideas.

She had no strong allies in the house, but she wondered whether Fred, Jack or even Lorna could be enlisted. Jack would hear soon enough through the Cowlers, if father didn't tell him. She might be able to rouse Lorna, but Fred was surely her best bet. He was due home on leave soon. She imagined him coming home in his naval uniform and driving out these invaders just as he had driven away those cannibals in the South Seas all those years ago.

She composed a letter to him in her mind, revised it leaving out some of the more graphic words, revised it again and finally fell into an uneasy sleep. She had been careful to appeal to Fred's protective nature and had included several references to their late mother. She showed skill beyond her seventeen years with her oblique inferences of ill-treatment, and left the detail to ferment in Fred's imagination during the long hours at sea. She included some of her girlish codes and signs, and suggested that they met at Maples before he went to the cottage. He could send his reply back to William Goss next door for her. William could be trusted with her life, as he was one of the several young men who were desperately in love with her.

The following day, July 17th, the letter went furtively into the post. For the first few days following, a wave of optimism calmed the deep, swirling hatred. But as July turned to August, and Fred did not appear or write, the tide of bile began to rise.

As she left Maples to go home the Friday before the August bank holiday, she was astounded to see Fred striding purposefully along the opposite pavement towards the Long Bridge. She called after him and had to run to overcome his formidable naval step. He stopped and turned to put his arms around her. Involuntarily she broke into a hysterical sobbing, and her saviour held her closer to him. She felt all the love and gentleness flowing from his strong arms. It intoxicated her, and she felt that if he did not hold her up, she would swoon there on the pavement.

"Come on now, my Wyn," he said quietly. He turned her, and they walked hand in hand into the nearby tea house where he had taken her before on his several war-time leaves.

They faced each other over the little square table. She adjusted her eyes and dried her face. How grown-up she was starting to look, but he could see the excited child in her eyes.

"What is it, Fred, what's happened?" she enquired in an unsteady voice.

"I went to the cottage straight off the train. When I got to the cottage that old woman was there with young Barbara and that boy. Then father appeared from his work. The reason I didn't reply to your letter is that I wanted to see it for myself. I already knew some of it, because a while back I wrote from the "Valiant" and asked Uncle Jack and Aunt Lena if I could stay with them. They wrote back and told me about Maria. The reason I wanted to stay with them is that cousin Ivy is there, staying too, on her annual holiday from Wales. Ivy and I have been writing for about six months now, and old Jack and Lena knows that. They said I could only stay if we were properly engaged, so I've been into Darke's and bought this with what was left. Ivy hasn't seen it yet."

He showed her a small, elegant diamond and sapphire ring.

She stared blankly. The ring glittered and the rays burned shafts into her mind as she struggled to absorb what he had just said.

"What d'you mean, what was left?"

"Well, you know that I've been sending money back for years and years from my naval pay for them to bank for me for when I finish."

She nodded sagely, although it was news to her.

"Well, it seems that it was put to other uses. I've asked them before on leaves to see the book but you know what I'm like with money. They'd just make some excuse; say it was at the bank or something, and I'd forget it. But this time I needed it for me and Ivy. When he realised that I wasn't going to listen to the excuses the old man got funny and fetched the book. When I looked in it, there isn't half a hundred left. First I thought he'd spent it on that old trollop, and didn't I go. Turns out they used it to kit Jack out at West Buckland so he was a proper credit to the Pow family. Now I need it for me and Ivy, it's not there. He don't care, because he don't want Ivy and me to marry anyway, us being cousins. Fine one he is to talk about suitable wives. I told him straight our dear mother would turn in her grave if she could see that pig-hole that used to be her home now. I couldn't stay, Wyn. I was choked. I think I'd have done something to him."

Silently, stealthily, tears rolled down her cheek again. First she had lost her mother, now the brother that she loved so much was leaving her too. He would not be there alongside her with his cutlass to drive the hated Maria out of Laurel Cottages. She felt the last sunny glow of her childhood dim and die. She looked again at his face, and he had aged. He was a man of thirty-two.

"But Fred, what will you do?" she falteringly asked him through her saucer eyes. "Ivy lives in Wales. Oh Fred, I'll never see you again." She dissolved into silent sobbing as the waitress deposited the teapot and cups, giving Fred a slightly hostile, quizzical look as she did so. Fred's natural straightforwardness of nature made him as ill-equipped at dealing with delicate matters of the heart as his father. Now he was becoming embarrassed at this public show of emotion by his sister. He silently cursed her for the fluke of having observed him from Maples. He decided to try and jolly her out of her mode.

"Now you should be glad for us," he said as cheerfully as he could. "Your favourite brother and your cousin. Aren't you going to wish us well?" He smiled tentatively, his deep blue eyes reflecting that boyish honesty that she had always found irresistible. She returned his smile. They were back at Fremington again for one last moment, listening to mother singing in the kitchen.

"Anyway, it won't be for a while. I don't know when I'm coming out. They're talking about sending us off to Russia."

They finished their tea in near silence. She observed his face closely, drinking in the handsome features as though she might never have another chance. Their conversation became contrived and stilted. When she confirmed that she had finished, Fred hailed the waitress. He tried not to seem too relieved as he paid the girl, who was still eyeing him suspiciously. He felt his face colouring.

They emerged into the warm sunlight. She mechanically wished him well, and Ivy too. She accepted Fred's invitation to go to tea with them at Jack and Lena's on Bank Holiday Monday. Although it was plainly an afterthought, she reasoned that by then the lead weight in her heart would have lifted enough for her to face them both.

As he kissed her goodbye he noticed that tears were rolling down her cheeks again, although she was still smiling. He would never understand women.

She had derived pleasure from her father and Maria's irritation when she had refused to tell them her destination Bank Holiday afternoon. They had retaliated clumsily by saying that she couldn't take Leah. She didn't want to anyway.

She had cycled happily up Sticklepath Hill by herself. The weather was kind, and she felt the warmth, and absence of conflict, when Lena welcomed her, and took her through to the garden, where she joined Fred and Ivy. She felt a small stabbing pang as she saw their hands entwined as they sat together on the old cane sofa.

She voiced great enthusiasm when Ivy showed her the ring, now gracing her third finger. The enthusiasm was not reflected in her eyes, and Ivy returned her neutral look with caution. As the day developed, Winnie noticed Ivy looking at her with even less warmth, particularly when Fred was paying her attention in his innocent, affectionate way.

Fred was in great humour, quite oblivious to the tight atmosphere around him. He told them of his latest adventures, and described some of his more colourful shipmates.

They sat down with Fat Jack and Lena and enjoyed their generous helping of cream tea. Their laughter rang out over Jack and Lena's fields of grazing cattle, past the railway, over the heads of the happy, waving passengers on their way back from the beach at Instow, and finished up amongst the keen-eyed gulls wheeling high above the silently spreading River Taw.

Had the Gods listened closely, they would have noticed that Winnie laughed less than the others. Try as she may, she could not escape her uncharitable thoughts that Ivy was taking Fred away when she needed him so much. It was as much as she could do to be civil as a writhing worm of jealousy wriggled and grew inside her. He couldn't really love Ivy. It was father's fault. It was a reaction of some sort to the situation at Laurel Cottages. She was terrified that her facade of forced goodwill would crumble. She thought she felt Ivy watching her with more and more hostility. Even Fred seemed to be becoming edgy and uncomfortable. Finally, she excused herself and made her way steadily home.

The late afternoon sun soaked into her back, but neither this nor the cheerful crowds making their way home from the Junction station over Long Bridge could warm away the cold hollowness inside her. Their collective happiness emphasised her despair. Her legs propelled her mechanically back to the cottage. She brushed her way past the unknowing Leah and retreated to her room, there to lay unstill as the faces of Fred, Ivy, her father and Maria formed a pageant to mock her.

The summer of 1918 drifted aimlessly on into a dank premature autumn. The trees wept silently with Winnie as she returned to her routine.

Finally the wretched War finished, and the whole Borough celebrated. Winnie joined in, of course. She helped to decorate Maples, and with her circle of friends she contrived to appear happy in the evenings. She watched the crowds milling around The Square and felt that everyone she saw must be happier than her. Her whole life now twisted itself around her desire to get even with those she held responsible for her unhappiness. Her father, the principal sinner, had now added Fred's engagement and absence to his long list of crimes.

Her boyfriends were a weapon that she employed. She had noticed the pride on her father's face when she had brought the likes of Geoff Jewell, the mayor's son, and Ronnie Darke to the house when her mother had been alive. She herself had felt proud, but truth to tell her affections were not very deep, and their main attraction was in the prestige that it brought her from being seen in their company. She could control them easily enough. They tried, in their genteel fumbling way, but she could cope. Now, she had announced that she could not bring decent boys back, with the house in the state it was now.

She stayed out later, made sure that near neighbours saw her when she was pretending, not always very convincingly, to be the worse for drink, or enjoying supposedly illicit encounters in the Rock Park. But none of it seemed to have any effect. The reaction was not, as she hoped, conflict and strife, but steadfast indifference. She began slowly to realise that *her father didn't care*.

The late autumn and pre-Christmas winter brought a new factor into her life. William Goss. It had started first as yet another scheme to annoy; to spend her time next door instead of at her own home. But she had always liked William, and had not taken that into account when she started her visits as a calculated insult to her father.

He had not made much of a sailor and had been sent home early. They had walked out together and spent ages talking about things that she could not remember later. The days at work had seemed more bearable as she looked forward to seeing him. They held hands. She had nearly suffocated him with one of her screen heroine's kisses. He seemed able to cope with her mood swings, and he saw through her extravagant postures. Most of all, she felt comfortable with him. She had no need to put on airs and graces for wealthy parents who viewed her with screwed up eyes. They joked, they laughed.

He would never come to much, of course. She would never be the wife of a mayor of Barnstaple or sit next to chain-wearers at dinner, like she'd seen in some of the photos of Ronnie and Geoff's parents. But with William, it didn't seem to matter. When he got over his nagging cough that he had brought home from the ship, and when he felt stronger, he would get a job with his dad at the pottery down the road. In the meantime he was always there.

Before she realised what was happening, and in spite of her wish to be miserable, she began to be glad to wake up again in the mornings. She sometimes secretly watched her father struggling in the bleak gloom of his little yard. Several times she felt herself wishing to take the few short steps down the passage to him, but still a mixture of pain and obstinacy kept her feet on the pavement of Trinity Street. Even in the house she scaled down to an armed truce. She never spoke to Maria unless she had to, but she took Barbara out and about. Even the persistent George, who seemed to think that her most savage scowl was a form of encouragement, tagged along, hanging onto her hand, and looking up and grinning all over his grubby face.

Had the vicar not said that the way to love and happiness was to be as a child? But she was not a child, and every day and week she saw more of William and she wanted him.

The teasing stopped and now all she wished for as Christmas approached was for him to get well. Sometimes he showed signs of improvement, but she cared enough for him now to notice the yellow-brown rings round his eyes, and his increasing tiredness. His father did not believe in the doctor. He had worked at the pottery, man and boy, all these years, and he had never had use for a doctor. If he didn't feel too good, he went down to Ceramic Terrace for one of old Woodbine Winnie's special remedies. That did the trick, although sometimes it was wise to make sure that the little room outside was free after you took them. She begged John Goss to fetch the doctor, but he would have none of it, and she was no diplomat.

Finally the 22nd December came, and she was eighteen. William was well enough to walk with her to Victoria Road station to meet Lorna, who was returning from Birmingham. The three of them walked back through the slush, dancing and laughing their way around the frozen puddles. Lorna was trying with difficulty to maintain her customary reserve with these two happy young fools.

They made their way to Eva's lodgings, where Lorna was staying. Eva was not home, but even

Vera seemed cheerful by her standards. What next.

Winnie and William looked a couple without a care in the world as they walked hand-in-hand back towards the brooding black silhouette of the spire of Trinity Church. The snow flakes began to fall again, and they cupped their hands to try to catch them as they fell.

She felt the hair on the nape of her neck rising. She looked up to see the dark ragged figure of the pauper in his old coat cowering against the blowing snow flurries as he led the "workhouse donkey" from Alexandra Road Workhouse with his little cart loaded with firewood. She shivered as William gave the aged figure a halfpenny, and was rewarded with a toothless smile as the man paused and raised his cap.

Children were playing happily in the street. Those that knew Winnie and William came round to tease them. It was all good natured, and could have graced a Christmas card. Suddenly, Winnie looked forward to 1919.

4

Winnie's optimism for the new year rapidly drained.

She had held her assistants job at Maples for three years. When the shop reopened after Christmas, she found herself looking at her colleagues more critically. Mr Naylor, with his wing collar and mild pretensions, May and Jennie with their "mustn't grumble" acceptance of their uneventful lives. There was nothing she could really complain about. They were not unpleasant or moody. They were just the same every day.

She felt her patience thinning with the customers. Most had celebrated the Christmas of 1918 with a sense of relief rather than joy. For those with husbands or sons still away in uniform the celebration sharpened the frustration and disappointment of continued separation.

Her own Christmas had been tolerable only because of her closeness to William. She had spent most of the day with him and his parents in their front room, trying not to notice the chill and the slightly musty smell. The Goss's financial caution extended to the small lumps of coal sprinkled in the fire, which gradually won its asthmatic battle for life.

The dampness and smoke from the fire aggravated William's cough, but he seemed cheerful and soon picked up. She wanted to go for a walk with him, just the two of them, but his mother persuaded them that William was not strong enough. So they stayed in and talked, and played card games.

She felt happy enough there, but as the day wore on, she found Mr Goss's cough, with William's occasional barks, increasingly irritating. By mid-afternoon Mr Goss was asleep in his armchair after his jug of ale. William seemed tired and lifeless. Mrs. Goss began her reminiscences - always a hazard, but especially so on this day.

As the the sky darkened, she looked at Mrs. Goss's mouth. Her teeth reminded her of a mincing device. The words emerging in such quantity were minced into undiluted, repetitive tedium. Winnie appeared to listen, but had long since ceased to hear.

Then it struck her. Mrs. Goss bored her. Her pinch-penny, self-opinionated husband bored her. Worse, far far worse, she realised that she was becoming bored with William, his continual illness, the fact that he never took them anywhere, his lack of money or ambition.

When she retired to bed that Christmas night, she told herself that she had just had a bad day, and that it would all seem different tomorrow. But a small nagging feeling in the corner of her mind told her otherwise.

The winter dragged dolefully on. In the shop the talk was all about when the men would return; why it was all taking so long; the shortages of this and that; how much more things cost when you finally obtained them.

Almost apologetically at first, the spring began to timidly drive back the endless darkness. It was chilly instead of bleakly cold in the mornings. The rain grew softer and warmer, then disappeared as suddenly spring cast off her coats and April blazed unseasonally, confusing the flowers and leading to speculation that the gas from the War had caused climatic change.

The few surviving flowers in the dark, neglected patch in front of 2 Laurel Cottages soon gave up their unequal struggle. The lack of interest in the little front garden, combined with the uncontrolled efforts of George and the other children had created a bare replica of the Flanders mud which rapidly hardened to resemble brown plasticine. Discarded toys, even twisted pieces of metal littered what had been only months earlier a neat little array of country flowers round a tiny lawn. A little bit of Fremington brought to the Borough. Mother had cared for it so much, small as it was. The front garden had one thing going for it. It did not mislead the few strangers who knocked at the door of the cottage as to the condition of the interior.

The first thing to strike the senses as the door creaked wearily open was the pungent smell. A combination of odours from uncleared meal plates, tobacco smoke and stale beer combined to produce this cocktail. A permanent film of dust seemed to coat everything on view. It was unwise to delve. Insects quietly invaded the larder; at night rodents could be heard fearlessly making provision for their families in the cosy nooks under the skirting boards.

Then there was Maria herself. Winnie was convinced that she could smell her physically. Certainly she never saw her bath. The food that Maria cooked seemed tainted to her, and as the months passed Winnie found it increasingly difficult to maintain her appetite.

She spent as little time in the house as possible. It depressed her to see her father sitting there in his chair with his inevitable clay pipe. He seemed to have lost the will to even try to govern his divided household now. He had become a hypochondriac. Bottles of all shapes containing quack remedies, mostly recommended by Maria, were all around the house. Small boxes of pills abounded. She was not interested enough to ask what ailments these pills and potions were supposed to be curing. She doubted if he knew himself.

Leah clung remorselessly to her, complaining about almost everything, but not loudly enough to arouse Maria's ire. She suspected that Leah was a good deal less critical when she wasn't there.

George got everywhere, spreading his grubby hands unchecked.

The one barrier to complete alienation was Barbara. The child had a lovely nature, and an outgoing unreserved kindness unusual in the Pow dynasty. Winnie loved her dearly, and would miss her greatly when the day came, as she was determined it would, for her to leave this wretched hovel.

Most evenings she spent with William. They stayed in and talked or, as the evenings became warmer, they would walk through the churchyard and down to the Rock Gardens. Those who saw them together saw a polite, slightly shabby, frail-looking young man with his attractive, concerned girlfriend. Whatever simmered privately in her mind, this was her public appearance, and the stability it suggested suited her purposes.

Less public were the evenings that she spent out, but not with William. It was not William's fault that he was unwell, and could not afford to take her out, but as the unusual fiery spring burnt into her, she knew that there had to be more to life than the walks in the Rock Gardens.

She had never lost contact completely with her friends in the higher circles of Barnstaple's social life. She would meet them in town. From there they would usually be driven fairly swiftly out of the Borough by their escorts in motor cars to another private rendezvous where a social event of some sort was being staged. The journey would transform her from the sullen, discontented shop assistant with an unhappy home into whoever she chose to be. Her smart set friends tolerated her as she amused them so much with her bubbly sense of fun, and cameos of characters to fascinate the under-occupied colonial servicemen from Canada, Australia or South Africa who were based around. With her cocktail glass containing sophisticated mixtures, and black cigarette holder held carefully between first and second finger, many an empire soldier returned home to relate his encounter with the daughter of the Earl and Countess of Fremington. Well, yes, they were certain. She had even gestured regally towards the family pile as they had whisked through Fremington in the car. She sometimes bought a few Woodbines with the small pay rise that she had concealed from her father and Maria. When she chose, these were offered to favoured female friends. It suited her independent nature to have her own financial means. She felt that it gave her an advantage over almost all of the girls in her set, who did not work, and therefore had no income of their own.

As spring bade its spectacular farewell to the west of England, her clandestine evenings became longer and more frequent.

The feeling of escape from the misery of her home life, combined with the effects of the extravagant cocktails, encouraged walks outside into the balmy night air. Sometimes it was with one of her known friends; more often with someone that she had met only that evening. The early crude fumblings with her more juvenile admirers were replaced by more deeply sensuous and sophisticated encounters in which she played a full part. More times than she cared to remember the heady combination of her awakened feelings, the cocktails and the magic of the distant music drifting across the starlit fields found her allowing her escorts to do the thing that her mother had warned her of so sternly - "don't finish up like Eva, Winnie." But mother was not here now. Indeed, sometimes the drink told her that had her mother not left her when she needed her most, she would not need to get away from the depressing mess that she now lived in. So in a way, her mother was to blame. If forbidden love was the price for the best of Barnstaple's male population to find her attractive, she would pay it. At least for those few snatched moments she felt wanted, and not just an intruder in her own home. And what the hell. All the modern girls in the set did it - or said they did. As one of the Canadian servicemen had said, life wasn't a bloody dress rehearsal.

Sometimes during the actual meaningless and unfeeling act, she felt herself wishing that her father could see her. Her escorts, panting through to their rapid conclusion, were perplexed by her sudden mood swings from unrestrained enthusiasm to floods of tears. All part of the blue-blooded temperament, no doubt.

The morning after the first time she had nearly died of fear. She avoided eye contact with everyone at the cottage, especially Maria. At Maples, she snapped and withdrew. She felt sure that her face would betray her. She covertly looked in the small mirror to see if a hideous boil was developing, or something similar.

But now she just brazened the mornings out. Nobody cared enough at home to question her, anyway.

She hardly noticed when she had a very light period in June. She had always been irregular, and even more so since the constant emotional turmoil at home. Anyway, the other girls had told her that there was no risk as long as the man took it out before it came, which she was sure, or thought she was, that they had always done. And she had never fallen into the trap of doing it standing up - Vera Gregory had warned her about that one.

Other matters were on her mind now. On July 21st her brother Jack was to marry Alice Cowler at Fremington Church. She had been flattered and a little surprised when she had been chosen to be Alice's bridesmaid. The event itself was a focus of happiness for the family, all the more so after the sadness of the previous year.

Of course, no wedding preparations would be complete without rows and disagreements, and the Pows and the Cowlers were ideal material for this. Maria tactfully avoided the most obvious one by stating that she would stay at Laurel Cottages to look after George. Father protested mildly, but they both knew that he was relieved.

Most hard to bear for Winnie was the absence of Fred. He had claimed that he could not leave the Cwmtillery Mine in South Wales, where he was training as a winder. She knew that the real reason was to avoid conflict on the day caused by the bitterness that he harboured. Ivy's parents had insisted that they could not marry until he went onto full earnings at the pit. This delaying tactic would have been impossible if he had still had his savings. Winnie wrote a pleading letter, but he remained unmoved.

This just left the more day to day problems, like keeping Tom Prust, Alice's maternal grandfather, sober, and persuading him to keep his hands off of the ladies, and also persuading Alice's mother not to moan loudly about the cost of everything.

Winnie realised that a dilemma faced her regarding William. She had progressively seen less and less of him as the spring had given way to summer. He seemed dull and shabby beside her more exciting and sophisticated friends, and his endless ill health was a bore. On the other hand, he plainly loved her and she did miss him when she hadn't seen him for any period of time. She never had to pretend with William. He might only be a habit, as her friend Kate Hardy had rather dismissively described their relationship, but he was a nice habit. All the rest of it was the icing which, sweet as it tasted, had no substance without William. There were times when, after some emotional battering at the cottage, or some hair-raising night out, she wondered why she did not just settle down with William.

As she attended the dress fitting with Alice she speculated whether she would be the next one looking into the mirror in a bridal dress. No-one need know about her other life. Her friends would be just as anxious to keep their moonlight forays secret.

Yes, that's what she would do. She had had her fling. No harm done. No tracks left, as her friend Kate would say. No-one would blame her anyway, if they ever got to know. She would certainly never blame herself. She was only human, and it wasn't her fault that mother had died, and her father had brought an old slut like Maria into her home.

She studied Alice's wide, innocent smile as she turned happily from side to side in front of the long mirror. She made up her mind there and then. Alice would be her maid of honour. She would speak to William as soon as this wedding was out of the way. There was no reason why not. She was Alice's age. And above all it would get her away from her father and Maria.

She felt an unfamiliar feeling of contentment flow through her body, easing the tension in her face and relaxing her. She almost felt tired. She could see ahead now, for the first time since mother's death. She would sleep well tonight.

Monday the 21st July approached with a crescendo of excitement. Kate had arrived the Saturday before and found lodgings near to Eva. Since her release by the armed forces she had persuaded Eva to put her in for a job on the railway. Eva had been reluctant, as the Great Western had enough problems with strikes and whatever else without Kate joining them, but finally she had given in under the barrage and Kate had now started at Exeter.

When Winnie arrived at Eva's rooms that Saturday evening she found Kate already there. Eva met her in the hallway. She looked flustered and explained in hushed tones that Kate had started off on best behaviour, but as she had felt more certain of her ground she had become her usual coarse, vulgar self, much to her own and Vera's disgust. Winnie found it hard to suppress her amusement, but made sympathetic noises before following Eva into her tiny sitting room / kitchen. Sure enough, Kate was holding forth in some detail about, apparently, the various latrines employed by the army, and the methods by which they had to be adapted for females; or, if, as happened, the men were less than co-operative, the measures a resourceful girl took. Winnie found this quite entertaining, but just as funny was the contrast between Kate's ruddy face, and Vera's pallid statue-like expression during Kate's frequent loud guffaws. She detected Eva's uneasy discomfort, and strove to convey an appropriate amount of sympathetic disapproval, without Kate noticing.

An idea formed in her mind. Her July period had shown no sign of starting, and she needed to talk to someone. Kate would know all about these things, and somehow she wouldn't feel embarrassed to discuss such a personal matter with Kate.

After Eva had fussily served them all a pot of tea, the consumption of which scarcely staunched the flow of Kate's rhetoric, Winnie suggested to Kate that she would be interested to see her lodgings, and would enjoy accompanying her on the short walk. She caught Eva's expression of gratitude and relief. There was a painful moment as Kate hesitated, but she then bowed to the unspoken will of her hosts and bid her older sister and niece goodnight, vowing to return soon so that they could enjoy another evening together. Had she not had the hide of a rhino, she would have noticed the slight over-enthusiasm in their voices as they wished her and Winnie goodnight.

Once out in the fresh air, Winnie wondered how she would approach this delicate matter without the whole of the Borough hearing Kate's responses. Rather than taking them out of their way to the Rock Park, which was a bit close to home, she suggested that they go onto the platform of the Town station and have a look at Eva's refreshment room, although it was closed. They walked briskly towards the station, Kate dealing abruptly with the few males commenting on either her or Winnie's appearance and possible availability.

Kate told the bemused clerk in the booking office where he could put his platform tickets, as she was an employee of the Great Western, a far superior organisation to his own. They sat on a bench looking towards the emptying River Taw. Winnie found herself hesitating more and more as she tried to make small talk. Suddenly Kate turned her ample frame and looked her straight in the face.

"Well, come on," she started, in her jerky loud voice. "What is it that you have brought me to this hole to discuss?"

Winnie explained falteringly about her friend who had missed her period, and asked her for advice.

"Happened all the time in the bloody Army," snorted Kate, adding several particularly gruesome examples of abortion attempts that had gone wrong. "Tell your friend to try codiene bio-morphine. If that fails tell her to go to old Poll Shambrook at Fremington. If she can't afford Poll Shambrook it'll have to be knitting needles. Christ, I remember one girl....."

Winnie heard no more as she fainted. When she refocused her eyes again Kate was looking intently at her and smiling kindly.

"Have you any other symptoms?" She asked softly.

Winnie realised that her fairly obvious attempt at deception was over. She suddenly felt relaxed, and poured out to Kate the causes of her anxieties. It seemed natural to tell Kate such intimate things. Kate interrupted now and again to clarify some detail, but otherwise listened with sympathetic nods and grunts.

After a short silence Kate pronounced that the chances were that the cause was nerves, but to write to her at once if the morning sickness or other symptoms appeared. She knew people in the services who still owed her favours. The relief relaxed Winnie, and she unselfconsciously cried on

Kate's shoulder. Kate wasn't so bad. At least she was approachable.

They made their way to Kate's dingy lodging house, then Winnie began her slow walk back to Trinity Street. She felt weary now, and tried to remember if Kate had listed that as a symptom. Depression reached out and grasped her in its cold arms. In the middle of Jack and Alice's joy, here she was again with something to get her down. She always seemed to be in someone else's dark shadow. Her face built up the required level of defiant indifference by the time she opened the door to 2 Laurel Cottages. That soon changed when her father told her that William had been taken into the North Devon Infirmary under observation as his breathing had become worse, and he was feverish.

For Winnie, Sunday July 20th was a day of unease and anxiety.

She presented herself at the Infirmary in the morning, only to be told that she would not be allowed to see William as she was not family. Nothing would move the Sister, and Winnie was left to storm back home, having been dismissed with a cursory wave of the hand. As she pounded past the church she glanced at the gaunt spire and wondered if William's illness was a judgement.

At Laurel Cottages, the children were trying on their outfits for the great day. Momentarily she forgot her troubles and helped Maria with the few alterations needed. In spite of herself, Barbara's innocent smiles melted her anger. However, the battle lines were redrawn for Sunday lunch. Her ire was particularly near the surface today, and she watched Maria eat with malign interest. The clumsy, unfamiliar use of the utensils, the shovel-like movements into the mouth which never closed completely. The downy facial hair which added to her uncouth appearance. The actions reminded her of a film that she had recently seen at the cinema in which a mad professor trained a monkey to see if he could become human. Although the monkey copied the movements, the whole procedure looked contrived and artificial. It was these day to day observations of Maria that developed Winnie's resentment into outright contempt.

She retreated upstairs and tried on the bridesmaid's outfit. The dress fitted well. Eva had skillfully adapted the sleeves and the collar sat down properly now. The black hat with its pink underlining added a touch of sophistication.

She wondered if somehow this outfit might betray her "other life" which she was now so anxious to put behind her. She adjusted the angle of the rim of the hat to a less jaunty position. She heard George start to grizzle downstairs, and this made up her mind to try the theory out by walking to Eva's. There were one or two extra questions that she had thought of for Kate, if the chance presented itself.

She smiled serenely at the admiring glances that her outfit brought from some of the others on the sunlit streets in their Sunday best. When Eva opened her door Winnie thought her face showed uneasiness. She even appeared to hesitate before quickly ushering her into the sitting room. Here Eva was preoccupied with last minute refinements to Vera's dress that the wheedling girl demanded. In response to Winnie's enquiry, her harassed sister informed her that Kate had called, but had left a few minutes before for an unstated destination. She sensed from Vera's cutting looks that her presence was not required as it was holding up the urgent work on her outfit. Winnie made her excuses and silently cursed Vera and her simpering mother as she walked round to Kate's, only to find an empty room. To salvage some use from her fruitless morning, on the way back she called on the Gosses, and was told that William was unchanged.

She entered the house thoughtfully. She looked into the sitting room and there they were each side of the fire hearth. As she entered, they stopped talking and looked down. Frederick volunteered a sort of grunt. He followed this with a sharp, penetrating look, then just as quickly turned away to resume his customary slumped posture in his threadbare chair. Winnie frowned as she turned to look at Maria. She sat sprawled in mother's chair, clumsily trying to knit over her distended stomach. She made no attempt to return Winnie's piercing stare, but Winnie could detect the suggestion of a self-satisfied smile around the creased edges of her mouth. Neither seemed to wish to engage Winnie in conversation. The silence seemed unusually deep, and she could hear the mantleshelf clock ticking relentlessly. She felt suddenly uncomfortable, and made her way moodily up the stairs.

The day of the wedding dawned with disappointing clouds.

After a chaotic breakfast, the party of Winnie, Leah and Barbara babbled noisily as they waited for the cab that Frederick had ordered. It would have been easier to go to the Square and hail one, of course, but Frederick was determined to show Trinity Street that the Pows knew how to do things properly. He allowed the cabbie to knock loudly twice to make sure that he was seen. They waved Maria and George goodbye and mounted the frail looking vehicle whilst the aged horse snorted its impatience. Then they were swaying off down the narrow street and out towards the Long Bridge. Winnie enjoyed the elevated position, and graciously acknowledged the friendly waves and expressions of goodwill from their friends and neighbours.

They arrived at Longhope, the Cowlers' cottage at Bickington and Leah jumped down and knocked on the wooden plank door. Winnie and Barbara alighted and followed her into the house. Their places in the cab were taken by Alice's father, her sullen-faced brother George and old Tom Prust, who were to proceed to the New Inn at Fremington to fortify themselves for the forthcoming event.

The time seemed to pass slowly at Longhope as the girls talked quietly and made minor adjustments to their finery. The knock on the door raised the volume to an excited chatter. Together with Mrs. Cowler they laughed as they squeezed into the little horse-drawn cab.

The sun was fighting some high cloud, and the cover was down on the cab as they moved gently off. The clear light painted the little cottages and few villas of Bickington village up like a watercolour. The local women watched them with upturned faces from their doorways as they wheeled slowly past. Mrs. Cowler took considerable pleasure in giving Winnie a detailed resumé of the various occupants, their estimated financial worth and any known or suspected indiscretions.

The girls chatted to each other as the cab rumbled along through the open countryside towards Fremington. As Winnie listened to the repetitive rolling of the wheels on the uneven road she found her mind wandering over the River Taw to Trinity. She searched vainly for William through the dark windows of the unbending stone Infirmary, then gazed down into the nearby churchyard and saw the moss and grass now edging gentle fingers around her mother's grave, to bind her firmly where she was to wait for her family.

Her flight of mind was rudely grounded by some good-natured raucous comments from some of the potters on the grass banks who were enjoying their dinner breaks in the warm sunshine. Most of the banter was directed at Winnie, who smiled and waved. Mrs. Cowler clucked in annoyance. Leah and Barbara giggled and joined vigorously in the waving. Alongside her, her face concealed by her handkerchief, Alice sat stony-faced.

Soon the centre of Fremington village came into view down the long hill. Winnie glanced left as she passed the estate cottage which for so long had been her home as a child. She remembered

Jack's uncomfortable visits home when he was a teenager at West Buckland; now he was inside the church waiting to get wed.

She smiled ruefully as they passed the proud red frontage of Fremington House basking in the sun. Mischievously, her mind sought the Earl and Countess through the shaded front windows, and she involuntarily chuckled. The cab stopped in front of the lytch gate leading to the church. Barbara got down, and smilingly passed her the bouquet of mauve sweet peas. The others followed, Alice's mother crustily brushing the dust and creases from her daughter's dress. They could hear the organ playing as they approached the open door.

Alice's pale blue dress was set off beautifully by her bouquet of pink carnations. As Winnie followed her to the door, Alice's father appeared, smiling, to link arms with his only daughter.

The organist, Mrs. Gillard, paused and then started the traditional music, and the little procession advanced towards the Vicar, Mr Dimond Hogg, and to where Jack and George Pennington, his best man, were standing. She had never seen Jack looking so smart. Not just his artificer's uniform; his whole bearing was upright and solid. The shy chrysalis of a naval student was now a man, and he looked it.

Winnie listened wistfully as the Vicar fussily performed the time-honoured rituals to transform a man and woman into a good Christian husband and wife. She could hear Tom Prust shifting in his pew alongside Alice's mother. She saw George Cowler's dark eyebrows furrowed. She caught sight of Eva and Vera dutifully listening. She wondered what Eva was thinking. Next to them Kate looked impatient as she gave Winnie a smile and an irreverent wink.

Suddenly it was all over. They moved off to sign the register in the small ante-room. Mr Cowler signed first as a witness, then Winnie's turn came. As she looked at the register, her mind went blank.

"Come on, Winnie." her father chided.

Finally she signed, Winnifred Norah Pow, giving the 'N' an extra roll to emphasise the importance of the occasion. Frederick then decided to add his illustrious signature to the document, but found that he had not room to sign his full name of Frederick Robert Jones Pow. He gave Winnie a withered look. Alice's mother started pushing in to ask where she was to sign, as if Frederick was included, she wasn't leaving without her name on the document. Sensing the Vicar's growing impatience, Frederick put his abbreviated name after Winnie's, and tersely used his thumb to indicate the space below to Emily Cowler, which she grudgingly accepted as suitable for the Cowlers.

As they left the church, Mrs. Gillard enthusiastically struck up Mendelsohn's Wedding March. They emerged smiling into the now full sunlight and, to those passing the church, the party presented an idyllic scene of family harmony. Those closely attached greeted and hugged each other, those less close exchanged cordial words and handshakes. Like a breeze that starts as a playful eddy, and then becomes naggingly cold, into Winnie's mind came the feeling that she felt eclipsed by the happy couple and their joyful halo of delirious guests. She wished Fred was with her now, and wondered whether he would be there when her turn came.

"Someone walk over your grave?" Kate enquired. "Come on, time to go and get stuck in to the drinks."

The handshakes with the Vicar over, they left him smiling and waving. He had in fact officiated at the marriage of his own daughter Florence prior to Jack and Alice, so the well-known local hazard of him following the party to the wedding breakfast was avoided.

They decanted happily from the motley collection of cabs and carts and went into the Cowlers cottage. The refreshments were covered to prevent the flies having a wedding breakfast of their own.

Mrs. Cowler vigorously directed the various operations to get the proceedings under way.

The photographer, hired at "no small cost", and who had scandalised them by charging extra to come out from Barnstaple, now attempted to assemble the party for the official photograph. Jack and Alice were centred, with Tom Prust and the bride's parents to their right. Winnie, her father and George Pennington were left. As the party settled Alice caught the smouldering eyes of her brother George. She brought him over and sat him in front of Jack, despite the entreaties about balance by the photographer.

"You'm charged plenty enough; you do as 'ee say," growled Mrs. Cowler, and he disappeared, chastised, under his black cloak. After two false alarms, the flash performed, and the stars returned to join their other guests.

The formalities were mercifully brief. The speeches, carefully rehearsed and neatly presented, were accompanied by toasts, and the cake-cutting ceremony.

The afternoon drifted by. Neighbours arrived to pay respects. Everyone seemed consumed in the pervading happiness, entering a mellow stage after the completion of the toasts. Even Winnie found herself relaxing into the atmosphere of carefree goodwill. She chatted happily with Lorna, Kate and Eva. She gently ticked off Tom Prust after his collision with her, which seemed to involve a well-directed grab at her backside.

Frederick was holding court. She noticed the respect in the listeners' faces as he set forth his forceful opinions about local and world matters. This was the father she knew as a child, not the strained and haunted figure who slumped by the fireside at Laurel Cottages now. For the first time for an age, she felt her old pride in him.

Only when Alice re-appeared in a navy blue costume and tagel hat to thank everyone as she prepared to leave, did it dawn on Winnie that this glorious day was waning. The bridal couple left in the motor taxi with cheering from the kerbside, and horns honking into the distance as they disappeared along the dusty road. Inside the house the atmosphere quietened. Neighbouring wives and mothers began to bid polite farewells to get tea for their husbands and sons returning dusty from the pottery. Winnie watched the mosquitoes playing above the water butt outside the window as the dipping sun backlit them.

As she sipped the cup of tea that Barbara had brought her, Winnie found herself listening to Lorna telling Eva and Kate all about the latest changes at the arms factory in Birmingham where she worked. Lorna did not notice that her enthusiasm was leading her into more and more detail, and her audience was losing concentration. Frederick noticed Kate starting to mimic her, and signalled that the time had come to leave the nuts and bolts of the factory to retire to the two cabs that were to deliver them back to Barnstaple.

Winnie did not want the day to end.

She bid a reluctant farewell to the Cowlers, and let Barbara proudly march the bouquet of sweet peas to the first waiting cab. They moved into their seats; she and her father facing; the less important Leah and Barbara with their backs to the driver.

The cabbie glanced round, Frederick raised an imperious hand, and they rolled steadily off into the fresher evening air. Kate, Lorna, Eva and Vera followed in their cab, and Winnie asked Frederick smilingly if he thought Lorna was still talking about the factory. He smiled back, and held her eyes in his gaze. She felt herself blushing, and looked away.

They watched the horses lazily flicking flies with their tails as the cab made its unhurried progress down Sticklepath Hill to the River Taw. Contentedly father and daughter sat in quiet togetherness, sometimes talking, or else simply taking in the last drops of happiness dripping from the day.

They waved farewells to Lorna's party as they went their separate ways at the Square and Winnie felt the darkness gathering as they rumbled down Trinity Street. They disembarked outside the house.

Winnie looked intently into Frederick's face. How could this plainly intelligent man also be so blind, stupid and insensitive?

She knew the magic of the day was over. She sensed the dark depression reaching towards her as the door of 2 Laurel Cottages began to open.

In a final defiant gesture she kissed her startled father warmly on the cheek. He stepped back slightly, partly in surprise and partly to conceal the tears forming in his eyes.

5

July 1919 ebbed quietly away, and with it, just as gently and unnoticed by the great leaders of nations, or even his native borough, went William's flickering life. The influenza epidemic, losing its vigour after months of indiscriminate slaughter of strong and weak, now had to select those like William, who had never been strong. The plague had unwitting allies in William's parents, whose stubborn refusal to involve the doctor allowed it the time it needed to overcome his frail body's unfortified defences. The end, when William's faint heartbeat simply ceased that warm early August evening, had a peaceful inevitability about it.

His parents, mercifully oblivious to their contribution to the loss of their only son, even found a form of quasi-religious reasoning in the event, arguing that William's prospects in life being reduced due to his ill health, some kind of superior intelligence had taken him now to save him further suffering.

Winnie listened to this explanation being related to Maria by her father with dismissive scorn. The funeral had been ordeal enough. The Gosses, shrewder financially than they appeared, had done well by William; everything good quality and properly done. She reflected that if they had been half as concerned about getting William medical help when he so needed it as they had been to see that all around saw that he was buried in style, he would still be there in his role as her anchor. She had visited William three times in the Infirmary. She was not a very good visitor, and had grown tired of the role quickly. Her brief dream of following Alice into blissful matrimony was now lying in Trinity Churchyard with William. Beside herself with grief as she had been when her father had told her of his passing, the truth was that she was unable to arouse any consistent emotion about William, or anyone else, at the moment. She simply felt fatigued mentally and physically. Her patience, never strong, became a bowstring. Nagging into her every day, the stubborn absence of her period symptoms made her restless and snappy.

Her publicity from the North Devon Journal report of Jack's wedding had made her a minor celebrity within her social circle for a week or so, but that had faded with the next triviality. Even the obvious escapism of partying with her scene friends did not appeal. The few times that she ventured out, she found them shallow and the conversation contrived.

Life inside 2 Laurel Cottages continued its progress into decay. As Maria stealthily drank, Frederick retreated into a philosophy that he had never totally left, namely that of a superior member of society who should not have to work manually if, indeed, he worked at all. He became more erratic with his work, and customers detected a change from amusing pretension to an altogether less agreeable combination of arrogance and indifference.

Into this unpromising scenario had come a new interest from a highly unlikely source.

Leah had appeared at Maples one afternoon with her friend Dora Smith, and Dora's father Henry.

Leah had apparently conveyed to the Smiths that Winnie would be a useful addition to the Amateur Dramatic Club. Mr Smith eyed Winnie appreciatively. Even allowing for the girl's assumed indifference, she had a mobile, expressive face and slim, tidy figure under her Maples outfit.

It did not take much persuasion for Winnie to agree to allow Henry Smith to take a detour on his walk to the little hall where the company met, and call for Winnie on the way the following evening. Although in his late forties, he was a handsome, well-dressed man. His hair showed no grey and his moustache was trimmed immaculately. His skin, though lightly lined, was that of a man who cared about his appearance.

She enjoyed their walks to and from the hall. She felt privileged as he described his plans and ambitions, and related his experiences from his own career in rep. Most of all she liked sitting with him in the hall whilst he directed the rehearsals with his clipboard. She would watch, fascinated, the different players and their reactions to each other, and to Mr Smith. Some nights he would devote his attention to general matters; other times he would concentrate on details, even down to facial expressions and speed and intonation of speech delivery.

Sometimes she would stand in for one or two of the minor characters, if the players were unavailable. She was surprised to learn how much thought had to be given to things like the positioning of the characters, arm movements, tone of voice. It wasn't just a matter of learning a few lines.

As August progressed the rehearsals began to become more disciplined. Mr Smith's control over the production became more firm, and he had less time to devote to her on a personal level. Although she had become quite competent at understudying the minor roles, she found the waiting around tedious. This affected her concentration, and her irritation began to speak through her characters.

Henry Smith had not the time to indulge her moods at this stage, and became correspondingly less patient. Some of the other members of the cast, sensing the deterioration in Smith's attitude to her from flattering young companion to irritant, turned from cliquey indifference to thinly disguised hostility in the knowledge that they were unlikely to receive his displeasure. They had seen the likes of her before.

As the opening night of the Monday of September Fair Week came closer, Mr Smith could not always call for her, as he had to be at the hall earlier for the increasingly hectic schedule. Gone, like the warm August evenings, were the intimate talks. The walks home, in gathering darkness, seemed hurried, awkward affairs now. When she sought to engage him in conversation about any of her personal matters, she sensed his lack of interest. She realised that this man, who had seemed to show an almost fatherly interest in her, was in fact only willing to give his attention to her if she shared his obsessional interest in the production. And the truth was that she didn't. The play had been a useful distraction whilst the healing process was in progress, but she had now absorbed the loss of William.

She began to miss rehearsals, preferring the less demanding pursuits that now gleamed brighter through the damp early September evenings. The beat of the jazz rhythms and the heady cocktails drowned out Laurel Cottages, William, and all the other boredom and misery. She still worried that there was no sign of her period, but she felt well in herself, and no other symptoms that Kate had described had developed. She could not spend the rest of her life at her miserable home, or sitting in a draughty hall waiting for a two minute walk on part in a two-penny halfpenny play. So if parties were offered, party she did.

The Tuesday before Fair Week, after a particularly fraught rehearsal, she walked stiffly homeward along Trinity Street with Henry Smith slightly behind her on the narrow pavement. They had hardly spoken since leaving the hall. As they passed Ceramic Terrace in the gathering gloom she noticed a gnome-like figure emerging from the dilapidated front gate of the garden to the cottage. After making futile attempts to close the gate, the man turned and started walking slowly and unevenly towards them. When his yellowed eyes engaged hers there was an unmistakable look of curiosity about them. The moment passed, and he repositioned his neck and upper body to meet Henry Smith's eyes. She was taken aback by Smith's reaction. The practised actor's face showed open surprise, recognition and embarrassment as he stammered out

"Good evening, Mr Goodrich," and received a grunt in response, as the other slowly limped away.

Before she could question him, Smith bade her a hurried goodnight.

She went quietly into the house. She looked stonily into the parlour, her indifferent expression now polished by her acting tuition. Her father was sitting in his usual position by the fireplace. He looked up towards her, whilst removing his discoloured clay pipe from his mouth. She saw him shoot a glance at Maria, who declined to engage Winnie in eye contact and continued her mending. She felt a warm draught on her back, and realised that this was coming from the front room, where a fire lay dying in the grate. She sought Frederick's eye again in vain.

She felt too apprehensive to overcome her curiosity and challenge them outright. She decided to leave them, and perhaps ask Henry Smith the following day if he knew what might bring the gnarled Mr. Goodrich to their house.

Slowly she closed the parlour door. She felt her heart beating uncomfortably as she trod the stairs heavily and deliberately. They creaked musically as she made her way up to her bedroom, where Leah slept the sleep of the good.

But Winnie did not sleep. Who the hell was this Mr Goodrich, who warranted an audience and a fire lit in the front room, a privilege seldom granted? Kate had mentioned people who could help her terminate an unwanted pregnancy. Her fertile imagination sharpened her mind to twist it into a spiralling nightmare. Vainly she struggled as Maria held her down, whilst Goodrich opened his bag of satanic instruments.

The following day being Wednesday, she left Maples at lunch time and walked thoughtfully through the ripe autumnal sunshine to the Town station, where she went to the refreshment room to have a cup of tea with Eva.

She had wondered whether to confide in Eva, in the absence of Kate, but as she listened to her eldest sister jabbering about the mundane events and good works that she made important to atone for the blight on her life, she realised that, despite Eva's situation, her constant handwringing could make her quite prudish. Indeed, listening to Eva's recital of daily events and fussing about her darling daughter Vera, she began to feel pangs of alarm that she was viewing her own future.

Almost as an afterthought, Eva enquired about the production.

If pressed, Winnie would have had to confess that she had somewhat exaggerated her part in the production when discussing it with friends and relatives. Her mind had gone into remote control listening to Eva's daily trials, and she had to employ her recently-acquired skills not to be taken by surprise "like a jockey left standing at the tape," as Henry Smith would have chided. Her mentor would have been well pleased with her vivid and well-delivered account of the latest rehearsals, and a little surprised at her description of her own importance in the proceedings. Eva listened enthralled. Others listened with interest, whilst a few exchanged knowing glances and nods.

Her oration reminded her that there was an extended rehearsal later that afternoon, and she bade farewell to Eva and her audience to complete her shopping expedition. She felt a surge of self-confidence from her performance in the refreshment room. Maybe she had been hasty. Perhaps a career on the stage was her destiny.

She was in a good frame of mind as she sauntered from shop to shop, swinging her parasol and exchanging pleasantries with those destined only to serve, as they lacked her gifts.

She retained her uncharacteristic jauntiness as she entered Laurel Cottages quietly and tiptoed into the parlour. She smiled at her father's sad, slightly comical face as he lay soundly asleep in his chair, the row of pills and potions guarding him sentry-like on the little table close by. He was there most afternoons now, having antagonised so many customers that mornings would suffice for the unsuitable toils that remained for him to perform. As she wondered whether to disturb his dreams, Maria entered from the scullery. Winnie, without speaking, grinned, and slowly but deliberately turned her back, almost shaking her rear, and retreated upstairs. Behind her, Maria stood erect, hands on hips, for a few seconds. A wistful smile crossed her face.

Winnie's evening went well, as did the rehearsal itself. Henry Smith seemed more relaxed, and they walked back happily, talking more than for some time. He smilingly avoided her questions about Mr Goodrich, though, despite praising her pleading facial expressions as she tried to interrogate him. Even a peck on the cheek failed to break his resolve, but she was in good humour when she approached the cottage, singing gently to herself.

She let herself in and heard voices behind the closed door of the front room. Father had another mystery visitor.

Before she had the chance to decide whether to listen outside the door, Maria appeared from the parlour and told her with some force in her voice to come through and wait with her in there.

Stunned by Maria's tone, she followed and sat in the chair as directed. She had never seen Maria like this before. She felt uneasy and vulnerable. She had always felt confidently superior in her dealings with Maria. Now, suddenly, something was happening that suggested that Maria was no longer cowed and defensive.

She sipped the grey, tepid tea that Maria passed to her, and they sat in silence. From time to time the sounds of the voices in the front room intruded. Sometimes they were raised, but mostly they were a bee-like hum.

About twenty minutes later, her father appeared framed in the doorway of the parlour. The slightly undersized doorframe emphasised his still-impressive build. His face did not look sad now, still less comical. Whatever this was all about, he had shaved and tidied himself up for it. He looked authoritive, if a little flustered, and he beckoned her curtly to follow him into the front room.

Inside the room, seated on one of the two high-backed wooden chairs, was the rotund figure of the local priest, Father le Haye.

She seated herself uneasily on the smaller easy chair. Between them, her father assumed his position on the sofa to conduct the proceedings.

Her senses, heightened by the play rehearsal, took her nerves to their ends. She frantically tried to calm her racing imagination by telling herself that what was now happening was part of a play.

"Act, girl, act!" she heard the exasperated Mr Smith echo into her mind.

But her legs became lead. She felt mesmerised like an animal that senses a trap closing over it.

Frederick asked her politely but firmly if she had any idea why the priest was present. Certain now of the forthcoming confirmation of her feelings of foreboding, her voice deserted her, and she meekly shook her head.

She listened with chilled horror as her father related as a series of facts the supposedly secret and intimate details of the events of her recent life.

How could she have been so foolish as to believe that she could confide in Kate, and that Kate could have resisted the temptation to relay this scandalous information to her father, Maria and God knew who else. From this treachery her father had conducted a series of discreet enquiries as to the possible origin of Winnie's condition (and, following the successful sponsorship of Vera, the possible financial benefits, she suspected). He had even visited a few of the fathers of her friends, she was horrified to learn.

He asked her sternly whether she thought she knew who the father might be.

She whispered "no" through her dry throat.

Father le Haye looked away towards his half-empty glass of sherry.

She thought that her father was about to slap her face, and flinched.

Instead, he went into a relentless verbal attack. Had she not the example of Eva and Vera to warn her? Who the hell did she think she was, treating other people like dirt when she was little better than a whore? When he asked her what her own dear mother would have thought, she dissolved into uncontrollable sobbing. Still he continued, on and on. Through her tears she wondered how many rehearsals he had made of this tirade. Despite the volume and vitriol, she recognised a controlled and constructed speech. She felt the colour return to her face. Somewhere deep inside her, she began to fight back. She dried her eyes, and asked him who Mr Goodrich was, and what did he have to with it.

The priest looked less uncomfortable, and listened intently as Frederick gave his explanation.

Being a Catholic, Frederick was not a Mason. He had been very surprised, therefore, when Mr Goodrich had visited the previous week. He had announced himself as representing certain people within the Borough in his capacity as the masonic almoner for a particular Lodge. He had explained, in a surprisingly matter-of-fact way to Frederick, that he was aware of the circumstances, and that arrangements were available in such situations, which were far from uncommon these days "when girls seemed to more or less do as they pleased". He had laid much blame on the war and its aftermath. He feared that the old order and discipline would never return. Frederick had listened with growing interest as the old almoner had moved from his opinions of the causes of post-war civil disorder onto the details of "the available arrangements".

Frederick now addressed Winnie directly to tell her that the Lodge would fund the removal of "the pregnant girl" for the pre-natal period of her "condition" and the three weeks confinement to follow the birth. Also the period prior to the baby being given up for adoption, normally another three weeks.

Winnie heard herself thanking him.

Frederick then told her that following the meeting with Mr Goodrich, he had contacted Father le Haye. The priest had contacted his colleague at St. Brigid's Hostel in Birmingham, where Lorna was resident. The sister in charge had confirmed that fewer working girls were now resident due to the decline in war work, and there would be accommodation available for Winnie to stay at the hostel until her time came, provided that she did not disclose the nature of her condition, or upset or show signs of corrupting the other residents.

She shot a glance at Frederick, silently enquiring whether Lorna was aware of all this. He just looked back at her with a steely look as he continued. "Arrangements will have to be put in hand at once, as you will be leaving for Birmingham on Saturday after the Fair next week."

In the short silence that followed she glanced at the priest shyly. He seemed about to speak, but confined himself to an enigmatic smile. Her eyes searched his slightly florid, kindly face in vain. She knew not what for. What did God's representative do an these occasions. Dispense guidance? Compassion? Apparently not.

Her father's words cannoned back and burst through the ice on her senses. She felt her blood racing, and her face perspiring. She needed to use all her acting talents to disguise her elation. She looked steadily back towards Frederick's firmly set face. He had just announced her freedom.

Their business concluded, her father dismissed her from the room.

She stood for a second in the passage outside, thinking it through.

So there it was. These three men, her father, this priest and a hunched freemason, had discussed her future between them, and reached their conclusions in the interests of those they represented. Everyone, that was, except her. Her father had obviously not considered that her views or feelings were of any importance.

She felt her anger rising, but just as she considered re-entering the room she was convulsed by a sharp, stabbing pain in her lower stomach. She rushed through the parlour past the startled Maria, and straight outside into the toilet, thanking God that it was unoccupied.

In the cool autumn air in the small closet she started shaking with uncontrollable laughter. Her period had started.

6

Ten days. Ten days. Just ten more days before, before what? Her bed was smaller. She was sure. She moved around attempting to sleep, but it evaded her. She gave up trying and instead began to try to figure it all out. Other emotions quickly joined the relief which had coursed through her veins in the outside toilet. She heard her heart beating. She was sure that the noise would wake Leah. She tried to hold her breath.

The obvious dilemma was that although it was tremendous of nature to give her this trump card, if she played it she would lose the chance to leave her hated home. Now that the opportunity to escape presented itself, she felt misgivings beginning to form like small black clouds.

She tried to imagine life in the hostel in Birmingham. In her mind it resembled the almshouses in Litchdon Street. She knew from Lorna that there were a few other girls from Devon there. Some were from Ireland even.

She tried to think what she might miss when she went. The shop was all right, but it never changed, and she had been thinking of leaving. She would miss some of her social friends. She couldn't imagine that she would have that kind of fun anywhere where Lorna was a resident. As she reflected on this, she realised that it had been some time since she had been out with them. This was partly her own choice, but no-one had called, or tried to find out if she was all right. With a chill of horror, she suddenly realised why. Her father's "discreet enquiries". It would be all round the Borough's smart set by now. She felt iron fingers grip her stomach.

She was glad that the time remaining was short, as it should avoid any chance of the truth being discovered. She had no real idea what the external physical signs of not really being pregnant were. She would die before she asked the one person who could easily have helped her, Maria, or even Eva. She felt sure that people would know the truth of her condition just by looking at her, just as she had felt certain that they could tell when she had thought herself pregnant. With such unscientific thoughts and reasoning, her conscious mind finally relaxed. The regular rhythmic beats of the rain outside on the hard pavement became the beating pistons of the locomotive that was taking her to Birmingham, and she joined the innocent Leah in belated rest.

The start of the remaining nine days passed in a kind of mental no-man's-land. She listed the business to be concluded. First there did not seem to be enough time to do everything. Then, just as suddenly, the days seemed too long. Time hung heavily on her.

She told Mr Smith that she had finally decided not to commit herself to his production. She sensed relief beneath his proclamation of devastation. Some of the cast didn't even feign disappointment.

Leaving Maples was harder, much harder than she expected. Unexciting and open to sly mimicry as her colleagues were, when she informed Mr Naylor that she would be leaving, she was surprised at his plainly sincere expression of regret. They were all genuine in their good wishes, and told her that the shop would be dull without her bizarre stories to get them through the days.

Friday September the nineteenth, the day of the Pleasure Fair, or Peace Fair this year, dawned.

The Pows made their way together to the entrance, where her father and Maria split away, leaving Winnie in reluctant charge of Leah, Barbara and George.

She soon decided that she could trust Leah to keep an eye on the two smaller children whilst she sought more mature entertainments. Little time passed before Leah would return to ask some question, or bother her with something. The heat of the day and the crush of the crowd made Leah's face red, and as Winnie studied Leah's ruddy countenance she doubted that this girl would ever be anything but dependant.

She escaped and passed down the familiar lines of stalls and entertainments. Somewhere in the distance she could hear the guest speaker, the Colonel of the Devons, recounting his war.

"Never heard one chap complain," caught an alley of sound and travelled through the hum and buzz to her.

"Can't have listened very bloody hard," commented the swarthy stallholder nearby, earning a scornful look from the middle-aged woman standing adjacent to him, who moved pointedly away.

She began to feel tired and claustrophobic in the heat. As she considered going back to find the younger children, across the crushed grass towards the edge of the park, she caught sight of an entertainment of some sort with a ring of admiring viewers. Her curiosity awakened, she went slowly over and found herself, for the first time in her life, looking at an aeroplane on the ground. She was surprised how small and frail it looked close up. It seemed incredible that the two wings with their flimsy struts were able to lift the contraption from the ground. In a playful moment she ran her hand under the lower wing.

She gasped as she felt a hand tap on her shoulder in mock admonition. Straightening up and turning in angry embarrassment, to the amusement of several watching children, she came face to face with the most handsome man she had ever seen. He did not look a lot older than she herself, but his face was attractively suntanned and had a mature expression beneath his beautiful blonde, wavy hair. He was only slightly above average height, but nicely built with wide shoulders which were concealed inside his immaculate airmans uniform.

Her face coloured as he conducted her around the flying machine. He might as well have been giving a recipe for a cake as she watched his face spellbound. She utilised all her acting resources to appear interested as he described the various parts of the plane in his accented English. She showed far more interest when he told her that he had been a volunteer flyer in the recent war. His name was John van de Leure and he was from South Africa. She was incredulous when he told her that he was now based at Birmingham. She could not summon the necessary composure to tell him that she would be there the coming week-end. Now fully in the grip of her fantasy, she imagined him collecting her and flying her up there. That would be some entrance. Mr Smith had always told her "Make an entrance, my dear, a real entrance." She pictured Lorna standing open mouthed on the airfield below.

She returned from her daydream to hear him describing that he had been in Birmingham recovering from a war wound, and some of his pals were still there. He was a free agent, so it was as good a place to be as any. Now that the war was over, he had decided to stay on in Britain and pursue his love of flying before returning to South Africa to his father's business.

He made to continue, but was distracted by the stumpy, half-formed figure of Leah staring fish-eyed up at them. Winnie looked at the hapless child with pure venom. Before anyone could speak, an upright military figure descended on them. Unaware or unconcerned about the intrusion he had made, he ushered the flyer away to commence his flying display. Van de Leure smiled at Winnie as he slipped with practised ease into the tiny cockpit.

The crowd stood back as he taxied and took off. They roared and cheered as he circled above them, but she heard them not. She died a thousand deaths as he looped the loop. She knew he was doing this just for her. When she could bear to watch, she loved the freedom of the plane soaring and weaving on its acrobatics.

All too soon the display was over, and her heart landed with him as the plane touched safely down and shuddered to a halt. To her chagrin she saw the machine immediately surrounded by strangers. She stood haughtily back from the throng and sought his eye as he struggled to remove his leather flying helmet amongst the closing mob. She would not compete with the herd, and strutted angrily away, turning on a small hillock to stand hands on hips and view the scene, and try to seem unconcerned. Leah's insistent tugs at her arm finally registered, and she made her way home, unfairly moody with the children.

For the rest of the day she was in a daze fuelled by her infatuation with the flyer. At Laurel Cottages she had to remind herself to appear appropriately downcast and contrite as the waves of ecstasy constantly passed over her, destroying her concentration and making her physically exhausted. Sometimes she felt feverishly hot, at others she shook with cold. All the time, a delicious nectar flowed through her.

She had no desire to rile her father at this late stage and put at risk her chance of joining her love in Birmingham, so, although her appetite had deserted her, she attempted to be civil, and to eat as much as she could manage.

She had never experienced anything like it before. She ached for van de Leure. The act of retrieving her case from the top of the wardrobe brought her to a new crescendo of excitement. Now it was really happening. She began to assemble her luggage for the journey. Lorna had written that the hostel lockers could only accommodate necessities, so drastic pruning was required. The clothes needed, and her substantial array of cosmetics, filled most of the available space. Lorna had told her that the hostel was supervised by nuns, but she discreetly slipped in some of her racier underwear, smoothing it for van de Leure as she did so. She carefully put in her favourite framed photograph of Fred and Jack with her parents, pausing to read the faces as she did so. Although only a few years old, the photograph showed her father as a stranger to the withered, almost defeated figure who now shambled round the cottage. Amongst the intelligence in the high foreheaded face in the picture, in his bright eyes she could see the now long-gone optimism. Her mother, never comfortable in photographs, sat straight-backed, staring apprehensively from the chair, her emotions not completely concealed beneath the stern determination in her expression. Between them Jack, confident, handsome, and Fred, tall, straight, hand on hip. What would she give now for an hour with Fred. Far away as he was, she knew that Fred would never desert her. A shaft of fear struck her as she wondered whether Kate's poison darts could reach Wales. She did not pursue this dark thought. She would have the last laugh when she told Fred that she was not pregnant, and it had all been malicious. He would never believe such a thing, anyway. She smiled at the thought, and continued her packing. Another, less likely picture to make the journey was the postcard that had arrived the previous morning from poor old Aunt Lyd on Exmoor. She had somehow learned of Winnie's impending departure and sent an uplifting study of a maiden crossing a flat stone bridge with the first four lines of the hymn "Abide with Me" printed below it. She presumed that Aunt Lyd saw significance in the symbolism, and decided that she would take it. Anyway, she slyly thought, the nuns might be impressed with her devotion.

She resisted an impassioned plea from Barbara, who was now fluttering about in the room, to take the remains of the bouquet of sweet peas with her. She picked up the dried and strangled flowers. They seemed to represent the passing of her life in Devon. She sadly handed the flowers back to Barbara, kissing her gently on the forehead as she did so.

After tea she left the house alone to pay one last visit to the churchyard. She paused at William's graveside. The contrast between the kind, thoughtful but shabby young man now lying peacefully in his premature resting place and the fit, exciting and mysterious van de Leure emphasised starkly the change about to transform her life. An unexpected twinge of guilt crept into her, and remained as she studied her mother's headstone.

The future intruded on the past suddenly as Barbara skipped happily towards her, ending her fleeting melancholy. The little heart-faced child entreated her not to leave them. Seeing Winnie's tear-stained face, she started weeping herself.

"I will try and be a better girl, if it will make you stay," she pleaded.

Winnie put her arms round the little girl's shoulders, and wiped her face with her handkerchief embroidered by her mother. She took her hand and walked back with her to the cottage. She promised Barbara faithfully that she would return to visit her soon.

It was over. She had won her freedom. There was nothing they could do now. Maria sat there, grubby, impassive. Her father was reclining peacefully in his old chair. In an impulsive act of defiance, she picked her way carefully through the scattered rubbish on the floor and kissed him tenderly on the forehead. He stirred and looked at her, looking puzzled and a little startled. She looked back at Maria, confidently expecting to see jealousy or anger. Instead she was stung and disappointed to see her stepmother give her a compassionate, almost patronising smile.

Confused, denied her final revenge, she turned abruptly and retreated upstairs to her bed, wishing her last night at Laurel Cottages gone. The boots of the returning drinkers outside in Trinity Street scraped an uneven tattoo on the damp, uneven pavement. They died like poisoned rodents as onto her night's stage van de Leure returned. They strolled together in the bright afternoon sunshine, past the Long Bridge and through the Square on their way back to the cottage for her to announce their betrothal.

Long before the appointed time of six o'clock Winnie was sitting on her bed fully dressed and wide awake. She carefully picked her way downstairs and ate her breakfast more heartily than she expected.

She returned upstairs and kissed the sleeping Leah and Barbara gently, before tiptoeing down the stairs and out into the dampness of September 20th 1919.

Her father carried her little case as they walked quietly together to the Victoria Road station. They passed unnoticed into the long gravelled drive leading to Trinity Church. To the right, she gave a slightly guilty glance towards the school. She paused silently as she studied her mother's gravestone. Then they were through the churchyard and into the narrow, tree-lined passage that led to Victoria Road.

She was pleased that the road was almost devoid of people, as she had no great wish to be noticed leaving the Borough in such an unceremonious way. It would all be different when she returned on van de Leure's arm. They would line the streets for that. She would show them.

Frederick tactfully assisted his flustered daughter as she purchased her single to Birmingham at the booking office. She looked at the destination on the buff coloured ticket. Snow Hill sounded romantic. It was all going to go well.

They walked the short distance along the decaying platform to where the carriages waited in silence. The dark sky, which had threatened them during their walk, now began to cry heavy drops of rain onto the corrugated roof of the station. Winnie frowned at the irregular but insistent tapping above her. Her mother was making a last tearful plea to her to stay in her home and abandon this adventure based on a wicked lie.

She started at the heavy metallic clang as the severe looking black locomotive backed onto the front carriage of the train. The elderly staff shouted for passengers to board, and waved flags. She glanced at her ticket again as she carefully placed it in her purse. She swallowed, then opened the heavy door and boarded the carriage near the front of the train. After leaving her case on one of the seats, she returned and spoke through the lowered window to Frederick. Unshaven as he was, he still cut a figure to compare well with the mostly agricultural passengers who were now filling the train to go to South Molton or Taunton.

The locomotive began to sigh impatiently, and they realised that the moment of their final goodbye had come. She saw his yellowed eyes filling, and felt the tears run down her lightly made-up cheek. They stretched and kissed, then, with a shudder, the train barked its way out of the station.

She waved until her father was a small beetle-like figure, then sat down on her seat as the train pulled her steadily out of Devonshire.

Part Two
Birmingham

1

The halting motion of the train roused Winnie from her cat-napping.

She massaged her slightly stiff neck as her eyes focused out of the window onto an alien, grey landscape.

They were passing a large locomotive depot. The engines were slumbering quietly in rows after their week's labour.

She spun in her seat as a large black locomotive at the head of a freight train hissed resentfully at them as they passed it on the adjacent track.

From her vantage point on an elevated section of the railway she sat transfixed. Between great work sheds she glimpsed a sea of slate-roofed dark brick buildings and forests of chimneys. Some of these were throwing out thick smoke of every shade, restricting visibility to the area near to the railway. A few blackened church spires broke the skyline. An unnaturally bright white clockface grinned ten-to-two crazily at her below its minaret. Little or no green was visible; just a few brownish coloured grassed areas on which ragged children were playing improvised games. Here and there a few stunted trees gasped for breath in the smoke-haze.

She felt depressed, and intimidated by the sheer scale of the city. How in God's name would she find van de Leure in this infernal maze?

The lights of the carriage twinkled as they plunged into a tunnel. The corona of smoke melted to reveal Snow Hill station. As the brakes squealed them to a halt, a shaft of daylight like that from a film projector framed Lorna staring firm-chinned towards the carriage windows. Winnie was seized with a mischievous desire to duck and avoid her, but Lorna caught her in her gaze, and moved purposefully towards the opening carriage door to prevent her escape.

She would not have minded a closer look at the enticing jewellery and fashion items displayed in the ornate windows of the shops in the Great Western Arcade as they marched through, but Lorna ignored her imploring looks and attempts to slow the pace, leading them imperiously on and out into the hazy daylight.

Everybody on the crowded pavements seemed to move more quickly and purposefully than she was used to back home. Lorna seemed to have adapted all right, and led her relentlessly on, swerving them round the wheedling street vendors. Winnie had genuine trouble keeping up the military pace as they completed their ten minute journey to the tram stop in Albert Street where they boarded the tram to take them to the hostel. When she complained that her feet hurt, Lorna glared at her fashionable footwear and told her stiffly that she should have worn more practical shoes.

Winnie decided to extract some revenge for the route march, and told Lorna that she had expected her to hire a taxi to take them from the station to St. Brigid's. She smiled secretly as Lorna told her sternly that she must learn economy, and might as well start right away.

Despite saying little that would not have appeared in a guide to the centre of the city after they left Snow Hill, Lorna conveyed all too clearly that she was to be employed again to do what she had so successfully achieved before in the family household; to keep a firm rein on her more wayward younger sister.

Winnie could almost visualise the correspondence. Father would have written in his still well-constructed style and neat script. Phrases like "needs a firm hand" and "put her back on the right lines" would have been involved. She presumed that Lorna knew why she was joining her in

Birmingham, or thought she knew. Like all the rest, some subtefuge would be needed to maintain the pretence. As she discreetly scrutinised Lorna's facial features, Winnie felt fairly sure that any biological knowledge that Lorna might possess would be limited to the theoretical, and, at least in that respect, she would not pose too much of a threat.

The tram clanked off for the short journey to Deritend. They disembarked, Winnie politely refusing the offer of help with her little case from the shabby but smiling young workman alighting behind them. She had caught his eye as he had sat down in front of them. He had exchanged glances with her as Lorna, oblivious of this impudent distraction, had continued single-mindedly with her monologue, moving from Birmingham's sights to the rules of the hostel, which seemed to be a fairly long list. Lorna, characteristically, had achieved a position of trust with those responsible for the running of St. Brigid's. It went without saying that under no circumstances would she allow Winnie to undermine that situation.

Lorna had a bed in one of the smaller rooms off of the main dormitory, so she showed Winnie to her bed at the busy end of the main room, and gave her the key to her small locker. She introduced her to a doe-eyed girl with rich dark brown hair called Sadie, who would be her "befriender". Sadie would show Winnie the layout of the hostel, and answer any questions that Winnie might have, before the evening meal at seven o'clock. Lorna then departed to attend to the several duties that she had to carry out prior to this event. Having been shown by Sadie the whereabouts of the showers and washroom Winnie sat down on her bed and sighed as she took stock of her new home.

In the short time that had elapsed since she had left the train she had realised that any thoughts she harboured of obtaining freedom after her elaborately and deceptively engineered escape from her father and Maria were sadly misplaced. No wonder they had been so apparently unconcerned about her welfare away from their grasp. This was the ideal situation for them. They did not have her at the cottage to disrupt their life there, but they knew that they had an able and willing keeper for her in Lorna, whose natural positive qualities of leadership and organisation would be reinforced by a less rational zeal to ensure that her errant sister slipped no further down the moral ladder.

Lorna's years away from the family home had added self-reliance to her other sterling qualities, and she was no doubt supremely confident of succeeding in her mission with Winnie. What her strong, unbending mind could not tell her, however, was that they were not at Fremington or Barnstaple now. Whatever changes and experiences Lorna had had since leaving Laurel Cottages, they were nothing compared to Winnie's. She would find, to her surprise and exasperation, that her own strength of character was reproduced now in a young woman who was no longer the schoolgirl in Lorna's mind.

All this, Winnie had by now reckoned up. As the unnatural mid-afternoon silence of the dormitory began to dissolve, with the arrival in stages of the other twenty or so girls, she started to try and work out how this position might be turned to her advantage.

She had feigned gratitude when Lorna had told her earlier that she, along with the other girls, would be allowed the privilege of staying up until 10pm as it was Saturday. After the solid but stodgy meal, she went to the common room, where most of the girls were gathered. Few, apparently, were out. The residents were talking, reading and playing board games. They acknowledged her with varying grades of enthusiasm. She sat with Lorna and Sadie. Even Lorna seemed more relaxed. She talked enthusiastically about her work at the armaments factory and then some of the voluntary work in which she was involved. Winnie felt that it would be diplomatic to express interest in this. Her apparent enthusiasm surprised and delighted Lorna, who then developed the subject into greater detail. Winnie's mind began to drift, and when Lorna was not facing her, she slyly studied the other inmates of her new home. She attempted to assess their possibilities as companions for mischief. Not very high, judging by their appearance, and their presence in the hostel on a Saturday night. Her attention suddenly became acute as Lorna described her visits to the wounded soldiers from Australia, New Zealand and South Africa, who were recovering in Dudley Road Hospital. South Africans! They might be the way for her to find John van de Leure, who was the other reason for her exile.

These visits were arranged with Father Parker of St. Patrick's in Dudley Road. Lorna would let Winnie know when the next visit was. Sadie sometimes went, and Winnie would get to know some of the other "nicer" girls. However none of the good works on Lorna's continuing long list could revive her interest, and her eyelids became heavy as the long journey slowly caught up with her. She noted for future reference the faces of the three girls sent to bed early for weekday infringements of the rules.

Soon afterwards she herself retired, not on this occasion to be tempted to break the firm rule of not looking out of the windows at night. The muffled rumble of the trams, the distant voices interspersed with unrestrained laughter, all spoke of a freedom a wall's width away outside in Deritend High Street. Singly or in groups the other girls quietly undressed and went to bed. Suddenly, and despite the activity around her, she felt very much alone. A tear crept silently down her cheek.

Sunday dawned, and with it, further unwelcome surprises. At Laurel Cottages she had risen on Sunday in her own good time. Of course the children might wake her, but she could remain in her bed reviewing in her mind what she could recall of Saturday night's events. Usually she could persuade Barbara to fetch her a cup of tea, which the child brought, smiling away, in her trembling little hands.

Here, she had become immune to the many new sounds around her and found sleep, it seemed, just in time to be awakened with a hearty "Good morning" by a towering figure. This turned out to be Sister Hilda, who she soon learned was responsible for most of the day to day running of the hostel.

The pre-breakfast routine allowed the minimum time for necessary hygiene and ablutions, let alone anything else. Activities dedicated to "vanity", she was primly informed by an anaemic looking older girl, were not encouraged, especially on Sundays.

Breakfast, and the resultant putting away of about two dozen porridge bowls and two oat pans, was followed by preparation for morning service. Sister Hilda paid keen attention to the girls' appearance, making sure that they were suitably tidy, clean-looking and modestly dressed. They followed her in pairs down the short street to the newly-built chapel by the railway viaduct. As Winnie drank in the pleasant autumnal sunshine, her companion waxed lyrical about the sermons of the priest, Father Lopes. Winnie's enthusiasms had never included sermons, but she became curious to hear this charismatic figure.

Once inside the chapel Winnie noticed that it smelled both new and musty.

Father Lopes smilingly commenced the service. Winnie studied the handsome lined face beneath the greying, slightly wavy hair. He did not attempt to invoke fear of hell fire, but addressed them more as a kindly father or trusted family friend. The sermons on this and subsequent occasions were nearly always on the themes of the welcome stranger or self-improvement. His manner of addressing his small congregation gave them the impression that he was talking to them personally. This led some, including Winnie, to believe that he was closer to them than was actually the case.

The service over, they returned to the hostel to prepare for Sunday lunch. She helped Sadie lay up the table, as everyone had to be useful. The meal itself was substantial. The numbers prevented the quality of cooking that she had been used to at home, but the beef was fairly tender and the vegetables only a little overcooked. After the pudding came "being useful" again, this time to help put away. She chatted happily to Sadie and a few others until Sadie told her that she would have to start to write to her widowed mother in Plymouth. This took ages, she told Winnie a little shamed-facedly, as she couldn't write very well.

Lorna caught her eye and motioned her to sit next to her on one of the old sofas. To her astonishment, Lorna informed Winnie that she would not be joining her at the armaments factory where she worked, as she had naturally assumed. Lorna explained that recruitment had stopped due to a slowdown in orders. She had instead arranged an interview for Winnie at R. & C. Wilson Bearings, one of her firm's main suppliers. She was to report at 9.15am the next day to Mr Charles Wilson, the owner's son, for an interview, at their Bordesley Green offices. She would tell her how to get there.

She studied Lorna's face and considered whether she was telling the complete truth. In her letters and visits home Lorna had never mentioned a slowdown of work. She wondered whether Lorna was trying to distance herself discreetly from her. However, nothing would be served by making an issue of this at this moment.

With fortuitous timing, they heard the call for the tea prior to evening service, which they responded to without delay.

Following the service there was a general meeting in the common room. She was introduced formally to her new companions. After various announcements there was a discussion on the relevance of prayer. The few enthusiasts who wished to debate the issue were soon the subject of glares from their less religious colleagues who were aware that supper would follow as soon as the talking ceased.

This turned out to be quite a sociable affair. Several of the girls welcomed her and she began to relax a little. Most of the girls seemed to have a quiet, almost resigned expression, and she sought in vain for twinkling eyes. She concluded that the regime at St. Brigid's together with the brooding presence of Lorna were unlikely to allow her the sort of freedoms that she had eagerly anticipated on leaving Barnstaple. Quite the reverse, in fact. She was still engaged on this depressing thought when the girls were reminded that bedtime was 8.45pm on Sundays.

She settled into her bed. She was not as tired as the previous night, and this heightened her sensibilities to the various noises emanating from the different parts of the room, and outside. This produced her characteristic intolerance and irritability with those around, most of whom she considered, in true Pow family tradition, to be her inferiors. Finally she joined her lesser mortals in sleep.

All too soon it was Monday morning. Another fitful night's sleep was followed by the breakfast scramble. This concluded, it was time to go out and see if Birmingham looked better.

The tram ride up to Bordesley Green was uneventful, but was of enough length to show that whatever impression Birmingham sought to make on Saturday or Sunday, when she was in her best finery, Monday was strictly working clothes. The tram clanged and squealed past rows of dingy, smoke-blackened terraced houses. At the ends of these terraces were tiny, gloomy little corner shops festooned with chipped enamel advertisements in a forlorn attempt to make them look colourful and attractive. Between the shops narrow cobbled streets climbed wearily up the slope to join the main road at numerous junctions. Down these cavernous gaps could be glimpsed the high, square shapes of factories, chimneys belching out smoke and blackened church steeples thrusting hopefully skyward like garden flowers choked by surrounding thistles.

Following Lorna's accurate instructions she made her way from the tram stop to the offices of R. & C. Wilson, whose elaborate and well-polished brass nameplate she identified on the wall of a three storey brick and slate building fronting the main road. She went through the open outer door and into the small dusty lobby that served as a reception area. She tapped timidly on a frosted glass sliding window and this slid half open to reveal a stern-looking bespectacled woman of indeterminate age. The woman told her that Mr Charles would see her shortly, and the window slid back. The door at the far end of the lobby then opened, and a younger, red-faced young woman beckoned her to follow her and led her through into a dark corridor. She knocked on a brown painted door, and upon receiving a "come" from the inhabitant inside, showed Winnie into Mr Wilson's office with no announcement and an indifferent wave of her hand.

Charles Wilson was seated behind a large, well-polished and tidy desk. His dark hair was neatly swept back, and he looked about 35. He seemed ill at ease as he explained, between frequent draws on his cigarette, that her duties would be to assist generally in the small factory behind the Bordesley Green offices, and to run errands to their forge, and to the railway works, who were the firm's biggest customer. From time to time she would also be required to go to the gun factory at Small Heath where Lorna worked. For these journeys a special bicycle was provided, much after the style of greengrocers' delivery bikes, as samples were often carried.

The pay, she noted with satisfaction, was exactly twice what she had received at Maples. She had just absorbed this comforting information when the door was opened without any warning knock and a younger version of Charles Wilson appeared framed in the doorway. The newcomer had thinner, slightly lighter hair and a correspondingly paler complexion. His eyes were less deepset but frighteningly piercing, and below them was a firm thin mouth and chin. He made no attempt to apologise for the obvious interruption and ignored Winnie as he asked his older brother if he was ready to join him at a meeting that Charles had plainly forgotten about. Charles appeared cowed, and replied to the abrupt enquiry by rising to his feet almost deferentially to join his brother James.

He mumbled something to her and left her in his office. She presumed that the interview was concluded, and that she was deemed acceptable. The red-faced girl reappeared, and took her through to the woman in the glasses, who was introduced as Miss Tilsley, the secretary to Mr Richard, the owner, and acting senior clerk, due to staff shortages caused by the war.

Miss Tilsley laid down the terms of her employment briskly, and then directed Clara, the red faced girl, to introduce Winnie to the people she would be working with, and the bicycle. This done, Winnie started her first day at R. & C. Wilson taking papers round to the various offices within the old, warren-like factory. It was not the type of work that she had done before. She didn't like the dirt and noise, but she soon enjoyed the friendly company of the staff. There were several other girls who had been drawn in to cover war shortages, two of them from Devon. They got her to ask the foreman, Tom, for the glass hammer, but were less fortunate a few days later when they tried to send her to the stores for the rubber nails. Tom looked a stern figure, and, being from the nearby Black Country, Winnie found him difficult to understand when he became agitated and lapsed into dialect. He was good natured and fatherly to the younger staff, despite uttering dire threats at times.

She saw less of the owners. The senior partner, Mr Richard, spent most of his time in his well-furnished office. He was an impressive, almost Dickensian figure in his winged collar and cravat with diamond pin. His clothes were well tailored and would have looked immaculate had he not been a chain-smoker. How his maids must have cursed as they brushed away the disfiguring ash. His appearances in the factory area caused everyone to examine what they were doing, however well, and produced an unnatural silence. He seldom intentionally interfered, but if he was not too busy would become something of a nuisance as he had done most of the jobs himself over the past thirty years. He did not always agree with the more mechanised ideas of his son James on some of the processes and was not averse to saying so. If contradiction and conflict about working methods loomed, Tom would normally waylay Mr Richard and diplomatically discuss how it was in days gone by when they were together building the firm.

James Wilson was a different prospect altogether. The money spent on his education, combined with an inherited business flair, had produced a young man of considerable business acumen. He it was who had been responsible for the acquisition of the forge to reduce their costs, and enable them to compete successfully for the lucrative war contracts. But, unlike many of his contemporaries, he had built contacts with people like the railway works, as he foresaw that the war work would have a limited life span. He seldom settled for long, and would stride purposefully around the works, sometimes standing silently to watch a particular process. He made no effort at communication with the staff, and his piercing eyes produced concern. When she was the subject of his interest Winnie would feel herself colouring up. He always seemed much closer than he actually was, and his presence made her feel that she was doing something wrong. At times he seemed more machine than human.

Mr Charles left his office only when he had to, and was plainly uncomfortable talking to any member of staff about anything except the most routine matters. Despite his natural difficulty in communication he was well-liked. His appearance did not inspire the fear that James's did.

The days passed and she got used to the routine. She looked forward to the journeys to the railway works and the gun factory, as they broke up the day and she saw some daylight. She had to be careful on the bicycle to avoid the tram lines, and the cobblestones were slippery in wet weather, of which there was more as September passed to October.

The only job she really hated was going to the forge. She had quickly accepted that this part of Birmingham was not beautiful, but the appearance and situation of the forge was the edge of hell to her. Down a narrow, twisting cobbled lane it would appear around the final bend, hissing like an angry monster. It had outgrown its site and sat partially on stilts where extensions had been built over an area now covered in simmering slag. This was adjacent to the confluence of two grey-brown waterways which still sometimes tried to reclaim their floodplain.

At any time of the day the buildings were partially hidden by the perpetual smoke, and after nightfall the flames from within the buildings gave them a truly infernal appearance. Even a short period of time near to the place resulted in a coating of grime on her skin and clothes and everywhere around there was a fine layer of dust deposited by the tall stacks above. The workers contained inside seemed dark and apelike. They spoke in accents so broad that she could not understand them. This, and her obvious distaste for their workplace, gave rise to crude, but good-natured jibes which were then replaced by outright hostility.

2

On Friday October 10th the world seemed about to end. The weather was dismal and she had delayed the bike journey for as long as she had dared. Despite much wishful thinking by her the rain simply increased in determination until there were quite noticeable clear centres on some of the grime-stained windows in the factory at Bordesley Green. Finally she imagined that she could feel James Wilson's eyes boring into her back wherever she went to waste time, and decided that the journey to the forge and the railway works could be delayed no longer.

She went out into the wet, grey afternoon with her cape on and set off moodily for the forge. The buildings looked more satanic than ever as they came into view. The coils of smoke combined with the dark grey haze from the river to give a parody of the mists she had seen over the pools on Exmoor.

She collected her sample and after the usual exchanges she set off up the hill. To the delight of those watching from the shelter of the forge entrance the bike wheels twisted on the irregular stone setts and sent her down the black mud of the river bank to the very edge of the evil-smelling water. She picked herself up and regaled those in hearing distance with some language that her sister Kate would have found familiar. Tears of both sorrow and rage trickled down her cheeks as she pushed the bike slowly up the rising gradient.

She arrived at the railway works twenty minutes later looking and feeling wet, dirty and depressed. She went to the reception area of the factory looking for Mr Gill, the storeman, to get him to sign the saturated delivery note and take the small sample. Mr Gill appeared with a companion. They both broke out into spontaneous laughter at the bedraggled sight before them. Despite herself, she began to smile and then laugh. Only then did she raise her eyes and look the stranger directly in the face. He returned her gaze with the most beautiful deep brown eyes that she had ever seen on a man. It was breathtaking. He removed his trilby hat to reveal a full head of jet-black hair. Below the eyes were a well-proportioned, slightly aqualine nose and a pair of smiling lips over a cleft chin. For what seemed an hour they held their gaze, and then the stranger spoke in a deep, melodic educated voice overlaid with a slight indeterminate accent.

"Who do we have here, Cinderella?" he enquired in a kindly, sympathetic tone.

Mr Gill produced a small and fairly clean towel, and she cleaned away most of the dirt from her face, only to reveal blushes.

"Now strangely, this could be your night, because I expect that you will be going to the ball tonight, like us." continued the stranger.

She knew that he meant the company dance that she had heard about. She had not thought much more about it as when she had mentioned it to Lorna, Lorna had raised objections to the lateness of the finish. Now, though, Lorna could have been in Barnstaple for all Winnie cared. She tried to blurt out her words but had to settle for a smile and a nod. She gathered her belongings with as much composure as she could manage in her flustered condition.

She set off back for Bordesley and suddenly nothing seemed to matter. The rain was now her friend, gently washing the remaining smuts from her smiling face. Her colleagues' friendly enquiries about the reasons for her obviously excited state produced little more than giggles. Her only enemy was the clock, which seemed to be trying to avoid reaching 5.45pm, which was the early finish time for Fridays.

Finally and grudgingly the clock gave in and released her into the queue forming in the gathering damp gloom of the evening. The tram rolled down the hill to Deritend and she hurried into St. Brigid's. Her ill-concealed excitement alerted Lorna who frowned when Winnie reminded her of the event. Lorna had made it plain, without saying so directly, during these few early weeks that she regarded anything that involved enjoying yourself, especially in the company of men, with deep suspicion. Winnie's assurances that she was meeting her friends from work and going in a group did not seem to convince her. Finally Winnie's patience snapped and she just told her that she was going and Lorna could please herself what she thought. Reinforcements arrived in the form of Sister Hilda.

To Winnie's surprise Sister Hilda raised no great objection on the basis that Winnie, more than most, should know what happened if she was foolish enough to "get herself into more trouble than she was already in, which would be difficult in the circumstances." This, Winnie realised with a start, was a reference to her assumed condition. The Sister's argument, therefore, could be turned to her advantage, as, as far as the good Sister knew, nothing could happen to make the situation worse, and Winnie was presumed beyond redemption. That suited her fine. Something of this conveyed itself to Lorna, who suddenly got up, and, to the astonishment of the few other residents present launched into a fierce verbal assault on her sister, involving the good name of the Pow family, the trouble that Winnie had already caused and several other more obscure topics. Winnie quite enjoyed this moment of notoriety, but her mild amusement rapidly turned to smouldering anger. She enquired what right Lorna had to adopt this position as her keeper, and by the time Lorna had turned her back on her and stormed off to her ante-room this had become a very spirited defence, culminating in the strangely unlinked statement that "Cinderella would go to the ball, whatever the ugly sisters thought."

Once Lorna had departed, though, and she had cooled down, it did remind her that she was supposed to be in Birmingham for a reason. If it became obvious that the reason was false, things could get quite difficult, possibly resulting in the ultimate disaster of being sent home to Laurel Cottages.

She pushed this uncomfortable line of thought to the back of her mind as she began to get ready. Although firm in her determination to go to the dance, she did not want to rock the boat any more, as plainly the argument with Lorna had not gone unnoticed. Most of the other girls appeared to show no reaction. A few seemed to view her with suspicion, whilst others seemed to give discreet encouraging looks or glances. She was unsure how far to go in making herself attractive for this event, or to be more exact for the dark handsome stranger she hoped to see. Whilst she was thinking this through in the little bathroom area she was stealthily joined by Sadie. Sadie was a little older than Winnie, but was by nature her follower. She shyly asked if there was any possibility of coming with her. Winnie accepted this offer with relish, as it overcame the possibility of the bluff of the imaginary meeting with her friends from work being exposed, or, far worse, of Lorna recovering her temper and offering to come with her.

This decided, they chatted happily as Winnie threw herself into her preparations with undiluted enthusiasm. Sadie watched with blank amazement as Winnie produced small quantities of "sinful" cosmetics that she had secreted in her locker. As Winnie washed the day's grime off of her face, she decided to use discreet amounts, and make the rest up at the dance hall. Sadie blushed as Winnie cleansed and powdered her face. They grinned conspiratorially.

Soon they were ready, and even detected a slight smile under Sister Hilda's contrived frown. They made their well-meant promises and departed, giggling nervously, into the cool, slightly sulphurous air.

Sadie worked in Sparkbrook, where the event was being held, and they soon boarded the 17 tram to take them.

They affected some decorum as they listened to the good-natured banter of the young men on their way out for their Friday night's entertainment. Winnie felt a sense of freedom as the tram rumbled past the villas and brightly-lit public houses.

The ballroom came into view set back a little from the small shops and premises around. It's exterior, in the fashionable mock-oriental style, disguised a warm, welcoming feeling inside. Trevor, one of the storemen who was acting as doorman, was only too pleased to let Sadie come in. They left their coats and entered the main ballroom. The dance floor was quite large and from the elliptical ceiling hung some chinese-looking decorations and the stained glass shades of the diffused lighting. To each side were archways of different sizes. To the left these led to a sort of lounge area, where Winnie exchanged waves with a few friends she recognised from work. Through the arches to the right was the bar, behind which stood a pretentious looking young man in a white jacket and bow tie, who was supervising the serving of many pints of ale and other drinks. Seeing her approach, he smirked and averted his eyes. This presented a challenge to her, and she marched resolutely to the bar with Sadie a lot less confidently in tow. Addressing herself deliberately to her adversary, she loudly ordered two of the cocktails popular with her former in-crowd friends in Barnstaple. The head barman fixed her with his best steely gaze. Even if he served personally, which he did not, and even if he considered it right for girls of Winnie's age to be ordering exotic drinks at his bar, which he did not, she would have to accept the limited choice on offer, which was what had been requested by the Company, and ask one of the bar staff to serve her in due course. To emphasise the point he gradually leant forward until by the end of this definitive statement his face was close enough for Winnie to notice the reddened blood vessels on his nose and cheeks, which showed him to be not as young as she had at first thought.

His face recoiled as though a string had been activated in the back of his neck. Behind her she felt the hair on the nape of her neck go up as she heard the smooth, yet intimidating voice of James Wilson. Her adversary behind the bar seemed physically to shrink as he executed her order. She felt her own face colour as she proffered the politely requested payment. She dared not turn behind her, and was relieved to find when she moved from the counter that Mr James had vanished as mysteriously as he had appeared.

Following this somewhat unnerving encounter the evening settled down to be quite enjoyable. She was in a situation that she liked; she had no threat to her position centre-stage from Sadie as she sat with several of her friends from work. The cocktails had blown a bit more of a hole in her limited finances than she expected for the evening, so she was more pleased than she tried to show when it was suggested that they had a drinks kitty. No reasonable offer of drinks from their respectable male colleagues was turned down. This generosity had to be repaid, of course, with dances on request, but apart from the sad lack of expertise from most of her partners, this presented no hazard. As the evening progressed the ale seemed to make the boys' feet larger and slower, but the drinks consumed by the girls made them more tolerant, so goodwill remained and their increasingly ungainly efforts produced mirth and unflattering commentary from those watching.

By half past nine she was enjoying herself so much that she had even forgotten the dark stranger, and there it might have stayed but for a call of nature. As she and Sadie made their way back inside from the cold toilet she almost bumped into him. He was standing with Mr Charles. As was normal with Mr Charles the stranger seemed to be making most of the conversation, and he seemed relieved when confronted with the inadvertent intrusion. Mr Charles began an attempt at an introduction. This was hampered because he had forgotten Winnie's name. She soon realised this and assisted her grateful employer with the appropriate information. She then realised that she did not know Sadie's surname. Her composure, so certain with her workmates, had now disappeared under the broadening smile of the stranger, who became known to her as Mr Roy something she didn't catch, the buyer for the Northern Railway of India. She studied him with even greater interest. He plainly wasn't Indian. She had seen Indians. She remembered the Indian girl burnt to death at Barnstaple Fair, and now in Trinity Churchyard. They were much darker than this man, and the men had beards, and wore turbans.

This idle speculation was abruptly swept aside when Roy asked her for a dance. He led her commandingly to the centre of the dance floor as the band struck up the slow waltz. She glimpsed Mr Charles talking surprisingly fluently to Sadie as she departed for cinema heaven in the powerful arms of this awesome figure. He said little as his obviously well-learned dancing skills and natural grace disguised her more limited ability. They stayed for two more dances, a foxtrot and another, even slower waltz, and he then led her back to Mr Charles and Sadie, who had by now exhausted their limited conversational talents, but seemed content enough.

She talked nervously and incessantly to Roy, who seemed to find her every word fascinating. She realised that she was talking too much and too loudly, but she could not stop herself. Mr Charles ordered them all drinks from the waiter who appeared deferentially at the table. On she went, fearing that if she stopped all this would end and she would wake up in her hospital-sized bed at St. Brigid's.

Then, of course, it did end. Unjustly, she hated Sadie as she reminded her that it was now a quarter past ten, and they had promised to be back by 10.30. Winnie's face coloured as she prepared to contest the decision, but Roy anticipated the situation and rose, announcing that he was also leaving. He would not hear of them catching the tram so late at night, and would be pleased to give them a lift in the car that he had hired for his stay in Birmingham. This admission of mortality brought an anxious enquiry from Winnie, but he smilingly reassured her that although he had many other places to visit in England and even Scotland, he would be returning to Birmingham, where he was based.

She muttered a slightly embarrassed goodnight to her workmates, who retaliated by assuring her that her share of the diminished kitty would be drunk and her health toasted. Roy asked them to wait a little while he said a proper goodnight to his hosts and suggested that they collected their coats. They waited in the small queue and at last she fell silent, replaying and savouring the events of this evening of all evenings. A snake-like hiss intruded into this mental Eden.

"He's an Anglo, you little fool." the serpent warned.

For a second she genuinely thought that it was part of her dream, but she then turned with a start to see the wraith-like features of Mr James' face, contorted with some form of vitriolic emotion, as he turned and denied her the chance of an explanation for this extraordinary intrusion into her private paradise.

Roy returned and they left the warm, smoky atmosphere of the ballroom to walk the short distance to the car. This was the first time that she had been in a car since leaving Barnstaple. My goodness, this feels right, she thought to herself, as they cruised past the lesser folk making their way home on foot. It was all very well being virtuous and fine doing good works, said the drink, but one saintly Pow was enough as a gift from Devon to this fiery city of smoke, metal and flames, some of which were now lighting the night sky in the valley behind the houses. She would leave that to Lorna. For herself, she rather fancied a few more car rides. All too soon St. Brigid's neat three-storey block came into view. Roy stopped the car outside and came round to open the rear doors for them. He was going to a concert the next night. He had two tickets and could get a third, he was sure. Would they like to come. If Sadie had been susceptible to the thoughts that were in Winnie's mind, she might have seen an early grave for accepting this polite but insincere offer. Fortunately she had the sense to realise the danger and explained that she had duties in the hostel that would prevent her attendance. Roy feigned persuasion until Winnie began to worry that Sadie really would change her mind, but she remained firm.

Seven o'clock then, he would call for her. She began to count the minutes.

Saturday passed surprisingly quickly. There was work at Wilsons as usual in the morning, of course. She was very glad that Mr Charles was in control this Saturday, which meant that Mr James would not have to be faced. On the other hand, she desperately wanted to ask James Wilson what he had meant by his unfathomable remark about Roy. She knew better than to try and discuss anything personal with Mr Charles, who in any case had buried himself in his office and would be difficult to engage in conversation.

She accepted the expected good-natured banter from her colleagues and responded in kind, taking care to emphasise the cultural superiority of the evening to come at the concert with Roy, in comparison with their more mundane activities. This made for more ribald exchanges, with Tom, their fatherly foreman, tut-tutting and everyone else laughing. As he heard her dispensing her wisdom, Tom wondered whether to quietly give her the benefit of his advice. But as he looked into her excited, open face, and saw the thrill of anticipation there, he decided against. The War had turned everything upside down, especially with girls. Best not. She'd find out soon enough what the world was about, then that fresh glow would leave her cheeks for ever.

From the works she took the tram straight into the city centre to spend as much of her pay as she dared, plus most of the savings that she had persuaded a reluctant Sister Hilda to return from the office safe to her. She had to look her best tonight, and although Sister Hilda had tried to calm her down and tell her that between them all at the hostel they could deck her out like "one of those film stars" this would involve borrowing, and she wanted this to be minimised. Buying new things was essential if the evening was going to be the unique occasion in the way that she desired so much. She had had a childhood of being clothed in hand-me-downs from older sisters and never felt comfortable dressed in things that were not exclusively hers.

She was skilled at shopping, and particularly good at obtaining items that looked better quality than they actually were for reasonable prices. She enjoyed looking round the large department stores, despite the condescending glances of some of the shop assistants at her working clothes. She always looked fairly presentable, whatever she wore, with her eye for colour match and contrast, and her fresh Devonian complexion turned a few heads. She actually bought most of her requirements in some of the smaller shops and stalls between the Bull Ring and Deritend itself.

By the time she returned to St. Brigid's she was satisfied that she had most of the requirements to produce the devastating appearance that the evening demanded. Word had spread amongst the other girls, of course, and the approving and disapproving camps had considerably enlarged since the argument with Lorna had begun the issue the previous day. Her supporters engaged in excited conversation as they examined the new purchases, paying particular attention to the underwear. This was variously described as "a bit daring, very light", or, by her less enthusiastic supporters as "brief or almost indecent."

She was not overconcerned with their opinions, but bore with the comments as she still needed a few items to complete her outfit. These were offered cheerfully and willingly.

Lorna had absented herself during this period, but was of course present at tea-time, where she was studiously civil and polite. Her disapproval was obvious to Winnie, but she had no intention of spoiling her evening with a row with Lorna before she went out. She did not join them for tea, claiming, truthfully, that her appetite had deserted her.

Lorna retired to her room after tea, and did not witness the crescendo of excitement as Winnie finally got changed and dressed. She had made Sadie almost into her servant for this enterprise, but Sadie enjoyed helping her. Sadie had told her more than once that she would be content with service in a house with a good master and mistress, when the factory work finished. This ambition puzzled Winnie, who could never think of herself as anyone else's servant, or visualise an end to places like Wilsons. This time Winnie made no concessions, and emerged in full war paint, allowing those so minded to express dumb disapproval.

Long before seven o'clock faces were peering shyly out of the windows, in direct defiance of the rules, and at about five to seven the look-outs reported Roy's car slowing down, so the knock on the door was not the dramatic moment that it might otherwise have been. Roy politely raised his hat to Sister Hilda, who, despite her calling, seemed more than a little impressed, and, upon his assurances, produced Winnie and wished them both a happy evening.

Before long they were in the Town Hall, where the concert was taking place. Like most other buildings she had seen in central Birmingham, the scale was awesome to her. In her mind she had imagined something like the old theatre at Barnstaple where they went to pantomimes. She wondered suddenly what Fred would think of all this, and a cloud crossed the starry sky of her mind. It soon passed, and they took their seats in the circle. She began to relax into the atmosphere created by the hum of conversation around them, and the distant tuning-up of the instruments. Roy had bought a programme and was telling her about the contents, but most of her attention was directed towards the appearance of the audience. They all seemed smartly dressed around them, the gentlemen in their dinner jackets and bow ties and their ladies in dresses of the type that she had looked at but not bought in the best department stores, set off by the heavy jewellery of their earrings, necklaces and bracelets. On stage, the shiny brass instruments reflected the lighting above as their players completed their fine tuning. The disjointed noises ceased abruptly and the audience became expectantly quiet. From the side of the stage a very tall man of stately bearing walked to the conductor's rostrum to loud, reverential applause. Although plainly into middle age he cut an impressive figure with his excellent head of greying hair and large moustache. He bowed to the audience and shook hands with the leader of the orchestra before assuming his place on the rostrum.

She watched fascinated as the conductor took the orchestra through the first piece, guiding them with movements of both his hands, his upper body and the baton in his right hand. The music ended and the audience began clapping.

Roy's hand on her arm discreetly prevented her rising to go. She blushed slightly and he smiled. She settled back for the next piece and secretly hoped that it would not last too long. The orchestra had rearranged and the cellist faced the conductor. She had no idea what to expect and was taken aback by the melancholy opening bars which seemed to reverberate from the auditorium through her very soul. Some around her were affected in the same way, judging by their expressions. As the work progressed she began to lose concentration, and looked further into the rows of listeners. Her eyesight, sharp as ever, arrowed in on the profile of someone that she had not expected to see. A few rows above them and across the aisle was Richard Wilson, the firm's senior partner. He looked almost asleep and alongside him she could recognise his wife's heavy figure, her ample bust decorated with some of the finest of Birmingham's jewellery. She wondered if their sons were also present, and felt a tightening of her body muscles at the thought.

The concerto ended to the expected applause, although she observed that those around them were not all clapping with unrestrained enthusiasm, and some were plainly discussing the work critically. She looked round gingerly to see if anyone was rising from their seat. Roy took her arm gently and lifted her to her feet.

They made their way to the aisle and then up towards the bar, where Roy had ordered them both drinks. Hers was the cocktail that she had favoured the previous evening. As she went up the last few stairs she anxiously sought the Wilsons, but she did not see them. They got into the bar and Roy went to fetch the drinks. The bar was cramped and was filling rapidly. She stood in a corner away from the door, as he had suggested. This avoided the crush of the incoming crowd, but was hot and airless. She remembered Roy bringing the cocktail, and her drinking thirstily from the distinctive stemmed glass. Then his comments and description of the music blended into the gaudy background of the bar. The lights seemed brighter and brighter and then went out.

She had no recollection of her faint and the work of the concerned, uniformed lady assistant who was now lifting her back slightly so that she could give her a glass of water whilst Roy looked anxiously down. They were in the small staff room adjacent to the bar.

He raised the palm of his hand to her as she attempted to apologise. He smilingly helped her to her feet. She felt shaken but well enough to walk. She could hear the muffled sound of the music. Roy prevented further discussion by thanking the assistant graciously and telling her that he would be taking his companion home, as obviously they could not re-enter the auditorium now with the concert in progress.

As they made their way to the exit Winnie felt that she would choke if she did not apologise soon. She began mumbling about having had no tea as they walked to his car in the cool but damp air.

He would hear none of it, and suggested that he took her to his hotel for her to recover in the comfortable lounge. The hotel was impressive outside. The dark appearance was no doubt the result of being so close to the adjacent railway station, but the entrance and lobby were high and well-decorated.

She sat in the lounge and as her senses returned fully a feeling of discomfort came into her consciousness. She began to convince herself that other people were looking at her. She started demurely sipping at the cocktail that Roy had brought her, despite her request for lemonade or ginger beer. Her confidence returned. She was with the most handsome man in the bar. She did not care who was looking or why. She drank her cocktail with more gusto and readily agreed when Roy suggested another. Whilst she drank this one she studied his face and realised what she knew she wanted to happen next. She conveyed this to him with her eyes and he whispered to her.

She left the lounge and went upstairs to wait by the first floor bathroom as he had told her to. He followed soon afterwards and, hand in hand, they went to Room 112. He unlocked the door quietly and they entered. The room was surprisingly plainly furnished, and, being a single room, was not very large.

He lit the gas mantle and there, accompanied by the low hiss of the flickering glow, they made love. This was the real thing, she knew. Her body reacted to his so spontaneously that he looked a little taken aback. She had no interest in explanations and nor, after a moment, had he. Time was too precious. This was the most delicious moment of her life. She had felt nothing like it before. During and after, she just wanted to hold him, hear him breathing, feel his body, look into his face. It was a lifetime away from the physical act that she had experienced before. That had been mechanical; this was a total joining together of two people. She wished, perversely, that they could die now, just like this, because she was sure that however long she might live, nothing would ever compare to the sweetness of this afterglow.

Drowsiness overtook her, and all too soon Roy was gently waking her. He kissed her tenderly on her cheek and whispered that it was time to return her to St. Brigid's or it really would be pumpkin time for Cinderella. She dressed and attempted to repair her make-up and hair.

They returned singly down the stairs, through the lounge and remet at the reception area. Roy spoke to the night porter and she saw him return the room key to him for safe keeping while he took her home. He gave the porter something else in an envelope. The porter smiled and furtively looked over Roy's shoulder where he met her gaze, which he then avoided. She frowned.

Roy dropped her back at the dimly-lit hostel at the promised time and Sister Hilda, again smiling more widely than normal, allowed him in to say a brief goodnight. The Sister tactfully withdrew to her little office.

Roy told her that he would call for her at three o'clock the next day to take her to Cannon Hill Park. They could have afternoon tea, listen to the band and take out one of the little rowing-boats on the lake.

He kissed her goodnight chastely on the cheek, perhaps even a little hurriedly.

She never saw him again.

3

She had, unknowingly, thrown down a challenge to the forces that surrounded her.

As she lay now, almost nine months later, in the narrow bed in the maternity ward of the Poor Law Infirmary in Dudley Road, she knew, even if she did not want to admit it to herself, who the winner had really been.

The early, pre-Christmas months now seemed far away, carefree almost.

She had soon recognised her condition. As she was supposed to be pregnant anyway, she considered that the Gods were favouring her.

The first shock had been Roy's failure to appear the next day. That had been bad enough.

She had not expected to be dismissed from Wilsons the following morning. No reason had been provided. She had simply been told to wait in the entrance lobby when she had arrived at 7.30 am that Monday. Miss Tilsley, the senior female clerk, had come out, given her her pay to date and told her that she was no longer welcome on the premises. The morning sun reflected from Miss Tilsley's Dr. Crippen spectacles, blanking out her piggy eyes and leaving Winnie to read the message conveyed by the thin, austere mouth. She felt her temper rising as she studied the lines round the mouth, but just took the packet of money, turned and stormed out, contenting herself with a partially successful attempt to slam the outside door. As she waited for the tram she concluded that this was the price of James Wilson's perceived snub for Roy at the dance.

No matter. She had soon obtained another job for less money in a similar, but smaller type of engineering company, but that had finished at the end of November when they lost a big contract.

By Christmas she was working in a small firm making bicycle components in a tiny, shabby converted workshop in Sparkbrook. Every day she tried not to glance at the ballroom as she passed it on the crowded, rumbling tram.

She had looked for Roy, of course. The day that she had been dismissed from Wilsons she had retraced her steps to the Town Hall and the grimy portals of the hotel by the station. She had gone to the highly polished reception desk and enquired, as though on behalf of a third party, the forwarding address of the gentleman in Room 112. She had been astonished to learn that, on checking their records, Room 112 had been unoccupied since the previous Thursday.

Her elementary theatrical training had failed her and her cheeks had coloured unstoppably. She had had to endure the ill-disguised smirks below the moustaches of the two receptionists.

After that debacle, and with no access to Wilsons, her enquiries could progress no further.

She had decided not to go home at Christmas. As the day had approached, nostalgic images had entered her mind of the days at home when her mother had awakened her, and the day had been one of excitement and security.

She wished that she could climb back into the shape of the child and wait under the sheets. But she was not now a child. She was a young woman; an unmarried, pregnant young woman, and would be viewed as such by those close to her, and by those who would view her only on paper.

Some of the girls, including Sadie, were staying at the hostel and there would be no questions asked there of the type that she might face in Devon. Even the unasked ones, like why the progress of the pregnancy seemed so remarkably slow.

Lorna was going to Devon, of course. She was staying with Jack and Alice at the Cowlers' cottage at Bickington. She was confident that nothing that Lorna said would arouse suspicions, as she was sure that Lorna knew nothing of the events of October 11th, or their result.

She waved Lorna off wistfully from the crowded platform of Snow Hill station and returned for the contrived jollity of the Hostel Christmas meal.

She had made the right decision. She had relaxed and enjoyed the two day break. She could not remember laughing so much. It was as though they were in a little hideaway, insulated from all the world's worries and torments.

The problems had really started in March.

That was when the strange, nocturnal visitor had appeared at St. Brigid's, most fortunately when she had been out visiting Dudley Road Hospital with Lorna's group. At least that had given her time to think before facing him.

Sister Hilda had reported quite factually to her that the visitor, a Mr Barnett, had called. He wished to discuss with her the making of "certain arrangements which must shortly be required".

Winnie's alarm had rapidly become almost total panic. She had been lulling herself with the strategy that she could support herself and her baby on the income provided through the masons as agreed at the meeting with Mr Goodrich and her father in Laurel Cottage, whatever that turned out to be. Then, after the adoption, she could return to Devon, whose fields now seemed greener and earth redder in her mind, and start again, a wiser woman.

Now all this was threatened by the appearance of this man here in Birmingham. She should have realised that this was bound to happen, and would have to put on the act of her life if her plan was not to disintegrate. This would most certainly happen if it was discovered that not only had she lied to get away from home in the first place, but that she had got herself pregnant three weeks later by a man whose name she did not know in a hotel where he did not stay.

Facing this problem had been difficult as she had nobody to confide in. She had begun to feel physically ill with worry, and decided on a drastic course of action. She would distance herself from those who would be in a position to question her bluff that she was about to have the world's longest known pregnancy. She had seen the hapless Mr Barnett, a pleasant, slightly crusty bachelor who seemed even more embarrassed about the whole matter than she was. She had achieved exactly the right mix of pathos and affected shyness to easily convince him that the time of arrival of the baby of an unwed mother was extremely difficult to predict because of the unordered nature of the conception, and the strain of the remorse that she felt. Mr Barnett had no reason, or comfortable way of checking this fallacious information, and she concentrated on continuing to look contrite as he told her not to worry, but to keep him informed, and let him know at once if she needed help.

The people at the hostel were another matter altogether. A few girls had been through there for the same reason as her, and even the Sisters were not going to buy an eleven month pregnancy, never mind Lorna.

The only solution had been to get away from the hostel before people began getting their calendars out, and trying to ensure that they were unable to follow her subsequent progress. This had been achieved with some difficulty; more than she had anticipated.

Mr Barnett was the chosen vehicle for this enterprise. She went to see him and asked whether he could arrange for her to be placed elsewhere until the time came for her to take her place at the Rescue Home in Ladywood run by the Salvation Army, where he had told her she would spend the pre-birth period. She still could not be sure when the baby would arrive, but she had to get away from St. Brigid's, where the girls were now being spiteful to her.

But she had overplayed her hand. Mr Barnett realised that he was now out of his depth and went to see Sister Hilda. The Sister listened to Mr Barnett's repetition of Winnie's conversations with him with emotions varying from scepticism to incredulity. She could see no reason not to comply with her request. She liked Winnie, but had grown tired of her histrionics, which had become even more pronounced during the pregnancy. She was also uneasy about her influence over some of the other girls, and the simmering feud between Winnie and Lorna, her reliable lieutenant. She would also be rid of the embarrassing questions arising from the symptoms of Winnie's condition from some of her less knowledgeable residents.

They had called her in, and to Winnie's acute discomfiture Mr Barnett had repeated almost word for word the unlikely reasons for the extended pregnancy. He left the hostel and the Sister called Winnie back into her office and attempted to obtain the truth from her. The Sister tried missionary kindness and comfort, but when this achieved only evasiveness and theatrical tears in response, she resorted to blunt questioning. This simply induced defensive outrage. Winnie told her that she would only tell Father Lopes the full facts as he was the only one she could trust, and this she did the following Sunday privately in the Sister's office.

Father Lopes listened carefully, showed sympathy and apparent understanding, and told her to follow her conscience.

Unknown to her, he added her name to the list that he quietly maintained for forwarding to his contact at the offices of the Birmingham Poor Law Union in Edmund Street. Through the Union's intricate web of committees, judgement would be pronounced on Winifred Pow. It would almost certainly finish up with the Boarding Out, Infant Life Protection and Maternity Cases committee. They would decide whether, subject to report, funding considerations and space available, her name should be included in the list of those to be detained for life (subject to five-yearly reviews) in the Asylum for mental enfeeblement under the 1913 Mental Deficiency Act. The act of giving birth to a baby whilst having no means to support the child was one of the most common qualifications for certification. Father Lopes had been thanked discreetly more than once by the chairman, Mrs. Bracey, for the information that he supplied that enabled them to get these degenerates out of circulation. He considered it to be "only his duty as a good Christian," he had told her.

None of this was known to Winnie as she went cheerfully to see Woman Sergeant Hartley of the Salvation Army at 'The Hawthorns' in Ladywood Road to discuss the arrangements for her confinement.

Sergeant Miss Gladys Hartley did not really like sinners very much, particularly unrepentant sinners, and Winnie did not come over as being very remorseful. She had not, as Winnie had erroneously assumed, heard from Father Lopes, and could not understand why the birth was not going to take place in late April or early May, as her records said it should. This was most inconvenient with these beds, so generously provided, in such demand. She certainly could not allow Winnie into the home for an undetermined length of time. It was out of the question. She blinked disdainfully over her half-moon glasses. She knew something was wrong, but had not the worldly experience, or time and interest to try to unravel the unsavoury details.

All she could offer were the names of several good Christian families in the city who would look after her and give her guidance until "her time". She uttered the last two words as though they caused her physical pain. She stroked her greying hair back to her tight bun, and sent Winnie on her way with a hastily written list with five names and addresses on it.

Winnie could not believe her luck. A godsend, she chuckled to herself, as she strode happily down to Five Ways in the tepid sunshine. She could disappear until early July, when she estimated that the baby would be born, and no-one except her and old tight-arse at the Sally Army office would know where she was; perhaps not even her.

Thus on Easter week-end, whilst most of the residents, including Lorna, were away, she slipped out of St. Brigid's to go and stay with her selected good Christians, Mr and Mrs. Samuel and Daphne Davis, at their neat semi-detached house in Harborne.

They had seemed a drippy couple when she had gone to see them, but they would suit her purpose. They were constantly anxious to give her advice based on Daphne's new baby, which they fawned over morning, noon and night. This suited Winnie, because they were so wrapped up with baby Matthew that they were not inquisitive about her, and did not constitute a threat.

She cultivated the Davises and showed interest in their wretched, gigantic baby. They began to trust her with Matthew. She took him to the park for them when Daphne had to lie down because of her anaemia, which seemed to be whenever any form of problem presented itself to her.

Finally, in early May, she put into action the audacious plan that was behind her smiling kindness to the Davises and baby Matthew. She took Matthew round to Mr Barnett's office. He concluded, as she had expected him to, that Matthew was her son. She asked for the payments to commence from April 24th, which she had decided had been his birthday. By a calculated ironic touch, it was also Lorna's birthday.

The big gamble, of course, had been that Mr Barnett would not contact the Salvation Army Home. But she judged, correctly, that Mr Barnett being an honest and straightforward man, it would never enter his mind to double check the facts of the birth. He told her that the allowance would be in an envelope addressed to her at his office reception every Thursday. It would be marked "Private and Confidential". When the baby was adopted, she must tell him.

She thanked him. It really had been so easy.

She had paid several uneventful visits to Mr Barnett's reception when he startled her by calling her back into his own office on June 17th. She had tried to avoid seeing him as even her loose fitting clothes were now bulging slightly. Her anxiety receded as he reached into his drawer and produced a letter that they had given him for her when he had called at St. Brigid's recently. She quickly put the letter in her apron and scuttled out of the building.

Later that evening, when the Davises had finished detaining her with their simpering trivia, she remembered the letter. The writing on the envelope seemed familiar, and she carefully opened it. Inside, in his large, slightly uneven hand, was a letter from her brother Fred. It was dated 25th May 1920 from an address in Abertillery, in South Wales.

My dearest Wyn

Father wrote to me, as Lorna has written to him to say that you have left the place she is living at, and she is not sure where you are. I hope and pray that if you do get this letter you have come to no harm and will let me know you are all right. I won't tell the others where you are if you don't want. It will just be between us, like when we had secrets when we were at home. You will always be my favourite, Wyn.

*You will see that I am now living here in Wales. In my last letter I told you I had got paid off
from the "Valiant". I got a job at Cwmtillery Colliery near here. Quite a few ex-naval men have
come to work in the mines round here. The mine owners like us because we get on with the work.
Also I am staying near to Ivy. We are getting married on Whit Monday, the 31st, at Newport
Register Office. The family don't agree with it because we are cousins. No one else will come. I
don't suppose you can get there, but it would make my day if you could. You know you will
always be in my heart.*
Please write when you get this. Am I doing the right thing, Wyn?
Your loving brother

Fredk.

She felt a searing convulsion engulf her, circling out from the pit of her stomach. She was certain
that Fred did not know why she was in Birmingham. She realised suddenly how heart-broken and
dejected she would feel if ever he found out. She felt alone and aware of the distance that now
separated her from him. The face of Sergeant Hartley flashed through her mind. She was being
punished for her wickedness and God would never let her see Fred again. She stared at the angel
on the 'Abide with Me' postcard that Aunt Lyd had given her, and she had left on her dressing table
to impress the Davises with her piety. She felt an awful cold feeling of emptiness, followed by a
surge of blood running upwards and round her brain. She began to cry uncontrollably and pound
the floor with her fists.

"Oh dear, oh dear," Daphne Davis had squeaked as she rushed through the box room door.
She had put her hand on the back of the hysterical figure crawling on all fours. The figure had
turned and, with some force, pushed her away. She remembered losing her balance before falling
heavily against the back wall of the little room.

The authorities had responded promptly to the hue and cry that the Davises had created. The
local police, in the burly form of Sergeant Lumsden, had arrived to collect the 'wild animal'
described by Mr Davis. The sergeant had walked her to the police station, written his obligatory
report, then sat down with her like a long-lost uncle to await the arrival of the area Poor Law
relieving officer, who had been called.

The sergeant was having a quiet evening, and he seemed happy to have someone to pass the
time with. He knew a young girl, he told her, just the same as her, who had got into trouble with a
Canadian. She had gone a bit mental at times, but she had got over it now the child had gone for
adoption, he reassured her.

She just sat and wept, silently.

When Mr Dent, the local relieving officer arrived, he, unlike the sergeant, had plainly not been
having a quiet evening. A conscientious, harassed and underpaid man, he had to decide what to
do with this new nuisance at minimum cost to the ratepayers, having established that the police
had no further interest in her. They were a difficult problem, these girls brought in to the city by
work, as none of the parishes wanted to pay for their upkeep in the 'House'. He knew Selly Oak
Workhouse was particularly full at the moment, with some wards closed for redecoration and
sanitation improvements. He asked her a few basic questions and as he wrote down the answers
on his standard form he was delighted to learn that she was due to take up her place at 'The
Hawthorns' with the Salvationists. Cost would not be an issue in this case.

He told her that he would contact Major Lee at the Salvation Army's shelter when he returned to the city centre directly. Major Lee would make arrangements as appropriate. In the meantime he would leave her in the sergeant's care. He even raised a thin smile on her pale, tear-stained face as he added that this was on condition that she did not try and overpower the sergeant to make an escape bid.

There had not been a day in the seventeen since that night when she had not wished that the sergeant had fallen completely asleep, instead of just dozing, and allowed her to escape the living nightmare that had followed.

The elderly Salvationist who had arrived around an hour and a half later had been businesslike and non-committal, almost to the point of silence. They had driven off in his old vehicle and collected her few possessions from the Davises, who had them ready by the front door. She peeped at them from inside the car as they glanced cautiously out of the door. She controlled a malicious desire to issue a piercing shriek and drive them inside.

They arrived at the shelter and Major Lee told her that she would have to spend the night in the female dormitory there as 'The Hawthorns' would not have her bed ready until the next morning. What fun that had been. She had not slept well, between the discomfort of the bed and listening to the many coughs brought out by the damp building in the warmth of the summer night. Eventually she took to trying to count the number of noises and this did release her to sleep.

Morning arrived, and after a bowl of green water described as soup and some fairly fresh bread, she departed for the 'Hawthorns', looking forward to the rest and relaxation that she imagined her pre-natal care would involve.

She was received by the staff of the Rescue Home for Women with all the enthusiasm normally reserved for pacifists at army recruiting offices in the recent conflict. She was placed in the 'secure room', the staff having obviously been warned prior to her arrival that she was likely to attack them on sight.

They took away her shoes and shut the stoutly-built door. She heard a bolt slide outside. Inside the room was a mattress set on a two-foot high base, a blanket, a plain enamelled washing bowl and jug, and a plain white chamber pot. Oh, and, of course, a bible. For some reason the presence of the good book in this spartan cell amused her and she started laughing. She imagined that they were listening and treated them to a number of gratuitous and most unflattering remarks about their organisation, their lack of attractiveness, and worst of all, the bible and some of their heroes contained therein.

Having relieved her tension, she attempted to sleep, which she achieved fitfully.

She had been quite correct in her assumption that they had overheard her remarks.

For the following sixteen days prior to her admission to Dudley Road Infirmary they made it their business to give her the most intensive instruction in how to love Jesus that any guest at the 'Hawthorns' had ever received.

All the girls who were favoured to be saved at the Rescue Home had to be taught that their fecklessness would not be rewarded. From six o'clock in the morning, when their lumpy porridge was consumed, to nightfall they would scrub and scrub to keep the 'Hawthorns' clean. Other work was brought in for them, and they were only normally allowed to rest during their brief meal breaks, or when the stern-looking visiting nurse examined them, which she seemed to do in surprising detail.

Winnie was singled out for special treatment. She was given as much outside work as possible, like scrubbing the steps and cleaning the windows, where they could be sure that the local inhabitants, particularly those worst qualified to do so, would pass judgement on her appearance and presumed character defects. Sometimes the locals were reinforced by the odd voyeur or two, or parents showing their errant offsprings the results of sin, and whispering cautions.

Sinners they were, and sinners they were made to feel. During the few breaks when even the most inventive of staff could find nothing physical to help purge their wickedness, they were treated to bible readings or morally beneficial lectures. She had received one of the several slaps across her face administered in the Lord's name after being removed from one of the lectures for bluntly questioning the likelihood of anyone wishing to sin with the matronly lecturer.

They never ran short of ideas, the good Salvationists. There was always a toilet to clean, a floor to scrub or the range to black and then black again. They only spoke to the girls in relation to the work being undertaken. The girls were not allowed to talk to each other whilst they worked, in case they spread 'degenerate knowledge'.

The women watching them looked fairly similar, even allowing for the fact they all proudly wore their uniform. They were almost all spinsters; most looked over fifty, she guessed, judging by their dated hair styling.

Some plainly found the girls downright distasteful, and would avoid physical proximity. It was a good game to work closer and closer to them, and drive them steadily round the room. Others were just indifferent, silent watchers on another world that they had been told about, but would never share, or wish to.

One or two were overtly physically or mentally sadistic. They shouted, they slapped, they poked accurately with sticks and plainly felt that the regime at the Rescue Home should add punishment to harshness as a cure for a lack of morality.

The worst type were the missionaries. They were not content with giving out the work. They had to explain how it would benefit the girls morally, and even help with the childbirth.

Between all of them, none of them spoke one word of kindness to her during her sixteen day stay at the Rescue Home.

She was relieved to be where she now was, awaiting her baby's arrival in the newly redecorated ward at Dudley Road Infirmary set aside for maternity purposes, following the departure earlier in the year of the last of the Commonwealth soldiers.

Just a tramride away from her, in the offices of the Birmingham Poor Law Union in Edmund Street, Mr Dent's hastily written report on her behaviour in Harborne lay awaiting filing, mostly because he did not seem to recommend a definite course of action, which was unusual for him.

In a filing cabinet in another office in the same building was the note from Father Lopes, and in a filing tray on the desk the memo that had arrived from the 'Hawthorns' that day offering enthusiastic support to any attempt to make an example of their recently departed charge, whom they described as stubborn, degenerate, a corrupting influence and totally unrepentant.

4

After the pains vented on Eve by the Salvationists' wrathful God had subsided, the actual birth in the early hours of Friday July 9th went surprisingly smoothly.

It mattered not that this particular baby was the product of wicked sinfulness. The euphoria that followed the delivery was as normal as for any other. In fact, the staff had found it difficult not to be consumed in the mother's total joy and fascination with the new little person that she had created.

They had been quite relieved when she had finally lapsed into sleep, giving them the opportunity to examine the baby more closely. The baby was perfectly formed, if somewhat undersize, but what drew the comments of the nurses was the skin pigmentation. From the early hours this seemed abnormally dark, and a cautionary note was attached to the little cot for jaundice. But they had seen jaundice all too often before, and grew more certain that this was not the cause. The ward Sister stared into the tiny face and the baby stared quizzically back, then returned her smile. She had seen faces like this one before, when she had trained as a nurse in Bombay during her father's posting there.

The staff used their practiced tact and experience to conceal their concerns from Winnie. Apart from the unusual skin colouring, the baby seemed weaker than average, and his mother had a lot of trouble feeding him. Winnie herself realised that the milk was difficult, but explained that she had lost her strength as she had not eaten well at 'The Hawthorns', having been unable to stomach a lot of the offerings due to her deteriorating nervous state. Even being shouted at and described as an ungrateful sinner in the sight of God's table had failed to revive her appetite, strangely enough.

The Sister grew more anxious about both baby and mother, and obtained consent to keep them both in the hospital for a few more days.

When John Barrow, the Infirmary Steward, arrived the following Thursday to obtain the details to register the birth, even he, as a non-medical man, could see that the baby lacked vitality. He was a thoughtful man with a caring manner, and had no difficulty in obtaining the information that he required. The baby's name was to be Roy, after his father, the mother explained. At Sister Radley's request he tactfully enquired about the father. The father's name was not necessary, he explained, for his records. In fact she could face severe legal penalties for wrongly naming a man on a birth certificate, he added. He listened smiling understandingly as she recited the story. He considered it likely to be true, as it was one of the most bizarre that he had listened to over the years. The girl was obviously not a common prostitute; she simply seemed to be naive. He would like to help her. The most obvious route, financial support by the father, was plainly not possible. This prevented another possibility, private medical treatment, which he was trying to encourage at the Infirmary.

He asked her if she knew anyone else in Birmingham, and she artfully took advantage of this question to ask if she could have a pen and paper later to post a letter to a family acquaintance who might be concerned. It had occurred to her before that Mr Barnett would be wondering where she was. She would write some tale to him and ask him to hold the payments at his office until she could collect them.

They decided to put down her last known regular occupation, cycle manufacturer's rubber worker, on Roy's birth certificate. She insisted that St. Brigid's was entered as her address as, irrationally, she wondered whether Mr Barnett might see the information, and did not want the hated 'Hawthorns' address on a public document.

Mr Barrow returned to his office and called Sister Radley in.

Sister Radley sat and listened as he repeated the information about the father that he had received from Winnie and his assessment of her financial situation, which he presented in his usual analytical and unjudgemental way.

The lines on the Sister's handsome face tightened as she listened.

"This sounds exactly like an Anglo," she quietly said.

Seeing John Barrow's uncomprehending face, she explained that there were many cases of mixed race "fraternising" in India, Anglos being almost exclusively the products of frustrated Empire civil servants and military men with native women. They were useful to the authorities, as they were invariably shunned by the Asian population, and were therefore pliable recruits to help run the admin of the Raj, especially strategic organisations like the railways. Some looked Asian, but many appeared totally European unless one was used to the tell-tale signs. There were also "springbacks", children who could be Asiatic but have white mothers, and so on. 'Roy' was just as likely to be the surname.

The conclusions of their well-intentioned discussion were bleak. There was no realistic possibility of tracing 'Roy' who was no doubt thousands of miles away. There appeared no financial support available for the baby. The only practical course of action was to place the baby for adoption. But who would accept a coloured-looking baby?

He was obliged to report the mother and baby's details to the Area Relieving Officer for the Birmingham Union, George Neal, who would take such action under the powers given to him under the Poor Laws as he thought necessary. The mother would certainly constitute on paper a candidate for the Asylum as 'feeble-minded' under the terms of the 1913 Act.

He decided to keep the report in his desk until he saw Mr Neal personally, rather than send it by post. By the time of Mr Neal's next visit on the 20th, all being well, Winifred and Roy Pow should be out of the hospital and, with luck, out of Mr Neal's district. The paperwork would then stay somewhere in the system at the Union offices at Edmund Street until someone had the time or interest to do anything with it. In his experience, that was unlikely unless she came to their attention for some other reason. It was the best he could do.

The baby's christening was arranged for Monday the 19th, the day before Mr Neal's visit. He wrote a short note to the Secretary at 'The Hawthorns' advising them that the most convenient time for them to collect mother and baby would be at 11am. after the service.

Just before leaving his office at seven o'clock, he explained his reasoning to Sister Radley. She was dubious about the baby, who seemed to be weakening steadily, and might not be well enough to leave the hospital on the 19th, but she agreed with his course of action, and understood the motives. She noticed the heavy lines around his reddened eyes. He always looked weary by the end of the day. She wished he would follow her advice and have a short break during the middle of the day. She did not want him as a patient, she gently chided with a sad smile that said more than he would ever realise.

Later that evening, as their maid served Mr and Mrs Barrow their evening meal, he told his wife about the strange young girl, whom he called W.N., who he had encountered. He stated his dislike of the draconian provisions of the Mental Deficiency Act and the unsuitable nature of its application to girls like W.N. He felt that the whole system of care in the city needed an overhaul; the hospital, the workhouse next door, the asylum up Lodge Road fighting old Ditchburn at the House for the less troublesome and more profitable lunatic paupers, and the prison at the top of the Heath for those who fell through those nets.

Mrs. Barrow listened silently to these views, as she had many times before. She had never told him, and never would, but she wished that he had not this complete dedication to his work at the Poor Law Infirmary.

It was not that she was by nature unkind, and she supported his efforts in public as a loyal wife. It was just that she could not understand his interest in improving and reforming the system. It paid his salary, after all. Why he seemed more interested at times in improving the lot of people who, from his descriptions, often seemed to be victims of their own folly and fecklessness, and undeserving and ungrateful for his tireless efforts on their behalf, was beyond her comprehension. Especially if, as it seemed to her, these were at the expense of his own health and attention to his family, and any ambitions that she might have for them.

On Monday July 19th Father William Parker dressed and made ready for the short journey across the road from St. Patrick's Roman Catholic Church to the small chapel in Dudley Road Infirmary. He tried to group the baptisms to save time. Sometimes this was not possible if there was uncertainty about the length of time that the forgiving God would allow these little innocents to stay on Earth before recalling them from their misery. He had three services to conduct today, Gladys Merryweather, Frank Irish, and firstly, at 10 o'clock, Roy Pow. In fact, John Barrow's secretary had expressed his employer's anxiety about Roy Pow when he had checked with him.

The baby was certainly still alive, whether well or not, judging by the volume of noise he was making in the little chapel. He was being gently rocked by his nervous looking mother, and was dressed in one of the two little robes recently made by charitable volunteers and given to the hospital for these services.

He carefully took the baby from the mother and began, in his quiet, lilting voice, the short liturgy dedicated, as always, to our Lady of All the Sorrows. The baby ceased his crying and gurgled. He was, indeed, very light to hold, and the whiteness of the robe emphasised his darker facial colour. The eyes were almost closed as the holy cross was made on his forehead. They opened momentarily and the face looked wizened, old as time itself.

The situation was as old as time, and as he mechanically concluded the text the priest found himself wondering what would become of this sickly-looking little mite, a thing he rarely now did. He added a silent prayer of his own for our Lady's protection for this blameless child born of sin.

Winnie thanked him, and he looked briefly into her tear-stained face. As he studied the hollowed cheeks and strained expression, her features seemed familiar. He blessed her, and again appealed to those above for their forgiveness for Winnie's sinfulness, and for kindness to her innocent baby.

He looked into her face again, more deeply. He saw apprehension gathering in her eyes. Oh well, perhaps he was imagining things.

He certainly was not imagining things. As soon as she had seen Father Parker she had recognised the potential for disaster. She had seen him several times before when she had visited the recovering servicemen in the hospital as a member of Lorna's group from the hostel. She had no wish for this day's events to be related back to Lorna.

To prevent the priest's memory improving any further she gave her 'abode' on the Infirmary record of baptisms as the 'Hawthorns'. She gave her 'quality, trade or profession' as 'examiner and checker'. Her natural irritability almost betrayed her when she insisted on correcting her middle name by removing the 'h' that they had added to Nora. She placed an 'e' on the end of Pow, as she had on the birth certificate, hoping that this might distance her from any checks that might be made.

Following the conclusion of the service, they returned to the ward. The nurse on duty told her that the transport was waiting to take her back to the 'Hawthorns'. Her heart sank. The next news turned her to near panic.

On the doctor's advice they had decided to keep Roy in the hospital a little longer, as they were concerned about his lack of body weight. Sister Radley, hearing Winnie's voice raised in protest, joined them and assured her that this was standard practice.

Winnie looked at the kind but firm features of the Sister's face and back down at her tiny baby sleeping uneasily in his cot. She promised herself that she would fight to keep this little speck of life, whatever it took. She trusted the Sister, who reassured her that it was for the best. She sullenly gathered her few possessions and made her way slowly to the hospital entrance and out into the mid-morning sun.

She returned in the car with the wheezing escort sent by the Salvationists, and depression descended on her as the 'Hawthorns' came into view. After the formalities she retired to the smaller of the two rooms set aside for the lying in period, the 'Reflection Room'. As she laid on one of the four beds in the sparsely furnished room she did indeed reflect that this room was more appropriate for her than the next door 'Repentance Room' as she did not feel very repentant at this moment, just very tired. Beneath the physical fatigue, though, burnt a new fiery determination. She now had something to live for. She was determined to hold on to Roy. She was going to have to think up a plan quickly if he was to avoid the normal fate reserved for children of evildoers like her, and repeated with relish by the "post-natal officer" on her arrival, which was that he would be put up for care with "decent people" when he was six weeks old. That would teach her and all like her not to bring innocent children into the world as products of sinful lust.

To achieve success, she was going to have to find a means of financing Roy and a way of getting him away from those who would take him from her. She had to get to see old Barnett and get the money from him. He would soon be asking when the child was to be adopted, and the payments would then cease. She would tell him that the baby could not yet be adopted as he was ill in hospital. She had no real idea whether that was fact, but as long as Roy was in Dudley Road Infirmary she felt that she had some time. If her baby arrived at the 'Hawthorns' she doubted that she would ever get him away from her vigilant guardians.

The Salvationists would not allow her to go to Dudley Road as her milk had dried right up. This, she was assured, gave the baby a better chance of life as it would not be contaminated with the evil inside her.

After three days of contemplation and surly compliance she could take no more. She had noticed that mid-morning, after breakfast was cleared, there was a quiet interval as people settled to their allotted tasks. She feigned illness. This meant no breakfast automatically, but she did not care. She was left alone in the 'Reflection Room'. She could hear the orders being barked, and gently opened the rattling sash window, raising the stubborn lower pane as quietly as she could.

Her heart pumping, she slid through the opening and shinned down the adjacent drainpipe. She landed at the side of the building, fortunately overlooked only by the window through which she had escaped. She walked as coolly as she could down the path that led to the tradesmens' entrance, through the gate and out into busy Ladywood Road. She could hardly believe how easy it had been.

She was still in her drab grey 'uniform' provided by the 'Hawthorns' but to the unknowing she looked more or less like most of the other young women thronging the road. Thank God they had not shaved her head, as they had once threatened. This would happen now, she was certain, if she returned to the 'Hawthorns'. Tension quickened her steps towards Mr Barnett's office as she concluded that this was almost certainly her one and only chance of freedom. She found herself looking for uniformed Salvationists in the few cars that passed, and tried to run.

The day was warm and humid, and she was a lot more weak and tired than she realised. She was almost fainting with fatigue when she arrived at Mr Barnett's office. This assisted her cause as he was shocked at her pallid appearance and got his secretary to bring her a drink of water. She had no difficulty persuading him of her pressing needs and he readily gave her the not inconsiderable sum of money due to her. She promised to let him know when the hospital would allow the adoption process to proceed. He hoped that the baby would soon be well; adding, to her discomfort, that it had looked all right when she had brought it before.

It was one thing to have the money; quite another to know where to keep it. One aspect of her plan lacking in detail was where she was going to live. She could not risk having all the money with her until this was settled. She decided that the only person that she could trust with the money that she didn't need now was Sadie. She had not seen her for some time, but, knowing her, she did not doubt that she would still be working at Sparkbrook. Stopping only to purchase some replacement clothes from a stall, she boarded the tram at Albert Street. She felt a strange pang of nostalgia as it rumbled away, just as the other tram had that far off day last October when she had been met by Lorna. She glanced furtively at St. Brigid's as the tram paused outside for what seemed an hour. The tram swung away from her familiar route to Wilsons and soon she was in Sparkbrook. She knew that Sadie was allowed a fifteen minute break at 12.45pm, and she just had time to change into her new clothes in a small park nearby before presenting herself, now feeling refreshed, at the reception of the little workshop where Sadie worked.

When Sadie appeared she was astonished at Winnie's changed appearance. Gone was the ruddy Devonian complexion and girlish mischief in her voice. Instead, this pallid, worldly young woman sat there in her shape, smoking and trying to make her life sound exciting. Sadie hardly understood much of what she listened to with increasing discomfort. Winnie was plainly as good a warning as the Sisters at Deritend could have contrived.

They sat on the bench seat nearby on the paved area, ignoring with practised ease the comments of the workmen who were walking by as they were changing shift.

Sadie gave Winnie an apple, but could not persuade her to share a sandwich, hungry as she looked. She would happily do what Winnie asked. She would tell Sister Hilda that her aunt had sent the money; she did not know anywhere that Winnie could stay, but would ask. All too soon the fifteen minutes had gone, and Winnie watched her uncomplicated friend walk back into the works.

She felt an unspoken wistfulness as she returned to Albert Street on the half empty tram. This left her mind and was replaced by tension as she saw the impressive outline of the Infirmary come into view. She had to take the chance and see Roy, but not get returned to the 'Hawthorns'. She cautiously entered the main entrance and enquired for Sister Radley. She calculated that she could turn and run out of the building if she needed to. She knew that Sister Radley was no fool and she would have to be careful how she presented herself. Her main aim was to keep Roy secure whilst she could make suitable accommodation arrangements for them both. Perversely, for the hospital to be the vehicle, her baby would have to be ill.

The Sister appeared in the entrance hall and motioned Winnie to follow her. She took her to the ward and into her small office, where they both sat down. Winnie took a calculated risk and turned on the water works.

The Sister remained in her chair, her face impassive.

Winnie explained that she could not face returning to the Hawthorns, and, wicked as she knew she had been, she still desperately wanted to have Roy.

Sister Radley offered far more encouragement for the first proposition than the second.

"What makes you think that they will come looking for you?" she enquired. "Are they that fond of you that they cannot bear to be without you?" She slowly smiled.

This thought had, of course, never occurred to Winnie, and she felt as though a huge rock had been lifted from her back.

About Roy the Sister was a lot more guarded. She knew of no facility for a mother to keep an illegitimate child unless financial support was forthcoming. In reply to Winnie's supplementary question, the normal other channels, as far as she knew, were adoption, boarding-out, the orphanage, a children's home or the Workhouse. If Roy remained weak and unwell, the strongest probability would be that he would be kept in the Western Road House round the corner from the Infirmary, so that he could be treated at Dudley Road if necessary.

Winnie listened to this information with intermingled shame and terror. She could recollect the paupers in Barnstaple with their cart full of firewood made from old railway sleepers. Now and again she had joined with the other children in their tormenting of the shabby inmates who they followed round the streets, even back to their forbidding home in the Workhouse in Alexandra Road. The Sister was called and had to leave the office briefly, giving Winnie just enough time to make herself feel physically ill at the thought of what the future might hold for Roy. She began to grasp, for the first time, her lack of control over the consequences of her actions. Her fragile confidence drained.

The Sister agreed to bend the rules and let her see Roy quickly, then Winnie really must go.

She looked at her baby. The wizened little face was relaxed in sleep. She felt a wild desire to lift him out of his railed cot and run for the entrance. As if sensing this, the Sister motioned her not to pick him up. She thanked Sister Radley with genuine sincerity and agreed to abide by the normal visiting times of 7.30 to 8.30pm. each weekday evening and 2.30 to 3.30 week-end afternoons.

The Sister knew of no accommodation herself, but there were lodging houses and hostels all round, so she should find somewhere if she kept quiet about Roy.

One final ceremony remained. She left the hospital, and, turning right into Dudley Road, made her way up past the railway bridge and, reaching up slightly, heaved the 'Hawthorns' uniform over the adjacent bridge into the dark, slow-moving chemical waters of the Birmingham & Wolverhampton Canal.

On Wednesday 3rd August John Barrow's secretary, Ernest Humphries, prepared his usual monthly lists to send to his opposite number at the offices of the Birmingham Union at Edmund Street. This was quite a detailed exercise, and involved giving particulars of all those patients in the Infirmary whose care was chargeable to the various parishes under the Poor Laws. There was a list of deaths, and also a list of new chargeable arrivals. He knew that this latter would be the most closely scrutinised when circulated, as the Infirmary was comparatively expensive, and some of the more parsimonious parishes would instruct their officers to seek to have the patients removed to cheaper accommodation, like the Workhouse, as soon as they could get away with it.

The new arrivals included a section for infants. This was sent in duplicate. The second copy of the list was for the consideration of the Boarding Out, Infant Life Protection and Maternity Cases Committee. They would decide the most suitable course for the upbringing of the children on their boarding out register at their meetings on the first Friday of each month. This was generally adoption for the babies and fostering for the older children. The less placeable went to Shenley or the other Childrens' Homes. Some teenage boys went to the trade schools, the girls to learn domestic service. Still others, if passed fit, would be considered for places on the emigration scheme to the colonies. The most damaged would go to the Institutions for their care.

As he signed the list, John Barrow noticed Roy Pow's name, and felt a sad inevitability cross his mind.

5

After all the drama surrounding Roy's birth, the rest of the summer passed in a strangely placid way for Winnie. The bizarre nature of the routine was obscured by the relief offered by its apparent stability.

She had obtained employment easily enough in some of the factories in Heath Street, near the hospital. Her nightly visits to the hospital had resulted in contact with a nurse whose landlady allowed her to rent a tiny room in one of the smoke-blackened terraces off of Icknield Port Road.

She called weekly at Mr Barnett's office for the support for Roy, upon which she began to depend for her own livelihood. The rented room, though damp and small, still cost a fortune compared to the hostel, and her earnings were reducing with most of her frequent changes of employment.

Independence came at a higher price than she had thought. Sometimes she helped at the local pub, the "Belle Vue", at week-ends to help stem the deteriorating financial situation.

She kept well away from Deritend. Her only contact with that period in her life were the occasional visits to Small Heath to see Sadie during her lunch breaks that she sometimes made when not employed. Sadie had been as good as her word, and had returned the money to Winnie when she had told Sadie that she needed it; rather earlier than Winnie had hoped. She liked Sadie, and was grateful to her, but as the weeks went by there seemed less to talk about, and she felt almost uncomfortable. She could not consider confiding in Sadie. Sadie seemed young for her age, and there was always the chance that she might let something slip at the hostel. For her part, Sadie would listen to her friend with a mixture of puzzlement and sadness. She would study Winnie's face with her large brown doe-eyes, trying in vain to understand her. She began to draw away from her mentally, physically almost, and was relieved when the meetings more or less ceased.

Roy remained weak and sickly. At the end of August Sister Radley called Winnie into her office and told her that Roy was to be moved into the Workhouse next door as soon as a bed was available for him in their nursery, as it was felt that there was nothing more medically that could be done for him at Dudley Road. Winnie felt her pulse rate quickening, but could discern no immediate threat from this. However, when the sister told her that visiting at the House was restricted to two hours on Sunday afternoons only she felt a lead weight in the pit of her stomach. She half anticipated the Sister's next and most distressing announcement, which was that she should regard the move to the Western Road House as a prelude to arrangements for Roy's adoption or boarding out. She got up and silently left the Sister's office. She looked once more at the tiny, undersized, sleeping baby and started to sob quietly.

She left the hospital and walked the short distance back to her little room. Her mind felt numb with worry. Again she had allowed a period of deceptive calm to lull her gently along without considering what must lay waiting at the end. She tried, amongst the intermittent flow of tears and even shaking, to focus her mind to try to deal with the new threat. She had brought Roy into the world. Her conscience demanded that she must try and keep him. To do that she would have to find somewhere to live with him, and someone to look after him whilst she went to work. This would cost money. To her, a lot of money. Her pay, and the money from Mr Barnett, were only just enough to support the present tenuous situation. It looked hopeless.

She washed her face, changed, and made her way to the "Belle Vue". She rarely visited the public house during the week. Indeed, she would have been turned away as an unaccompanied female, but for the fact that she was known there as she worked some week-ends. She did not know the people well at the "Belle Vue", but if she was to stand any chance of saving Roy she had to start making enquiries about possible accommodation and local child minders. They must exist in an area where quite a lot of married women were employed, especially since the outbreak of the war. She did not enter the public, which was the men's bar, so she cautiously entered the dimly lit snug. The only other occupant was old Queenie, who she had heard Mr Irons, the landlord, curse as the only woman in Ladywood who could make one glass of stout last from opening to closing time.

She felt nonplussed, and was about to turn and leave when the smiling figure of Ernest, the barman, appeared behind the bar as he took one of his infrequent glances into the snug from his hectic duties in the public. She liked Ernest, and he served her with her ginger beer shandy. He was a tall, broad-shouldered man in his mid-thirties. He was quiet, yet she had never known any of the men who became aggressive after their drink to want to take him on. He had an unspoken authority about him. She took a swig of her drink and looked into his handsome face. Even the developing faint lines on his forehead and around his firm mouth only added an air of distinction. She decided to gamble on an approach.

She told him that a friend of hers was in trouble and had to leave her present accommodation. This friend was a war widow and wished to work, so she needed help to look after her child. It was not very original, but was the best she could think of in her present state of stress.

He appeared to listen attentively, then enquired how the friend proposed to pay for the baby's keep, as work was becoming scarcer and a lot of firms were getting rid of women to provide jobs for the men, who were still returning from the services. She had not thought this through, and mumbled about pensions and private funds.

Ernest turned sharply as the figure of the landlady, Mrs Irons, appeared behind him and told him to return to the public, where customers were waiting. Mrs Irons glared from beneath her dyed blonde hair at Winnie, and continued to do so after Ernest's abrupt departure. She had plainly misread the situation, but her action confirmed to Winnie the relationship that she had suspected existed between the older woman and Ernest.

She sipped her ginger beer shandy slowly, chatting to Queenie and pacing her drinking to last until she knew Ernest would eventually return to clear away. This was closer to the legal time than usual owing to the presence of Detective Sergeant Hallam in the public, who had selected the "Belle Vue" for his after-duty pint, much to the annoyance of some of the local rogues, who felt obliged to abandon their dubious transactions and gambling in his company. As she was about to get up to leave, Ernest appeared through the adjoining door to the public bar with his cloth. He took her glass, told Queenie to drink up, to the latter's muttered protests, gave Winnie's table a wipe, and pushed a piece of paper onto her lap. Mrs Irons appeared behind the bar and he turned slowly, almost insolently, as a man does when he feels that he has the upper hand, and smilingly retreated back into the other bar. Another glare followed from the landlady, which Winnie returned with a demure smile. She had already worked out that her week-end job was gone, so she might as well engage in some female point-scoring.

She graciously bade the now furious landlady goodnight, and walked the short distance home. In her room, she opened out the folded paper. On it, in large capital letters, she read "MRS COOTE, 37 OSLER TERRACE".

Wherever close-knit communities exist, so there are Dora Cootes to be found amongst them. They are an essential part of the fabric the area. Aged enough to be accepted as dispensers of wisdom and advice, arbitrators, facilitators of business contacts, even match-makers, the societies in which they live depend on them, frequently as a substitute for more formal but less approachable organisations deemed as outside the community, like the police and local authority officials.

Mrs Coote lived alone in her small but surprisingly well-furnished home in a quieter part of the area. It was said, by those who troubled to speculate, that someone in her family had another house elsewhere in another, more prosperous part of the city, where she retreated from time to time. Certainly she was sometimes absent with no explanation offered. She was always out early in the morning. She went down to the flower market, returning to the small outhouse at the back of her house with the items needed to make up the floral decorations and arrangements which she then took during the morning to the many shops in Ladywood and Winson Green where she had customers. The shops were a most useful source of information and gossip, as well as giving her an income.

It was just after 4 o'clock in the afternoon, and she was now enjoying her favourite part of the day. She was relaxing in her chair by the fireplace in the parlour. Her cat Felix was at her feet and she was drinking her cup of tea steadily whilst she considered the strange events of the afternoon.

It was not uncommon for someone to be waiting at her door when she returned from her morning round, but the thin, almost hysterical girl who had been on the doorstep today had taken an abnormal amount of calming down. Dora had assumed, wrongly, that this was a routine paternity or pregnancy termination matter. When she had finally coaxed some sort of information out of Winnie Pow it had been difficult, even for her, to give any practical advice or help, given that the proposition was that the girl wanted to live with and keep her baby but had no apparent means of financing this absurd notion.

She had not wanted her lapsing back into panic, so she had employed one of her favourite cooling tactics, that of gently asking leading questions in a quiet voice. This gave her time to think, and also made the girl concentrate and therefore begin to think for herself.

The story had appeared to be meandering to a repetitive dead-end. Dora had felt her mind beginning to switch off. She had continued the conversation more out of politeness than genuine interest, whilst she waited for an opportunity to show Winnie the door. In reply to Dora's question about how she came to be in Birmingham in the first place, the girl had blurted out the name John van de Leure. Dora's mind had galvanised itself from the agreeable doze that she had been sinking into. She hoped that she had not betrayed the electricity in her voice as she enquired further about the South African who seemed to fascinate Winnie so much.

When she felt that there was no more to be learned, she had told Winnie that she must leave, as she was expecting someone else at 4 o'clock. She had taken her address and promised to contact her shortly, answering her frantic pleas with reassurance that she wished she felt as decisively as she stated.

No doubt something could be arranged, and Winnie Pow would never know how lucky she was. Dora's still nimble mind went into overdrive. The motive would not be altruism. She looked at the recently framed photograph of Fay, her only grand-daughter, on her sideboard and, as she did so, muttered a promise to herself. Even with the official co-operation she believed that she could, by the most fantastic chance, call on, the enterprise would be difficult and possibly dangerous.

She stirred herself reluctantly from her chair, and made her way to her friend Mr Haines's tobacconist's shop at the end of the terrace. His recently installed telephone was a godsend for her, and she asked the operator for the number that she had been given and told to memorise. She made sure that nobody but Percy Haines was in the shop whilst she made the call. She left with a small purchase as usual, and returned to her parlour to continue relaxing with Felix whilst she planned her approach to the meeting arranged for early the next morning at the Flower Market.

She felt less calm than usual as she edged her way around the cramped market. Whilst making her normal purchases she had to keep an eye open for the person who she was meeting. She did not want him looking conspicuous, and attracting unwanted attention to their rendezvous. She was not even certain who it would be. As she worked her way outside to load her little cart with another smaller than normal bundle of flowers she was reassured to see the tall figure of Detective Sergeant John Legg walking in his straight-backed way across the wet cobblestones. She intercepted him before he reached the main market area, and motioned him to follow her, with the cart, to an area concealed from the gaze of the curious.

The sergeant grinned from under his almost totally bald head.

"This had better be good," he chided as the rain ran down his face.

"I've got a lead on van de Leure," she announced, trying to control the excitement she felt by speaking more quietly than usual.

"What sort of a lead?" asked the sergeant in his accented melodic tone.

This was the bit she would have to sell.

"Well, a contact from outside the city who would provide the sort of cover that we have been seeking."

She recited the story that she had extracted from Winnie, slightly exaggerating the very limited extent of Winnie's meeting with the handsome flyer.

"And you say that this girl has come to Birmingham to be with van de Leure?"

She could see scepticism beginning to form in his face, and decided that the end she desired justified a little manipulation of the truth, even to this most agreeable representative of the force. By the time she had finished she had explained the arrangements necessary to achieve the end that they both, for completely different reasons, desired.

"That's a bloody tall order, Dora," he commented, but she could see that he had bought the idea. She knew that he would have to sell it to Inspector Davey, but John Legg was a man who could sell anything if he had confidence in it. He had told her that when he retired he would start a new career selling insurance, and she was sure that he would be successful.

"I need a quick answer, Mr Legg," she advanced.

This he promised, and, smiling in his usual engaging way, disappeared between the empty stalls of the open market.

She looked around cautiously and was sure that their exchange had not been noticed or overheard. She finished loading the cart and began wheeling it steadily towards Ladywood. It seemed to grow heavier every week, especially when having been saturated by the persistent drizzle. When she got home, she allowed herself the unusual luxury of a cup of tea with Felix whilst she re-ran in her mind an apparently successful encounter. She had been so lucky that it had been John Legg. It really was true what they said. There was nobody easier to sell to than a salesman.

Later that day, at her favoured time, an unkempt messenger knocked on her door and handed her a sealed envelope that he had been told to give to her personally. She thanked him and watched him disappear into the gathering gloom of the light rain and smoke-haze.

They had certainly acted with unusual speed. They had contacted John Barrow at Dudley Road Hospital and put him in the picture. The Public Health authorities had a considerable interest in this matter, so the co-operation that she desired was readily forthcoming. They would place Winnie Pow in one of their addresses in Tennant Street where she could be easily observed. Dora would make the arrangements for the baby once the 'escape' from the Western Road House had been arranged. The Force and Dora would then have to engineer the meeting between John van de Leure and the strange, rather naive-sounding young woman who had unknowingly become their bait.

To Winnie, Dora Coote had seemed like the Fairy Godmother.

Within a week Dora had found her the remarkably cheap, if basic, lodgings in Mr & Mrs Wakelam's house in Tennant Street. The house, like the street itself, was run down and shabby. Sarah Wakelam was anxious to inform Winnie that she only took in her lodgers, or guests as she preferred to term them, due to her husband Mr Austin's illness, which prevented him from obtaining gainful employment. She never explained what Austin Wakelam was suffering from. Certainly it did not prevent him from drinking his ale that Sarah fetched him every night in a cracked, discoloured jug from the local. It involved a lot of coughing, which her landlady emphasised was not consumptive. Mrs Wakelam herself always seemed to be slumped in her rickety old chair between the front door and the fireplace in the living room. By positioning herself there it was impossible for Winnie to avoid her landlady's enthusiastic attempts to engage her in conversation whenever she returned to the house. Winnie would have enjoyed these chats more if Sarah Wakelam had not carried before her an aroma composed of stale cigarettes, beer and body odour.

The day after Winnie's move to Tennant Street, Dora told her that she had obtained Roy's discharge from the nursery at the Western Road House. She knew the Sister in charge of the nursery, and had told her that Winnie was in a position to support Roy. To save the delays of going through the appropriate channels, the Sister had agreed to release Roy into Winnie's care as Dora had pointed out that the ratepayers would be saved the costs of Roy's keep.

Dora had expected a show of gratitude from Winnie, but still had bruises on her arms and neck several days later from the bearhugs. She also did not claim Winnie's description of her as a saint.

Sarah Wakelam was not approved for fostering, so Roy was to be boarded out with her cousin, Mrs Malloy, in Freeth Street. Dora emphasised to Winnie that she must keep the arrangements secret. It was not an authorised fostering. If the authorities found out that she was not looking after Roy herself, they would almost certainly return him to the Workhouse. She was satisfied with the glint of fear in Winnie's eyes as she turned to go.

Mrs Malloy had been a nurse at one time, Sarah Wakelam informed Winnie when she took her to her cousin's tiny terraced house.

"Wonderful, she was. Had to give it up due to her back trouble. Couldn't do the lifting."

Despite Mrs Wakelam's enthusiastic recommendation, their visit gave Winnie a sense of unease about the Malloys. Certainly the general appearance and lack of cleanliness of their home gave no indication of Mrs Malloy's competence as a nurse. Also, almost from the first visit, she became irritated at Mrs Malloy's constant whinging about the seven shillings a week allowance they agreed for looking after Roy.

Sarah Wakelam could see that Winnie was unconvinced. On the walk back to Tennant Street she reminded Winnie that Roy was weak and he needed round the clock attendance. As she had to work, Winnie was not in a position to give that to him herself.

Dora had also found her a job with a components company in Icknield Square, close to Freeth Street. Some of the parts were for the growing local aviation industry. Whenever she worked on these she thought of the blonde flier who would one day rescue her from her present plight.

On paper, the situation was as convenient as it could be, given Winnie's circumstances.

Just sometimes, mostly at night when Mr Austin's cough was unusually persistent, or she thought she could hear the rodents under the floorboards digesting their trophies carried from the unwashed plates, her mind would trace its way back to the origin of these arrangements, and she would feel a nagging sense of unease. But she could not pin it down, and by the morning it would pass.

She still made her regular calls on Mr Barnett. It was strange about him. He had seemed for a while to be getting quite concerned about the lack of progress with the adoption, then all of a sudden he had stopped asking about it. More surprisingly, he accepted without question that she needed her allowance to pay the family looking after Roy for special nursing until he was well enough to be considered for formal adoption. Had she stopped to think about it, she would have realised that his change of attitude dated from shortly after her tea-time chat with Dora when she had told Dora about him.

It seemed impossible not to confide in Dora. When you sat by Dora's fire with the kettle simmering on the range it seemed natural to tell her everything.

As the days shortened her health improved and she felt stronger. Like a bird recovering from a damaged wing, she wanted to fly again.

Indoors, her room at Tennant Street was damp, gloomy and claustrophobic. Outside, the soot-stained rain added a new ingredient to the cocktail of smoke and acrid smells that emanated from the factories all round the area as they produced their various industrial and chemical products. The sun fought a daily battle to pierce this umbrella of grey above West Birmingham. Some days it gave up the unequal struggle in mid-afternoon and a premature night fell, revealing a new panorama of flame-lit smoke billowing around the shadowy, gas-lit cobbled streets.

She settled into her routine of work, calling at Dora's after work two or three nights a week and visiting Roy almost nightly. She enjoyed the week-ends when she usually took Roy out, normally to Summerfield Park, but sometimes further afield.

It was during one of these excursions, to make the best of a warm autumn Sunday, that she saw, high above her head, a small plane performing aerobatics. Her mind instantly went back to John van de Leure. This was the omen that she had been waiting for.

Dora listened carefully as she stirred the tea in the pot, while Winnie excitedly recounted the events of the previous Sunday. Not just that. Joyners, the company she worked for, was taking part in a three day exhibition. Many local companies would be there, both suppliers and customers. She had heard today that the organisers had invited many aviation companies. The omen in the park was plainly to tell her that John van de Leure would be there. She was certain.

Dora settled back in her chair. She knew instinctively that this would be the crucial moment that would determine whether the operation would get off the ground. For her sake, and that of her friends in the Force, who were becoming increasingly anxious about the lack of tangible results, she prayed for luck and success.

She need not have worried. Seldom had Dora Coote succeeded so spectacularly.

Winnie threw herself into the work at the exhibition with an enthusiasm that she had not felt since her move from Devon. Every day she saw the stand taking shape, and had to wait no longer than the opening minutes of the exhibition to see John van de Leure. She could not believe her luck. There he was, in the same casual pose that she recalled from what seemed like half a lifetime ago at Barnstaple Fair. This time, however, there was no admiring throng of adolescent girls to compete with, as the exhibition had yet to open. He was standing in front of a small aircraft, talking quietly to a couple of friends. He seemed a little older than she recalled, but just as handsome. To her he was like one of those Greek gods that she had seen recently on the screen at the Picture House in Dudley Road come to life.

She studied him during the opening hour. He did not detect her covert observations, and she noticed that as the exhibition hall slowly filled he acknowledged some of the visitors, mostly young men, as well as some of the other exhibitors. As he talked in his relaxed manner he spontaneously broke into a wide, engaging smile, reminding her of the postcard picture of the Prince of Wales on her dresser at Tennant Street. He certainly seemed to be popular, and to know a lot of well-dressed people. She fancied herself in their company. She was sure that their social life offered a great deal more pleasure than her present drab routine.

To reach that happy situation she realised that she would need to employ all her natural charm and guile, supplemented by her underestimated acting ability, to ingratiate herself to her quarry.

Admiring the plane during the mid-morning lull solicited the necessary introduction. Flatteringly, he claimed to remember her from Barnstaple, and she found herself on the receiving end of his not inconsiderable resources of qualities to match her own. He told her that he was not on this stand all day, as it was his two friends who ran Manor Aviation and Trading who were the actual exhibitors. John was employed by them as and when required for certain flights, or display purposes. It was a fairly loose arrangement, much favoured by these impecunious pioneers of air transport.

For the three days whilst the exhibition was on, Winnie felt like she was floating on air. She could not wait to get to the hall. She ate little, and fretted if van de Leure was absent. When he was there, he charged her with life. It was like looking into a kaleidoscope. They talked, they shared cups of tea and sandwiches. Just to look at him made her heart race.

As the closure of the exhibition approached, it crossed her mind that this match with John van de Leure might also end, like a curtain coming down on the final night of a theatre production. But her efforts had been successful. He was sufficiently intrigued to ask her for her address so that he could call that evening and take her out. She hesitated momentarily as her baby corkscrewed into her mind and out again. It was no contest.

The late autumn of 1920 and the winter that followed were not the time of high excitement that Winnie had looked forward to.

After her first outing with John, a disappointingly tame evening at a suburban cinema, events did not progress at anything like the pace that she had expected and hoped. In her imagination, he was going to succumb to her attractions and they would enjoy a whirlwind romance, culminating in their marriage; truly one of the social events of the Birmingham calendar. In practice, her routine changed remarkably little in the first months of their relationship.

He took her out most week-ends, and sometimes during the week. One of the major disappointments to her was the solitary nature of their dates. She had confidently expected to be at social gatherings with the type of people with whom he had seemed so closely acquainted at the exhibition, but on almost every occasion they spent the evening together at the cinema or sometimes drove to a quiet country pub. Even though she enjoyed his company, she began to feel that the relationship was not progressing, and speculate on the reasons. He made few attempts to approach her physically. He was gentle and kind, a model of good manners, and considerate in his every action. He was also almost unfairly attractive. Sometimes she wanted him so much that it hurt. Most of the time, however, she was grateful for the fact that she did not have to face refusing him, with the consequent risk of losing him. She had made up her mind that there would be no repetition of the events leading up to Roy's birth if she could help it.

As the weeks went by, she realised that she knew little more about him than she had the day the exhibition opened. She knew he was South African, she knew he flew aeroplanes, he had a nice car, was plainly not short of money and was very charming. He lived alone, apparently, apart from a servant, in a large house in one of the better roads in leafy Edgbaston. She had seen the house once when he had called there hurriedly on their way out for a drink one Saturday evening. He had driven round the semi-circular front drive and collected a small parcel from his man, who had opened the door. This he had then deposited at a dingy-looking pub in an industrial area of the Aston district on their way out of the city.

Sometimes he was not even around at the week-ends, business being the stated reason. More than once she had walked the road outside his house, but Dora had cautioned her against this as it achieved nothing, and might offend him.

Dora was like a kindly older sister to her. Despite the considerable disparity in their ages she never felt uncomfortable discussing her various problems with her. It did not matter whether it was the characters at Charles Joyners, her workplace in Icknield Square, Roy's continuing weakness and health problems, or the saga of her slow-burning love affair with John van de Leure.

She was sometimes surprised how interested Dora was in this latter topic. She listened to Winnie with endless patience, and offered advice on how to progress the campaign. She was particularly helpful in suggesting subtle ways of asking questions to try to learn more about him. From this, she suggested, Winnie would come to learn the best approach to win his love. Perhaps he had been hurt in the past, or, like Winnie herself, had had an episode that he wished to keep quiet about. Once he learned that he could trust Winnie, no doubt he would open up.

Most evenings she made her way to Freeth Street, where Roy lay in his cot. He showed recognition of her, but, love him as she did, she began to become impatient with his lack of vitality. Sometimes, usually on her walk back to Tennant Street after seeing him, she tried to think what would happen if things developed with John. She felt a cold guilt, but sometimes this was overlaid with a kind of anger against her helpless baby, as though he might become an obstacle to her future happiness. When this died down, the guilt resurfaced with a vengeance, usually as she was extinguishing the dim finger of light from the hissing gas mantle in her room.

She was not the only one frustrated by her slow progress with John van de Leure. Inspector Davey was a good chief, but he was also a results man. It was accepted that patience was not his strongest characteristic. This was now evident to Sergeant Legg, who was telling his unimpressed senior of the problems being encountered in piercing the wall of secrecy that surrounded the activities of John van de Leure.

Legg's report was nothing much more than a restatement of information already known. Van de Leure's address, his known associates, details of some of his latest movements above and on ground level. The rest was just the results of diligent observation and good, honest, old-fashioned police work. The only matter of definite interest was the episode of the parcel dropped at the pub in Aston. As no vehicle had been available to follow them on the night concerned, Legg only had this vague description that the passenger had given his informant to go on. The rest of the report was speculation based on Legg's well-known imaginative powers.

The Inspector always knew when Legg was on the defensive. Although the sergeant was a persuasive arguer, his normally cheerful face would cloud with concern and his cheeks would almost blow into a pout. Davey was in a dilemma. Left to his own judgement he would have called the whole expensive farce off, but he had to be seen by the considerable forces interested in the operation to be doing all he could, and at the moment this was his only lead.

He listened to the persistent December rain beating on his window, and, after appearing to consider the matter, issued the expected warnings to Legg. He told him that he would review the position at the end of January. Legg left his office a relieved man. He told Davey that he was sure he was onto something, and that maybe the forthcoming Christmas season, with its attendant festivities, would result in a careless release of information.

Close by, in the offices of the Birmingham Poor Law Union in Edmund Street, a quite different discussion took place.

The Committee discussed the welfare of the various children on the agenda of the meeting. Usually they listened to or read the submissions of the Clerk, James Curtis, and agreed to his recommended course of action. In the matter of Roy Pow the Clerk took the unusual step of passing a letter to the Chairman. The Chairman, Joshua Whiteley, was not going to give the other members, especially the ferret-like new chief woman visitor, the satisfaction of a visible reaction, so he just announced that for reasons that were confidential the case of Roy Pow was adjourned. He proposed closure of the meeting and instructed the Clerk to get the refreshments prepared for their usual sherry and biscuits prior to the Christmas break. He concluded by wishing them all a Merry Christmas, and thanking them for their diligent work throughout the year.

6

As the tired, murky days of December 1920 made their shorter and shorter appearances, it was not just the unseen audience who were becoming restless with the continuing lack of action in the drama of Winnie Pow and John van de Leure.

Winnie herself was becoming exasperated that their almost brother and sister relationship showed few signs of blossoming into the full romance that she desired; also with the unpredictable pattern of his availability, with no real explanation offered; almost as though she was someone to pass his idle time with. She even began to wonder whether he was married.

Typically, the enjoyment of sharing the evening of her twentieth birthday on Wednesday 22nd with him was promptly followed on the 23rd by the disappointment of learning that he would be unavoidably away for Christmas.

He had been very generous with the gifts that he bought her at Lewis's. She had enjoyed choosing the clothes and perfumes. She had understood when his attention had been diverted while she took her time looking at the counters, and was again interested to note that several people acknowledged him. He had seemed annoyed when she had asked him when she could meet some of his friends, but the moment had passed.

She made the best of Christmas, accepting Dora's invitation to spend most of the day with her. She had met Dora's younger sister, who gave the impression of quiet contentment, and also Dora's daughter Lily, a strangely subdued woman in her forties, who seemed to lack Dora's vitality.

John's absence at least meant that she did not have to worry about spending time with Roy, an increasingly infrequent pastime. Try as she did, the baby showed no real response to her attempts at contact. He was no substitute for van de Leure. She soon became irritated and bad-tempered with him. She spent every penny she could afford, and more, on little presents that owed more to guilt than generosity.

On Christmas day she took him out to the park during the damp afternoon, and spent an hour there exchanging pleasantries with the local inhabitants who were walking off their lunch and ale. This ended abruptly when a boy of about eight, with childish innocence, enquired "who'm the little coloured boy."

John had perhaps detected her impatient mood on his return the Tuesday after Christmas. He had called unexpectedly at Tennant Street and announced that they would be going to the New Year's Ball at the Midland Hotel. She told Dora excitedly that she would be able to show off her new dress, and that on Friday he would be taking her to a jeweller in Vyse Street that he knew, who would bedeck her in suitable glittering finery.

She could not remember being so happy. She begged her indulgent employer for an extended dinner break, and, to the envy of her colleagues, was whisked off to Vyse Street by John, who collected her from outside Joyners' main entrance in the car.

She took so long to choose her jewellery that he threatened to drive off and make her walk back, but eventually she decided on a cultured pearl necklace and matching earrings. She was so happily absorbed in making her choices and teasing John that she did not notice the tall, balding man with his back to her at the end counter. He seemed equally undecided about the choice of an anniversary present for his wife. To her astonishment John did not pay for the items, or even mention an account. He just wished the young man serving them a jovial goodbye and they left to return to Joyners, where she endured one of the longest afternoons of her life.

The New Year's Ball marked a considerable change in their relationship.

John behaved in a totally different way. After a cautious start, when he seemed thoughtful and absorbed, he began to introduce her to some of his friends. She sat with a small group of them whilst he left them to engage in conversation with others here and there. The three girls and two men at her table brought her into their conversation, and she realised how little she had to contribute in such company. They seemed not unlike her good-time companions in Barnstaple, with their attempts at sophistication in dress and speech. Although they were about her age, she found herself considering them to be immature and shallow.

She was aware, though, that this was a test of some sort, and she tolerated their affected talk and mannerisms with as much grace as she could muster. As the evening progressed, they all relaxed and by the time 1921 arrived she could tell that she had been accepted. John seemed to have lost the tension of the earlier evening, and, as they danced the last waltz she felt a closeness to him mentally and physically that she had despaired of ever reaching.

She sensed her confidence returning, and as she flung her arms around him as he drove her home through the good-natured crowds, all seemed well with the world.

Her New Year's resolution, she loudly announced to him, was to do three years' living in the year. He laughingly promised to assist her with that aim.

They parked a little down Tennant Street from her room, and she attempted, with only limited success, to get him to share the passion that was now coursing through her. Finally they disengaged and she re-arranged her hair with some deliberation. He seemed strangely unruffled, and she noticed his unbroken composure reflected in the face dimly illuminated by the gas lamp above them. They exchanged one last, chaste, goodnight kiss. He drove slowly by, waving gently as she reached the door of no. 154.

In the weeks that followed she saw him more and more. During the week he would call for her and take her to fashionable cocktail lounges in the city. She began to feel more comfortable with the other four or five girls in their tightly knit set. She listened carefully to their references to the shops that they patronised, and was soon exchanging lightweight conversation with them whilst their escorts talked to each other.

Sometimes at the week-ends he took her on his car journeys. One bleak Saturday afternoon in February they went up to deliver something to a man at a place near Stoke-on-Trent. They did not go into the five towns itself, but skirted it on a higher road. Despite the distance, the smell of coke ovens and sulphur climbed its way up and entwined itself around them. As John talked with the older man she gazed down on the unsorted maze of chapels, squalid-looking streets and strange, beehive-shaped kilns. She could never remember seeing anywhere so brazenly ugly. In the distance she could see smoke rising from a steel plant, and a little closer, the gaunt rusty headgear of an apparently disused coalmine broke the smoke-laden skyline.

With a jolt, she heard John in heated discussion with the stranger, and turned to look. The other man looked swarthy and unkempt, quite unlike most of the people that John met. She saw him raise the small package that John had given him in an angry gesture. John lifted his arms protectively. For a moment she feared that they were about to come to blows, but their voices receded.

She watched anxiously as the shabby figure disappeared down a track laid with uneven cinders. John returned to drive them back to Birmingham. He seemed unruffled by the encounter, and politely evaded her enquiries.

He always seemed to be in control. She looked at his handsome profile as he drove. She realised that she would go to the ends of the earth for him. She had been so determined, after her other fiasco, to keep the stakes high. She had maintained, with more difficulty on her part than his, her policy of allowing no major physical intimacy until acceptable formalities had been undertaken. She knew that this must involve marriage, but there was no sign of a proposal from John. She wanted him so much. She wondered how she would react if he were to ask her to live with him, but not as a married couple. Whatever might be in her mind, she had learnt from several encounters that John was not someone who would be pushed.

More enjoyable Saturday or Sunday jaunts took them to several other neighbouring towns. She would irritate Dora by not even knowing where they had been when she related the week-end's adventures to her at Osler Terrace. She saw less of Dora now, as her social engagements with John developed and grew, and took up more of her evenings.

She saw less still of Roy. He never seemed to change. Her frustration at his lack of reaction began to uproot her conscience. She lived with a gnawing fear that John would somehow discover Roy, and, like the pantomime that they had gone to, all would end at midnight. She would call at Freeth Street furtively on her way home from work.

By the time of the unseasonably early Easter in late March she had begun to balance these guilt-ridden visits against the consequences if she was discovered, and lost her ever-increasing social life.

Some nights she would return to Tennant Street and lie awake, thinking of the various dreams that now had come closer to forming definite shapes in her mind. She fancied herself as the hostess at the house in Edgbaston. Whilst she enjoyed her work at Joyners, she began to envy the other girls in their social circle, who either did not work, or else worked purely for their own amusement. Some were actively interested in charity work. She always politely declined their invitations to join them, fearing a chance meeting with former acquaintances who would provide embarrassment terminal to her new life.

Once again, as at Christmas, he seemed to sense her frustration building up, and on Easter Monday the proposition appeared to materialise in the second possibility as he blurted out:

"Would she be interested in sharing the house at Edgbaston with him?"

She had enquired quietly what status he had in mind for her, and he had stared at her nonplussed, as though he had not thought that important or relevant.

After an uncomfortable silence he had slowly and deliberately told her that he would make arrangements for them to be married by a minister of the South African Dutch Reform Church. It would take some time to arrange, as the man he had in mind covered a wide area, but he would organise it.

She could not disguise some misgivings deep in her consciousness. He had definitely been reluctant to commit himself. Although this African minister sounded exotic, it seemed odd. Also odd was the fact that he had not mentioned his family. She thought once again how little she really knew about him. She had realised over the months that her dream of a grand white wedding, and being given away by Fred in his naval uniform was a hopeless fantasy, but this was something else. On the other hand, this might be the only opportunity she got of moving into his residence in Wellington Road, which was daily a more appealing prospect than the dingy slum in Tennant Street.

Even Dora seemed unable to offer definite advice on this issue when Winnie called on her after work the following night. She had not foreseen this development, at least not this soon, and for once she was unsure of herself.

"Just keep me informed," she told Winnie. Her anxiety made her overemphasise the words, and made them sound like an instruction.

This triggered a latent anger in Winnie. On her last few visits, she had felt that she no longer needed Dora in the way that she once had. Indeed, she associated Dora with a past that she was now trying hard to put behind her.

Gone was the waif who had called Dora a saint.

"I don't have to report to you, that nosy old bitch in Tennant Street or anybody else," she blazed.

Dora realised she was on dangerous ground.

"I know, I know, Winnie," she replied, trying to gain thinking time.

"But if you go and live with him you will need someone to keep you informed about Roy. I've heard he's very weak."

Winne read a disguised tone of menace in this statement - an unspoken threat of exposure in some form. She rose and stormed haughtily out of the house, startling Felix from his agreeable slumber with the suddenness of her movement. As she walked briskly back down Icknield Port Road she felt her cheeks smarting with indignation. She did not need Dora. She did not need anyone. Dora had unwittingly decided her course of action for her.

When van de Leure called for her that evening he noticed that, even by her own standards, her appearance was immaculate.

After a particularly enjoyable evening, she told him to park the car slightly down from 154 Tennant Street. He looked a little apprehensive. He did not like surprises.

He looked relieved when she told him to put his recent not very convincing and bizarre marriage proposal on ice. She would come and live with him as his live-in housekeeper. Let the world think what it liked.

"Yes - yes, of course." he stumblingly replied.

"Next Saturday, then," she stated in an unfamiliar clipped tone.

He nodded assent mechanically. As he drove away, he thought he detected a new certainty in her goodnight wave and smile. He felt the steering wheel slide slightly in his hands. Unusually, his palms were damp.

Winnie had scarcely left the Terrace before Dora, with less care than normal, was making her way to the tobacconist for her usual telephone call. Events were getting out of control, and she needed to have an urgent meeting with Legg.

7

Happily unaware of the confusion that her actions were causing others Winnie left the caterpillar population and emerged into the unprecedentedly warm days of Spring 1921 as the butterfly that she had wished herself ever since the liaison with John van de Leure had started. And a beautiful butterfly she was. Her innate sense of colour and dress combined with the new vital ingredient of financial resources gave her a stunning appearance at the many social engagements that they attended.

John held accounts at a number of remarkably varied places. Even if he did not, he or his manservant Victor always seemed to know someone who would supply her needs on account. Even old Caleb Chambers had eyed her warily and allowed her to leave his shop in Corporation Street with the finest underwear when she had mentioned the name "John van de Leure."

She loved her hand-made shoes from Skinner & Son in Broad Street. She spent hours there.

With selected friends, she spent many happy afternoons at the fashion parades organised by the large department stores.

Her regular visits to Vyse Street provided the jewellery to set off the fashionable items that adorned her slim figure. She was relieved to note that her stomach was as flat as before Roy's birth. To ensure this, and help her appearance, she took advantage of one of John's more unusual accounts - Herr Schenkel's City Hydro & Massage Establishment. However many times she went, Herr Schenkel would always remind her when she phoned that he was "opposite ze Prince of Vales Seatre." It became one of her favourite impersonations.

At last her life was changing for the better. Her confidence returned. This was accompanied by a new, slight caution which she held at the back of her mind; a sort of instinctive wariness that there were experiences from which lessons needed to be learned, and that her salad days were gone, never to return.

The move to Edgbaston was the icing on the cake. Within their social circle they were accepted as amongst the leaders, and her unlimited access to funds meant that she was keenly watched, and often imitated, in fashion and colour. Not all were uncritically flattering about her and her doings, of course, but living as she now did with constant access to the car when John was there to drive her, or taxis when he was away on his frequent trips, she felt able to ignore her critics. She was particularly happy when up in the sky with him in the plane. She felt literally away from them all, her critics, Roy, Lorna, the lot of them. What a magical feeling it was to sit there watching John in his leather flying helmet calmly controlling the little two winged plane. This really was living. It even surpassed the many Balls, Dances, visits to the Theatre, and all the other social functions that they were now embroiled in. Some week-ends they went to the country for gatherings of the local elite, even the occasional minor member of the peerage being present. Many envied John van de Leure his attractive young escort, and she discreetly refused the many propositions that she received.

What never happened was that functions were held at their imposing red-brick villa near the top of fashionable Wellington Road. She did not know the reason for this, but John quickly became petulant if she persevered in suggesting social events there.

One thing she learned quickly was not to rock the very luxurious boat that she was now cruising in.

During the three weeks since she had moved in, John had been out a lot. She hadn't minded too much. It had given her time to get used to her surroundings. She had quickly adapted to not working. She concluded that she was never meant to work, if this was the alternative.

She decided to indulge herself, and poured herself a glass of sherry. Gazing out of the window of the spacious drawing room, she noticed the pink May blossom decorating the trees swaying in the breeze. It felt as though she had always lived at Edgbaston. The change from the depressing scenery of Tennant Street and Ladywood seemed to illustrate her new status.

Like a caterpillar over a leaf, Roy crawled over her mind and reminded her of the ease with which all that now shone so brightly could become tarnished and unpleasant. Truth to tell she had no real idea what to do about Roy, but hoped that as things continued to develop at Edgbaston some scheme would formulate itself.

Still Roy persisted.

She looked at the time on the grandfather clock in the corner of the room. She checked on Victor's whereabouts, then tiptoed upstairs to her room. Selecting the older clothes that she retained for the purpose, she decided to pay a visit to Roy. On the way, she would call on Mr Barnett to collect the money for the Malloys. This was a problem that she had not thought of. Although John gave her a small cash allowance, virtually everything was paid for on his accounts, so she depended on old Barnett more than before.

She called a taxi and got the driver to drop her at a discreet distance from Mr Barnett's office. Climbing the stairs, she checked her appearance to make sure that she did not show signs of her new status. She need not have worried. Less than five minutes later she was back at the taxi rank with the money in her pocket.

She mused aimlessly about her clothes for the evening to come as the taxi dropped her at the end of Freeth Street.

She noticed the grime and acrid smell more keenly than before as she walked the short distance to the Malloys.

She knocked twice before she heard Mrs Malloy shuffling towards the door. The door opened a few inches, seemed to hesitate, then opened fully. Never attractive, Mrs Malloy looked aggressively hideous. From her blotched face came pure vitriol.

"You'm too bloody late," she bellowed, as Winnie glanced round to see the curtains of the adjacent houses starting to twitch.

"What do you mean?" Winnie replied quietly, determined to use this encounter to reinforce her enhanced status.

"Well, don't tell me yow don't know. They bin here and carted him off back to the Workhouse. Some bloody interfering woman, it was. Bloody nonsense about him looking starved. Oi told her. Him bein' a bit black and what have yer. But no. Off he went. Yow owe uzz. Three bloody weeks. Twenty-one bob, and you'm not leaving her till oi get it."

To Winnie's horror she felt her collar being lifted off the ground by Mrs Malloy's bulbous hand. She struggled free, and, reaching into her bag, counted out the money.

"Bugger off, yow, and don't come back here no more with youm black bastards," Mrs Malloy's words followed her down almost to the junction with Icknield Port Road.

Dora had just arrived back from her round when Winnie stormed into her living room after a cursory tap at the door. Her visitor did not waste time on pleasantries.

"You're behind this, aren't you?" Winnie rasped.

"Sit down." Dora was not going to tolerate this. "Sit down and listen."

Winnie obeyed, her confidence evaporating as she waited for the onslaught.

"After our last meeting here I took it on myself to go to Freeth Street. How could you have left your baby in a place like that? You selfish, immature little fool. You are Roy's mother. Doesn't that mean anything to you? How could you? How could you?" Dora repeated, swallowing to choke back her emotion. "When I saw him there, his bones almost poking through his skin, the lice, the ringworm, I couldn't ignore it, Winnie. I contacted Mrs Biggs, the Chief Woman Visitor for the children. She had him admitted to the Western Road House last week."

Winnie listened in silence. She felt a deadness inside. But the force of Dora's attack had negated her feelings of conscience, and her new-found arrogance asserted itself. The words rolled from her tongue like hot lead.

"Dora, I did not ask Roy to be born, but as you correctly say, he is my son. I hope to make arrangements for him in the near future. Until that time the care he can get in an institution might be the best thing for him. In the meantime, please oblige me by staying out of my business."

Dora watched in stunned amazement as Winnie opened her bag, adjusted her make-up in a small, ornate handmirror, snapped the bag closed, rose, and left her home without another word.

She walked steadily home, surprising herself with her outward calmness. The events of the morning, traumatic as they had been, had released her from Dora's grasp. The worst Dora could do, were she so minded, would be to turn up at Wellington Road and tell John about Roy. She would back herself to convince John that Dora had come from the asylum in Lodge Road.

She felt a quiet contentment as she arrived back at the house.

John was still out.

She put a cigarette in her holder and lit it, then ordered afternoon tea from Victor, and went back to reviewing her new life.

She had been treated with studious civility by Victor since her arrival on April the second. She had soon overcome her initial nervousness in her dealings with him. After a few days it seemed natural to her to have servants.

The manservant had never shown outright enthusiasm for her since her arrival, but she paid no heed to this, putting it down to Victor being an old man and set in his ways. What made her wild was not Victor, but John's way of talking with him in their strange native tongue, which was totally unintelligible to her.

But it was not John and Victor talking afrikaans that would have shocked their friends. When she had told John that she would come and live with him as his housekeeper, she had assumed that he had accepted her on the basis used by many men, even priests, so it was said, that this would be little more than a device to cover their living "as man and wife" without the complications involved in a formal marriage. In fact, John had shown no desire whatsoever to consummate the relationship. He seemed perfectly happy to live with her, in separate well furnished rooms, have her on his arm when they were out, infer to the world at large that they had a full modern relationship, but not actually have one. That was not what she had expected when she had brazenly proposed the arrangement, but she had not doubted that all would change once John got used to her being there with him.

But all did not change, and spring gave way to summer.

At first, the gnawing pain that this rejection caused her was hidden under the relief that she felt to have left her more run-down surroundings. As the hot summer wore on, however, the frustration burnt into her and became a mind-numbing humiliation sucking away at her new found self-confidence.

Finally, on the last balmy Saturday evening in late August, she could stand it no longer.

They had both had plenty to drink at the dinner party they had returned from, but she had deliberately disguised the lower amount that she herself had consumed. After making sure that Victor had trudged his weary way to his attic room she crept barefoot across the hall and into John's room. He was sitting in his expensive underwear looking into the mirror on his dressing table. Hearing the click on the door he turned sharply round. The flames that were burning lower in her excited body must have been clearly visible in her face, dimly though it was reflected in the subdued light. He looked like a startled rabbit, but she was taking no prisoners and advanced relentlessly towards him. Before he could argue they were on the bed together. She made a crude lunge for his manhood and began working skillfully and instinctively with her hands. She felt his arousal starting and pushed closer. He did not fend her off but seemed totally traumatised by this female version of rape.

Whatever he really thought that night, her determination and his physical reactions overcame any other feelings. They were quickly engaged in the mechanics of the sex act. Soon, too soon for her, he had finished, and as he showed no inclination to please her further, she climbed off of him and lay by his side on the large bed, aroused and panting. He just lay there, motionless. If his eyes had not been open, she would have thought him unconscious. For a wild, irrational moment, she wanted to kick him or beat him with her fists. She looked into his inexpressive face, her heartbeat slowly returning to normal. Gradually she became aware of the sounds around her. Amongst them was the uneven hissing of the gas jet in the wall light. Suddenly she felt that she was back in Room 112 with Roy's absent father. No words were needed. The depression induced by the comparison hit her like a giant's fist. She slowly rose, left her inert and silent companion in his territory, and just managed to close her own door before breaking down into uncontrolled sobbing.

Sunday mornings were always leisurely, but inside the house Winnie was anything but relaxed. She had not ordered her usual breakfast in bed from Victor, as she had not expected to be in her own room.

She heard the old man's heavy, uneven footfall as he descended the creaking stairs to the first floor. Cautiously she peered out onto the wide landing and asked him for some toast and tea. As she tried vainly to eat, she wondered whether this would be her last meal at the house. After a seemingly interminable time, she heard the familiar click of the door and knew that John had left his room. She opened her door slightly and watched him walk down the wide central staircase to the ground floor and disappear from view. Wrapping her silken housecoat around her to counter the slight autumnal chill in the air, she followed him to the spacious rear drawing room. There he was, just like any other Sunday, hidden behind the"Times".

She sat in her usual chair on the opposite side of the fire, and waited. Had she a match, she would have cheerfully set fire to his newspaper, but there he sat, and there he remained.

Every sound seemed magnified. A cup being put down sounded like a window breaking to her. Like a child, she began to make various noises to gain attention, but to no avail. Finally, at twelve o'clock, the paper was put down, and he reminded her that it was time for their usual Sunday drive into the country to meet some of their well set up friends in the exclusive pub that they usually attended.

He drove normally. They discussed the events of the previous week normally; he appeared completely unaware of the fretful glances she darted in his direction, willing him to give her a sign of what the consequences were to be for her.

The conversation in the pub was the usual combination of affected chatter, joviality and, in John's case, short, subdued discussions devoted to business with some of those present, with odd sorties to the car park.

They spent the rest of the day in their usual fashion, walking in the park, returning for the early evening cocktail before dinner, listening to their new gramophone and then retiring to their separate rooms.

It was as though the events of the previous night had never happened. More than once in the following weeks she wondered if she had, indeed, imagined it. Life, with its pleasant if superficial round of social events, returned to normal.

As the summer's ferocious heat finally gave way to autumnal dampness a couple of weeks later, the past shuffled shabbily up the front drive. Victor opened the door to a particularly persistent and aggravating flower-seller who he had warned off the previous day. This time Winnie heard the raised voices and, looking over Victor's curved shoulders, found herself staring into Dora's angry eyes. Dismissing the muttering servant she pulled the door to and moved outside, announcing that she would make a purchase to be rid of the obstinate pedlar.

Dora almost hissed at her that Roy was very ill and had been taken into Dudley Road Infirmary. She snatched Winnie's arm and made an impassioned plea for her to call on her. She left Winnie with a small bunch of heather, rearranged her ragged shawl and made her way slowly back down the immaculate drive. Winnie returned the gardener's withering stare but did not see the erect outline of John van de Leure observing her with anxious curiosity from the upstairs landing window.

Winnie watched the diminishing cottage-loaf shape with gloom and foreboding. She had seemingly just overcome her final obstacle to future happiness, and now, just when she didn't need it, her past had made a re-appearance.

A wave of unreasoning resentment broke over her mind. She knew that she had neglected Roy, but she had told herself that her contact with him was inhibiting her total enjoyment of her new life. She had not exactly forgotten him, but had comforted herself with the proposition that if she was needed, she would somehow instinctively know. Instead of which, this gaunt intruder from Hades had appeared.

She returned thoughtfully to her room. From her window she watched the yellow and brown leaves steadily falling from the trees in the garden. She saw the gardener sweeping them carefully into heaps. Later, when the wind was right, he would make a fire and burn them. Here was a man with certainties. All she had were dilemmas. She felt as though her head would burst.

John watched with puzzled interest as, uncharacteristically, she put her new warm winter coat on and left to walk the short distance to the park. She noticed the children in their prams, mostly with attentive nannies, some with their mothers. How she envied them. Why couldn't it be like that for her?

Feeling even more depressed she walked quickly back to the house as the fine rain began to penetrate. She had made her decision and her head had cleared. For better or worse she would let events take their course with Roy. She had started off with loving intentions but she had got no recognition from him in return for the sacrifices that she had made. If only Roy had been more responsive. She saw him in her mind momentarily, dark, lifeless, lying in his old cot. She was sorry, of course, but she had done all she could at some personal risk. Yes, that was it. She would not give in to Dora's moral blackmail. If Roy was in Dudley Road, they would look after him.

The best thing she could do for Roy was to keep her own life together and wait for an opportunity when she could help him. In any case, she was entitled to enjoy her life. It was not as if she had asked for him to be born, she reminded herself.

As soon as the chance presented itself she would get whatever money was owed to her from old Barnett and give it to Dora for Roy. That would shut Dora up. In the circles she now mixed in, money seemed the answer to most problems with those kind of people.

October 1921 was an eventful month.

Winnie threw herself into the social whirl with tremendous zest, even for her. It was as though the cold chill produced by Dora's impertinent intrusion had left a feeling that every day and evening might be the last, so best enjoy it.

The month sparkled and shone, and on the final Saturday evening was moving to a peaceful conclusion with a small dinner party at their friends, the de Graafs, in their new home in nearby Westbourne Road. The six guests were called for dinner, and began chatting happily as they waited for the soup to be served by the maid "borrowed" for the evening. Winnie liked Paul and Lydia de Graaf. Paul was like John in build, but as dark in colouring as John was fair. He was a business associate of John, and obviously did very well, judging by the very latest in furnishings and tableware on show. Lydia amused her slightly. She sometimes teased Winnie about her Devonian accent, but this was really a defence mechanism to cover the fact that her own cultivated tones lapsed into her native Black Country now and again. As the large silver plate tureen was placed a little heavily on the table, Lydia was entertaining them with her account of the shopping expedition to London to buy the new furnishings.

Nothing, nothing was available in Birmingham like the new purchases, according to Lydia. This, with the accompanying exaggerated hand movements, would be parodied at forthcoming social events.

Even as she casually observed the maid filling the soup bowls with the ladle it did not dawn on Winnie. It was only when she observed the servant's solid profile and the slightly clumsy movements that she studied the face. There was no doubt about it. It was Lorna.

She was consumed by a mixture of malicious triumph and panic.

Luckily, she was genuinely hungry, and ate heartily. For a while she was a little subdued, but she nervously consumed her wine more quickly than usual and became effervescent as the evening progressed. She had no intention of giving Lorna the satisfaction of having taken the edge off of her exhilaration, and made a particular point of thanking her for her attentive service as they were getting ready to leave. She saw her sister's eyes fill with smouldering anger, as she hoped, but could also see a kind of disturbing confidence in their deep blueness; a niggling defiance that seemed to say that this was just an aberration in their respective positions in the Pow pecking order.

The following morning she woke to savour her triumph, but it was not long before it seemed hollow. She wondered what the consequences of her meeting and behaviour to Lorna would be.

Then it was time to get up and go to the sink in the corner of the room. She had not worried when she had no period in September. That was not unusual for her. But October had come and gone. Now the sickness had started. She was sure now. She was pregnant again.

She looked into the new heavy oval silvered mirror in her hand. She didn't know whether to laugh or cry. Her reluctant stallion had scored on his only attempt.

Should she tell him? How would he react? Would he now marry her? Would this make him into a true husband? Was there any chance that he would accept Roy? There was a better chance that he would not want his own offspring.

She needed to make plans in case she decided to terminate the pregnancy. She knew these things happened. Some of the girls in their set claimed to have had abortions, although you never knew how much was just talk. She did know at least one person to talk to, though.

There was an unnatural jollity in the busy city centre streets as night fell on Friday 4th November, caused mostly by the presence of the numerous guys and their guardians who solicited donations with varying amounts of courtesy and menace. Between two rivals she walked the familiar stairs up to Mr Barnett's office. The receptionist's mouth narrowed and she seemed to squint behind her glasses, as though making quite certain of Winnie's identity. With a forced smile, she retreated into Mr Barnett's office. Winnie did not want to face Mr Barnett, and was relieved when the receptionist reappeared and handed her an envelope which was unlike all the previous ones in size and shape. It should contain a fair amount, probably enough for the cost of an abortion if that was the way things went. She opened the envelope in the taxi taking her to Ladywood. She could not believe the contents.

Written personally by Mr Barnett in his neat, straight handwriting, she read

Madam

It has been brought to my attention that you have indulged in a deception of the lowest kind. There is no need for me to give the details, as you are only too well aware of what I refer to. Suffice it to say that, were it not for the delicate nature of the transaction that has been the cause of our unwanted association, the police would now be involved.
Do not seek to contact me again.

Yours faithfully

A. Barnett

She finished reading the short page with its hammerheaded words as the cab slowed by the end of Osler Street. The cabbie prompted her twice before she emerged and paid him, forgetting her usual tip and inviting a comment similar to that given to her by the disappointed boys with their guys that she drifted past in a trance-like state.

She knew Dora would be in. It was a quarter to five. She would be by the fire relaxing with Felix.

And so she was. Dora listened with apparent sympathy to Winnie's tale of woe. She had not loved Winnie overmuch when she was poor; being rich had not improved her.

The only consolation for this unwanted intrusion was that John Legg's idea of cutting off the money supply had worked and forced Winnie to make contact again with Dora. It was amusing really that the chance meeting between Winnie and her sister had provided such a convenient scapegoat. How Lorna's ears must have burnt as Winnie poured out her animated, if less than logical, explanation of how Lorna had been behind the unfortunate events that had resulted in her not being able to use the money provided fraudulently for Roy's upkeep for her own illegal abortion. Dora was interested in the pregnancy. This might certainly give possible angles. She tried not to ask too many direct questions about van de Leure, but got, she thought, a fairly accurate picture of their rather unorthodox relationship. On and on Winnie went. She was crying in her self-pitying way, making her voice an irritating wheedling tone. Incredibly, she did not ask once about Roy, and finally Dora had to tell her that on the 13th October, some three weeks ago, her son had been moved from Dudley Road Hospital to the nearby Western Road House. Winnie broke out into deeper sobbing, but still had the mental composure to whine that it would be unwise for her to visit him as if they traced her it would be all over with John.

Dora looked at her with barely disguised incredulity and some contempt. But she had to remember the purpose of the exercise, and nodded agreement with the wisdom of these self-centred thoughts. Thoughtfully, she offered to keep Winnie updated about Roy's condition through her contacts in the Workhouse. This, of course, would require regular contact between them. How much and often would depend on whether Winnie ever developed an interest based on motherly love, or even guilt, in her hapless little boy.

She had regained her position of influence, which is what had been intended. She let her guest cry herself to a standstill, and then waited with gathering impatience for her to leave. Winnie's main concern was to repair the damage to her expensively coloured hair and her make-up. Having helped her with this important task, Dora let her out into the now completely dark night.

She watched her strike out confidently into the blackness, catching sight of her as she passed through the little islands of yellow light beneath the gas lamps. Expensively clothed, well fed, straight-backed and hollow-hearted.

There would be much to report to John Legg, and she was soon off down the road to the tobacconist's cosy little shop.

Although with the end of the early signs of the pregnancy her condition was not obvious, Winnie knew from Dora that she would have to either have the termination or tell John about her condition. His lack of interest in her physically served her purpose well as she made up her mind. He seemed content with her as as his mistress in name only. She decided to see if he would consider being a husband in name only, for obviously now they had to marry for the child. If he said no, there was still just time for the termination.

She had to choose her moment carefully. She now knew him well enough to know when he was relaxed and receptive. She led into it by telling him that the coming 22nd December would be her twenty-first birthday. He said that he would have guessed her younger and she realised that they had never discussed their ages. She was equally surprised with his disclosure that he was twenty-eight, for the opposite reason.

He made the expected announcement that they would have to celebrate in suitable style, and seemed delighted.

She had rehearsed her other announcement, and delivered it with as little emotion as she could manage. She anxiously watched the flames illuminating his face and waited for his reaction. Although at first quiet and withdrawn, he soon reacted with surprising enthusiasm. He would contact the minister early in the New Year and make the arrangements. The wedding would have to be a quiet affair, given the circumstances. Her relief far outweighed any momentary disappointment.

The twenty-first birthday celebration was to be a surprise, John insisted. He refused to tell her where they were going, even when they got into the car. It was a surprise all right. He drove her straight to the hotel by the railway station where Roy had been conceived. It hadn't been his first choice, he explained, but even with his contacts it had been difficult to find somewhere willing to take a party of eighteen at relatively short notice. Outside the entrance she felt almost sick, but once inside her drama training saw her through the initial stages. After a couple of cocktails before the meal she began to relax, and as the evening progressed she threw herself into her role as queen bee with relish. The champagne flowed. Their friends expressed their undying affection and flattered her. If it was hollow, it was still enjoyable, and she lapped it up.

During a short interlude when no-one spoke directly to her she reflected contentedly on how her lot had improved since her last enjoyable but rather sordid visit to the hotel. Life may not be ideal in all ways, especially one that she was reminded of there, but there was a lot to be said for "the fast life" as the nuns had referred to it, usually in diminished voices. What did they know. She would enjoy her life to the full. If there was a bill to pay, they could put it on her account. Sod the lot of them.

She took another deep draught of champagne, and the smiling waiter moved catlike to refill her glass.

The afternoon of Christmas Day 1921 produced some interesting contrasts.

In the front drawing room of the house in Wellington Road, Winnie and John were curled up together on the large sofa in front of the roaring fire. They had enjoyed their excellent lunch served as always by Victor.

She had offered to help him, but John had become almost ridiculously protective now, and would not let her.

About a mile away from this scene of comfort and contentment, Roy was enjoying his second Christmas in the world as well as he knew how. The ward housemother had dressed him in his best for the day, just like the other seventeen babies and young children in her care. As he was too weak to even begin to walk, he was in his cot when Matron brought the three Poor Law Guardians round in the afternoon. They had joined the paupers in the main dining room of the Workhouse for their Christmas Dinner.

They brought nuts, apples and some toys donated by the Friends of the Workhouse Children. The Chairman, Caleb Chambers, later wrote in the Visitors Report Book that all the children seemed happy and well-fed. Some were playing games organised by the staff; others rested contentedly in their beds and cots.

Lying alone in his cot, Roy Pow stared unknowingly at the white ceiling. He heard the excited noises around him and sensed the happiness of others. He was aware of the faces that periodically looked down at him. All smiled at first. Some frowned and quickly went, but others stared and carried on smiling kindly. He waited for the familiar face that he knew to come. She was the one who sometimes held him closer than the others. He knew she could be angry, but he had never known why. But when she was nice it was like nothing else.

Whilst Roy waited vainly for his mother to visit him in the Western Road House, a quite different gathering was taking place many miles away in Barnstaple.

The Pow family, including Fred who was visiting, were listening open-mouthed as Lorna related the latest goings-on in Birmingham. They knew from her letters that the job at the gun factory had finished. She had had to own up to the fact that she had taken the menial work as a maid in order to relate her version of the events of the late October evening at the de Graafs. She added her own colourful conclusions about what Winnie was doing, partly gained from stories from other domestics. She was cut short by Fred who, with an explosion of anger, rose from his chair and told her to wash her bloody mouth out and made several other suggestions before he stormed out of the cottage.

Lorna was well satisfied. She had the comfort of knowing that she was not returning to Birmingham as she was going to take up the appointment in London that her grateful last employer in Handsworth had obtained for her. She had found an unexpected satisfaction in her work for him. He had been sorely used by other servants and had been so grateful to find someone with Lorna's qualities of honesty and reliability that he had been happy for her to rule the house. His sister from Moseley, who had suspected Lorna of having financial ambitions with her elderly and partly senile employer, had, however, finally won the day and arranged for him to go into a nursing home. His last act, the least he could do for her, he anxiously assured Lorna, was to give her glowing references and recommend her to his cousin, Alfred Adamson, in Wimbledon.

Father resumed his slumbers. Maria contented herself with a silent observation that she had been proved right when she had told him that she was glad to see the back of Winnie, and so would he be in time.

8

One of the qualities that had sustained John van de Leure in his business enterprises was his remarkable memory. He could almost always remember names after one introduction, and never forgot a face. This, combined with his considerable personal charm and innate sense of danger, had kept him clear of many a financial whirlpool. He was less certain in his dealings at a personal level, but tended to instinctively employ the same approach that served him so well in his more detached contacts.

As he watched the birds busy amongst the budding spring daffodils in the garden he had an indefinable sense of unease.

He knew that he had to make the arrangements that he had promised Winnie. She had known better than to start pestering him about it, but he sensed her unspoken anxiety in her eyes. That was not the source of his disquiet.

The whole economy of the country had slowed down dramatically during the autumn and winter of 1921 and this had been reflected in his own fields of activity. As he travelled around, people were less carefree and seemed less willing to commit themselves. Some even seemed edgy, as though they were uncomfortable to be seen in conversation with him.

Then there was the appearance of the old woman selling flowers last autumn. Something had taken place between her and Winnie. She had known Winnie before her call. He had observed them talking, and seen the recognition in her eyes. That had made him more watchful at other times. He was sure that sometimes he was followed in the car. One or two faces turned up too often when he was in shops. They were not serious buyers; he could tell.

The wild animals in his native land had this sense. The blacks who worked for his father often remarked that when they went into the bush from their villages to deal with a ferocious predator they would find it gone "with the bed still warm".

Perhaps the time had come to move his lair. He could not yet return to South Africa, but he just knew that the time was right to leave the existing scene. He didn't want to lose all the lucrative contacts that he had cultivated. Suddenly it came to him. They would go away to marry and have an extended honeymoon. It was perfect.

As she felt the wheels of the plane touch down, Winnie's breathing returned to normal. The flight had been a fairly short one. She guessed that they had been airborne for less time than their most common journey to the windswept airfield on the coast near Liverpool. As usual after take-off they had to cope with the restricted visibility from the rising smoke over Birmingham, and for some way the low cloud kept them close to the ground. Winnie did not mind this too much. However many times she flew, she was always fascinated by the view of the ground below, and if they were low she could see details like people working in the fields. John pointed out Worcester to the right. Beyond it she could see the clear mounds of the Malvern Hills. As the cloud lifted they crossed the greenery where the fruit grew, and minutes later, in full sunshine, she caught sight of the beautiful little villages nestling in the Cotswolds.

All too soon they began to lose height, and here they were on the flat, bleak waste of the airstrip north of Swindon where John had arranged to land. He had only told her his plans the night before. She had had no chance to see Dora to tell her. In a way she was relieved. When she saw Dora she inevitably felt obliged to ask about Roy, and the news was never any better. If she was away from her, the subject would be removed as well.

The plane taxied to the end of the gravelled airstrip and he parked it on the grass. Vague directions were given by a large, smiling ruddy-faced man in a battered greatcoat waving his arms between puffs on his cigar. He had emerged from a nearby small, rusting hangar. They got out, stretched and made their way towards the two primitive looking huts that served as a reception area. Outside the nearer one was an open-topped touring car which she assumed correctly John had hired. She sat in this whilst he went into the hut and exchanged some friendly banter with the two men inside. The airfield was plainly of military origin, and she listened with interest as she overheard John discussing with them his experiences of flying from the aerodrome during his service with the Royal Flying Corps.

It was chilly waiting, and she was glad when they drove off. He navigated them expertly from the map balanced on her lap, and she drank in the fresh, clean air as they drove the five miles or so over progressively narrower roads to their destination. This came into view over a small stone bridge as a small gabled and turreted country hotel, not much bigger than some of the county manor houses where they relaxed at week-ends. It was so unlike the large hotels that they had in Birmingham that she was a bit taken aback.

They unloaded their considerable luggage and Winnie wondered whether she had wasted her time packing her finery. It all seemed very small scale and rural. She need not have worried. Scale it might lack, but the hotel plainly had class, and she was glad that she had one of her smarter travelling outfits on as she was appraised critically by the reception clerk. Well well well, they were signing in as Mr and Mrs van de Leure. She wondered how long this would remain a pretence.

She did not have long to wait for an answer to her question. As they enjoyed a pre-dinner stroll amongst the shrubs before the meal, John told her that he had obtained the required licence and that they would be married in Swindon the following day. The Minister, Alan van Meher, had telegrammed him at the hotel to confirm his availability just before they had arrived.

Involuntarily, she threw her arms around him and engaged him in a passionate kiss. He had anticipated her response, if not the ferocity of it, and, for a moment in time, under the gently whispering trees in the fading dusk, they looked the idyllic lovers of stage and screen that Winnie wished them. The moment passed, and she contented herself with joyfully holding his hand as they walked the paths in the professionally landscaped gardens. They carefully tiptoed across the immaculately striped lawn to the recently installed fountain in the middle where they embraced again. They made their way back, balancing like children in the footmarks left in the dew by their outward journey. As they slowly returned through the grounds she cupped some of the foliage on the shrubs in her free hand. She noticed how clean the greenery was. How different from the grime of Birmingham. Even in Edgbaston dirt and smut found its way into everything, discolouring clothes and choking the very plants. She asked him excitedly whether they could live somewhere else. Far off in her mind she was driving up to Laurel Cottages in Barnstaple with him on her arm. What matter if they had to be a little vague about their baby's birthday. How well John would fit in with her erstwhile in-crowd friends in the Borough.

As if in warning, her pleasant daydream was shattered by several heavy rainspots on her head. By the time they reached the hotel the storm had begun. They laughed happily as they ran through the impressive entrance and into the reception area, attracting a variety of amused or disapproving stares from the other fourteen guests who were gathering for dinner.

Catching sight of the assemblage of glitter and cut of the dresses as they rushed in meant that no amount of exhortations would make Winnie hurry her preparations. As the seemingly endless process continued John produced a small box from his inside pocket and placed it rather solemnly on the dressing table. For a few seconds she ignored it, then, realising what it must contain, she snatched it up and opened it. Sure enough it was a wedding ring, but it was much lighter in colour than any others that she had seen. Sensing her puzzlement, he smilingly told her that it was platinum. She stared at it for a short time, then slowly removed it from the box. He reached over her shoulder and taking it from between her fingers, gently placed it over her third finger on her right hand. Frowning, she replaced it on her left hand. As she did so he kissed the back of her neck. She felt tears rolling down her cheeks. Then they both laughed. Back to the make-up mirror again. This was too much for John. He told her he would come up for her in ten minutes, and went down to the small bar.

They finally made their entrance for dinner a good half hour after the rest of the guests, to the thinly-disguised displeasure of the staff. Once they had informed the elderly waiter of their choices from the few alternatives on the menu, Winnie began to examine the other guests and their surroundings. She and John were the youngest by a good twenty years. Most of the others looked semi-rural types, rather like those she had seen around the Imperial Hotel in Barnstaple. She remembered how grand they had seemed to her then, and now here she was in amongst them. She realised that some of the men were giving her sly glances of appreciation. Their wives, plainly aware of their husbands' activities, mostly showed amused indifference, although malice was clear on one or two faces. Her expensive clothes, deliberately chosen to disguise her condition, were now being appraised by the older women.

She swallowed self-consciously and blushed a little. The new ring seemed to burn on her finger. She noted self-satisfaction on one or two of the surrounding female faces. She excused herself and went to the nearest bathroom. She toned down her make-up a little, and returned to the dining room with renewed determination.

As they consumed the overcooked mediocre food she noticed the strange decor of the room. John explained that the shields represented the various army regiments which presumably had been based locally during the Great War. Several countries were represented, including his own, South Africa. She attempted to get him to talk about South Africa but he immediately became defensive. A frost ensued, and remained for the rest of the meal. Later he only reluctantly joined her for a walk in the moonlight, complaining about the damp, and appeared delighted when he detected fine rain, which meant a retreat to the hotel lounge.

He engaged in conversation with some of the other male guests. The wives made only the most obligatory attempts at talking to her. Visible or not, her condition still made her tired. She excused herself fairly abruptly, and went upstairs to the room. She knew that there was no physical purpose in waiting for John, and she did feel genuinely drained.

She woke to find him asleep with his back to her. She had been awakened by the dawnsong of the garden birds. The last time she could remember that happening, she had been a child in Fremington.

As she lay still she listened to John's gentle breathing and saw his body rise and fall rhythmically.

So this was her wedding day. The day all girls looked forward to more than any other. She edged comparisons out of her mind. With John at her side she would be more than a match for Jack and Alice or any other competition.

She wished so much that Fred could have been there, but knew that he would like John and be proud of her. From Devon her thoughts took flight and landed amongst the slates and chimneys of Birmingham.

She assured herself that this day could only benefit Roy in the long run. One day she would be able to show him that she was a good mother really, and how much she had tried to look after him. She saw him in his cot. He was smiling approval. Then he faded and was gone.

Again she looked at John. Nerves suddenly gripped her in an iron vice. She felt sick. She asked herself the questions that she had avoided for the last year. Why wasn't he interested in her body? What did she know about him really? Why had he become so on edge last night when she asked him about South Africa? Where did his apparent wealth come from?

She called up all her resources of mental strength to cease this destructive torment. The light beating of a shower of rain at the window reminded her that she did not even know where she was. The fact was that there was no alternative to going ahead with the wedding. Perhaps he would become more open with her after the marriage. Yes, that was it. He would change.

Whatever she imagined the wedding would be like, nothing prepared her for the actual event. As they approached Swindon, the pleasant greenery gave way to the sort of industrial scenery familiar to her from Birmingham.

They passed a huge railway works that proudly proclaimed its ownership by the Great Western Railway. This brought Kate back to her. She knew what she'd say. She could hear her.

"Go on, girl. If he's got money, and he's offering you a ring, bloody take it."

John looked quizzically at her as she broke into a quiet chuckle.

The sky blackened as they dipped under two huge bridges carrying the railway over the road. He grinned as she ducked, and clung on to her white and primrose hat with her elegantly-gloved hand. They skirted a small park, and slowed as they arrived in an area of uniform little houses in rows, whose one redeeming feature was that beneath the dark slate roofs was an attractive, if smoke-stained light yellow stone, not the dingy red brick of Birmingham.

On the corner of two rows of houses was a small chapel. Outside on the pavement were three men. One, a straight-backed neatly dressed man in a long black coat and trilby hat, acknowledged John's greeting with a formal nod. His two companions were in working mens' attire, and stared furtively around, as though unsure what they engaged in. They seemed an ill-assorted trio.

John got out first and spoke to the tall youngish, moustached figure in the trilby, who glanced in her direction from time to time. The two men had plainly met before, and appeared even to share a joke as they talked. The stranger reached beneath his coat and consulted his watch, and she could see a dog collar. The other two men looked slyly at her from time to time and grinned with yellowed teeth. She heard them coughing and talking in low, subdued tones broken by loud, uncouth guffawing. She felt uncomfortable. She caught sight of the local beat bobby strolling down the opposite side of the street, resplendent with his Lord Kitchener moustache and row of medal ribbons. She had an irrational desire to yell to him. She noticed that the two older men with them were quite deliberately facing away from the policeman with their shabby coats up.

As her nerves began to resurface like rocks at low tide John returned and led her out of the car. It was five to eleven.

He had told her on the way in the car that it was a different service from the Church of England, less formal, more like a civil ceremony. The minister unlocked the door to the Chapel with some difficulty, and asked them to wait in the porch while he got everything ready. A nearby clock dolefully struck eleven as they entered, adjusting their eyes to the half-light.

She felt a sense of emptiness as the Reverend van Meher uttered the familiar liturgy in the musty, deserted chapel. She tried to read John's eyes, which remained firmly focused on the minister's face. She studied his enigmatic expression. Her heart cried out for one small gesture or mannerism that would drive away the fancies and doubts clinging like limpets to the corners of her mind.

Ridiculously, she glanced behind to see whether Fred was there during the short silence following the enquiry as to the validity of the parties to the ceremony. Her eye caught the simultaneous upward glances of the two goblin-like figures hunched together in the front pew. They grinned as they quickly cast their eyes downwards.

The bride and groom signed the register at the top of the newly-opened page.

"Not used often these days for weddings, then, Alan," commented John.

"No,unfortunately not. First since the War. Everything went. We've even had to buy a new register," commented the minister conversationally in his flat, slightly-accented, voice as he assisted the two witnesses to add their signatures.

The bride and groom left the building with the minister and went out into the light drizzle. Their witnesses had already scuttled away into the surrounding grid of mean little cottages. John handed the minister an envelope. He placed it in his inside pocket without checking the contents. Winnie surveyed the bleak, empty street and tried to prevent her eyes misting over as she shook hands with van Meher. He wished them good luck and safe journey and then he, too, disappeared into the maze. And that was it. She was now, from this day forth, to be known as Mrs Winifred Nora van de Leure. It sounded very grand. She repeated it to herself a few times. It sounded powerful and important.

They drove back past the railway works, their path impeded by the huge swarm of men on bicycles and foot coming away for their weekend. How she would have loved to have been recognised as a bride, like Alice with the potters at Fremington. But, apart from the ring on her finger, they were just what they had been before the formalities, an attractive well-dressed couple.

On the way back to their hotel, they noticed a new building that they took to be one of the new "road houses" for car tourists. In an uncharacteristically spontaneous action, John suggested they have their own wedding breakfast there, just the two of them.

It was glorious. She gazed out through the glass of the new-style metal window by their table. Outside, on the back terrace the sun streamed down onto the lawn where a pair of peacocks were strutting, plainly lovebirds. She rested her eyes and soaked up the warmth. Suddenly, she remembered one of Father Lopes's sermons. She had been too occupied studying the detail and defects of the window and its glass. She had not observed the beauty that lay beyond the hard, imperfect pane and it's surround. The peacock, right on cue, thrust out his gorgeous tail feathers, and turned to face her, proud of his finery.

She studied the ring again and her doubts began to evaporate. She liked the informal ambience of the dining room, with its clientele of young travellers. The up to date decor contrasted with the stuffy hotel that they were staying in and she asked John if they could move there. He shook his head dismissively. Her new name was not as powerful as it sounded, obviously. She delicately resumed her consumption of the fish course with the new, shining fish fork, and demurely sipped her glass of Muscadet.

Following this enjoyable interlude, they made their way in leisurely style back to the hotel in time for afternoon tea. As they quietly chatted, for the first time she felt relaxed in her role as John's wife. Tea was well patronised, and they assumed correctly that most of the new arrivals would also swell the attendance at dinner.

They took the hint from the previous evening not to be late again, and were rewarded with less overcooked, warmer mediocre food. The pretentious wine waiter appeared to have uncommon difficulty finding the champagne that John requested, producing an indifferent vintage that John reluctantly accepted. They were not about to enlighten the other guests on the reason for the celebration, and attracted scornful looks from those who plainly considered them brash and showy. In a deliberate show of defiance, they linked fingers and clinked glasses as they toasted each others everlasting joy and happiness.

The next day being Sunday they relaxed with breakfast in their room. Winnie enjoyed the sensation of security generated by this act of domesticity. No matter that seasonal showers battered the hotel and grounds for most of the day, making it impossible to walk out until the evening. They both felt tired and contentedly agreed a programme of inactivity.

The week that followed was blissful for Winnie after the crescendo of nervous tension that she had felt prior to her wedding.

Technically they were on honeymoon, but her condition ruled out full intimacy.

The only real signs of her pregnancy were occasional sudden attacks of nausea and more prolonged spells of tiredness.

John was as attentive as ever. They seemed totally at peace with each other. Gently he would hold her, caress her body and hair, explore her almost medically in a way that he had not attempted previously. It was as though he was reaching out to her mentally through his physical actions.

The hotel became an island of happiness for them. She loved the clean, green grounds, the lack of noise and distractions, and, for virtually the first time, being the recipient of John's undivided attention.

They got around in the car. Most days they spent exploring the nearby villages or, if the weather permitted, sharing picnics prepared for them by the now more friendly staff. Those were Winnie's favourite days; she would sing as she unrolled the rug to share with him their basket before returning to the car and driving back with the hood down.

The solitude of the picnics gave him to her more completely even than the hotel. She would seek to please him, sometimes feeding him like a baby. Other times she would slowly disrobe, noting with great satisfaction his obvious arousal in response to her improvised shows, and then carefully knead him to a conclusion. She wondered if Mr Smith would be pleased to learn that his acting tuition was being put to such use. When he was at his most relaxed, she toyed with the idea of trying to prise information about his family out of him. But she wanted nothing to take away the sheer pleasure of the week. Plus the fact that she did not want to invite questions about her own family. She had great plans for the day he would meet them, but that was a little way in the future. For now, this was all she wanted.

On the Friday they decided to visit a Roman Villa a few miles away, at Chedworth, that one of two elderly sisters had recommended to them from their guide book. The sisters had then, of course, invited themselves, brushing aside John's concerns that the rear seat of the car was so uncomfortable. Winnie had been amused that John had fallen for such an obvious ambush.

Superstition was never far from Winnie's mind, and she frowned as she drew back the curtains to reveal that a dark, clouded sky had replaced the painted blue and white that they had been favoured with for the previous four days. She asked John to call the whole thing off, but he said he did not want to let the old ladies down. This produced a hormonal tantrum from his wife about who he cared about most.

She realised that she was behaving irrationally, and allowed him to persuade her.

She did not like the imagery conjured up by the ruins of the villa. As old Eva read extracts from the red guide book, the emphasis seemed to be on the mortality of all things. It reminded her that the magic of her last few days was bound to end. She began to feel the mosaic floor heave and tilt.

It was Edith who caught Winnie as she fainted and nearly fell badly. She was not a spinster as Winnie had assumed, but a widow and mother who had served as a Red Cross volunteer nurse during the last year of the war. She knew immediately what the trouble was. She was surprised to learn how advanced the pregnancy was, so few signs being evident, but told her that nature was only being kind to her, and that she really should make preparations and take it easy.

From that day onwards, the stay at the hotel seemed to become tarnished. The sounds and routine of the hotel, so pleasant and sometimes amusing the previous week, became tiresome and irritating to her.

The weather became more seasonal, ambushing them on their attempts at picnics. John used Edith's 'good advice' to enable him to leave her, urging her to rest at the hotel while he went out for part of the day by himself several times.

During the week the hotel was almost empty, and in her boredom she noticed as the week went on that the management retaliated with cheeseparing cuts in the heating and food.

The following weekend was more bearable, if only because the weekend guests arrived to give the place a semblance of life.

Along with some of the other better-heeled weekenders, they were invited to join Colonel Longhurst, the owner, and his wife for a pre-lunch sherry in the drawing room at twelve noon sharp on Sunday.

She tried to show interest as the Colonel gave his address to the guests. The pair of them were almost a caricature; the Colonel with his port-coloured nose, monocle and handlebar moustache, and his wife with her tweeds and fleshy, motionless expression standing to attention at his side.

He told the assembled ranks that they had been pleased to help the cause during the recent conflict by making their family home available for officers posted from the Empire. This had continued after the cessation of hostilities. Yes, and I bet you got bloody well paid for it too, she mutinously thought. Since the standing-down of the men, a mistake in the Colonel's opinion, fewer military guests had come, but they still intended to keep up their standards. They would rather close than entertain "tradesmen, hikers and those type of people".

As several of the audience guffawed appreciation, her blood rose.

So that was it. They'd rather have their hotel cold and empty for most of the week than cater for the increasingly mobile commercial classes.

She had had more than enough.

On the Sunday night, they had the first out-and-out row of their married life. John was surprised and somewhat alarmed at the ferocity of her verbal assault, which he genuinely felt at times would become translated into physical violence. Reluctantly, he agreed to return to Birmingham the next day.

He put some of her "hysteria" down to her condition, but reflected that, whatever the cause, she had got her own way. He didn't like it.

9

Whatever she had gained from winning the argument to return to Edgbaston, Winnie soon regretted her insistence on leaving their leafy retreat.

She felt uncharacteristically on the edge of her nerves in the plane. It seemed so fragile as it weaved them through the rain squalls. She felt heavy and vulnerable, and conscious of the load inside her body.

As they approached Birmingham she saw Roy's contorted face staring at her amongst the palls of dark smoke that reached up like giant's fingers. She begged him to forgive her, and not to drag them from the clear blue sky and down onto the grime-laden streets that formed the lines of the city's grubby working hands. The plane engine spluttered. She gripped the seat with white knuckles.

John's friend Gilbert met them at the grassed airstrip and drove them the short distance along the Bristol Road to Edgbaston. He seemed agitated, and above the engine noise and the rhythmic beating of the rain on the canvas hood of the car, she could hear him in animated conversation with John. John was in control of the situation, as usual. He quietly calmed and reassured Gilbert, emphasising here and there with his hands. She was proud of her husband.

She wondered suddenly whether John had laid on any kind of celebration at Wellington Road for them.

As they got out of the car, and Victor hurried from the house fussily to help with the cases, she realised that she had to be content with his formally delivered congratulations on behalf of the staff. "The staff." All four of them. As Mrs van de Leure she felt more secure in her role as their mistress. This was a fairly nominal position as she would not have risked trying to order Victor around, the cook never took any notice of anyone, and the maid and cleaner continued with their duties in their normal sullen way.

Considerate as John continued to be, even during her now frequent mood swings and nausea, she sensed a certain wariness in his dealings with her. She had hoped that the invisible bonds of their marriage vows would bind her into his heart in the way that only true lovers know; the ecstasy that they had shared during their first week at the hotel. But, although kind to her at all times, the coolness that had always kept that last completeness from her now returned, as wide a barrier as ever. She wondered if it was her fault in some way. Perhaps she should not have shouted at him at the hotel as she had.

Her condition heightened her emotions and made the emptiness and pain a sharper, deeper, hurt. It was there when she awoke. During the day she ached for his company. Sometimes he was at home, but even he could not disguise his restlessness. He did not seem to understand that just his presence took her to the start of the path to the special place that they had visited so briefly.

As May progressed she seldom left the house, and became increasingly anxious when John went out.

She tired more and more quickly, and took to spending more of the day sitting and looking fretfully out of the front window, where she would wait restlessly to see him returning.

She was thus occupied at about ten o'clock on Wednesday the 17th when she caught sight of a figure in an unseasonal heavy, threadbare coat and shawl advancing slowly down the immaculate front drive towards the house. She felt the power in her muscles melt as she recognised Dora's shuffling gait.

She raised her unwilling legs from the seat and went down to the front door before Dora had time to go round the side of the house to the trades entrance. Only the gardener was uncomfortably close by when she intercepted her by opening the large studded door. After the same ritual as before of a pretended purchase, Dora told her that Roy was very ill again and had been transferred from the Workhouse to the new children's ward at Selly Oak Hospital. Winnie could not think what to say, and her momentary hesitation was interpreted by Dora as indifference. She raised her voice and implored Winnie to visit him. Winnie found her voice now and told Dora to get off her property and never return. Seeing Dora's dumbfounded expression she flamboyantly waved her hand to her, showing the platinum wedding ring, which had been joined the previous week by a somewhat belated engagement ring consisting of the same precious metal, and including three large diamonds.

Dora retreated more swiftly than she had advanced, and Winnie, still smarting with emotion, watched her with satisfaction until the rhythmic clipping of the hedge reminded her of the gardener's presence. He returned her gaze with an expression that she construed as dumb insolence. She glared and considered dismissing him. Her head suddenly felt as though it would burst. She turned, and, slamming the door, retreated into the house.

She went up to her room and sat on the small sofa by the window. She felt herself trembling.

Beyond the gently waving trees she could see the tops of three particularly tall chimneys that rose above the green skyline. She had noticed them many times. It was as though they were there peering over the sighing greenery to remind her of the falseness of her escape from the grime and industry of the city. Somewhere in that grubby anthill was her child, and as she stared aimlessly out, she tried to think what to do about him.

A blankness came over her mind. She was now in the last stages of her pregnancy. With the best will in the world she was not fit mentally or physically to deal with the problems created by Roy's unplanned and unfortunate existence. Certainly she could not begin to approach John about him.

The debate was short and uneven. Again she comforted herself with the idea that Roy's welfare was best served by her continuing good health and prosperity.

She relaxed again and pressed the bell for the maid to bring her a pot of tea. As she waited impatiently, sharp iron claws closed suddenly somewhere inside her.

She jumped up and went over to her new rosewood bureau. She uncovered the five pound note that John had given her for emergencies. Her hands seemed to double in size as she scribbled "for Roy" on a loose piece of paper, and fumblingly pushed the money and note into an envelope addressed to Dora.

After her tea she found new springs in her legs and walked smartly down to the pillar box on the corner. She felt all right now. She had done her duty by Roy.

John had been very generous with the more material items of the world since their return. Apart from the ring he had given her other presents of jewellery. She mused that it might be better to live in cold emotional comfort than passionate poverty with a Rudolf Valentino. She could go to the Picture House to see him.

John had arranged for her to have all the medical nursing that she needed, or imagined that she required. He had shown a surprising new talent of his own by mixing relaxants for her, which she grew more dependant on each day.

The day after Dora's visit he told her that he had made arrangements for the actual birth and lying in to be at the 'Marlands' private Maternity and Surgical Nursing House in Erdington. This had been recommended by some friends of the deGraafs. Even this favourable endorsement did not allay her anxiety, and into her already fevered imagination loomed the 'Hawthorns'. John reassured her by telling her that he had arranged for them to visit the 'Marlands' that afternoon so that she could see it for herself and meet the staff.

She felt a sense of foreboding as soon as she they turned into the gravel drive and drove though the well-tended grounds towards the handsome white-painted front elevation of the 'Marlands'. The house seemed to crouch secretively behind the large trees hiding it from Sutton Road.

Despite the freshly-painted rendered finish, the large square bays combined with the balconied flat-topped entrance portico to convey the impression of enforced detention. The dividers in the small-paned Georgian windows became metal bars in her racing mind. At the sides of the house, tall castellated chimney stacks looked down on her like sentries with grotesque medieval helmets. As they climbed out of the car, two trams rolled past each other in Sutton Road, as though patrolling the boundary.

John pressed the entrance bell. Panic overtook her, and she gripped his arm and slid her bulging body as close to him as possible. A pleasant, pale-faced young nurse opened the door, and showed them into the matron's well-furnished private drawing room.

She studied the array of gaudy china ornaments on the shelves around the room as she listened with amused disdain to the clumsy attempts of the middle-aged and heavily made up matron, Agnes Brist, to flirt with John. Mrs Brist turned suddenly and spoke to Winnie in her ingratiating tones. Winnie had not time to make the facial adjustments to prevent Mrs Brist detecting her scorn, and the matron's florid features flushed with anger. She unconsciously spoke more quickly, the vowels flattened and some aitches were forgotten as her breathing became louder. Strongly-scented cheap perfume radiated from her perspiring body.

Winnie concluded that she had not made a new friend, but Mrs Brist was no doubt being well paid for her services and could please herself what she thought of her.

The 'Marlands' seemed warm and comfortable inside. She reminded herself that it was regarded as one of the best private maternity homes in the city. She really tried to accept Mrs Brist's gushing assurances of her happiness during the forthcoming stay, but still doubts gnawed at the back of her mind. She studied Agnes Brist's face again. The broadness of the matron's painted smile was not reflected in her cold blue-grey eyes. On the drive back she amused John with her impressions of Agnes Brist.

During the night the images conjured up by Dora's visit melted with the fancies of the day to produce nightmare and terror during her disturbed attempts at sleep. The hallucinations intruded into her waking hours the next day. John became increasingly anxious. Hearing her screams, he mixed her a relaxant. As she sipped his latest creation, she asked where he had acquired his skills.

"From a good Zulu witch doctor," he reassured her. His smile lit up her soul.

Whatever the cure might have been, she recovered her composure sufficiently by the late afternoon for him to feel able to announce to her in his usual factual but definite way that he had arranged for her to go to the 'Marlands' the following Monday, the 22nd. The doctor expected the birth later that week.

She accepted the news calmly, almost placidly. Her theatrical temperament, never slow to surface, brought forth a dramatic "last request" for a walk to the park the following day.

The weather was balmy as they set out and walked hand in hand past their unknown neighbours' villas to the park entrance. They walked in almost complete silence towards the Cricket Ground, then back along by the pool, before sitting down on one of the benches.

They returned the smiles of the other week-end promenaders, most of whom were parents or nannies with their little charges.

Winnie felt a relaxed contentment, even a thrill of anticipation, as she felt herself about to join them after the bother of the childbirth and lying-in was completed. She would have her place amongst them as of right.

John sensed her improved state of mind and decided that he could risk passing on some of the useful information given to him by the doctor and the visiting nurse which would be of assistance to her in the new adventure of childbirth. She listened to him intently, trying not to let her detached amusement show through, or betray by some loose word or gesture her own first-hand knowledge of the subject.

As he earnestly dispensed the well meant but superfluous information she leaned back and studied his handsome face, with the deep blue eyes and Prince of Wales smile that had attracted her at the Peace Fair so long ago. She really did love him, and would do anything to keep him, even if it meant living with the present imperfect physical side of their marriage. She just knew that when he saw the baby and became a proud father he would be held to her with bonds that would never break. Then he would want her. She knew he would.

Sitting still as they were she gradually became aware of a chilling breeze on her legs. Suddenly she felt an overpowering need to return home.

She had seen a vision of the future, and she wanted nothing to spoil it. She even began to think which room the nanny would occupy. She made John laugh on the slow walk back by trying to imagine Victor's reaction to the intrusion. How on earth would he adapt to the newcomer? John replied casually, but a little too quickly, that he would cope perfectly well. She turned and gazed into his face. His cheeks were taut and his eyes desperately sought her reaction. For a brief second he was at bay, and she waited, willing him to speak. He swallowed self-consciously, but no words escaped his quivering lips. She knew that, just for that fleeting moment, the key had been in his hand to open the gate to that last path. Again she searched his face, but the mask had returned.

She felt the curtain falling on the happy scene in the park. The darkness pushed the light from her mind.

She was still mulling this incident over as she lay in bed listening to the rain beating on her window. She knew that she could not approach him directly. She told herself that he would tell her when the time was right. Also, some things were best left unsaid. She should know that, of all people.

The sleeping draught began to melt her senses. The curtain in her mind began to rise again. In place of the park, with its smiling middle-class strollers and their pampered children, the familiar nightly cast of half-formed horror beckoned and teased her from the stage. She tried vainly to escape back to the woken world, but they advanced relentlessly until they surrounded her, grinning and reaching their diseased hands out to engulf her. The louder she screamed, the more they shrieked and chanted their abuse at her. She wished them back to the hell that they emerged from, and which, every night, they triumphantly carried her to.

Sunday was an anti-climax after Saturday.

They had their lunch quietly at home, and relaxed by the fire during the afternoon. They were outside the house only for a brief early evening walk amongst the dripping trees whose shadows were briefly visible on the garden paths as the sun made a belated appearance.

Their evening was difficult as she could not help being overcome with emotion and a gathering sense of apprehension. She demanded increasingly impossible assurances from her husband until he finally became exasperated and suggested that she laid down.

He brought her a cocoa drink which included one of his potions and she sank into her best and longest sleep of recent days.

She woke with a heavy headache to greet the Monday morning allotted for her to go to the 'Marlands'.

The maid helped her with her packing, gently persuading her, with John's assistance, that she was going to have a baby, not on a world cruise. John would be over to see her each day and could reinforce her clothing and other requirements as the time went on.

She observed the scenery on the journey as though she might never have another chance. They went on a different route from her previous visit, and the only things she noticed were some signs to Bordesley and Deritend as they drove steadily through the terraces, factories, carts and motor lorries of the inner suburbs. The terraces became fewer and neat villas began appearing, stepped further back from the kerb. She stiffened as she recognised the end of the journey coming into view - the straight, tree-lined Sutton Road, Erdington. As they turned into the drive, the stout, cunningly corseted figure of Mrs Brist appeared at the door in a slightly tight black dress with pink trim. She greeted them with her fleshy smile.

She reminded Winnie of a spider. A cold shudder went down her neck.

Winnie soon found that her instinctive doubts about the 'Marlands' and its matron were well founded.

Although the single room accommodation that she occupied was spacious and well furnished she did not have to delve deeply to find evidence of the slovenly regime over which Mrs Brist presided.

Like other arriving visitors they had been impressed by the neat, well stocked gardens and comfortable residents' lounge. The appearance conveyed had led them not to consider more detailed examination of the premises. Winnie's insatiable curiosity soon led her to discover the thick dust under the beds and the unhygienic conditions in the kitchen.

When John visited her two nights later she whispered her misgivings to him. She had been foolish enough to make an angry remark about the state of cleanliness of her room to the girl who 'called herself the cleaner' that morning. The girl had abruptly left and promptly brought Mrs Brist back with her, who loudly directed the girl to clean Winnie's room to 'Moddom's satisfaction.'

She had almost lost her appetite after her furtive visit to the kitchens.

She did not want John to think that she was ungrateful. He didn't really know what to say. He would smuggle in some of her favourite cakes, the ones that she had taught cook to make like her own mother. He turned her tears to laughter by adding that that was providing that Mrs Brist did not start searching him. The doctor, who he had seen on his way in, had told him that it might now be hours rather than days, so he begged her to stick it out until the birth. The lying in could perhaps be somewhere else.

She reluctantly agreed to this course of action. She realised that as she was now almost bedridden with what the elderly visiting doctor had diagnosed as 'pre-natal hysteria and nervous weakness,' there wasn't really any choice.

The baby did not rush to make an appearance, and by the time the midwife appeared at six o'clock on Monday morning Winnie needed all the skill of the woman's profession to complete the birth. After the relative ease of Roy's illicit arrival, Winnie was unprepared for the agony visited on her. Truly, God moved in mysterious ways.

The nurse presented her with the small bundle; not much bigger than Roy. The baby's most striking feature was the thin wispy corn blonde hair, plainly his father's.

John arrived late in the afternoon. She watched his face anxiously as he came in, carefully lifted his son into his arms and gazed at him. His face broke into a wide smile. Exhausted as she felt, her tiredness left her as she shared his ecstasy. She could see the glow of pride in his face as he gently rocked his son in his arms, talking to him in the baby talk that men know that babies understand. Flowers appeared in the room. John had brought a bottle of champagne with him, and also a bottle of sherry for Mrs Brist to thank her for her personal attention to his wife's needs during her difficult time. Weak as Winnie was, she gave him a very wry smile as Mrs Brist made her well rehearsed "you shouldn't have" reply.

Mrs Brist, Nurse Halling, Sally from the next room, all toasted the health of mother and child enthusiastically with the delighted parents. One by one they left, Mrs Brist, the last, thanking John again for her sherry and assuring him that it would be put in a safe place, away from the staff. You couldn't be too careful these days, she added confidentially. She congratulated them again, John being the victim of her sloppy kiss on his cheek. When she left, they both burst out laughing as he attempted to wipe off the lipstick and rouge.

Then it was their own time. Although nearly asleep, she sensed the peace, love even, that was between them and the little fair-haired baby. It would work. The baby was the seal that would bind them inextricably for the rest of their lives.

She could sense John talking gently to her, or the baby, but she heard nothing that he said. She was in the park with the other mothers, then they were in the car - no, the plane, on their way to Devon. She would persuade John to buy a large house, Fremington House, why not, and they would invite her family who would come like Joseph's brothers to the Pharoah's palace to pay homage.

Gently he released his grip on her hand. The sleeping draft had worked. He kissed her tenderly on the cheek and left quietly, thanking the nurse for her help. Mrs Brist had retired to her room. She was also asleep, the sherry bottle now almost half empty by her side.

The difficulties of the birth had produced a kind of togetherness between the staff and Winnie, and the days that followed were a lot easier.

Although she naturally wanted to get home, she did not view the three week lying-in with the dread that she had before the birth. She looked forward to the afternoons, when the nurse who had welcomed them to the 'Marlands', Jane Halling, was on duty. She seemed a pleasant girl, interested in her charges. She chatted cheerfully to Winnie about her boyfriend Arthur, and how she hoped to continue nursing when they married, if he allowed her.

John was as attentive as ever, paying his daily visits, bringing gifts and flattering the matron. He seemed relaxed, happy and carefree in a way that she had never seen him.

When he called on Friday the second of June, Mrs Brist reminded him that he must remember to register the birth, for which he had taken the details the previous day. He apologised, and as he left he promised, literally hand on heart, to attend to it first thing Monday morning. He had been a very naughty boy, he agreed.

He left the finger-wagging matron waving in the doorway and drove out into leafy Sutton Road.

It was a pleasant evening, and the worst of the traffic had gone. Although the trams were still a hazard, he decided to go through the city centre. He whistled happily as he drove through Aston.

The grassy verges and trees gave way to the denser terraces and narrow pavements. Outside many of the houses the residents were relaxing in their tiny front gardens. Some of the men had jugs of ale on small tables, enjoying a pint whilst their wives chatted before the evening routine of getting the children to bed. The children were everywhere, happily playing their games of hopscotch and with small toys. They were blissfully unaware of their shabby, unhealthy appearance as they cheerfully waved to him. He looked at them with genuine pity. His son would want for nothing. He would have the best. Life was perfect in a way that he would never have believed possible.

Nearer the city centre some of the businessmen in their trilbys were making their way to the bus and tram stops for the evening journey home. Give it a few years, that would be him. Who'd have thought it.

Some twenty minutes after he had set off from Erdington he made the familiar right turn off of Bristol Street and into Wellington Road. There were few people out on the tree-lined pavements here. The children of Edgbaston did not play in the street.

A young couple were walking towards him hand in hand, presumably returning from the park. Unusually, a policeman was walking slowly towards the house on the opposite side of the road. He turned and respectfully touched his helmet as the car passed. Strangely, for the time of year, the policeman had a cape over his uniform.

He turned into the drive and drew up in his usual lazy way on the hardstanding by the side of the door. Before he had a chance to open it, Victor appeared anxiously at the door to inform him that two gentlemen were waiting to see him in the drawing room. He was not expecting company, and looked anxiously back down the drive. The uniformed policeman was standing motionless at the entrance to the drive looking straight back at him. The cape was now open at the front, and to John's shock and amazement, he saw quite clearly glinting in the evening sunlight the barrel of a pistol in the policeman's right hand.

He weighed up his chances.

"Don't even think about it, sir, we have cars posted at both ends of the road." said John Legg calmly but firmly behind him.

It was his own fault. He had become so preoccupied with the baby that he had forgotten all his good habits. His movements had become too predictable. He had been flying straight with the sun behind him. This was the price for dropping his guard for even a short time. He would have to see which way they wanted to play it. They might only be fishing.

He swore under his breath as he turned and followed the detective sergeant into the house. He carefully placed his hat on the stand and walked across the hall into the drawing room, where he found Inspector Davey standing. Davey managed a thin-lipped smile, then in his usual businesslike way, having established John's identity, told him that he would like him to accompany them to Ladywood police station. He was not under arrest, but it would be in his interests to assist with their enquiries.

John showed no visible reaction, and after courteously obtaining Davey's permission, he gave Victor some instructions. They left the astonished servant to look after the house, and got into the unmarked car which had appeared in the drive.

10

The match started as soon as they left in the car. Hoping to capitalise on van de Leure's surprise at being taken in, Davey had instructed Legg to engage him in friendly conversation on the short journey. This would prevent him thinking too much, and work Legg into his confidence as the approachable face of the law. This strategy failed miserably. Legg, at his chatty best, was a lightweight compared to the man they were transporting. He could almost hear van de Leure's brain wheels turning as he fielded Legg's sociable banter in neutral. The only useful outcome from this preliminary skirmish was to convince Davey of the magnitude of the task before him. This man was, as all the available intelligence had predicted, a very cool customer.

Whilst their guest awaited them in the witness room, Davey and Legg were in their customary positions in the inspector's office. Legg was organising the tea, and as the kettle simmered gently he kept quiet, busying himself with re-checking unimportant reports.

Davey was also quiet, sitting behind his desk. He relished these contests. The difficulty with this one was knowing where to aim. It seemed highly unlikely that van de Leure could be bought, judging by his apparent wealth, so he could not be turned by money, the most common lever. He could not see him confessing, and evidence usable in a court against him was sparse in the extreme.

This really only left bluff and threat, with all the unpredictability that entailed, if real unpleasantness was going to be avoided. Before the war his father in Dundee would have softened up van de Leure in the old manly way, but these forms of interrogation were now frowned on by the new hierarchy.

Time was moving on. He had no intention of letting van de Leure go, and sent a duty constable out to get the nearby friendly J. P. to sign the ticket enabling him to keep van de Leure in custody as an Empire citizen likely to abscond by plane. That would make old Caleb Chambers' thick eyebrows rise when he read it.

Van de Leure was brought into the interview room. He looked calm. His face betrayed nothing. Not a man to play poker with, mused Legg. Legg took the notes as usual; he knew his boss's style so only noted verbatim the particularly important matters in the conversations of each interview.

After the brief introductions, Davey tried to lead his suspect into the main thrust of his attack. Legg noticed that his voice was rising; not a good sign. If he felt on top, Davey was quiet and analytical, usually lulling the miscreant into a deadly ambush. Soon Legg found himself having to write faster.

"So, you are a trader, Mr van de Leure, in commodities. And what commodities in particular?"

"Whatever people want to buy."

"Would that include illegal items?"

"Not that I am aware of."

"Mr van de Leure, you do not have a job as such, do you?"

"If you mean an 8 to 5 job, no."

"How do you support yourself then?"

"I operate as a freelance pilot, normally on commission. I learned that skill fighting for Britain as a volunteer, as you may be aware."

Oh, he'd have to throw that in. Half the villains in the city that they got to court claimed immunity as bloody war heroes.

"Come on, Mr van de Leure, this does not bring you the money for a house in one of the best roads in Edgbaston." The bluster was building up again.

"I also have a private income."

"From what?"

"Am I under arrest?"

'Well -"

"No is the word that you are seeking, Inspector."

"Oh, it is, is it?" snapped Davey, sitting straighter in his chair. "I'll tell you what I'm seeking, Van de Leure. I'm seeking to find out exactly what you have been up to, how you support yourself in your opulent lifestyle, and who pays for it in the end. That's what I'm going to find out, and, guess what, you're going to tell me!"

I don't think so, thought Legg, as the Inspector's voice built up to a crescendo of controlled aggression that intimidated most of their regular clientele.

Van de Leure sat, hands still, face expressionless apart from his thin, natural smile. He maintained this posture effortlessly for the next twenty or so minutes as the Inspector continued his fruitless verbal assault. Davey disclosed little acquired information. Legg knew that would come next time, but he tried to intimidate van de Leure by inferences about knowledge or disloyal contacts. He might as well have stayed in bed, thought Legg.

Legg's other role in these interviews was to spot reactions for further sessions. He could not later recall anything that disturbed van de Leure.

The duty constable's face appeared at the small glass window let into the door, and his nod indicated that Caleb Chambers had signed the necessary papers.

Davey relaxed back into his chair, which was significantly and deliberately upholstered and comfortable in a way denied to his suspect.

"Well, Mr van de Leure, it seems that some hospitality has been arranged for you here tonight, and for a while longer if we deem it necessary," he said with as much barb as he could fashion.

For the first time van de Leure seemed to stiffen.

"How long will I be here, I have - commitments?" he said slowly, and a little crossly.

"How long will you be here?" Davey repeated quizzically as he perceived his opponent's discomfort. "Well, John, that rather depends on you, and how quickly we progress. It's getting late, and we are both tired. We'll call a halt to it now, and resume tomorrow. Sergeant Legg here and I have commitments, too, but we'll be here tomorrow to talk to you again, and we'll give you all the time you need. Perhaps overnight you will recall some of the answers to the questions I've asked tonight. We can have a chat about your commitments, too," he added, with a malicious smile.

He called the duty sergeant, and had van de Leure booked in. Then the two detectives retired to the office, where the kettle was still simmering, to bounce their thoughts off of each other.

"Well, John, the only thing I picked up was that he doesn't seem to like our hospitality. Rather ungrateful of him, really, when we've gone to such trouble."

"I thought we finished the stronger," commented Legg enthusiastically, much after the style of a sports reporter who had popularised the saying in his forlorn attempt to rake something out of a Villa 5 -1 defeat back in the spring.

Davey hardly heard him. He not only saw problems in convicting van de Leure, or even persuading his seniors to charge him, but he saw hazards too.

The prize for success was his yearned for promotion to Chief Inspector; that much had been made clear. But what if it all blew up in his face? He knew from the copious reports of van de Leure's movements that plenty of the self-appointed elite of Birmingham were well known to him. What if he got van de Leure to court, and the defence called them and obtained an acquittal, or, more likely, the withdrawal of the case? That would go down like a lead Zeppelin upstairs.

And so would his chances of an enhanced pension.

He had put a great deal of his time into the operation since being chosen to spearhead Operation Pipe Dreams in the area. He had attended all the meetings since the operation had moved north to Liverpool and the Midlands. He still retained much of his initial scepticism about the whole dope girls proposition. The idea of innocent, clean-living white girls being lured into drug addiction and slavery by mysterious turbanned foreigners belonged to the picture palaces as far as he was concerned. But someone believed it, and the operation had been passed down from Scotland Yard to his Chief, and he had entrusted Davey with the groundwork. Every few days, especially at the beginning, they had pestered the life out of him. Even the bloody Mayor and Corporation had got involved.

"Forces in other towns and cities were making arrests. Why wasn't he?"

As an experienced policeman he had seen none of the build up of the web of activity that formed round illicit operations, and finally brought evidence into the light after being glimpsed dimly by the eyes of his network of informers. As the months had gone by his doubts had increased. It just didn't feel right.

The initial excitement had been replaced by lack of interest when the expected nest of exotic Arabs had not been found. Now, the whole thing was just a bloody embarrassment. He had been relieved when the Chief Super had told him that the Op was being stood down.

He did not have to be told to engage in a damage limitation exercise. Although funded by Scotland Yard, the Watch Committee were always sensitive about the use of their police time on "wild and woolly schemes from London."

He knew that he had to get a result of some sort with van de Leure. But what? Perhaps it would all be clearer in the morning.

He suggested they adjourned to the nearest civilised hostelry; an idea that soon had his junior ranked colleague turning out the gas under the kettle.

The gas had been lit for half an hour or so when Davey appeared in the office on the stormy morning of Saturday June 3rd. He had been awake for some hours, awakened by the thunder, and then kept awake by the early dawn and mental rehearsals of the next round with van de Leure.

Legg studied his boss's face and did not like what he read. Davey, normally the most surefooted of interrogators, seemed uncharacteristically unsure of himself. He watched him brooding over his first cuppa, and waited for what Davey called the "workings of the overnight subconscious" which had provided inspiration many times. The only announcement was that he had decided to let van de Leure stew until about ten o'clock. This was further evidence of uncertainty in Legg's opinion.

Half an hour before the appointed time, the intercom went, and Davey was summoned upstairs. When he returned, Legg could see he was angry.

"The bastard's even more organised than I thought. When he was giving old Methuselah at his house that list so he could look after things, it included the name of Solly James for him to phone. Need I tell you more?"

There was no further discussion before ten o'clock. None was necessary. Solly James was senior partner in one of the most respected legal firms in Birmingham. Davey's game of cat and mouse with time was now reversed. They both knew that they were now the ones with the time limit. The only glimmer was that van de Leure would not be sure that Victor had succeeded in his mission.

Ten o'clock came, and they made their way with no great enthusiasm to the interview room.

Rather like bowlers facing a top batsman resuming the crease the second morning of a cricket test match, they knew that they had to try and make their breakthrough before he settled.

The doubts in Davey's mind never made this likely. Whatever qualms might have been in van de Leure's mind, he soon picked out the repetition, the uneven approach, the lack of solid facts in Davey's questioning, and was quickly blocking or dispatching him to the boundary at will. It was painful to watch and listen to. After an hour and a half of almost total stalemate, Davey called a halt, and they retreated to the pavilion, or in their case, Davey's office.

Davey and Legg sat in sombre silence. Neither wanted to discuss the fiasco of the morning, and, worse, neither knew what to do to break this man down. Unconsciously they both realised that they had just one more session left.

Finally Legg could take no more of it.

"You can't just let this bastard walk away from it, Sir, can you?" he asked with unusual earnestness.

"You tell me how to nail him, John, and I will be delighted to do it." Davey flatly replied.

"Well, Dora Coote is sure that he was behind that opium business that her grand-daughter got involved in."

"She could well be right, John, but where is the bloody evidence?"

"Well, her grand-daughter is six foot under in Lodge Hill Cemetery, and none of her other contacts have made themselves known."

"Well of course they bloody haven't. They don't want to be there with her. I know this swine is involved in this dope business, if it exists at all. If I persevere long enough I will probably also get a disclosure from that bloody jeweller in Vyse Street that he has been purchasing diamonds from our friend, mostly to supply various council members and their assorted floosies. By that time, he'll have receipts for every last chip. Then there's happy families up at the 'Marlands'. If I need to, I'll just have to play that one."

Legg looked at his colleague uncomprehendingly.

The increasing humidity reminded them that it was now past midday. They adjourned to the canteen, having long ago discovered that a well-fed detective is more likely to be relaxed and in control of events. Legg attempted to take their conversation away from van de Leure, but he knew he was talking to himself. At one thirty Davey made a pronouncement. From his tone Legg knew he was now resolute in his pursuit of van de Leure.

"I've worked it out, John. If I can't win, I'm not having that bastard waving to me from his bloody car in this city."

"Oh," said Legg flatly. He knew that Davey was party to information that he did not share with his junior, but he would be highly interested to learn how he was going to shake the seemingly unflappable Mr van de Leure. At least the afternoon now held interest.

At two o'clock precisely, they were back in the interview room.

Davey looked fresh and relaxed. He exuded more self-confidence, and Legg could see a determination deep in Davey's eyes not visible to van de Leure, who, despite his fair stubbly chin, seemed cool and collected as ever. Legg felt that surge of adrenalin that always came when the climax of an interrogation approached. The oldest instinct in the world. The hunter closing in for the kill. The prey, in this case arrogantly defiant, unaware of the attack to be launched.

When he was on top form, when he allied tenacity to his analytical powers, Davey was a real master of his trade.

From the opening exchanges Legg knew that, one way or another, he would witness the destruction of van de Leure during the afternoon. Davey started routinely enough, restating the paltry disclosures that he had ground out from van de Leure in the previous two sessions. Van de Leure settled back and was as startled as Legg when, without warning, Davey calmly, almost politely asked:

"Well, John, you obviously don't want to talk about your business affairs, so before we let you go, why don't you tell us about your marriage?"

"Why should I? It's none of your business."

"Oh but it is, John. Bigamy is a serious offence."

"I haven't committed bigamy."

"Well now, you'd better explain these, which were found during the search of your house."

From the top drawer in the desk Davey produced two documents. Legg could see from his position at Davey's side that both appeared to be certificates of marriage.

He watched van de Leure's face intently. To his astonishment a smile spread across it.

"All right, gentlemen. I have a confession to make."

Both detectives faces mirrored suspicion and anticipation.

"I have indulged in a little harmless deception on Miss Pow to please her. She wanted to be married. I knew that was impossible, for, as you rightly said, Inspector, bigamy is a serious offence, so I arranged a little ceremony for her with a friend of mine. She got what she wanted, or thought she did, and I broke no laws, did I, gentlemen?"

If Davey was put off, he didn't show it, and continued.

"All right, John? Lets talk about your real marriage. You were something of a problem to your family, according to my South African colleagues. Your parents despaired of ever marrying you off, didn't they, John? You showed little interest in girls. Families like yours, owners of substantial mining and land interests, need good matches, don't they John. And here you were, twenty-one gone, and no sign of a match. We know that you were made to marry Myra van Haas. Suitable match with an only child; ugly as sin, I'm told, John. How the hell did you produce that beautiful little baby girl with her? You must have thrown a bag over her head."

If Davey had been trying to anger van de Leure into a mistake, he was disappointed. Van de Leure's mouth broadened into a thin, ingratiating smile.

"But then it didn't really matter to you, did it John? Your ideas of sin were, and are, quite different," the detective continued, trying not to let his irritation show. "And when your marriage failed to provide the cure for what your parents assumed was your illness, they decided that manly combat would be the remedy. So they paid for you to come over to England and, to give you credit, you did them proud with your efforts against the Kaiser. Proper little von Richtofen, you turned out to be, didn't you? But you couldn't face going home to lead a lie, could you? You stayed, and found another talent. You had inherited your father's business acumen. A deal here, a trade there. And you could practice your other, more healthy love - flying planes. But you still had the old desires, didn't you? And they had to be catered for, and financed. We know about your little parties, John. We know where you have been going, who finds the young lads for you, who else goes, who you pay hush money to, the lot. And that sort of thing *is* an offence under the law.

Van de Leure had listened studiously to Davey's oratory. Legg thought he saw admiration at times in the younger man's face for the thoroughness of the research and the authoritative presentation. There was a short silence before van de Leure spoke. His voice was perfectly controlled.

"How many witnesses do you think you will get to court? Also, the defence can call witnesses. I could surprise you with some of the people my lawyer could send for."

Davey knew that van de Leure was gambling. They both were. The stakes were now almost at their limit. He had only one card left.

He looked into van de Leure's face. He could sense a slight unease within the young man's projected self-confidence.

He would try and avoid the final unpleasantness.

"Mr van de Leure, I have a proposition for you. We will not proceed with any charges against you or your funny friends if you are on the 12.15 from New Street on Monday. That will take you to Southampton Terminus station on the 'South Express' from Cheltenham. There is a good hotel at the terminus. We will provide you with a first class single for the journey, your servant obviously a third, and suitable accommodation for you both to wait the next sailing for Cape Town."

Van de Leure appeared to weigh the Inspector's offer carefully. When he spoke, it was with care and deliberation.

"I am minded not to take up your offer. You are forgetting one fact that you stated in your excellent summary. I do not wish to return to my life in South Africa. I can live without my ugly wife and crying girlchild. I have all I need here. I am building a happiness I never thought I could have. And anyway, we both know you are bluffing. You would never even get past the magistrates - oh, before you think about it, two of them are regular attenders at our little entertainments. No, I think I will continue my convenient and comfortable home life here in Birmingham. I have found a lady who I am genuinely fond of in my own way. She enables me to present myself as I wish, but is also uninquisitive, a little naive, even."

There was nothing of the arrogance that van de Leure had conveyed in the earlier interviews as he enunciated his words carefully. He looked into Davey's face, hoping that his obvious respect for his interrogator would now produce an honourable end to the matter.

For the first time, Davey saw something else in van de Leure than the demonically evil trader in crime that he had needed to create in his mind to sustain himself mentally against van de Leure's formidable intellect. He was a man who was reaching out for a new life.

Davey could call it a draw and let him go. The price would be high.

Seeing van de Leure driving past him in his car and grinning down at him.

No arrests or even results from an extensive operation.

No guesses for who would be left to carry the can.

No promotion.

Davey lit a cigarette. For a second, a split-second, Davey hesitated as van de Leure's magnetic eyes challenged Kenneth Davey of Hall Green, good husband and father, keen gardener, to overrule Inspector Davey, ambitious policeman.

Inspector Davey knew that he had no real choice. Slowly he opened the drawer, and placed the photograph carefully in front of van de Leure. Legg could not make out clearly what the subject was. It looked like some kind of small animal in a blanket.

Van de Leure was obviously puzzled.

"What does this mean?"

"That, Mr van de Leure, is your naive and uninquisitive lady's other son."

Disbelief registered on the young man's face.

"Oh yes, it's true. I wouldn't insult a man of your intelligence by trying to pull a stunt. This is Master Roy Pow. He was born at Dudley Road Infirmary on July 9th 1920. You can see his birth certificate if you want. I have a copy."

He waited to watch van de Leure mentally reeling before delivering the knockout blow. He rose from his chair and stood behind van de Leure's chair. In an almost fatherly tone, he continued,

"Who is the father, I hear you asking? They have various names across the Empire. In India, a lot of them work for the railways, apparently, like he did. Where he came from, they are called Anglos. I think you call them Cape Coloureds. She was unlucky with this one. It's quite black."

Van de Leure stared with eyes of glass at the photograph of the ugly little undersized baby. He raised his eyes and spoke slowly, falteringly almost, to Davey's empty chair.

"What time was that train?"

Legg shot a smile of satisfaction at Davey, and was surprised not to see the look reflected in his senior's expression. Davey looked almost sad. Maybe he was just tired.

Legg settled back into his chair. He glanced at the clock. It was almost ten to three. It had taken just under fifty minutes.

Davey quietly told van de Leure to stand up.

"You are free to go, Mr van de Leure."

Legg thought he saw Davey put his arm on van de Leure's shoulder as they left the room together.

Legg hummed quietly to himself as he worked on the final report for Davey to present to the Chief. It didn't take him very long. Presenting matters that were not much more than monumental wastes of police resources as being well-planned contributions to the public wellbeing was a routine duty for him.

"You should be in politics, John," Davey commented as he had so often before on reading Legg's well-crafted efforts.

He finished making the few amendments and lit a woodbine as he re-read it.

Legg could not understand why his boss was not in higher spirits. He had, after all, broken a formidable opponent.

Suddenly they both felt fatigued, and Davey told Legg to leave the typing-up for the following morning. As he left, he turned his heal on the pitted lino to stub out the last sparks of his cigarette end.

They shone accusingly and brightly back at him, then died. Innocent victims of Operation Pipe Dreams. Like the love of Winnie Pow and John van de Leure.

The Chief frowned as he read Davey's report.

It might be hard for him to explain that the sum total of the results of the whole operation had been to frighten off one South African. He raised his eyebrows as he read Davey's conclusion that the lack of arrests was accounted for by the fact that, despite an exhaustive operation, there was no real evidence of a "Dope Girls" operation in the city, probably due to the high reputation that the City Constabulary enjoyed.

He thought about the possible repercussions on those involved, especially himself.

Scotland Yard had paid the bills. No financial loss to report. Good. The two, influential, sweaty members of the Council who had held a confidential meeting with him the previous Friday would be relieved to know that the source of their concern had left the city. They would square any muttering in the Council House.

He would recommend that Davey get his desired promotion. He had undoubtedly worked hard. And he was a good Lodge man.

The Chief signed the report and put it in his *out* tray.

11

The two detectives would have hardly recognised the sullen figure of John van de Leure sitting on the bench in the park the following morning. The upright, confident-looking character who had strode into the police station less than three days before was still unshaven. His shoulders were slightly sloped forward as he sat there trying to make sense of the events.

He still could hardly believe it. He would have trusted Winnie with his life. He had given her everything a woman could want. And she had repaid him with falseness and treachery. His friends had always told him that women were fickle, sly and unreasoning. He had argued with them. He had not wanted to believe it. Well, he did now.

The noise from a nearby game of cricket being played on an improvised pitch intruded. He saw the father, his jacket removed in the heat, laughing as he bowled the ball slowly to his fair-haired son. The boy's brother was fielding. All this, the everyday domestic happiness accepted by the world, that had been there for him only the day before, that he had fought Davey for, had been snatched away by the woman's treachery.

Suddenly, sitting on the very bench where it had all seemed so appealing and possible just two weeks before, he realised what an unreal dream it had always been for him.

His mind turned to more practical matters. He had already instructed Victor to commence packing. The rent was paid to the end of June. He had sent a note to the agent.

He felt the wrenching pain in his stomach as he reminded himself of the price he had agreed.

He would never see his son again. If he wanted another one now, he would have to service that fat sow at home in South Africa.

It was inconceivable to see Winnie again, of course. From his inside pocket he took out the letter that he had already written to her. He re-read it, made one addition, and sealed the envelope. He would post it at the railway station. She would get it later that day, or first post Tuesday. The cheque for Mrs Brist was with it in the envelope. That would pay for the rest of her lying-in. Then she could sort it out herself. Served her right, the deceiving bitch.

As arranged, John van de Leure called at the police station shortly before twelve o'clock and collected the two railway tickets to take him and Victor to Southampton.

They arrived at Southampton Terminus station in the early evening and found their pre-booked accommodation in the impressive South Western Hotel comfortable.

As he undressed to prepare to go to the bathroom down the corridor, John noticed the small bulge in his jacket pocket. It was the letter to Winnie. He summoned the reception. The attractive young boy in the page boy's uniform who tapped at his door assured him that the letter would definitely make the evening post.

John studied the boy's ruddy, sea-fresh complexion, and asked him to wait. He felt the old, forbidden excitement rising, and as he returned with the generous tip, he allowed his bathrobe to part. The boy blushed, but did not look away. They both smiled.

After his solitary meal, he retired to his room to wait for his young companion to finish duty. As he undressed for bed he searched his pockets for the coins that he had promised him. From the bottom of one of the jacket pockets, he brought out a dog-eared piece of cheap lined paper. He realised it was the information that he was supposed to have taken to the Register of Births office in Birmingham. He read it once, hesitated, then, noticing the large ashtray on his table, tore up the sheet, and placed the pieces in it. As he waited he smoked a cigarette, and passed the time by setting light to the ends of the paper.

Overnight he decided not to go to South Africa.

A couple of days later he and Victor were on the boat to France. John found the French more tolerant of his passions than the cold, inhibited, hypocritical British. He soon built up a very profitable Cross-Channel airfreight business.

He kept in touch fitfully with his family.

A few years later, shortly after Victor died, a letter arrived to say that his father was dying.

Africa had been calling him. Every damp French winter the sights, smells and sounds of his homeland grew clearer during his frequent sleepless nights. He accepted the generous offer for the airfreight business that he had been considering, and returned home on the steamer in some luxury.

He could face his father now that he had a successful business behind him. He had given his father a reason to respect him at last, and the old man obligingly died content shortly afterwards, happy that John could now run his business interests.

John fitted in as best he could with the claustrophobic society that he had shunned for so long. He was polite and considerate to his wife, and spoiled his daughter.

They had no more children. In his mind, his son in England grew up fair and strong. He needed no other.

Some evenings, though, he would feel the old stirrings.

He would go to parts of nearby Mafeking not usually frequented by people of his class, or in some cases, race.

It was in one of the 'B' grade hotel bars one night several years later that he overheard a group of local, good drinking, war veterans, some known to him, exchanging stories with a hotel guest. He stood at the back of the group and studied the stranger, who was holding centre stage. The visitor, who was plainly a practiced raconteur, was a tall well-groomed man who looked in his late thirties. In the smoke-filled light, he looked slightly dark in complexion, a feature emphasised by the silver fleck in his immaculate jet-black hair. He was recalling his visit just after the war to England, and the easy pickings among the sex-starved girls and war widows.

John moved closer until he could read the speaker's badge on his lapel. He was evidently one of the representatives at the conference of railway engineers that was being held locally. With his now slightly imperfect eyesight, he made out the name "S. Roy, Esq., Senior Buyer, Great Indian Peninsular Railway." He listened on until the bragging became more obviously exaggerated, the guffawing louder and coarser. He wanted to ask the man where in England all this was supposed to have happened. But he didn't.

* * * * * *

"Letter, dearie," announced Mrs Brist cheerfully, as she woke Winnie at half past seven. Winnie had lurched back to sleep after her third almost sleepless night wondering where John was. He had seemed so happy on Friday night, and she just could not begin to think what had happened to him. As usual, her imagination had gone into overdrive. The last waking nightmare before sheer fatigue had released her back to light sleep again had involved Lorna bringing mother and Baby Roy to see her.

"Such wickedness, such wickedness," her mother's face had shaken with anger and pity for her weak and sick little infant. Far, far, worse, she could see the contempt for her in her mother's eyes. How pleased Lorna had looked. How smugly she had smiled.

Winnie started as she realised that the smile that looked down on her now was painted on the matron's bloated face still heavy with the previous day's make-up. Above it the eyes were not smiling.

She wagged the letter tantalisingly in front of Winnie, and Winnie's drained senses recovered sharply, anger being the first. She snatched the letter from her startled tormentor, and impatiently tore the top of the envelope open. As she unfolded the single sheet of plain unheaded paper, the cheque fell out and slid over the side of the bed. Before she could move, the matron's plump ringed fingers had expertly grasped the cheque. Her eyes narrowed as she scrutinised it avidly.

"Excellent, my dear, I knew your nice young man would not let us down. Such a good class bank, too." She was plainly impressed and, her concern allayed, rose and turned to leave the room. Her progress was arrested by the shriek from the bed.

"Bad news, my dear; oh dear." She reached down to share the information that had so distressed her patient, and read.

My dear Wyn

I regret that I have been called home on urgent family business.
I can give you no indication of how long I will be gone, and when I will be able to return.
I have made the necessary financial arrangements with Mrs Brist for the remainder of your lying-in.
I have been told that you have other contacts in Birmingham, so you must look to them for your welfare after that.
Look after our son better than your other one.

The last five words had plainly been added later. The handwriting looked completely different to the rest of the letter, including the simple "John" that appeared below the devastating text.

Winnie read the letter several times. She looked again at the envelope, and tried to read the postmark. The combination of the smudged ink and her impatient tearing open made this almost impossible, but eventually she deciphered Southampton, 5 June 22 and 7.30pm. Where was Southampton? Whatever was John doing there?

With a shudder she remembered that when she was a child the 'Titanic' had left from Southampton. It was a port. There could be only one reason for John being in Southampton. He was leaving the country. She felt herself beginning to retch.

She struggled to rise from the bed. Mrs Brist called for the nurse.

"You need rest, my dear. You're overwrought. You've had a terrible shock," she told Winnie, trying to keep the malice and satisfaction out of her voice.

The nurse, the sour-faced one, appeared. Agnes Brist whispered instructions to her, and she disappeared, promptly reappearing with a heavy syringe. Winnie sensed their purpose, but they were too fast for her.

"Now then, dear," she could hear Agnes Brist's crowing tones as they turned her on her front and wrenched her expensive knickers down past her backside.

"You'll feel a lot better soon," said the matron, smiling as Winnie stiffened on receiving the full impact of the clumsily inserted syringe.

"Now pull your knickers up like a good girl." Mrs Brist added condescendingly as the nurse collected her cotton wool and needle. They grinned to each other as they watched Winnie struggling to re-adjust her underwear. They had enjoyed themselves.

When Winnie awoke several hours later she could feel the soreness in her backside from the injection. But there was more to it than that; a sort of dull pain in her leg. She called the nurse. Sour-face had gone off duty, and the afternoon nurse, who had been present when the baby had been born, came into the room. Winnie began crying, and told the nurse that she wanted to see the doctor. The nurse told her that the doctor would not be available until the next day, but she would tell Matron.

She could hear Mrs Brist marching purposefully down the linoed hall, and was unsurprised when she appeared stone-faced in the room.

"What do you want the doctor for?" she snapped. "He is a busy man. We gave you a sedative because you were threatening to become hysterical. That's why we have taken your baby away until we think he is safe with you. I do hope you don't intend to complain about the care you are receiving," she added menacingly.

It had not occurred to Winnie that John was not in his cot.

"Where is he?" she whimpered.

"He is safe in one of the spare rooms. Nurse Broadhurst took him away for his own safety when you started your demented behaviour this morning. And also, of course, we need to be sure that he is safe with you, physically and morally, before we return him, so you'd better tell us what the last line of that letter means."

Winnie began to sob. She read the excitement of the hunter closing for the kill in the Matron's perspiring face and forced smile, and looked for pity to the sympathetic eyes of the young nurse standing slightly behind her. She addressed herself to the nurse.

"Roy is ill in Selly Oak Hospital." she whispered.

Unsatisfied, Agnes Brist pointed to the last sentence in John's letter.

"But that refers to your *other* son, doesn't it?"

It was obvious that Mrs Brist intended to strip her naked emotionally, and enjoy each layer as it came off. She decided to deprive her of the pleasure.

"All right, I had another child out of wedlock two years ago. Satisfied now?" she grinned defiance at the matron.

A nervous giggle escaped as she saw her tormentor's reddened face contort with frustrated rage.

"You're getting hysterical again. Perhaps you need another injection."

Winnie curled into the foetal position away from them.

"Oh that *is* a bad sign," said the matron venomously.

"I can keep an eye on her for you," volunteered the nurse. "We must watch the sedative quantities. I trust Nurse Broadhurst recorded the previous dosage in the book."

Agnes Brist knew very well that Nurse Halling was drawing attention to the lack of proper records. Her face became pinched.

"Very well, then, I'll let you take responsibility for our honoured guest," she hissed, and left the two younger women together.

Winnie burst into tears. The nurse put her arm around her shoulders, and noticed how bony they had become.

"You really must eat properly, mother," she tenderly told her.

Gradually she talked Winnie round. It was certainly puzzling about her young man. She promised to take the note that Winnie scribbled to Mrs Coote as soon as she could, but that would be tomorrow after she finished duty and had had her morning sleep.

The next seven days were for Winnie how she imagined purgatory.

The nights brought a succession of nightmares from which she frequently woke drenched with sweat and gasping for breath.

The mornings brought the twin threat of the quietly malicious matron and the openly sadistic Nurse Broadhurst. They had been obliged to behave whilst John was around, but now that he had plainly deserted her, they missed no opportunity to humiliate her in every way possible. Intimate physical examinations, injections and medicines, mostly laxatives, of dubious value to treat her now more painful leg, combined with sneering innuendoes about her morals, her clothes, even her voice made her mornings a torment bearable only by Winnie's intense will-power, and an increasingly desperate belief that someone, somewhere would take her away from all this.

The afternoons were more endurable because of the kind nature of Nurse Halling, but even she seemed a little more distant after her apparently fruitless attempt to contact Dora Coote.

Constantly stabbing at her through all her waking hours was her sense of grief caused by the enigma of John's departure, and the daily reminder of him provided by the beautiful, fair-haired baby who was so peaceful in his cot.

The night of Tuesday the thirteenth was stormy.

The humidity added to all the other trials to make sleep impossible. Finally she got up and jerked the reluctant window sash up. She lifted her baby gently out of his cot to share with her his first view in this world of the fingers of lightning flashing over the featureless countryside.

The storm was subsiding, and the cool breeze was calming the angry, restless atmosphere. The turbulence had chased away the persistent whiff of sulphur in the wind, and she drank in joyfully the clean, fresh air. John's eyes closed as she peacefully rocked him. They felt as one to her as they listened happily to the last of the rain tiptoeing down the drainpipe by their window.

Somewhere in the middle distance she could hear the rhythmic plodding sound of a train in the railway cutting. From time to time she caught a glimpse of flame-lit wisps of smoke as the locomotive battled up the gradient. The engine paused, as if catching its breath, and then continued its wheezing progress. Its sheer dogged determination impressed her, and she agreeably admired a kindred spirit.

Suddenly, and unexpectedly, a bright flash of lightning made her involuntarily turn away from the first floor window. She almost released baby John from her arms in sheer terror.

Mrs Brist must have come silently into her room whilst she was observing the train's struggle. Her painted and plastered face, illuminated by the stark lightning, reminded Winnie of the hideous masks used at Halloween by the less God-fearing.

She could see her uninvited visitor gently swaying.

"Enjoying the view, are we?" said the matron, making a conscious effort to avoid slurring her words. "Let me point out a few local landmarks for you."

She moved to the window and grasped Winnie's arm to turn her to face out with her. Winnie's whole body froze rigidly.

"Over there are the reservoirs, very picturesque in the spring," she waved exaggeratedly at the empty space. "and there, you can just see the lights glowing, what do you think that is?"

The grotesque but menacing figure gripped Winnie harder for support.

"That, my dear, is the ever-burning gas lights of the Aston Workhouse. I expect that will be your home after this Friday. I don't think you will like it very much. It hasn't the luxury of our lovely home here, and you won't find the same high standard of company. Oh dear, no. You will be put in a ward with the simple ones. They do that now with bad lots like you who don't learn their lesson. They will keep you awake at night, but during the day they will mostly just shout and yell and stare at you. If you keep on about that leg of yours, they'll put you in the female venereal ward, with all the whores and worse. Covered in scabs, some of them are. You'll like it in there. Lucky they'll take all that finery away from you when you have your visit to the wash-house. Wouldn't like to be you sitting in your fancy clothes in there with half the scum of the city for company."

The pain returned to Winnie's leg. She felt feverish. She shook herself free of the matron's grasp and sat on the bed, cradling her baby protectively.

Agnes Brist pulled the window sash back down as the breeze stiffened.

"You'll be glad of my advice when you get there, dear. I know what I'm talking about. I was the assistant matron there for seven years."

From deep inside her throat, rumbled a stifled gurgling laugh. She turned and grinned maliciously at Winnie's turkey-like expression, then left, content with her successful efforts to shred Winnie's moment of contentment.

Winnie drank unsteadily from her tumbler of warm water. She placed John gently back in his cot and returned to bed. Her resolution was now totally concentrated by her persecutor. She had to get a message to Dora, whatever the cost.

When the dawn chorus woke her she wondered whether she had just had an abnormally realistic nightmare, but the faint malodorous fragrance of stale whisky convinced her of the reality of the events.

She took advantage of the early hour and crept downstairs. The office was unlocked. She took the two sheets of paper and envelopes that she needed. She was lucky with the stamps, which were where she guessed, in the top drawer.

She returned stealthily to her room and wrote the two notes. One was a final plea to Dora, the other a letter to her brother Fred at the Laurel Cottages address for forwarding. She gave Dora's Osler Terrace address for his reply.

She heard the sounds of the breakfast being prepared, and hid the letters in the bedding in case her tormentors paid her an early call. This proved a wise precaution, as shortly after 8 o'clock Nurse Broadhurst entered the room with a cup of tea and some toast. This was because Doctor Erskine would be seeing her at 8.30, and she must look her best and happiest.

Winnie's suspicions were immediately aroused. When she had asked to see the doctor, they had refused. Why was he available now?

A little late, the old doctor arrived, accompanied, as always, by the fawning matron. He was plainly here for a purpose, and commenced a rudimentary physical examination. He spoke almost exclusively to the matron. When he came to Winnie's left leg he hesitated. He looked again and Winnie winced as he pressed and straightened the leg. He took her temperature again, and this time looked at the thermometer with more attention. "Hmm," he communicated.

He rose creakingly from the chair provided earlier by the matron and motioned her to leave the room with him. They left Winnie's room and stood outside in the corridor. The doctor's slight deafness gave his educated voice the added volume Winnie needed to overhear the conversation from the other side of the door, where she stood painfully.

"She's developing white leg, I'm sure of it," she heard Erskine declare.

"White leg? But that's caused through bad hygiene. It can't be, not here!" rasped the alarmed matron, her veins projecting against the fake pearls around her throat.

"She should be out of here, Agnes. She needs the hospital."

"She is not going to the bloody hospital from here with a diagnosis of white leg. She isn't!" screeched Mrs Brist, shedding her veneer of decorum. "I'd lose all my referrals."

A silence ensued.

"You've got a short memory, James, but I haven't," she glared at the doctor desperately.

Another pause followed.

"Not that, surely, Agnes. You wouldn't."

"Yes I damned well would, if it was the end here. She's hysterical, that's all. Has been since she got here. Have her committed."

"I'm afraid that under our new enlightened masters that is no longer so easy. You need two signatures. I'll put her up for the House as being destitute with a child. That'll be easier."

"I don't care what you do. Just get rid of her for me."

They walked off, and the voices faded.

Winnie knew that she had only one last chance.

Nurse Halling still seemed distant when Winnie gave her the letters. She was curious about the origin of the stamp on Fred's letter, and when Winnie admitted that she had taken the stamp from the office drawer the young nurse realised that she was carrying her own dismissal notice. She would not be persuaded by Winnie's tearful pleading. Winnie then slowly and solemnly removed from her now bony finger the engagement ring that John had bought her. She held it in her trembling hand, and invoked the all-forgiving God as she looked up with imploring eyes. The nurse, not dishonest by nature, was not overpaid, and she knew that her Arthur was struggling to save for their engagement ring. The diamonds shone and glistened in their expensive setting.

After all, she was putting her job at risk. She accepted the ring, and tried to ignore the tearful kisses planted on her cheek.

Late the following morning she made the journey to Osler Terrace, and found the old woman in. The young nurse had been shocked the previous time she had called on her with Winnie's other note. She had not dared to tell Winnie that Dora had simply read it, and told her that Winnie had made her bed and must now lie on it, before curtly closing the door. This time Mrs Coote was more sympathetic. She told the nurse that she now realised that Winnie was a foolish, vain young woman who had been swept off her feet by van de Leure, just as her own grand-daughter had been. At least Winnie was still alive, unlike her own beloved Fay.

She spoke the words aloud as she scribbled the note for Jane Halling to take back to the 'Marlands' with her. She told the astonished nurse that she would have to somehow inform Winnie that Dora had found out that she was not Mrs van de Leure. A reliable contact had told her that the wedding was a sham. She must register as Winnie Pow when she went into the workhouse, as she certainly now would. If she came out with the story about the fake wedding, she would be sent straight to the Asylum. She would never be let out or see her children again.

She got Jane to promise to inform her at once when she knew where Winnie was sent.

When she returned to the 'Marlands' that afternoon and had her cup of tea prior to starting her shift, Jane Halling reflected on how strangely entwined people's lives were, and how rarely they matched up to appearances. Her own Arthur's cap would fly off when he knew the real reason why she had, against her nature, accepted that ring from the desperate and pathetic woman.

She had received the results of her tests that morning, which now made it urgent for their engagement and marriage to proceed. She would explain that at the right time to him, but it could not be delayed.

But when was the right time to tell this young mother that she was not married as she had thought?

She checked the board for the following mornings duties. She saw the admission slip on the clip above the desk. Transport was arranged for W. van de Leure at 8.30 am. Just after breakfast, as usual for the workhouse. She was a little surprised to see that the destination was the Western Road House. At least that would save Winnie having to sample the delights of Erdington House, as the local Aston Workhouse was now known. Just the outside of that place was enough.

She felt her heart pounding as she set off down the corridor clutching Dora's note.

12

Quite unintentionally, Agnes Brist's lurid remarks about the Aston Workhouse served to soften the shock when at just after nine o'clock on the morning of Friday the 16th June, Winnie and John Pow passed through the impressive archway of the Western Road House.

Winnie winced as she stepped down from the back of the van that had been sent to fetch her. She hobbled over the uneven stone setts of the cobbled yard. John stirred and stretched as she made her way into the female reception area. She stood painfully as the uniformed assistant behind the desk looked closely at the admission order and the attached note, glancing quizzically up at Winnie from time to time.

Truth to tell, May Palmer was still fighting off the last of her hangover, and was finding it difficult to concentrate. The white, clinical walls of the reception area seemed to glare and dazzle her when she felt like this, which was becoming more often. Living with her mother had a few compensations, one of the main ones being that the nominal amount she gave her for housekeeping left her a few shillings, even on May's modest pay, to drink away the depressing days.

She tried to focus her mind again on the admission order. It was signed by Aldeous Lye, the relieving officer for Erdington district. The note with it was from a Doctor Erskine, who wrote that he thought that the woman had something called white leg, and would soon need Dudley Road Infirmary. Additionally, someone else had written in a plainly uneducated hand the words "*Twice fallen*" across the front of the admission order in thick blue crayon. Yet another amendment had been made, in a tidier hand in pencil, to change the name on the form from the exotic sounding "van de Leure" to the plainer, and somehow familiar, "Pow".

She had to get on.

"So what's your name?" she rattled out like a machine gun.

The woman stared back. This could take all day.

"Well, I'll give you a choice of two. Is it Pow, or van de something?"

"Pow. Winifred Nora Pow." Winnie whispered back carefully.

"You must speak up, my love," May told her more sharply than she intended. She looked again at Winnie's blank, defeated face, and continued.

"Have you really twice fallen?" she asked Winnie incredulously.

Seeing Winnie's incomprehension, she asked quietly. "Is this your second illegitimate?"

"Yes," Winnie simply replied, a silent tear caressing her pale cheek as she pulled her baby to her chest.

May could see that Winnie appeared to be in genuine distress. She softened her tone and completed the rest of the entries as quickly as possible, motioning her to sit and wait on the bench. At least the baby was quiet.

The woman seemed half stupid. Not only could she not seem to remember her date of birth, or that of her son, but she appeared to have no idea what she did to earn her keep. Finally May Palmer had got tired of waiting, and put down "Bar attendant". Thank God it was the quiet period of the day. She wouldn't want these two turning up in the six o'clock queue. The woman was a certainty for the Mental ward, or Epileptic ward as they called it. She pitied her. The first time in the House was always a nightmare, especially in there. But it had been policy since April last year to put the second fallens into the Mental Block so that they didn't contaminate the first-timers. She still had the instruction in her desk. This one didn't seem a threat to anyone.

She didn't even trouble to search her, just asked her the regulation questions about possession of knives, matches or tobacco.

The three of them waited quietly. The mother stared aimlessly or rocked her baby while May filled in some of the never-ending paperwork. A few minutes later the outside door opened, and the porter deposited a ragged bundle into the reception room.

"Not you again, Maudie," enquired May in a good-natured tone of resignation. "What have you been up to now?"

"I got thrown out, Mrs Palmer. You know how it is."

"I know how it is for you, Maud. Just remind me."

"Maud Phipps, 19th September 1893, Room 4, 316 Gooch Street, C of E, put me down as a table hand."

May Palmer's face broke into an involuntary grin. She liked Maud.

"Some table hand you are. I'd tell them to count the knives if you turned up where I was."

She completed the familiar paperwork, then came out from behind the desk.

"Come on now, Maudie. You know the drill."

To Winnie's astonishment, May proceeded to give Maud Phipps a fairly detailed body search right in front of her. Maud did not complain, but exchanged increasingly ribald remarks with May as the assistant's searching hands probed ever more intimate parts of her scrawny body, and just grinned toothily when the search produced no result. Then, without warning, she collapsed, as if in slow motion, onto the floor.

May ran to the inside door, and two female orderlies entered the room.

"Not again" was one of the kinder comments Winnie overheard.

A tall woman with high, hollow cheeks, plainly a senior orderly, followed them into the room. She scrutinised the admission forms and abruptly barked out her orders.

"Take her downstairs till we decide where to put her," she directed her two assistants, pointing to the unconscious bundle on the floor.

"You follow me." she snapped at Winnie.

Winnie and John followed the rhythmic clicking of the keys hanging from the orderly's belt to a huge, high ceilinged wash-house. She told Winnie to undress, plainly not an invitation, and returned shortly afterwards with a well-used towel. She was luckier than she deserved, Winnie was told. She could use the personal bath with fresh water, not follow others into the big communal tub as was usual, and the water was as warm as it got at this time of day. She told her not to be too long as it wasn't the Queen's Hotel.

Following her brief soak and cursory soaping with the remains of a hard slab of carbolic, she was presented with a worn but well-washed cotton uniform.

"Not much meat on you, but our wholesome food and a bit of hard work will soon cure that," was the appraisal from her companion as she studied Winnie's body much like a local farmer might view a new addition to his stock.

"No sign of pox on you anywhere. We'll skip the venereal check. There's no-one available anyway," she added casually.

Winnie struggled self-consciously into her ill-fitting garb.

John began to cry. The orderly told her to hurry up and finish drying him. They would sort his nappies out later. She hadn't got all day.

They left the bath house and turned left into the long, bare corridor of the female side of the Workhouse. Winnie could not see where it ended. They began a relentless, fatiguing walk along the unpainted redbrick corridor. To her left was a handrail. It was cold to touch ,with white-painted metal diagonal bracing under it, and too high to give adequate support. Beneath her feet, her uneven steps echoed from the stone floor. In the space between the corridor that they were walking and a parallel similar one about fifteen feet away, over the handrail, she caught glimpses of similar floors above them.

Mrs Mason pointed out the huge kitchen as the smell of boiling cabbage floated to meet them.

From time to time they passed through large iron gates. The ancient, animal fear of enclosure began to engulf her. She sensed a feeling of demeaning anonymity. With every painful step into the bowels of the Workhouse, she was ceasing to be Winifred Pow. The uniform was growing onto her skin.

The inmates that they encountered held their heads down, as if in fear of recognition by an obvious new arrival. The supervising staff straightened from their casual postures as they approached. Some almost stood to attention. All said "Morning, Maam," or, less commonly, "Morning, Mrs Mason," to her escort. Thankfully, several engaged her briefly in conversation, which gave Winnie desperately needed moments of relief. During these fleeting interludes the sounds and smells of her new home became apparent.

A kind of cool, sanitised dampness pervaded the corridors. This was reinforced by the astringent waves of disinfectant coming from the battered metallic pails scraping along the floors as an army of women of all ages shuffled around them, the muffled rustling of their scrubbing brushes and brooms increasing on Ida Mason's approach.

It was obvious to Winnie that Mrs Mason viewed the army of forced labour around her as less than human. She did not hesitate to push or even gently kick them out of her way, and offered no apology when she trod on a gnarled hand, blue from the cold water and disinfectant.

As they passed rooms leading from the corridor, Winnie detected the sounds of sewing machines and then the humid, muggy atmosphere of a large laundry took her breath away.

Most of Winnie's concentration was absorbed in trying to match the painful military pace being set by Ida Mason, who seemed totally oblivious or unconcerned by Winnie's obvious struggle to keep up.

Suddenly they stopped outside a large room with 'NURSERY' above the door.

"How old's the baby?" snapped Mrs Mason.

"Three weeks, ma'am," Winnie replied as respectfully as she could, trying to keep the fear out of her voice.

The orderly hesitated for what seemed an age.

"Normally they don't let you keep the baby with you where you're going, but the nursery's full, so we'll see what Sister says when we get there," she stated, resuming the march without further comment.

They turned right into yet another corridor. At the end Ida Mason pointed Winnie to a flight of well worn stone steps. She followed her as Winnie struggled up the agonising climb, pushing and poking her as she faltered and tried to grip the handrail for support.

At the top they came to a large ward. It was so long that Winnie could barely see the other end. It looked spartan with whitewashed brickwork instead of plastered walls, and was divided into three sections. Ida Mason led her into a small office just inside the entrance to the ward.

"Here's another one that didn't learn her lesson first time round, Miss Sketchley," she announced almost cheerfully to a thin-faced woman in a grey uniform. For the first time, Winnie saw Mrs Mason smile.

After she had turned and left them, Winnie told Maria Sketchley in a conspiratorial tone:

"I shouldn't be here really. It's all a mistake. I've got a big house in Edgbaston to go to when this is cleared up."

The orderly appeared to nod and smile in sympathetic agreement. Then she suddenly straightened up behind her desk. Winnie saw that the smile was one of total contempt.

"Oh, is that right? Well, Mrs Big House in Edgbaston, until that time comes, you will be in our care here. And you will obey the rules."

Winnie looked into the woman's prematurely aged face. She felt the mocking eyes radiating red scorn back at her.

"It's amazing how many of you immorals are here by mistake, and you should really be in castles or palaces. Well, most of us in this ward would be only too pleased to see the backs of the likes of you. We had enough problems in here with the bloody loonies, without being given a bunch of immorals to look after. Now let me show you to your residence. I do hope it is up to your high Edgbaston standards," she added, curling the words as deeply into Winnie as she could.

She directed Winnie to a bed in the first section of forty or so beds, set out closely in two parallel lines from each wall. She watched with amused indifference as Winnie painfully humped a thin black and white striped flock mattress from the bedstore to the minimum-width bed that she had been allocated, and looked equally unconcerned as Winnie hobbled back to the store cupboard and clumsily carried the little cot for John to its allocated position at the foot of her bed. In response to Winnie's whispered enquiry, she loudly pronounced:

"Oh yes, of course, madam's bathing facilities," before telling Winnie that the annexe containing the toilets and sinks was at the opposite end of the ward.

Unfortunately, some of the more mentally handicapped inmates weren't very skilled at using the facilities, but she hoped that they would suit Winnie.

"I might even arrange a little job for you, keeping them in good order," she told her terrified prey with a croaking laugh.

There were no other inmates present, except for two young women, one of whom looked simple. The orderly explained that most of the others were at their tasks. Only those considered too old or mentally feeble were in the ward during the day. She had noticed that Winnie appeared to be limping a bit, and hoped that that was not affected to avoid work. If that was the idea, she had better know now that, soft as the Guardians and management had now become in her opinion, able-bodied malingerers were still severely dealt with. She would give Winnie five minutes to settle John in his cot before returning to direct her to her tasks.

Winnie sat on her bed, trying to ignore the throbbing pain in her leg. She began to tremble as she fought the gathering fear inside her. She was so absorbed with the pain in her leg and the fear of Miss Sketchley's imminent return that she did not notice the ward Sister enter the room and study her with concern.

Sister Butler was a recent appointment. She presided over the inmates in her care with kindness and patience. She had not considered herself a natural nurse, but had become involved as a Red Cross volunteer. She had helped with the Empire war wounded at Dudley Road, then followed the overflow somewhat unwillingly into the neighbouring Workhouse when the carnage of Passchendaele had made that a necessity. She had been impressed with the caring attitude and enthusiasm of some of the younger staff amidst the traditional repressive atmosphere of the Workhouse ethic. She had happily volunteered to return when the chance presented itself during

Dudley Road's reconversion for civilian use. Her pay was less, but she had achieved the rank of Sister earlier, and enjoyed the responsibility.

She was one of several appointments made by the board of Guardians of the workhouse to introduce a more caring approach for those of the genuinely destitute sick and old whose only refuge was the House. They stoically withstood the criticism from those critics of their "soft" approach that such notions encouraged entry to the House, thereby defeating the long-established object of the Union system of deterring the undeserving.

She read again the admission slip in front of her. The twice-fallens like Winnie were becoming less common now that the War workers had largely disappeared. The city authorities had coped reasonably well with finding adoptive parents or foster homes for the offsprings of these itinerant nuisances, who were a drain on the rates of the unlucky parishes who were billed for their keep if they happened to live within their boundaries on the all important admission date.

Now it was mostly the destitute coming into the House, since the war work had ground almost to a halt. The old aim of deterrence could only work if there was somewhere for people to be deterred to as well as from. For some months it had been apparent that the quality of working age inmates admitted had been above the level of tramps and others interested in the regular meals, even relative comfort and security offered by the House compared to what was available to them outside.

The majority of the beds in Sister Butler's ward contained the elderly able-bodied senile, some of whom had been in and out of the House since the 1860s. The mentally simple formed the other group of more or less permanent residents. Both these groups included people who would no doubt have been better catered for in the Asylum in Lodge Road, but successive workhouse masters were keen to hold on to these docile people, and the costs to the city ratepayers was less per head in the House. They were no trouble, did unpleasant jobs uncomplainingly, and eventually finished their days in one of the bedridden wards.

The two gentle Downs syndrome twins, Louise and Ellen, had been residents in the House since having been left outside the archway as four year olds fourteen years before. They never lost their good nature, despite being the butt of the unkind and ignorantly fearful.

Well worth the House hanging on to were the four or five younger women in the ward whose health had broken under the strain of their positions as maid of all work to overdemanding families of limited means. Most had started their lives in the workhouse or an orphanage and were servile, and glad to return to the security and routine of the House.

More difficult to control were the half dozen or so diagnosed epileptics.

Deliberate violence was rare, but two of the beds in the ward were in the form of strapped cots to control brief fits. Longer or more violent attacks were dealt with by confinement in the basement cells for the protection of the patient and those around. The strait-jackets were used then, but otherwise rarely left their hooks.

More transient occupants included those who displayed disturbed symptoms on arrival. The most bewildered were those who were misdirected or arrived at a busy time when more appropriate wards were full.

Since April 1921 these groups had been joined by the twice-fallen unmarried mothers, who were kept there until the time came for their baby to be taken away, normally at the age of six weeks. The staff were trained to keep a close watch on these moral degenerates. It was likely that they would be sent to the Asylum at the end of their time in the ward. If they realised their fate, they might try and escape. If that was attempted, they were unlikely to succeed. One of the reasons that the FEP block had been selected for their incarceration was that it was the furthest ward from the entrance. Those foolish enough to attempt to de-camp spent the rest of their time in the basement cells, and lost the right to see their baby. This brainwave of the Boarding-Out, Infant Life Protection and Maternity Cases Committee of the Union had brought considerable headaches for Sister Butler and her staff. They were used to dealing with the mad, not the bad, and many of them resented having to give time to a bunch of devious sluts who were, by common consent, only in the House because of their own sinfulness.

These, then, were the varied inhabitants of Winnie's new home, the FEP ward. They formed part of the hidden world of sixteen hundred or so diverse souls, united only in their total poverty, who comprised the small village known as the Birmingham Workhouse. Other than those favoured inmates working outside in the grounds, they were rarely glimpsed by the outside world. Sometimes passengers would point at them, usually with derision, sometimes with sympathy, from their seats on the top deck of the trams ploughing freely up and down Dudley Road on their way to or from the city.

She became aware of her surroundings again as she heard the voices of Sister Butler and Maria Sketchley. They were speaking sharply to each other. In their postures they bore a strange resemblance to the prehistoric monsters in one of the films that John had taken her to see. The Sister, shoulders sloped, was staring up at the other woman's willowy figure above her, who abruptly turned and walked through the ward, clicking her heals noisily on the floor lino as defiantly as she dared. As she passed Winnie, she cast a predatory eye over her, like a beast denied its prey by a weak animal's mother.

Sister Butler watched her adversary depart. She told Winnie to spend the rest of the day getting used to her surroundings. Spartan as they were, they had a strangely calming effect on her after the nightmare of the 'Marlands'.

She finally left the ward in the early evening to go to the dining room. The two women from the adjacent beds helped her with the walk.

By the time that they had reached the huge dining area she had heard their life histories.

The blonde, painfully thin woman in her thirties surprised her by being well spoken. Hazel had had parents who travelled, and when small she had been sent to a boarding prep school reputed to be one of the best in the city. The teachers had beaten her daily. When she had foolishly mentioned this to her father on one of his infrequent visits, the headmistress had had little difficulty in persuading him that Hazel was given to fantasising, "a common trait amongst the girls". When he had left the school premises she found out the price for her comments. She was thrown into a bath of almost scalding hot water and held underneath. Her mouth was washed and washed again with soap, to 'purge her of her lying ways'. Since then she had retained a morbid hatred of baths, and had to control the urge to scream when they had their compulsory weekly visit to the large communal wash-house; also Winnie's least favourite ritual, with the staff gazing with varying degrees of curiosity at their naked bodies, some plainly passing sly comments below their breath. Hazel's mother had died, and with her the small annuity that paid for the school. The Workhouse had been her only refuge when her father had taken up with his new wife, who disliked Hazel as a "stupid, hysterical, girl and a compulsive liar."

Helena in the bed the other side had been taken in when she could not give a good account of herself in Livery Street late one evening. She had never been able to speak properly since the accident at her birth, and, also being unable to write, had no way of explaining this to the unsympathetic relieving officer. That had been seven years ago. Since then, she had spent almost every evening staring blankly at the wall.

The meal was plain enough. It was not overloaded with meat, but the heavy bread and potatoes rapidly filled her. The brooding presence of the staff discouraged leaving food. Hazel warned her not to do this, as this ingratitude was usually cured by a prolonged spell of scraping out cooking pots and pans, or cleaning the kitchen.

The two Downs girls never left her. They followed her back to the ward, and stood, smiling innocently, while she got ready for bed.

She struggled with the threadbare blanket, and woke during a brief nap to find them staring intently at her each side of the bed. Instinctively she cried out. This woke the night nurse, who, on discovering the cause of the commotion, pushed the girls roughly down to the strapped cots and fastened them in. The result of this was counterproductive, as they could not see each other and began shrieking. The nurse then gave them several hard slaps on the face, reducing them to a petrified silence. When Winnie protested at the harshness of her action, the stockily-built nurse straightened up to her full height and walked slowly and deliberately to loom up over her bed. She reached into John's cot, and held him roughly to her chest.

"What are you going to do about it, then?" she snarled, bringing her ruddy face to within inches of Winnie's. Winnie felt her courage dissolve.

"Please don't hurt my baby, please," she whimpered.

Slowly, keeping her eyes firmly on Winnie's terrified face, the nurse returned John to his cot. As he began to cry, she turned and whispered loudly to Winnie.

"Get him quiet now, or he'll get what those mongol freaks got."

Winnie calmed her baby and returned, cowed and shaking with fear, to her bed.

After that introduction, she dreaded the nights. It was at night that the phantoms raised themselves. After the lights were dimmed at nine, she would feel herself shrinking as the shadows grew into grotesque shapes on the walls around her. As she entered the half-life between wake and sleep, the sounds, distant at first, crept ever closer and fought to reach her from underneath the other beds. She wanted to cry out, but feared the two night nurses.

The days in the FEP Block were a lot more bearable. The ward might have been a little short of life's recent luxuries, but there was an inextinguishable spirit amongst the inmates. Those with minds suffered more, but the equality of poverty and dark humour bound them together.

The Sister prescribed that she only did light work due to her medical condition, and the supervisory staff knew better than to put their jobs at risk by disobeying her instructions. Most of the staff were disapproving, one or two even openly judgemental, but at least they didn't try to ram their religious fervour down her throat like the Salvationists.

Winnie rapidly rose within the ward hierarchy. Compared to most, she had received a good basic education, and was soon helping to write letters.

The first few days passed fairly uneventfully. The only major interruption to the routine was a visit by several members of the local Eugenics Society.

The Assistant Matron accompanied the party. She explained to the inmates that the Society aimed to improve the lot of everyone by promoting better breeding. To this end, it was necessary to obtain information about those who had shown signs of moral or physical degeneracy.

Along with several others on a list, Winnie found her head being examined in some detail and measurements being taken. The Society members went into animated discussion as they referred to the charts and tables that they carried.

The visit went along smoothly enough until Harriet, one of the twice-fallens, loudly told her examiners to "bugger off." She received a sharp slap across the face from the orderly accompanying the erudite visitors for her lack of courteous co-operation. A struggle ensued, and the object of the visitors' research became hysterical.

Winnie could not conceal a measure of wry amusement as the members of the Society to improve the nation's stock scuttled out of the ward carrying their tape measures, callipers and thermometers. She doubted that Harriet would get a good score.

13

On Wednesday 21st the staff were even more fastidious than usual in ensuring the obsessive cleanliness of the ward.

As Hazel predicted, a party of visitors appeared. They were not the usual visitors who came to check the conditions of the inmates, but were announced by the handsome, upstanding Matron, Miss Higginson, as the Soho Women's Guild. As they passed the gleaming matt blacked heater in the centre of the ward some noticed Winnie and John. Several came over and asked Winnie how old the baby was. One told her that God had forgiven her sin by giving her such a beautiful child, and Winnie smiled.

The smile faded abruptly when her companion leaned over the cot and peered intently into it. She straightened, and asked from beneath the large green brim of her hat,

"What a frightfully nice child. Such a pity. Has his adoption been arranged, my dear?"

The words struck Winnie like an arrowshaft.

As the final group of good ladies passed, one of them hung back. Winnie was still reeling from the adoption comment and only as she felt the letter being pushed into her hand did she recognise Dora in her finery. She sat heavily back on her bed. Dora smiled and walked on, stooping slightly in her characteristic way.

As soon as the party had moved out, she opened the letter. The lack of privacy now grated heavily, but there was nothing else for it. Hazel watched inquisitively and the Downs twins smiled blankly as she examined the writing on the envelope before sliding her hand under the rear flap to open it.

So Fred *had* received her letter from the 'Marlands', and replied to her at Dora's address. The writing on his reply was less steady than she recalled. Still less the contents.

My dear Sister Wyn

I am back in the Service as an instructor at Devonport.
I can hardly believe the things I have heard.
When I was home last Christmas someone you can guess was telling all who listened how you were a kept woman and leading a fast life.
This person has now been telling Ivy that she heard from a friend up in Birmingham that you have gone and got yourself married in the spring to a foreigner, or that you are living openly with him as man and wife.
I cannot believe this, my dearest Sister.
Write to me and say it isn't true.
All I can say is thank God dear mother's not here to hear such wicked things.
Always your loving brother

Fred.

She felt light-headed and told the girls roughly to go away. Sister Butler became aware of her distress, and came quietly over. Without being asked, Winnie passed her the letter. The Sister frowned as she read the contents.

"Don't write back yet," she advised.

But it was too late. Winnie's shock had been replaced by an uncontrollable defensive rage. Lorna had done her work well. She would answer Fred all right, and bloody Lorna with him.

The Sister decided that it would be better on balance to let Winnie vent her anger in print and quickly fetched her her pencil and the small sheet of paper that she had noticed in her desk earlier in the day. Winnie was plainly bordering on hysteria, and her hand trembled as she raised the pencil to start writing.

"I can't let him know I'm in here. I can't!" she screeched.

Sister Butler saw the tears of pride and panic forming a mist over Winnie's eyes, and took a decision.

"Put my address down, dear. 57, Wood Lane, Harborne."

Winnie pressed hard on the paper to work her anger out, breaking the pencil lead twice. She read the letter to herself aloud, emphasising the parts that she felt most strongly about, before rising unsteadily and giving the letter to the Sister.

Dear Fred

You will find that during the months of March & April that I was at Swindon.
If you do not believe me please write to find out for yourself.
This person had better take care & not mix things up. Please tell her to be careful what she is saying.
As for you taking any notice of such a thing, I am rather surprised.

Winnie
You can please yourself if you answer this

She slid down in her chair and made one final alteration. "Dear Fred" was heavily pencilled out, and replaced with "To Fred".

Mary Butler suggested calmly that Winnie slept on it, but her eyes blazed as she impertinently told the Sister sharply to get it posted as soon as she could. Sister Butler summoned a thin smile and told Winnie that she would obtain a stamp and post the letter on her way home.

She had had enough of this now. The noise level in the ward was rising; always a warning sign. She told Winnie sternly to return to her bed and stay there until she recovered her temperament.

Winnie lay on the bed panting and moaning. The Sister ignored her, and shepherded away the small gaping audience gathering around the bed.

Later that day, in the early evening gloom, she posted Winnie's hasty reply.

At seven the following morning at their naval home in Devonport, Ivy brought the letter in to Fred while he was having his breakfast. He opened it and frowned. He passed it to Ivy as it was time for him to go, and he was never late at the base.

Ivy read the letter carefully. She knew that Fred was devoted to Winnie, and had a soft spot for her herself. Winnie had been the only one who had not been openly antagonistic to their wedding, and had sent belated congratulations. On the other hand, if she and Fred were ever to join the great and the good of the Pow family, was it wise to get involved with Winnie, who was plainly some form of black sheep.

Then there was the question of Fred's health. The headaches had got worse lately, and some days he could not drive them off at all. The last thing he needed was to get involved in an emotional conflict.

She thought about it whilst she finished her tea and toast. She put the letter away in the drawer in the sideboard. If Fred brought the subject up, she would discuss it with him. If not, it might be just as well for them both.

* * * * * *

The visitors from the Soho Women's Guild were delighted with their visit to the Workhouse, and the Hon. Secretary, Alice Exton, took the trouble to comment favourably in the Visitors Report Book on the courtesy shown to them. Her brother Wilfred, the Guardian who had accompanied the visit, added that "if the public knew how the inmates were looked after, a great deal of prejudice and misconception would be removed".

They had enjoyed their visit a great deal more than Winnie. From that day the casual comment about John being adopted spiralled her into a deepening depression. She would cradle him for hours, hug him, or just stare into his clear, unquestioning blue eyes. If she left the ward for any reason she would rush back and frantically check that he was still in his cot. Her tolerance of her surroundings, and those around her, evaporated, and the sights and sounds that had previously mildly amused her now produced only annoyance and low spirits. She shouted at the harmless for daring to stare at her; she reminded the reducing number who cared to listen to her that she came from a good family in Devon, and had a large house in Edgbaston waiting when the present misunderstanding was over.

Her histrionics became more frequent and tiresome. She invoked official wrath by almost refusing to eat. She was finally persuaded by a threat that John would be taken away if she showed signs of neglecting her health.

Her natural irritability was added to by her determination not to sleep at night. She felt certain that if she lapsed into unconsciousness, they would take John.

"What a frightfully nice child. Such a pity." She saw them standing at the entrance to the ward, waiting for her to slumber before pouncing. Her eyes felt permanently heavy and sore, she cried a lot and felt drained and devoid of energy.

The worst problem was the searing pain now spreading in her left leg. She constantly called for the doctor, who came reluctantly and pronounced her "hysterical with a physical symptom of her mental degeneracy".

Finally even Sister Butler's patience snapped and on the following Tuesday, the 27th, she handed Winnie over to Maria Sketchley, who had suggested previously to the Sister that if Winnie were more occupied, she would have less time to be self-obsessed and depressed, and therefore a nuisance to others, including Mary Butler.

Winnie told Mrs Sketchley plaintively that she could hardly stand up. Maria paused momentarily, then grinned. She told Winnie to follow her, and, seeing that Winnie appeared hardly able to walk, led her slowly out of the ward, and along the corridor a short way. She enquired with mock thoughtfulness several times whether she was walking too fast. They passed through the double gates onto the small landing that led to the three turn staircase stretching down to the ground floor. Fetching a pail of water and a heavily worn scrubbing brush from a store nearby, she told Winnie to clean thoroughly the entire staircase. She would not need to stand for that, she added smilingly. She left, promising to be there when Winnie reached the bottom landing. Kneeling painfully, Winnie began carefully cleaning the wide stone steps. The icy water contained a slab of carbolic soap and a strong-smelling disinfectant.

Her hands quickly became sore. Her knees ached on the cold, hard surface beneath her. On the second landing she paused, and looked back up the sharply rising middle flight. She could see where generations of paupers had worn down the centre of the steptreads. She saw a vision of herself in the drab cotton uniform wearing these steps down year on year, and finally dying in one of the depressing urine-smelling female bedridden wards further down the corridor.

She could hear the familiar sounds of the House; the distant clangs and scraping of pails. It was a warm day. Behind her, through a slightly open window on the landing, she heard a bird singing. Such a familiar cheerful noise, but it sounded out of place in the harsh coldness that was now her home. A warm tear rolled slowly down her cheek.

She felt dizzy and feverish. She resumed her labours and finally she reached the bottom. Right on cue, she heard firm footsteps descending towards her. To her horror, the tall, gaunt figure of Ida Mason appeared. Maria Sketchley stood grinning behind her, having tiptoed down to watch the fun. The senior orderly closely examined the bottom three steps, staring intently at the corners by the wall.

"No time to rest and admire," she commented curtly. "I can see where you have missed the corners and edges. Back you go."

She dared Winnie to retaliate. She need not have worried. Winnie was broken, mentally and physically.

The two orderlies watched with satisfaction, their arms loosely folded, as Winnie began the slow ascent. Ida Mason turned to go, paused, and looked again. She pursed her lips, and crept silently closer. She watched the thin arm revolving mechanically, struggling to reach the corners, and put her hand on Winnie's back. She was shocked to feel how bony Winnie was. Without saying anything, she took the scrubbing brush from her hand, put it in the pail, and took it back to the store. Then she came down the staircase again. Winnie looked up at her with real fear in her face. She felt her lips tremble. To her amazement, Mrs Mason helped Winnie to her feet and with unexpected gentleness shouldered her back to the ward. Mary Butler looked up with true astonishment as Ida helped Winnie to her bed.

Later that day, the Sister persuaded the Assistant Matron to examine Winnie herself. They called the relief doctor who confirmed their fears. Winnie definitely had white leg, no doubt aggravated by her recent exercise.

By the time the Guardians visited on the following Friday, June 30th, Winnie was bedbound. She was feverish, and scarcely noticed the concerned look of the acting Chairman, Caleb Chambers, as he blinked owl-like at her and John over his half-moon spectacles.

In reply to his question, Sister Butler told him that she expected Winnie to be transferred to Dudley Road Infirmary as soon as the paperwork came through to confirm that a bed was available. He nodded sagely and trusted that this would not be too long. The mother could plainly contribute little or nothing to her baby's welfare, and he would be better cared for in the newly decorated nursery.

"You should try and eat, young woman," he told Winnie brightly. "Nice fish dinner today." She stared back, aware of his kind concern but unable to co-ordinate a response. "Good, good," he commented as he moved on.

Before leaving, the Guardians had tea as usual with Miss Higginson in the Matron's office. Chambers always enjoyed the rest after the long walk. He told her smilingly, as he did on almost every visit, that he was sure that the Victorians had specially hardened the stone floors in the corridors. As usual, he balanced the Visitors' Book precariously on his knees and filled it in as he ate his biscuits. In addition to listing the wards visited, Aged & Infirm, Sick, Nursery, Church of England Male & Female Merit, Female Epileptic, Female Bedridden 1, 2, 3, 4, 11, 12, he added that "the ages of the residents we saw varied from five weeks to 95 years & irrespective of age they seemed as well cared for as possible and as happy as their circumstances permit."

Sister Butler regretted that she had allowed Winnie to nettle her into punishing her with the staircase cleaning. She wondered whether Ida Mason would use her error of judgement against her in some way. It was highly unlikely that any enquiry would be held about the staircase episode, but the Guardians had expressed concern about the baby's welfare, and it would be prudent to be seen to be taking prompt action. John was in any case due to be transferred to the nursery on July 10th, when he was six weeks old.

She observed anxiously that Winnie's face looked thinner and more drained than ever. Her left leg was now almost entirely swollen and white. Her fever had died down, which in some ways made her worse, because she was more aware of her surroundings and frustrated and even frenzied from time to time. It could be considered that she was a danger to her baby in her present unstable frame of mind. Mary Butler would have no friends if Winnie harmed John, even accidentally.

The debate in her mind was over. She realised the effect that her action would have on Winnie, but the welfare of the baby had to come first. She went down the long corridor to the floor administrator's office. She told her the position, including Caleb Chambers' interest in it. The clerk reminded her that the nursery was technically full, but in the circumstances she would arrange accommodation for Monday for John Pow.

It was always difficult to know how the immorals would react when the baby was taken. Mary Butler had dealt with quite a few now, and by the time the day came, she usually knew how to play it. All would protest, of course. The hard cases would protest loudest and most vehemently, but once the baby went they did not take long to settle, and, given the chance, be on their way out of the House to resume their previous activities. Some of the working girls or servants who had "been led" were more pathetic. Most, sinners or sinned against, finished up in the Asylum.

She decided that it would be better to tell Winnie before the nurse arrived. In her condition Winnie was hardly able to turn to violence. Winnie just stared numbly and whimpered at Sister Butler when she gently told her after breakfast that John was being taken from her to the nursery until she was stronger again, and able to look after him properly. They would bring him to see her each day.

When, half an hour later, the grey uniformed nurse arrived to take John, Winnie attempted to get out of bed. Between them, the nurse and Sister strapped her in with restrainers. After several piercing screams, she simply lay there trembling and calling for her baby.

The ward emptied as the day progressed. As the noise level reduced, it became more difficult for the Sister to ignore Winnie's pathetic weeping. She considered a sedative, but decided that she would serve her patient better if she could occupy her mind.

She went over to Winnie's bed and looked down at the empty, defeated face. She took with her the yellowed pack of cards that she kept in her desk. As they played a few hands of rummy, she engaged Winnie in conversation. Gradually Winnie's voice returned to something like it's normal tone. She asked about Winnie's family. Without warning, Winnie began sobbing hysterically. She held Winnie to her chest. When she calmed down, she told the Sister that it went back to that day that they made her clean the steps. As she had looked up those steps trodden down by generations of paupers it had dawned on her that she would die in the Workhouse because her family would never want her now. Even her beloved brother Fred had not replied to her letter. Having read the letter sent on June 18th, the Sister did not consider this a great surprise, but it gave her an idea. She suggested that Winnie write again. Reluctantly, Winnie agreed. She returned to her desk and brought the top half of a piece of lined paper.

Winnie ceased crying, dried her eyes and, with Mary Butler's encouragement, began slowly to write in a surprisingly neat, composed hand.

F E P Ward
Western Rd House
July 3rd 1922   *Spring Hill*
Birmingham

My Dear Brother Fred,

I received a letter from you a little while ago & I answered it, but I don't know if you received it. Well Fred you are my brother & I feel that I want to tell you everything, but I can't explain it all to you in this note, the letter which you wrote to me before upset me very much, you will see by the above address where I am. I have been ill & Fred perhaps I shall never get better anymore. I wish I were dead. I have nothing to live for now, but the Sister in this ward told me to write to you. She has been very kind to me, so I thought I would do as she told me & write to you. If only I could see you & tell you everything as I could never make you understand in this letter. One thing Fred, you told me in your letter that you were glad dear mother was dead, but I say this now to you that if mother had lived I should never have come to this. There was a time Fred when you used to tell me all, when I was younger and at home, so I want to tell you this that the person who told you that I had been living a fast life has told you a wicked lie, and the Sister here will tell you the same, also other people who have known me since I have been in Birmingham.
All I hope Fred is that you will never have the misfortune that I've had.
I feel too upset to write more now. How I wish I could see you just once again but I don't suppose I ever shall, as you will never forgive me.
My love to Ivy
Goodbye Fred
Your loving Sister

Winnie
Do write to me Fred if you can.

She handed the letter to the Sister and asked her to check it for spelling mistakes. Mary Butler read the letter and turned her face to avoid Winnie seeing the tear trickling slowly down her cheek. She had presumed that she had trained herself to be immune from the human feeling now running through her. She cleared her throat and pronounced the letter "fine" and promised faithfully to post it on the way home.

She knew that she had overstepped the line and become personally involved with Winnie. As she put the letter into the box, in time for the 5.50pm collection, she offered a silent wish that the results of her actions would justify the professional risk that she knew she was taking. If these people did not respond to a letter like that, they must be as hard as nails.

* * * * * *

As the letter had caught the second last collection, it was down to Plymouth by the night mail train, and Ivy found it in her hall early Tuesday morning when she came down to make Fred's breakfast.

She recognised the writing, and decided to put it in her apron and wait until Fred went to the dockyard before opening it.

She read the letter with a sense of gathering gloom, panic almost. She felt even more deeply in her heart that this Winnie business posed a threat. Their marriage had its difficulties, with the difference in their ages, Fred's drinking, headaches, tempers and jealousies. Siding with Winnie could deepen even further their isolation from the family. At all costs she must avoid making Fred choose between his undoubted loyalty to her and his lifelong devotion to his wayward sister. Now, more than ever, she counted the cost of her family's disapproval. They were not there to ask for advice.

She looked at the letter and would have willingly borne the pain if it had burnt itself before her eyes. She knew that she could not conceal its arrival from Fred. She tried to guess what his reaction would be. The best thing she could do was to consider the matter during the day, and have some ideas ready when he returned from work.

At tea she anxiously studied Fred's expression as he slowly read the letter. His eyes narrowed as he concentrated, and his face set into the deep, resolute expression that usually led to a pronouncement of action, often the wrong action. When he finished reading, he sat glumly silent. She took the chance to suggest that they think about it overnight. To her surprise, he quietly accepted her suggestion. For most of the evening he sat with a glazed expression, motionless in his chair, moving only to refill his ale jug, or drink from it. He did this quite a lot now, and it worried her. Wherever he was at these times, he was not with her.

The next evening they sat down at the kitchen table together.

Fred seemed divided between going up there and "sorting it out" and trying to contact other family members. After much discussion, he accepted Ivy's suggestion that she first write to the Matron at the Western Road House for further information, particularly about the life-threatening illness, which Ivy privately viewed with scepticism.

Ivy wrote her brief letter to the Matron, and posted it after Fred had seen it Wednesday evening.

On Saturday morning she received a reply dated 7th July from the Matron's secretary at the Western Road House informing her "that Winifred Pow was transferred to Dudley Road Hospital yesterday the 6th inst. All enquiries should be addressed to the Matron, Dudley Road Hospital, Spring Hill, Birmingham."

Ivy sat at the kitchen table and wondered what Fred would say when he came home.

As Fred read the note, his face coloured. Slowly, in a voice deepened by emotion, he told her simply.

"Now we have got to do something."

Whilst Freda Judge, the matron's secretary, had been typing the letter to Ivy, Winnie's name had come up somewhere quite different.

The Western Road House Sub-committee of the Birmingham Union were having their monthly meeting at Edmund Street.

The minutes of the previous meeting were approved, and the Visitor's Reports read and stamped.

The usual business of the committee, staff appointments, reported matters of discipline, approval of punishments, placements of children for adoption or fostering, accident reports, formal reports of deaths, were all dealt with in the polite but businesslike way that Caleb Chambers ran the committee. He expressed particular satisfaction at the progress of the decoration of the House that he had noted during his recent visit, especially the nursery.

During the light refreshments that followed the formal business, the new clerk, Ezra Keeley, overheard Chambers telling other sympathetic members about the small baby called Pow and his sick mother. Keeley knew the name Pow from the thorough examination of the files that he was undertaking, and made a mental note to collate the information for consideration at the next meeting.

Keeley did not share Chambers' charitable thoughts for the welfare of the paupers. To him they were another manifestation of the weakness of the post-war state. This would all change when a strong man came to power. Then, the people like Keeley, whose administrative abilities had won the War, would be recognised and given positions of authority. In the meantime, he enjoyed his work at the Union offices.

To him, the paupers were names on cards. They were a burden on tax and ratepayers like him. It was his ambition to minimise that burden. He noticed some names repeating themselves on the different registers. It angered him that they seemed to be able to claim relief because of the chaotic state of the files.

When he had brought the filing system up to its pre-war standard, he would be able to cross-reference these scroungers, and set special investigation units on them.

For his own carefully concealed reasons, he particularly hated the unmarried mothers. He determined to make an example of this Pow woman.

14

Though now slightly diffused by the piercing light of the "reformers" torches, the Workhouse still threw out the dark, threatening, judgmental shadow of its Victorian parents over the likes of Winnie Pow.

The neighbouring Poor Law Infirmary in Dudley Road, built in the 1890s to take the old and sick away from the punitive regime of the Workhouse, now reached out with gentle hands to heal Winnie's sick body and mind.

For fifty-four days, from her admission sedated on a stretcher on the morning of July 6th 1922 to her discharge on 29th August, her mind experienced just about every human emotion as, together with her frail body, they fought with the strength given only to a mother to overcome the mortal danger that threatened to take her stunted young life and make John and Roy orphans.

Of the first fortnight she had little conscious knowledge, as the danger to her body focused all her mind's efforts on its needs. Had she later possessed the required powers of recall, she would have known that her condition had been unusually life-threatening, and had frequently required all the skill and attention of the senior medical staff.

Few visitors had appeared, but Sister Radley had learned of her presence and spoken to her, although the morphine had deadened the recollection. Dora had turned up and attempted conversation, but quickly realised that it was a waste of time, and Dora always had things to do.

Even Father Parker, who had last seen her at Roy's christening, and recognised her unusual surname on the end of the metal bed, had paused on his pastoral round, although she would not have heard his prayer for her, as she was deeply cradled in the arms of Morpheus.

The hospital advised Ivy weekly on Winnie's condition. They told her that Winnie was heavily sedated for much of the time. Whilst this did not give Fred and Ivy comfort, it did at least mean that there was time to engage in correspondence with other family members to solicit assistance for Winnie.

Fred wrote to Jack in the only language he knew. He simply asked his brother for support, both directly and with other family members. He realised as he penned the letter that the contents would be related to Lorna as quickly as Alice could send her version to Hammersmith, where Lorna was in domestic service.

He struggled to compose his letter to his father. He realised with heavy-hearted resignation that the family, from being close and as one when his mother had been alive, was now a fragmented shambles riven by petty jealousies and alliances. Half way through he almost tore up the letter, but persevered and finished with an unsatisfactory plea for his father to rally the dissenting parties to a cause that Fred knew that most would be indifferent to, or even openly or covertly hostile.

One by one the replies arrived during the days that followed. The story had obviously spread around the family with varying degrees of exaggeration and distortion. It was clear that the great and the good had established a "party line" and taken quite a lot of trouble to make sure that the natural sympathy of some of their lesser brethren should not be misplaced or wasted.

Some responses were predictable, including the first. Lorna wrote to say that she was sure that the authorities in Birmingham would be well able to deal with Winnie's difficulties. She had herself found the councillors and their officers very competent during her dealings with them in her role as an organiser of charitable events. Sorry as Lorna was to hear that her sister was ill, she was particularly glad that she was in the Infirmary, which was regarded as one of the finest in the country, bearing in mind, of course, that it was a Poor Law Institution. More surprising was Lorna's announcement that she was now engaged to Mr Arthur Adamson, the nephew of the couple to whom she was "a companion."

"Companion. Bloody maid." Ivy heard Fred chortle.

They would shortly be informing such family members as could attend of their wedding day. She presumed that Fred and Ivy would not be able to make the journey, bearing in mind the distance, and Fred's comparatively low rank in the Service. They were invited to send a suitable small gift instead, which would be gratefully received.

Eva wrote a letter which read as though it had been scripted by Lorna. In her careful, heavy hand she wrote that much as she would like to help, there was nothing practical that she could do, and financially she was unable to assist. She added the comment that sorry as she was for whatever had happened to Winnie, she ought have taken Eva's situation as a warning, and therefore must bear some of the blame herself.

More surprising was the garbled note he received from Kate. She considered that she had taken the trouble to give Winnie her best available advice on a confidential basis when she had first heard of her problems. If she had chosen to disregard it, that was her own misfortune, and even if she had the means to help, she felt disinclined to do so. Plainly she meant what she said. She had not even invested in a proper sheet of writing paper, feeling that a piece of creased scrap paper was adequate to convey her sentiments.

Fred was no historian, but he read just the first two paragraphs of his father's letter before telling Ivy that, as he had predicted, Pontius Pilate could have done no better. Expressions of regret for Winnie's plight abounded in the well-formed if shaky script, but there were several pointed references to the difficulties created by Winnie when she had been at home. It was crystal clear that it was easier for him to let his daughter be crucified than risk the wrath of Maria, and prejudice the little influence that he still had with his other children.

This just left Jack to reply. Fred waited with growing impatience. He counted every day as a bad one. If he could only have seen Jack personally he might have been able to reason with him as his older brother like when they had been boys at home.

But Fred was no longer at home, and Jack was now subject to other influences. The letter, when it finally crawled through the letter-box, was no surprise. Expressions, deeply felt and no doubt genuine, of sorrow and pity for Winnie's predicament, but the need to take into account the feelings of other family members, and most of all his dear wife Alice, etc., etc., but do keep them posted, and if there was anything that they could do, bearing in mind Jack's frequent long absences at sea......Fred could hardly bring himself to finish reading the letter.

Ivy saw the anger and frustration in his face. She moved quickly to avoid a hasty reply being sent to Jack and Alice that would do terminal damage to their growing acceptance of Fred and Ivy.

She reminded Fred that there seemed to be nothing that they could do at this stage. The last bulletin from Dudley Road had told of substantial improvements in Winnie's general condition. They were confident that the danger had passed, but she was still semi-conscious and sedated a lot of the time.

Ivy had felt mildly resentful when Fred had responded so unquestioningly to his sister's pathetic plea for help. She now studied the mixture of determination and exasperation in his face, and felt nothing but a deep love and admiration for him. Once again he was prepared to stand alone against the rest of the family, as they had both done when they had wed. Any doubts that she may have harboured vanished when she looked into his clear, steely-blue eyes.

By her third week-end Winnie had entered the second, and longest, period of the fifty-four days. The acute treatment had ceased, and been replaced by a daily regime of absolute rest in bed and elevation of her swollen left leg with pillows and bolsters. Apart from the glycerine and belladonna mixture applied to relieve the pain, the only other medication was the daily use of laxatives which led to her continual state of debilitation and depression caused by the frequent requirement for bedpans.

She was still almost oblivious to the days of the week, or their dates. Only the changes of staff and increase in the number of visitors distinguished the week-ends.

During the long hours of daylight, she was now conscious of her visitors, both medical and non-medical. The staff were a dedicated and cheerful lot. They gave her as much time as their duties allowed, and did their best to keep her spirits up.

An unexpected companion was Maudie Phipps, who recognised Winnie from their brief encounter in the Female Reception Area of the Workhouse, when Maud had collapsed during the search. Maud was recovering in the ward from her latest very unprofessional attempt at abortion. As soon as she could walk again, she came to Winnie's bedside daily and chatted to her like an old friend. She shared with her her store of illicit drink and cigarettes that were smuggled in daily by her visitors. She assumed that Winnie was engaged on similar activities to her own, and entertained her with lurid tales of her own colourful experiences. Winnie found herself revaluing her own sorrows by listening to Maud's stories. As the girl dug into her memory, Winnie realised that here was someone who had never had anything going for her. From her childhood in the home of drunk, violent parents, through her spells in the children's home to her systematic abuse by the husband of the foster mother who had reminded her on an almost daily basis of how they had "rescued her and taken her to their villa", she had not stood a chance.

And yet, here she was, with her coarse laugh, nudging Winnie's gloom away. If Winnie had asked her for her last halfpenny, she did not doubt that Maud would have given it to her.

Winnie missed her cheerful, toothy smile when she discharged herself after only six days, telling Winnie that "if she was going to lie flat on her back all bloody day, she was going to get paid for it."

Dora called in once or twice a week. She reassured Winnie that John was still in the nursery at the House, and gave her news of the outside world. Despite Winnie's repeated heartfelt enquiries about John van de Leure, she had not the heart to relate the detail that she had heard from John Legg to the silly, sick young woman. She did, however, remind her that Roy was still weak and unwell at Selly Oak Hospital. Winnie looked concerned, but could not conceal that her interest was staged. It puzzled them both that she could not find in her heart natural maternal feelings for Roy. It was almost as though she was trying to blot him out of her mind and pretend that he had never existed.

Her other visitors were the regular ecclesiastical gentlemen, to most of whom she would willingly give the time of day, and, with less enthusiasm, the do-gooders. One afternoon, the all too familiar bonnets of the Salvationists appeared at the entrance to the ward. Instinctively, she shrank under the bedclothes. It was not only the Salvationists who caused her to want to hide beneath the bed covers.

The nights were short and generally warm. Most nights she took a mild sedative to encourage sleep and wipe away the noises of the ward. As in the Workhouse, in that mental half-light where the fight to stay awake is lost, from out of the shadows of her mind came other visitors.

Sometimes they were quite casual acquaintances, like Sadie from the Hostel. Now and again her long lost boon companions from Barnstaple appeared to ask her when she would party with them again. But mostly they were uninvited shades of her own guilt and sin.

The corn-blonde hair of baby John, fading into the darkness, slipping from her reach as she groped frantically for him as he cried.

Worse, far worse, Roy crawling, dark and unformed, over her legs and body and relentlessly towards her face. She would desperately push out at his probing arms, but always he would rise over her neck until his swarthy, diseased face was level with hers. She would scream in terror as his eyelids would roll open and reveal the empty sockets. She would stare into the empty, yawning blackness. It would grow and envelop her. She would be falling, falling faster. Then she would see him above her. Always gaining. Soon he would catch her. He would drag them both down. She must wake up. She felt the warmth of the earth. It was her own sweat-soaked body.

Members of her family; mother, stiff-chinned, unsmiling, came and just stared. Lorna, smiling smugly, self-righteous, triumphant. Lorna would have been upset to learn that when this apparition appeared, it had a stimulating effect on Winnie's resolution to recover. Even her father, smart and neat in his suit and waistcoat as he had once been, came and shook his head sadly over his errant daughter. She could smell his old clay pipe long after his visits.

Poor, shabby William, who she had tried so hard to love, who had lost out to the bright lights, still unquestioningly loyal to her from the churchyard where he lay, stared dolefully at her from the gloom.

Roy's father livened up one or two bedtimes. She would have found the fifty-four days a lot more bearable with a nightly visit from him.

Only once did the person her heart really bled to see turn up. Although his face was shaded, she could feel the presence of John van de Leure. She felt herself reaching out to him, and as she did so, he slid back. The harder and more desperately she sought his embrace, the more indistinct he became; then he was gone, and she was being chided by the night nurse for sitting up suddenly in bed. The nurse asked her why she was crying.

She slept through the day when there was nothing to keep her attention. She felt herself sliding back into the melancholia that Maud had helped to lift. The Day Sister had told her that it was the week-end, but it had only depressed her more. She was lying back remembering the week-ends of her early teens, when they would go on picnics or to Fat Jack and Lena's farm. She heard the girlish laughter echoing over the meadows. She particularly looked forward to those days when Jack or Fred were home. How proud she felt to be seen with them.

She could see Fred now, handsome and upright in his uniform. He was standing by the bed.

She checked mentally. Her eyes were open. Panic seized her and she grasped the rail of the metal bedhead.

"Hello Wyn," he calmly said.

For a few, interminable, seconds she just stared up into his face. Then, they embraced and, like a dam bursting, she felt the warmth of the undemanding love that she had forgotten existed.

The spell was broken by the appearance of the voluntary tea lady. Winnie noticed with amusement that on seeing Fred the handsome young war widow's posture straightened. Her figure became more pronounced, and she seemed unusually solicitous of their needs.

Winnie was glad of the intrusion to give her emotions time to calm down, and to try to decide what to tell Fred. She just kept looking at him. She really couldn't believe it was him sitting by her bed.

She composed herself and told Fred an edited version of the events that had led to her being in the Workhouse and now the Infirmary. She showed him the brief note that she had received at the 'Marlands' from van de Leure, stating that he had returned to South Africa. She cried as she told him how she had been duped into thinking that she was married, and had borne him a child. She assumed that she still had a home to go to in Edgbaston when she was well again, there to wait until van de Leure returned.

As Fred listened to Winnie's story his eyes narrowed with gathering anger. He suggested that he could best use his time by going to the house and finding out whether this van de Leure was there or, if not, where he could be found.

As he rose to leave he reached into his inside pocket, and produced a bundle of dog-eared letters.

"Kept them. Every single one you ever sent," he told her with pride.

He left his rucksack and strode purposefully from the ward to hail a cab.

He had not been gone ten minutes when Dora appeared. Dora was amazed by Winnie's news; indeed, had Fred's rucksack not been there she would have wondered whether the fever had returned to Winnie's brain. She reluctantly agreed to Winnie's anxious entreaties to conceal Roy's existence from Fred, viewing with scepticism Winnie's claim that she wanted to tell Fred about Roy herself in her own time and way. She was not going to leave without seeing Fred, and had to conceal her aching feelings of pity as Winnie told her so enthusiastically and confidently that Fred had gone straight to Edgbaston and how he would "sort it all out". She knew the sickening inevitability of the outcome of this futile expedition and mentally rehearsed her reactions.

Less than an hour and a half after he had left, Fred was back.

He told them that he had found the house occupied by a well set-up couple who had viewed his appearance with disdainful suspicion. After her maid had announced his arrival as "some kind of sailor at the door" the lady of the house had informed him that they were renting the property through an agent from a Mr and Mrs de Graaf. Mrs de Graaf, such an elegant woman, with her harlequin parasol, had walked round once with a key. They had no idea where the previous occupier had gone or where the de Graafs lived. The agent might know, but such information was confidential. He had asked if there was any forwarding address or other information left in the house that might help him trace his ex-service chum. The woman had given him an icy stare and wandered off into the hall. She had returned and given Fred a brown paper bag, making it clear that, as they were shortly expecting guests, the interview must now end.

Winnie stared at him, then Dora, with a blank expression. Dora, consumed with her own tension, wondered what lay in the brown paper bag on the floor.

"You can't have gone to the right house." Winnie told Fred quietly.

Fred lifted up and held open the paper bag from the house. Inside Winnie saw a small brown leather object. She stared unknowingly. Only when he took it out and it unfolded into John's flying helmet did she burst into tears and throw herself on Dora's shoulder.

Dora felt herself in an uncomfortable position. These people had no claim on her, but she had been responsible for Winnie's involvement with van de Leure in the first place, and she felt that she owed it to Winnie and this pleasant young man to try and help. She asked Fred how long he would be staying, and where. He smilingly told her that it had been all he could do to get the railway fare together, so he had thought in terms of a couple of nights under the stars until he had to return on Monday. She told him coyly that she would risk her reputation and he could stay on her sofa in the sitting room at Osler Terrace. He thanked her graciously.

Winnie implored him to see her baby, and make sure he was all right. Dora told her that she would take Fred round to the Western Road House herself. She promised that she would try and locate the de Graafs from Winnie's description of their palatial house. She was already familiar with the name, which Legg had mentioned as one of the suspected "dope set", and could easily have located them. But she would gamble on Fred not finding them, or, if he somehow did, not obtaining any information about van de Leure that would add to his sister's pain.

She left Winnie and walked round with Fred to the Western Road House. They passed under the archway and entered the female reception area.

It was mid-afternoon and the uniformed female clerk told them abruptly that no visiting was allowed. If they returned the following day between 2pm and 4pm, it would be possible to visit baby John as long as Fred could prove his identity as a relative. The clerk was fortunate not to engage Fred's fiery eyes. Fred shared the serviceman's usual disdain for "civvies," especially officious civvies.

They walked back through the slightly hazy sunlight to return to the Infirmary. To make conversation Dora asked Fred whether he had any other leads to follow apart from the de Graafs.

"Oh, dear me, yes," he told her, lowering his voice to emphasise his new role as the Sherlock Holmes of Birmingham. "I just didn't want to raise Wyn's hopes too much."

"Bit of luck, really. When I walked back down Wellington Road, I noticed a police house. Believe it or not, there was an Inspector Lane in there. He remembered this van de Leure business all right. I showed him Wyn's letters. He thinks van de Leure's done a runner. He looked through some of my letters from Wyn. Only thing we could come up with was to try Wyn's old address. That place in Tennant Street. The inspector gave me directions, so I called there on my way back. What a dump that was. I could hear children crying in there, but no bugger would answer the door. Time was a bit short, so I left them to it, but I'll be off there again tomorrow morning."

He kicked a stone as he walked on.

Dora felt the ground freeze under her feet.

Winnie was anxiously awaiting them, and Dora could see signs of panic in her eyes. She told her that she would leave them together while she went back to prepare for her unexpected guest. She could have added that she had an urgent call to make in Tennant Street on her way home.

When Fred arrived at Osler Terrace to find a well filled plate of meat and potato stew cooking on the range for him he was more than ready for it. Dora had enjoyed preparing it for him, and he was fulsome in his praises for the food and also the jug of ale that she thoughtfully provided, and regularly refilled. After she had cleared the meal she joined him in the fireside chairs. Here was a type of man that she had forgotten existed. Most of the people she dealt with were devious, even on the police side. You had to read between the lines. Fred was plainly as straight as a die, and spoke so. As she listened to him, his loyalty to his sister shone through. He plainly did not know all the facts, and it would serve no useful purpose to enlighten him. She had to agree with Winnie about that. But as she heard his vivid description of the destruction of their family, she began to feel a new sympathy for Winnie. Her own grand-daughter had got involved with the dope gang because of the conflict at home; who was she to be judgemental about Winnie now? She was a victim too.

Fred accepted gratefully when Dora offered to accompany him the following morning. She knew the area and might be able to save him time; an offer about as genuine as King Herod's to come and worship the infant Jesus, but made with kinder motives.

The next morning Fred visited Winnie at the Infirmary and returned to Osler Terrace at eleven o'clock to take Dora up on her offer.

He returned from Winnie's bedside with yet more detail of the de Graafs' house. Winnie pinned great hopes on the de Graafs. They had been *such* friends. Winnie's visits seemed to have been mostly in darkness, and her description was more of the sumptuous interior of the property. Also the never-to-be-forgotten evening when Lorna turned up as a servant. All interesting, Dora pointed out, but unhelpful for identification from the outside.

Dora suggested that they went to Tennant Street first. They walked together slowly down grimy Icknield Port Road and Ladywood Road to Five Ways. Being Sunday, most of the factory chimneys were idle, but Fred still remarked on how dirty everywhere looked. Dora rallied to the support of her adopted city, and reminded him that without the arms made in Birmingham, his ships wouldn't have anything to fire. They'd have looked silly shouting "bang" at the Kaiser and Tirpitz. How boyishly he laughed. He was like fresh air to her.

Dora was not looking forward to the visit to Sarah Wakelam in Tennant Street. She was breaking her own rules and becoming emotionally involved with Winnie and Fred Pow. Perhaps she really was getting too old for the game.

Fred's clear, firm knock produced a result this time.

He did not detect the conspiratorial gleam in Sarah Wakelam's eye as she ushered him in, with a nod to Dora.

She told Fred over a cup of grey tea that she would like to help him. Trying not to catch Dora's tense expression, she smiled as she recounted her happy times when Winnie was staying with her. She remembered the smart young man who used to call to collect her. The whole street noticed him. That had been when her husband Mr Austin was alive, she told them with reverence. Since he had gone, she continued, she had struggled, and had to resort to caring for children during the day to supplement her income from her "paying guests."

"Miss Pow would have a job to recognise the place now. It was spotless when she stayed here." Sarah Wakelam looked into the distance. Dora presumed that she must have exceptional vision, or imagination.

Fred looked thoughtful as they left Tennant Street for the brisk walk to Inspector Lane's house in Wellington Road. To Fred's chagrin and Dora's relief, the Inspector was not in. He was not expected back until about half past two. Dora reminded Fred that they had to be at the Western Road House at about two to visit baby John, as they had promised Winnie. She would go and see the Inspector herself during the week, and let Winnie know anything that she learnt. After a slight hesitation, he thanked her and accepted her offer.

The Sunday relief clerk at the Western Road House was an insipid looking woman who gave the impression of being harassed, although plainly was not busy. She did not ask Fred for identification, merely tore them off a ticket and gave them brief directions. They arrived at the nursery and the smiling nurse on duty took them to John Pow. To Dora and the nurse's great amusement, Fred then looked at the baby and blushed, wondering what to do. Seeing his embarrassment, the nurse helpfully lifted the baby out of his cot. Inexpert as Fred was about babies, he could see that this was a perfect beautiful child. His corn blonde hair and pale-skinned face could have graced a biscuit tin. Fred uncomfortably accepted him into his arms, until Dora put him out of his discomfiture and took the baby for a spell. He was gorgeous, and responded to her gentle rocking with a smile. As she rocked, she casually asked the nurse if she knew if any adoption plans had been made. The girl did not; she was only the relief. But she had heard the Sister telling an interested visitor that there was a meeting on August the fourth about adoptions.

Dora replaced the baby in the cot, and only then did the one thing happen to take away the faultlessness of the baby. He coughed; a sickeningly familiar catarrhal noise, followed by heavy breathing. She knew that sound.

When they returned to Dudley Road Infirmary, the seed that she had planted, apparently casually, quickly took root. Fred told Winnie that he had not realised that the baby would be taken for adoption. He could not allow that to happen. He promised her on their mother's life that he would get the family to take on his upbringing. Dora told Fred that he must get the person who was to adopt the baby to write to the Boarding Out Committee of the Union at Edmund Street, and make sure the letter arrived in time to be considered at their meeting on August the fourth. Time was short.

Dora left the brother and sister together and went home to get the meal for herself and Fred. It had to be the rest of the stew, but Fred was a polite and grateful guest. She enjoyed looking after him.

When she watched his upright figure striding away the following morning to catch the 10.30 through to Plymouth she felt genuine regret. She had not given Mr Coote a son. He had never expressed the disappointment she knew he felt. Their daughter had never taken the place of "a lad who might play for the Villa." Perhaps that had conveyed itself to the unfortunate girl. Who knew.

Fred wrote again to his father. Three times he started the letter; twice it went into the bin. Finally he contented himself with a straightforward and, by his standards, tactful and polite plea for Winnie's baby to be brought up at Laurel Cottages until Winnie was well again, and able to look after him herself. Less diplomatically, he reinforced his argument by pointing out that the cottage was full of other people's children anyway.

To his despair and anger, his father replied that Fred must understand that, as he himself had pointed out so delicately, the house was quite full. Also, who was going to pay for the baby's keep? The plumbing business was not doing too well, and money was tight.

He wrote to Jack, suggesting that he and Jack could help, at least for a short period until Winnie recovered. The following Monday, July 31st, Fred received a letter to say that Jack could not commit himself to such an arrangement. He knew that Winnie was his sister, as Fred had put in his letter, but he and Alice could not be seen to condone her actions, which were the results of the 'fast life' she had led.

Finally, and desperately, he wrote again on Wednesday August 2nd to his father, begging him to save Winnie's baby from adoption for her. The child was his grandson. Surely he would help the blameless infant, whatever he thought of Winnie.

During the week following Fred's visit Dora visited Winnie with increased frequency and enthusiasm. She noticed with concern that as the days passed, Winnie's optimism began to fade.

Dora hid her anxieties about the time that Fred was taking to send the all important letter for the meeting on August 4th. When she had heard nothing by Thursday 3rd August, she took matters into her own hands.

Having ascertained discreetly that Caleb Chambers would be chairing the meeting, she wrote him a note, which she took to his well-known corsetry shop in the North Western Arcade. Chambers read the note, sucking his lower lip in a characteristic gesture as his eyes zig-zagged back and forth behind the powerful half-moon lenses.

"I'd heard you were giving up all this, Dora." He gave her an enquiring smile.

"Yes, sort of, Mr Chambers. This is not exactly my usual line of work."

Chambers thought again. Ezra Keeley had made a point of mentioning this case to him earlier in the week. He didn't like the way Keeley seemed to apply his undoubted administrative ability so zealously to hounding these helpless people. He had seen the sick mother and her little baby himself in the House, and felt sorry for them. It might be opportune to teach young Keeley a lesson.

Dora now had her head slightly on one side. He smiled.

"All right, Dora. Leave it to me." He grinned as she chastely pecked him on the cheek.

Dora would have derived considerable pleasure had she been at Edmund Street the next day to see the expression on Ezra Keeley's face when, after his damning presentation about Winnie Pow, the acting chairman had announced to the meeting that he had received information from a reliable source that a private adoption was likely. As this would obviously save the Union money and time, the matter was to be adjourned to the next meeting on Friday September the eighth.

Winnie's morale was now ebbing away rapidly. The deterioration in her mental state was hindering her physically. She was losing the will to recover. Whenever Dora visited she asked her, with increasing desperation, why Fred did not reply. Her self-pity, never far from the surface, began to emerge. She cried for her baby, and, increasingly, for herself. Then stories of plots by Lorna and others began to spring up. Dora started to dread visiting her.

On August 19th Winnie told her, with real terror in her voice, that John was now also in the hospital. Dora was prepared for this news. She had been to see the Workhouse nursery Sister following her visit with Fred. She knew the early signs of whooping cough. So did the authorities, the Sister told her, but shortage of available beds due to the epidemic and cost per bed meant that priority could not be given to a pauper child.

Dora attempted to reassure Winnie, but convinced neither of them.

John's admission to the hospital did reinforce Winnie's efforts to get fit and out of the hospital. She had lost most of the swelling now, and was with difficulty getting the leg muscles moving after their long redundancy. She knew that she must at all costs avoid a return to the Workhouse if John was ill. She was certain that if that happened she would never see him again. She asked Dora for advice. Dora suggested that she got Fred to write to the matron of the Infirmary and say that she had a home elsewhere to go to when she was discharged. The authorities would almost certainly accept this without question, as if she returned to the House she was one more charge on the rates. She could stay with Dora until Fred succeeded in his efforts to get baby John down to the family. In a way, John's illness might help, she reasoned. It would certainly delay any proposed placement of John for adoption.

On her return from the Infirmary Dora dashed off a note to Fred. She told him that the hospitals were swamped with the victims of the whooping cough epidemic. John could not get the treatment he needed in the Infirmary. She implored him to get his family's agreement to get the baby to Devon. Dora was sure that the only way that he would get the care he so desperately needed would be if they took over looking after him without delay.

At the stroke of 10am on Tuesday the 29th August Winnie left the Infirmary with Dora, having given the registrar's clerk Fred's letter to read.

Winnie amused Dora by stretching uncomfortably in her returned clothes, which were now several sizes oversize.

The clerk carefully copied down that she was leaving to live with her aunt, Mrs Edwards, at "The Cottage, Trinity Street, Barnstaple." Funny that Fred should have chosen old "Woodbine Winnie" for her escape. The old lady would have been surprised.

She smiled at this idea as they emerged into the clouded daylight.

They came through the impressive entrance to the Infirmary and Winnie stopped, momentarily dazed. A male pauper was mowing the grass. There had been a recent shower, and she drank in the pungent aroma of the cut grass.

She looked again. The person behind the old mower was not a male pauper. He was a man. He looked about the same age as her father, although he was almost certainly younger. Despite being engaged on one of the most prized jobs in the House, his face carried the depressed, crestfallen look that the inmates shared. A wave of pity crossed her mind.

As she cautiously limped forward, leaning heavily on her stick, she caught sight of the FEP Block. It glowered back at her, resentful of her escape. She felt its shadow creeping across the grass towards her. Panic seized her. She leaned heavily on Dora to propel herself towards the opening in the outside perimeter wall, and freedom.

She looked around gingerly at the traffic in Dudley Road. As she hobbled slowly and painfully towards Dora's house she kept imagining that people were looking at her. She felt as though she was still wearing the drab uniform of the House, not struggling clownlike in her own clothes.

She smelt the humid decay in the water as they crossed the canal bridge where, so long ago, she had gleefully thrown her 'Hawthorns' uniform. No-one would ever put her into a uniform again.

As she passed them, the mean, smoke-stained houses and corner shops of Icknield Port Road looked alien to her now. From behind them she heard the insistent metallic sounds of industry, and from time to time fingers of sooty smoke clouded her view.

She quickly became physically exhausted, and they had to stop several times on the short journey. Once a shabby local wag enquired where her war medals were. She couldn't prevent a grin spreading, despite her exhaustion. Birmingham, the grubby child with the smiling face.

She felt her mind pulsating with fresh energy. During her enforced pauses, the last three months ran through her mind like a newsreel. Since her entry into the apparent luxury of the 'Marlands' on May 22nd she had endured the submerged callous cruelty of that place, the austere surroundings of the Western Road House, and the enforced frustration and physical idleness of her fifty-four days in the Infirmary. She had survived all three institutions, and emerged the stronger.

She had received unkindness from some, and been almost totally ignored by those who could surely have come to her aid.

The few oases of kindness had appeared from the most unexpected sources, or those who could least afford to help her. The underpaid and overworked Sister in the FEP ward of the Workhouse; the penniless prostitute who, she had learned from the staff at the hospital, had died of blood poisoning from her premature return to her art a few days after her discharge. Poor, Fred.

Only her own steely determine to survive, almost to spite the world that had abandoned her, and her mother's love for her baby, had seen her through.

She looked down quickly as the sun, with unexpected harshness, dazzled her as it broke through the clouds for a brief moment. The cracked and hardened pavement beneath her feet reflected the cold anger she felt growing deep within her.

She had not expected support from her fashionable friends in Edgbaston. Even van de Leure himself had become a strangely peripheral figure in her mind compared to her own struggle for survival and her baby.

But her family she could not forgive. She would remember. She would pay them back.

Never again would she depend on those who professed to care for her and love her, and finish up in an institution.

The one institution that she could not escape from was her own mind. She knew that, according to the normal rules of conduct, and fairly basic religious teaching that she had received at Fremington and Barnstaple, she had committed wicked sins. But surely she had paid for her transgressions. Surely, if there was a forgiving God, he would look at her account and consider her debts repaid.

As they paused for the final time before turning into Osler Terrace she uttered a silent prayer and looked hopefully for a sign. To her horror, on the pavement, a little to her left, a large black crow was playing a macabre game with a wounded, flightless young pigeon. The pigeon would hobble away, dragging its damaged wing. The crow would wait, steel-eyed, before judging its jump onto the back of the other bird's neck. Winnie drove the feathered undertaker off with her stick. It stared at her insolently from the gaslamp standard, firm in the knowledge that as soon as she was gone, it was free to resume its deadly sport.

15

In some ways being on the outside was more of a frustration to Winnie than her recent enforced incarcerations. She found herself trying to contain intermittent spells of manic energy between long bouts of severe tiredness and depression. She could hardly eat or sleep. Her concentration was shot to pieces as she worried constantly about John.

Ironically, the contrived story of going back to Devon, invented to prevent her being returned to the Workhouse, now prevented her from taking the risk of being seen visiting her baby in Dudley Road Infirmary. Some days she would use her daily exercise walk to pass the hospital. She would stare up at the massive entrance, scan the rows of windows and will her baby well. He would know that his mother was as close as she could be. She did not linger. Dora had warned her that it was not unknown for a bored relieving officer to stop ditherers in the street and have them committed to the Workhouse or even the Asylum for "failing to give a good account of themselves".

She sorely tried Dora's patience. Dora had helped many destitute people. Most were a lot more humble than Winnie Pow.

As her strength recovered Winnie began to complain about just about everything, from the size of the rooms in the house and its inferior toilet and bathing facilities to the basic diet that she shared with Dora.

When she felt well, she did not feel well enough to assist Dora with her cart. When she did not feel well, she would sit sobbing in a pit of depression, sorrowing over her misfortunes, none of which were apparently her fault in any way.

Dora waited anxiously to hear from her contact that John's adoption by his grandfather had been approved. She could not understand the delay.

She informed Winnie on Tuesday the 12th that John had left Dudley Road for Selly Oak Hospital the previous day. They both realised that this offered them the chance for her to see John. With difficulty, Dora persuaded her to let her visit John alone first. She reminded Winnie that she was supposed to be in Devon. If she was recognised, they would take her back to the Workhouse. As usual, Winnie wanted action without delay, and Dora wearily set off for Selly Oak after her modest lunch.

She had to lie and say that she had come up from Devon to finalise the adoption arrangements to overcome the resolute refusal of the ward Sister to let her visit the baby out of normal visiting time. She was shocked with what she saw. The baby was a pallid colour, and was plainly a lot weaker. The cough now had the characteristic 'whoop'. Enthusiastic as the nursing was, he needed more constant attention than could be financed by a Poor Law Hospital.

Whilst she tried to resolve this, she asked the ward Sister if she knew where the other boy, Roy, was. The Sister told her that, with the whooping cough now reaching epidemic proportions in the city, they needed every bed, so Roy had been moved that very day to the next door Workhouse until permanent boarding out arrangements could be made. It had all happened a bit sudden, like. She had only noticed because Roy was so much darker than the others, and seemed a cheerful little soul, for all he couldn't walk with the rickets. Mr Wastlow in the registrar's office was dealing with it.

She found the clerk helpful and obliging, partly because, more by luck than judgement, she had called on Roger Wastlow at his quietest time of day. He was a pleasant man of military bearing. He had been given the job as registrar's assistant by a grateful nation as part of the policy of finding jobs for the returning soldiers at the expense of the women who had filled them whilst they had been away on their country's service.

Roger did not intend to die of overwork. He had learned from the Army that there was a lot to be said for being politely helpful, and not stirring up trouble.

Dora explained the purpose of her visit, and stressed how the proposed move for John Pow to Devon would save the ratepayers money.

The name Pow rang a bell, he told Dora. Time not being an issue, he put down his pipe carefully and looked through the 'in' tray on his oak desk.

"There it is, thought I'd come across that name just lately," he exclaimed.

"Ah yes. Here's chapter and verse from Union H.Q. Bad lot, the mother. Had two illegitimates. That young whippersnapper Keeley is after her. If he finds her, she's for the Asylum. She was a very lucky woman. Apparently there was a delay in the system, or something. By the time they went to find her, she'd done a bunk. Supposed to be in Devon."

He passed a copy of the memo to Dora. Under the formal heading she read:

Winifred, Roy and John Pow

Consideration was given to the case of the above named unmarried mother and her two illegitimate children, all chargeable at the House.
The Clerk reported that the mother had first come to the attention of the authorities in 1920, when she had given birth to her first illegitimate child, Roy Pow. She had subsequently absconded from the Salvation Army Rescue Home place provided for her lying-in.
She had been admitted to the Western Road House with her second son, John, on 16th June 1922. Both mother and baby had become unwell, and been admitted to Dudley Road Infirmary on 6th July and 19th August respectively.
Her other infant, (Roy Pow) had been admitted to the House in April 1921 suffering from severe malnutrition. He had subsequently been admitted to the Infirmary, returned to the House on 13th Oct. 1921, then fallen ill once more.
He had been in Selly Oak Hospital since 1st May 1922.
After discussion it was Resolved:

1) That Winifred Nora Pow, presently in Dudley Road Hospital, be committed on her discharge not to the Western Road House, but to the Birmingham City Lunatic Asylum for life (subject to the usual five-yearly reviews) as being mentally feeble under the terms of the 1913 Mental Deficiency Act.
2) That Roy Pow be placed in suitable boarded-out accommodation as soon as he was fit to be discharged from hospital.
3) That the application by Mr & Mrs F.R.J. Pow, grandparents, to adopt John Pow under the terms of the Poor Law Act 1899 be acceded to.

Dora stared at the stark indictment of Winnie.

Roger Wastlow suddenly looked up, and asked Dora what her interest was in the matter.

Dora had anticipated the question, and replied smilingly that she was an old friend of the family, acting on behalf of the grandparents. They wanted to assist discreetly as far as they could for the good name of the family, one of the oldest in North Devon.

"Very good, nice to know such good Christian people still exist," Roger Wastlow commented, as he loudly banged his pipe on the large ashtray.

"By the way, where is Roy Pow, the other boy?" Dora chanced.

"Oh, right, yes, I've just been trying to deal with that." Wastlow looked down and again read from the memo from the Birmingham Union. "Roy Pow is to be placed in suitable boarded out accommodation as soon as he is fit for discharge. The hospital told me that he was all right to move. Mind you, I think that was because they wanted the bed. I've seen him, and he looks pretty weak to me. Difficult to tell, mind, because he's so dark. Anyway, we tried to place him. But with him still not well and looking a bit coloured to boot, we couldn't find anyone, so we've put him in the House until we can sort it out. Ugly little cove. Nobody will want him."

Dora decided to assist her new friend.

"I *might* be able to solve your problem," she announced.

She was encouraged to see his eyes shine with interest. Anyone who offered solutions to Roger Wastlow's problems at no risk to himself was always worth listening to.

"Try Mrs Wakelam, of 154 Tennant Street," she told him. "If your people mention my name, I think she'll do it for you."

Wastlow thanked her profusely, and was making a note of the details as she left his office.

She knew she was taking a chance, but she still entertained the idea that Winnie might one day take an interest in Roy. If he was in the Workhouse, she would never be able to see him.

She returned to Osler Terrace and told Winnie that she had seen John, and he looked a bit pale. It might have been the reduced light, as the evening had been quite dark and autumnal. She told Winnie the news about Roy, and this produced a long overdue bout of guilt-driven hand-wringing.

Finally, at last, this vain, arrogant yet vulnerable young woman moved away the shield that had blotted Roy from her mind. Although she had ignored Roy these long months, the prospect of someone else caring for him produced loud indignation and floods of tears.

This belated display of maternal concern was too much for Dora, who told Winnie that she was all in, and retired to bed.

The following night, with great difficulty, Dora again persuaded Winnie that it would be very unwise for her to visit John, as if she was recognised, she would now be put straight into the Asylum, and she would never see him again. All she had to do was wait the short time until he was taken to Devon, and then she would be able to take him out as often as she wanted to the green fields and red earth that she had told Dora so much about.

When Dora visited John on Thursday she was horrified. He was plainly sinking fast. The nurse doubted that he would see the week-end out.

An agonising dilemma now faced her. If Winnie came to the hospital and was recognised, she would book her ticket for the asylum in Lodge Road. On the other hand, she might never see her baby again.

She decided that she had not the right to deny a mother that; they would have to risk it. In any case, Friday night was a popular visiting night, so they would be less conspicuous.

Winnie had not attempted a long journey since her discharge, but summoned enough strength and determination the following night to take on the walking involved both in travel, and down the long corridors of the hospital.

The hospital was lighter than Dudley Road, and had recently been redecorated and improved. This lifted her spirits, and by the time they arrived at the ward she was looking forward to seeing John. She peered smiling into his cot.

Dora caught her as she fell. She sat Winnie down with her head down between her knees. She asked the duty nurse to bring a glass of water, explaining that Winnie was suffering from the effects of pain-relieving pills.

Winnie was many things, but she was not stupid. She knew that she had seen the mask of death on her baby's face, and when they finally returned to Osler Terrace she dissolved completely; more completely than Dora could recall anyone in her long life.

Gone was the vanity and the irritating pretentiousness. The tiresome references to her family in Devon, who had become almost minor nobility in some of her earlier stories, now became bitter accusations, with lurid descriptions of desertion in her hour of need and "stabs in the back." She was calling to her dead mother amongst her ramblings, and also to her brother Fred, over and over again. Most strange were references to "the crow on the cradle."

Winnie had written to Fred the previous day. Her visit to Selly Oak now turned impatient anticipation into desperation. The following morning she wrote to her father.

Dear Father

My baby is very ill, and he must go somewhere where there is fresh air. Please, please write to me and let me know when you are coming to collect him. It must be soon, by Saturday if you can. I know I have done some wicked things, but you must help me. If not for my sake, then for your little grandson.

Please, Father, forgive me
If mother had lived, none of this would have happened, and it is not my innocent baby's fault.
Your daughter

Winifred

Winnie had taken the news that she was a fugitive from the Asylum with comparative calm. She almost seemed to think that it was a game of some sort, until Dora reminded her that she would be there for life if they caught her. She decided that her new status as a wanted woman meant that it was far too risky for her to go to Mr Haynes's shop for one of the stamps that he kept under his counter for regulars, and drove Dora from her chair to carry out this chore, and post the letter.

By now Dora had reached a point where at times she almost felt like arranging for Winnie to go into the Asylum before she drove her into it herself. She calmed herself and suggested that they visited John on Sunday afternoon. This was when most visitors went, and they should be able to see him without attracting too much attention.

As Sunday was a fine day, they decide to walk down to Five Ways and catch the train from there. Winnie wanted to test her leg, and until they reached Ladywood Road it seemed like nothing had ever gone wrong for her.

As she chattered, mostly to criticise other peoples' fashions, Dora marvelled at Winnie's apparent ability to detach herself and shut out all the devastation of her situation. She behaved as though her only care was that she was wearing an out of fashion hat. All that changed, however, when 'The Hawthorns' came into view. It looked innocent enough to Dora, but she could feel Winnie's terror as they crept past the high hedges of the front garden. Winnie actually cringed. Winnie then noticed the beat policeman on his leisurely Sunday afternoon round. She made them detour conspicuously across the road; an action which, had her name and face really been on a "wanted" poster in the police station, as she evidently imagined it was, would have got her arrested for certain. After this excitement, the rest of the journey to Selly Oak passed uneventfully.

They made their way to the ward as casually as they could, even walking separately sometimes.

John was in the same place, and looked little different. He was coughing less, but looked a little thinner in the face. They peered into the cot.

Dora was startled by a tap on her shoulder.

She looked up into the smiling face of George Raymond, relieving officer for the Ladywood area for the Birmingham Union. Normally a very useful contact, he was probably at this moment about top on her list of people she did not wish to encounter.

"Hello, Dora. What brings you here?" he enquired in his unusually attractive local accent.

"Oh, you know me, George. I can't always tell everyone what I'm doing and why." She hoped she didn't sound curt.

"Oh, by God no, I understand. And who's this young lady?"

"This is my niece from Worcester, Celia. She's staying with me a few days while she recovers from a bout of flu."

"Yes, you do look a bit under the weather, Celia is it. Still, you're in good hands. I've had many a nourishing cuppa with your aunt. She's something of an institution in this city, you know," he told the white-faced girl, his voice building up, and attracting glances from staff and visitors around.

The last thing Dora wanted was to be recognised as an institution at this moment. She silently wished the affable George Raymond in hell, and looked round furtively to give him the impression that he might be blowing her cover. Taking the hint, he wished "Celia" a speedy recovery, and went on his way.

The two nerve-shattered women made their way out of the hospital as fast as they could without being noticed. The return journey was accomplished without further incident.

For the rest of the day Winnie was noticeably quieter than at the start of their journey from Ladywood. If she had realised at last what it would be like if she stayed in Birmingham much longer, Dora reflected, it would encourage her to leave as soon as she could, which would be in both their interests.

When she returned home after her round the following day, she found Winnie framed by the open front door, peering anxiously out. With her sunken eyes and deadpan expression, she resembled an ailing bloodhound.

Being a Monday, Dora's round with the cart had been heavy going.

With difficulty she persuaded Winnie to give her time to take her coat off, and fill the kettle. It annoyed her intensely that each day Winnie knew the time that Dora would normally be expected home, but never once had she arrived to find the kettle simmering on the range.

Dora stirred her tea slowly. She read the heavy script of the well punctuated letter with gathering gloom and horror.

Dear Winifred.

I do not think you have any idea how much trouble you have caused your family.
I would like to help you, but I simply do not have the money for the journey. You surely know that Lorna is being married to Arthur Adamson Esq. this Saturday at 11am in Hammersmith in London. We have had to buy her a present. We are fortunate that Arthur's family have undertaken most of the expense for the wedding.
In any case, I am no person to collect and look after a small baby on a long journey. Maria will come if you send us the fare or a ticket. She knows about children.
I would suggest Thursday, the 28th. That will give us time to make the necessary arrangements. I'm sorry Winnie, but thats the best I can offer.
I did not ask you to lead the life you have, and nor did your dear mother, who I'll thank you to keep out of these letters.

Father

Dora waited for the eruption. It was not long coming.

Winnie became genuinely distraught. The neighbours, tolerant though they were, banged on the wall for some time before Dora ended Winnie's ceaseless ranting and almost epileptic behaviour with a resounding slap round the face. The noise was greater than the actual force, but at least the screaming gave way to a muffled sobbing. This in turn gave way to angry dogmatic statements that whatever else happened she would not hand her baby over to *that* woman.

Dora had listened at greater length than she had ever wanted to to Winnie's accounts of her father's seduction by the wicked Maria. As a woman and a mother, Dora could understand her feelings. On the other hand, she had really had enough of all this.

She decided that Winnie would not be persuaded in her present state of mind, and just switched off as the denunciation of Maria was followed by the more usual accusations of treason by her family, and the less than rational idea that Lorna had deliberately arranged her marriage date in order to prevent John being collected.

All Dora could see ahead was further delay whilst this feuding family squabbled. The baby would die, and Winnie would finish up in the Asylum. Dora decided ruefully that the only way she was ever going to rid herself of her cuckoo was at her own cost. She had not forgotten, as Winnie obviously had, that Winnie had sent her five pounds "for Roy" from Edgbaston before she went into the 'Marlands'. Dora had considered that she might keep this to offset the cost of Winnie's keep, but now she was prepared to sacrifice this modest sum to regain possession of her home.

Winnie was ecstatic when Dora produced the five pound note from the back of her bureau. Completely ignoring the fact that she had sent Dora the money for Roy's welfare, she waxed lyrical about this solution to the financial problem of getting John to Devon. She even chided Dora for not suggesting it earlier.

Suddenly she seemed drained of all emotion. She sat down wearily on the sofa, and spent the rest of the afternoon almost in silence gazing into the fire that Dora had lit to keep out the autumnal chill. As the sun ducked below the house roofs, the starker light from the fire painted the bags under her eyes. Her cheekbones appeared to project through her marbled skin. Dora was looking at her in old age.

The gentle humming and occasional crackling of the fire pushed Winnie and the world's troubles, which were now nearly the same thing to Dora, from her mind. She started as through the window she saw the gas lamp burst into light outside, and illuminate the lamp-lighter's bearded face. She pulled the curtains.

By the following morning some kind of calm had restored itself to Winnie's tangled mind. Dora considered it safe to take the initiative. She told Winnie that she would be going to Snow Hill after she finished her round and buying a 3rd class return ticket for the following Thursday. The ticket would be for the 7.00am from Barnstaple, and the 4.10pm from Snow Hill. This would give the person using the ticket over two hours in the city, during which time John could easily be picked up and transported to Snow Hill, by cab if necessary. She wrote the train times down for Winnie.

She told Winnie to write a covering letter to her father for Dora to post with the ticket on her return. Winnie continued looking at her from the bed with a pained expression.

Dora decided that all that needed to be said had been said and wended her way out into the gloomy dampness of the morning. Tuesday was a quiet day, and she returned at half past three to find Winnie still in bed. She had evidently decided that she was suffering from a wasting illness, and felt unfit to rise for the day. Judging by the larder, she had not eaten, either. The illness had prevented the letter being written.

Dora told her heatedly to write it straight away, as she had not stood at the booking office at Snow Hill for minutes on end to have the ticket sitting on the mantleshelf.

This brought an accusation of bullying, but she would not be deflected. She waited with growing impatience whilst Winnie ladled on protests about the choice of Maria, asking why Leah or Eva could not come.

Dora retorted that she did not now care whether Satan came to the station. It had to be resolved. It was time that Winnie realised that she had her own life. She meant to continue, but caught sight of Winnie's crushed expression. This was not the time. Flustered, she turned and went into the scullery.

From the parlour she heard the metallic scraping of the pen nib as Winnie scratched out the reply to her father that took away the little of her self respect that the Workhouse had not ground out of her.

Dora just hoped that the contents of the letter did not antagonise her father, who from the tone of his last letter was fast getting tired of Winnie. She breathed a sigh of relief as she posted the envelope into the grime-pitted post box at the corner of Osler Street and Icknield Port Road.

When she returned, she asked Winnie whether she wanted to visit the hospital that evening.

Winnie shook her head. She started quietly crying, claiming that she couldn't face it because Dora had got her in such a state. Dora should have understood better. She had not needed Dora losing her temper with her on top of the final humiliation of having to give her baby to Maria.

Having transferred her guilt to Dora, Winnie found the sensation of dozing in front of the fire very agreeable. The day's traumas retreated, and a warm spirit of optimism spread through her relaxing mind.

She saw them waiting on the platform at Barnstaple Victoria Road station, where it had all begun. Her father, sad-faced but forgiving and delighted with his beautiful blonde grandson.

Fred, in his uniform, smiling, triumphant, celebrating their triumph over all the odds against the great and the good.

Then she saw her son John, a little older, recovering quickly with the good, clean air of Devon, growing stronger and taller, more like his father every year. His father...

16

Strangely, the accidental intertwining of the lives of the two occupants of 37 Osler Terrace had become a catalyst for the great changes that awaited them.

Dora had provided Winnie's hiding-place from the forces that would engulf her and her baby if she stayed much longer in Birmingham.

Likewise, having Winnie as a houseguest had finally convinced Dora that the time had come for her to abandon her life in Ladywood and retire to her Severnside cottage.

The daily routine continued. Dora left early each morning. Each day the cart felt heavier.

Winnie rose late, long after Dora's departure to the market. The sound that brought her down from her bed in the mornings was the post landing on the cold brown lino in the front parlour.

She became resentful when Dora suggested that a visit to the nearby public baths might be worth the risk, preferring to refer to the lack of Dora's facilities in house.

Each evening they made their way cautiously to Selly Oak Hospital. Dora had warned Winnie to be careful in case the regularity of their visits became noticed. She would keep lookout as Winnie spent what time she could, depending on the staff around, looking at or, when she felt safe to, holding her baby. His coughing seemed to be more frequent and violent. She felt helpless as she strained against Dora's strict instructions not to call the staff or draw attention to herself. Dora complained timidly on her behalf, but was terrified that she would draw out some figure of authority.

On the morning of Wednesday the 20th Dora told a crestfallen John Legg that the van de Leure fiasco had put the lid on it for her. She had lost her enthusiasm. She had only stayed on to see if van de Leure could be nailed, and her grand-daughter Fay's death explained. She would not be persuaded.

Legg reported to his new chief that he would be using the new informant he had recruited recently. He had noticed that Dora was becoming increasingly negative. Life went on.

When Dora returned to Osler Terrace on Wednesday afternoon, almost as an afterthought, Winnie handed Dora a letter which had been delivered by the morning post. It was from Dora's niece Agnes Petch. Dora read it with interest and amusement. Agnes's letters were a source of refreshment to her. It was reassuring to know that there was life out there, and optimism, certainly if you were young. Dora was aware through her other activities that a social revolution had taken place since the War. Her generation neither took part in or understood it. Some tried to pretend that nothing had changed, but to Dora it was another signal that the time had come for her to retire.

Agnes had been the darling of the family until she had "got herself into trouble" by taking "comforting the on-leave officers" rather too far in the frantic whirl following the end of the War. She had then been shunned by her parents, and, like the rest of the world, it seemed, had turned to Aunt Dora for help.

It had been impossible to refuse the saucer-eyed requests, and she had repaid Dora's faith in her by making her own way, and was writing to tell her indulgent aunt of her latest enterprise. She had moved to London three years before, partly to have baby Joyce, and partly to join in the "endless party" that she assured Dora was taking place there.

Agnes had never been silly with money; she shared Dora's shrewdness. The result of this was that she was now renting a house in Torrington Square, in Bloomsbury, and was making the rooms ready for renting out to students and tutors at the nearby university. This project, she assured her aunt, would definitely enable her to repay the modest loan that Dora had discreetly made her to enable her to support herself and the baby.

Dora read the rest of the letter and chuckled. Attracted by the sound, Winnie, unable to comprehend that Dora could be involved with anything not directly concerned with her, asked Dora if she had been to the hospital to confirm John's discharge.

Dora told her that this was pointless until her father wrote and finally confirmed that he had received the ticket, and that Maria would be coming the following Thursday. She could have added that she had other things to do.

The weather being damp and still the following day, it was getting murky by half past four when Dora turned into the Terrace. She had had a productive day, and been sustained by the knowledge that the pieces were now falling into place to enable her to regain her home, but she was tired.

The post had arrived at the crack of dawn. She had recognised Frederick's handwriting, and woken Winnie. Winnie's euphoria at the confirmation of Thursday 28th had been followed by the expected reaction when she realised that Maria was coming. Dora had not needed any further cues to leave the house.

At Selly Oak Hospital Mr Wastlow could not have been more helpful. He had phoned Mr Curtis at Edmund Street whilst she waited, and established that as the committee had resolved to allow John Pow's discharge and, subject to medical approval, his adoption and transport to Devon, Thursday 28th September was fine. Mr Wastlow could give Dora the discharge ticket to save her returning unnecessarily again. She just needed to present that at the office when she arrived, he told her with a smile as she carefully placed it in her bag.

He also thanked Dora profusely for the tip about Sarah Wakelam. That had already been authorised. Really got him out of a hole.

So, all was now in place, she mused contentedly, as her home came into view.

For the first time for days, she felt relaxed.

A little later than normal, Felix was on her lap as she dozed by the fire.

Winnie's wheedling voice faded. As it did so, she was off to the little cottage. Soon she was sitting on the green garden seat watching the fast-flowing Severn gently elbowing the reeds on the bank with its muscular arms.

Winnie was mentally and physically exhausted. Listening to the torrential rain outside, she allowed Dora to persuade her that they would gain nothing by taking the risk of visiting John that evening. They would go tomorrow evening. It was only twenty-four hours. She was sure John would understand.

Friday 22nd September dawned.

It was the date for the official start of the autumn, but the sun had grown weary of its fight with the sulphurous atmosphere of Ladywood a week or two earlier. Its stunted children, the damp, dripping trees, were depositing their starved leaves onto the browned grass as Dora returned from her lengthy round.

She felt happy, almost light-headed, as she had now formalised the irrevocable decision that she had already mentally taken.

She had called on her friend Frances, who sometimes helped her with her round. Frances had expressed an interest in taking over the round. Dora had accepted the twenty-five pounds offered by her parents. She knew the round was worth more, but she had had enough.

Then she had called on her landlady, Mrs Turner, in Monument Road, and given in her notice on the house.

As she made her way back, Dora's mind travelled back to the early days. She and Mr Coote had struggled. They had been very happy together. He had been a good man, sober, unexciting perhaps, but a good provider. They had never had to go to her family for anything. She had been so sad and empty when he died suddenly, but after her period of mourning had found her new life surprisingly fulfilling with the flowers and the police work.

But she knew now, like the trees, that the season was changing. She looked at her hands. The fingers were already starting to split with the damp and cold of the early mornings.

She wondered what would become of her house guest. An idea formed.

The evening was warmer than some recent, and the darkening of the dusk was held at bay by the orange glow from the metal forges. As they set off for Selly Oak, Dora, slightly stooping as usual, comfortably held her pace walking with the wraith-like figure by her side. Her attempts at small talk not finding a response, Dora settled for near silence.

As they walked up the short approach to the three-storey orange-red block of the hospital, the last embers of the sun's rays left the slate roof of the impressive three-storey building.

Winnie seemed hesitant, even physically stiff. Dora became slightly alarmed. She did not want any unsolicited enquiries about their presence.

Their shoes seemed to tap and scrape as they made their way up the stairs to the ward.

The baby was not in his usual place. Dora looked into Winnie's face more directly and deeply than she intended. They both knew.

Dora had to act swiftly to avoid chaos. She shepherded Winnie into the nearby toilet and told her to stay there. She told her that if she felt faint, to put her head between her knees, but at all costs not to get involved with the staff.

She walked as calmly as she could to the Sister on duty. The news, though expected, still gave her a stabbing pain. Baby John had died quietly at half past four that afternoon. He had been taken to the mortuary. The whooping cough had taken him. Third one that week. The medical certificate would be available from about half past nine the next day, and the death should be registered tomorrow morning if possible.

She returned to Winnie as fast as she could. In the cramped washroom she cradled her head as she gently told her. Winnie accepted the news in silence. She looked helplessly at Dora. Dora steeled herself against her own conscience for persuading her not to visit John the previous evening. She led her quietly from the ward.

They left the hospital as silently as they had come, and returned to Ladywood.

Dora stoked up the slumbering fire, and both women sat gazing into the flickering shapes that lit the grate, Dora in her chair and Winnie on the small sofa.

Dora looked at Winnie's face, still, turkey-like, staring ahead, alternately bright in the reflected fire or dark in the room lit only by a gas wall jet. She went to the sofa and put her arms round Winnie's bony shoulders. She felt Winnie's frail body quiver, then vibrate violently as tears trickled down her emaciated cheeks.

Winnie whispered that she should have gone to see her baby the previous evening. Maybe she, as his mother, would have spotted something. It was a judgement. It was all a verdict on her wickedness. She should be the one lying in the mortuary, not her innocent baby, that had been in the world for less than four months. He had never seen the fresh green grass or heard the birds singing in the trees, or felt the warmth of the sun. Now he never would.

It was her family's fault. She knew from the frustration in Fred's letters that since his visit they had done nothing but argue and dither. They could have collected John in August if they had wanted. He wouldn't have got the whooping cough then. If they had only come for him the previous week, as she had begged her father, he might still be alive. But instead, he had argued about train fares, and gone gallivanting to London for Lorna's wedding. Why the hell hadn't he asked this Arthur Adamson's family to loan him the money, if they were as well off as he made out? She would never, never, forgive them.

Dora listened patiently as Winnie tried to work the pain through the top layer of her mind. Finally, she saw Winnie to her bed and turned in herself. Her brain was already working on a plan that she had had in the back of her mind since she had first heard the "whoop" in the baby's cough.

Waking early from habit, Dora left Winnie and was at Selly Oak before Oliver Hooper had arrived to certify the death.

She found Winnie up and surprisingly alert on her return.

Despite Dora's reservations, Winnie insisted on accompanying her to the Register office. The clerk copied the detail from the medical certificate, asking the necessary questions quietly as he proceeded.

John was spared the label of the Workhouse child by being put down on the death certificate as a resident of 'The Marlands'.

With considerable speed of mind, Winnie replied that she was a "Refreshment Room Waitress" and lived at 154, Tennant Street, her old address in those far off days when she had done her courting with John van de Leure.

Jonas Robotham signed the form and gave them a copy.

They emerged from the dark, wood-panelled office blinking into the daylight. The clock in the nearby tower struck eleven o'clock.

The sun broke through and lit up the scene of people hurrying about their business for a few seconds like the flash of a camera, before hiding shyly behind the veil of light clouds again.

Winnie wondered whether it was sunny at Hammersmith for Lorna's wedding.

They returned to Osler Terrace.

Winnie seemed at peace with herself. Whatever her inner thoughts, she was at least compliant and appeared calm.

"Who will arrange my baby's funeral?" she asked, without looking up.

Dora had been dreading the question.

"I had no choice, Winnie. I had to tell them it will be the Parish."

"A pauper's funeral," Winnie flatly commented.

Had Winnie not caught sight of the little blue booties that she had knitted, with much advice and cajoling from Dora, to take to the baby for his journey to Devon, she might have been able to accept the news with some composure.

After she finished crying, she told Dora that she must see the baby in his coffin. She would insist on this to make sure that his little body was not taken by the doctors. She had been told about this in the Western Road House. Old Helena had told her that two of her nine infants had been taken under the Anatomy Act, it was called. They didn't have to ask. She grasped Dora's sleeve and implored her to make the hospital promise that she could see John.

Dora had not the heart to refuse Winnie's request, although she realised that by the necessary contact that this would involve, more attention would be drawn to the macabre event, and therefore risk to Winnie. She told Winnie that she thought her fears were groundless, but she would sort that out when she went to the hospital on Monday to get the details for the funeral. She certainly hoped to herself that Winnie would be spared that one, final horror.

Sunday morning Dora slipped quietly out of the house. When she returned an hour later her eyes were glassy with rage, and she had plainly been crying. Consumed as she was with her own sorrow, Winnie noticed Dora's unusual disposition and was alarmed.

She had suggested earlier that they attend the local church, wherever that was. When she repeated the request, she could hear the barely controlled anger in Dora's voice as she agreed. She had never seen her in this frame of mind. Plainly she would disclose the reason when it suited her, and questions would certainly not be welcome in the meantime.

They walked the short distance to the gloomy church off of Monument Road.

Winnie could not absorb what the elderly Vicar was saying. All she was conscious of was how out of place she was with the rest of the congregation. One or two had nodded to Dora, but they might as well have been from the planet Mars to Winnie. Most looked like local shopfolk and clericals, many with their unwilling children alongside them.

They plainly had their own pecking order. Some had their own family pews marked. Winnie and Dora tucked in at the end of one of the back pews. From her seat she could read on the cold walls the names on the memorials to local worthies who had donated sums so that their eternal souls would be looked after by this stone and brick building and its incumbent. Her eyes moved to the adjacent stained glass window. The figures appeared to move in the combination of the last of the sunlight outside and the flickering candlelight. There was baby John, his cherubic face smiling back serenely at her. Did coming here mean that John would be there waiting for her when, finally, she was released from this living torment that she was suffering for her sinfulness. She asked God's forgiveness, for herself and her innocent baby, but, deep deep down, she thought that if there really was a God who was there to listen, he would have answered her long before this. Her Christian beliefs had always owed more to superstition than enthusiastic faith, and at that moment she became a confirmed sceptic.

Unusually for a Monday, Dora completed her round quite early.

She was glad not to be too exhausted, as she was going to need all the accumulated guile, and what was left of her charm, to get what she wanted, but she was determined as she arrived at Roger Wastlow's office.

"Come in, come in."

Roger welcomed his guest like an old friend, annoying his young clerk by telling him to fetch them a pot of tea without delay.

He accepted the bunch of chrysanths enthusiastically; they were his wife's favourite.

They settled with their tea. With uncharacteristic forcefulness he asked Dora why the unfortunate baby's funeral was to be "a Parish job."

"Oh, Mr Wastlow, it's so sad," she replied, producing a handkerchief for added effect.

"The family feel strongly that the circumstances are such that, given their standing in the county, they can take no direct part in it."

"Hm. And there's no-one else, to, er, help with the cost as friends?"

"No, sir." she sat uncomfortably on the undeserved guilt she felt.

She waited for the announcement that must follow like a bell clanging.

"Have to be the Parish, then, I suppose. Most unfortunate, most unfortunate." He shook his head sadly.

She nodded. "Will you be able to attend?"

This was the moment.

"Mr Wastlow, can I ask you something in confidence?"

"Well, yes." He wondered what intrigue this inoffensive old flower lady could be involved in.

"Well, the baby's mother, as you know, is not available."

"Just as well, from what I've heard."

"But her sister would be willing to come along to discreetly represent the family as long as nobody gets to know about it."

Wastlow did not have to think for long.

"Can't see a problem with that," he said, mildly puzzled.

He picked up the phone.

Replacing it, he told her in hushed tones that the funeral was to be at 10.30 the following day at Lodge Hill Cemetery.

"Is that too soon for the aunt to get there?"

"No. I can send a telegram to her this afternoon."

She went the final step.

"The baby's aunt has a strange request. I hope you don't think it's impertinent."

"Go on."

"Well, she wants the coffin lid unsecured so that she can see the baby."

"Oh, that old story. Parish funeral. Coffin full of stones. No, that's all right." He laughed heartily, and decided to add some information for Dora's benefit.

"The mortuary have made the coffin. Just bare wood, of course, planed one side. Very small, I'm told. Poor little mite weighed next to nothing at the end. Just too weak to resist, I suppose," he speculated.

"Glucksteins are doing the funeral under their contract. Normally there's no-one, and they just pick up the coffin from the mortuary and take it straight up to Lodge Hill. I'll phone them and tell them to be outside the hospital entrance in Raddle Barn Road at 10.15 tomorrow. You and this aunt can go up with them in the car. They'll screw the lid down when they get there. Lovely chrysanths."

Dora sipped the last of her tea demurely. She had kept her promise to Winnie. She thanked Roger Wastlow and left his office well satisfied. It was comforting to know that, even in her swansong, she could still exercise her arts when needed. Goodness, though, she felt tired. And her hands were sweating.

David Gluckstein sat waiting in the passenger seat of the mourners car outside the lodge in Raddlebarn Road. He wondered whether he was cut out for his latest occupation.

He had only joined his brother Leon full time in the funeral business reluctantly after the end of his involvement with Manor Aviation. He had helped out from time to time before, when the flying was quiet. Flying had been his real love. He had left the RFC in 1919 and invested his bounty towards the second plane. Gilbert and Bunny had convinced him when they told him how they charged what they liked during the railway strike, just before he arrived. With all these bolsheviks and anarchists about, it was only a matter of time before another strike, and then they would all make another fortune. But there had not been another national rail strike, and they had found themselves in increasingly ferocious competition for the diminishing contracts available.

That was when the South African had appeared. David had never trusted him, but Gilbert and Bunny had overruled his misgivings, and anyway they needed the business. Without realising it they had become dependant on him. Now he had vanished, and with him most of their work.

Thus it was that he was an unwilling undertaker's assistant. This was the first baby. It had been bad enough collecting the tiny coffin from the mortuary. Even the carpenter had remarked that he thought the coffin was the smallest he had made, 2'2" x 15". He had seen the little sleeping child curled up inside. He looked like a doll, perfect, unblemished. He had felt his heart race and thud, and was relieved when he had put the coffin on the back seat. He had the six screws in his pocket, and the small screwdriver to drive them into the pre-made holes once they got to the cemetery.

The sooner this was over the better. Leon said you got used to it, but he doubted that he would ever be able to be detached enough to get used to seeing a small child buried.

His nerves were still on edge and he recoiled when the window was tapped. This was no good; he must pull himself together.

He got out onto the leaf-strewn pavement, taking care not to slip as he did so.

Before he opened the rear door Leon carefully transferred the coffin to the front seat. David opened the rear doors and the two women got in and sat in the seats. He looked at the younger woman and could not prevent a raw wave of shocked pity crossing his unhardened mind. Her eyes were dry but empty, and her arms projected like a scarecrow's from the ill-fitting dark dress that she had plainly borrowed for the day. Nevertheless, she asked if she could have the coffin on her lap. He looked at Leon, who nodded assent, and he gently laid it on her bony knees.

The older woman carried a quite well made small wreath.

Leon eased the car smoothly into motion and they made their way up to the main Bristol Road. They waited while a nearly empty tram rumbled solemnly south along the central reservation. The crew were presumably on their way off shift and he could see them talking to each other on the front platform as they swayed gently along.

As they drove up Weoley Park Road towards the cemetery gates he studied the young woman's face in the car's mirror. She looked transfixed as she stared down at the tiny coffin rocking gently on her lap.

They passed through the wrought iron gates of the cemetery into the tree-lined grounds. Leon parked the car outside the cemetery offices just inside the gates, and David motioned the women to wait whilst he checked that everything was ready.

The indifferent registrar confirmed that the grave had been dug as ordered.

"Plot 378, sector C6." he announced flatly. "At least he's last in - shan't have to dig him up and bury him deeper."

Seeing the young undertaker's puzzled expression, he explained that 378 was a public baby plot dug to hold five. John Pow was to be buried above four other babies.

"The whooping cough's filling them as fast as we can dig them," he commented dryly, before turning to refill his blackened kettle.

As he returned to the car to complete the short journey to the grave David again wondered whether he was cut out for a profession where the small talk was about the details of graves.

They parked by the harsh-looking double-ended red sandstone chapel.

He opened the rear door of the car and gently attempted to remove the small plain box from the mother's lap. The lid was slightly open, and Winnie gave a last lingering look at her smiling fair-haired son. Gluckstein gently took the light weight from her. He discreetly shielded the coffin from her as he carefully screwed down the lid. As he lifted the lid of the oblong box to position it for the screws, he could not resist a final glance inside. The baby was still in the foetal position. His feet were now concealed beneath a pair of little blue booties.

David started as a dark shadow bathed him in blackness. He was momentarily dwarfed by the tall, lean figure of the Reverend Walter Stillwell in his customary homburg hat and long black coat.

Leon and David helped the two women out of the car. David wondered if the mother was going to pass out as she seemed to stagger, but she straightened up and took a step expectantly towards the open doors of the chapel.

Leon moved quickly to divert her path away from the chapel entrance, trying as he did so to avoid the disparaging looks of the two women entering the North Chapel. He explained to Winnie that he was sorry that the service for a Parish funeral could not include the cost of using the chapel.

They regrouped, and silently followed the ageing cleric out of the long shadow of the chapel. Despite the sunlight, Winnie felt suddenly cold. She followed the priest's swaying coat as he led them past the first two sectors full of well-kept headstones and neatly tended grass.

Across the path from the second of these was a single row of similar headstones. Behind these lay a large area of lightly clumped grass between mature trees. Winnie frowned as they walked across this wasteland. The uneven surface was only broken by a few crudely erected wooden crosses or simple wooden stakes. Some had names scrawled on them, others simply numbers. Here and there were graves roughly marked out with small stones, or rusting tins with a few fading garden flowers in them.

This, she suddenly comprehended, was the area reserved for paupers. David saw her reel unsteadily again as she realised that her son, the hard-won fruit of her barren love for John van de Leure, was to join these pitiful souls, the poor who were of no more value to the world in the ground than they had been above it. They were deemed unworthy even of their own memorials to say that they had once made the journey, however short like John's, from their mother's womb to this resting place. Winnie felt a numbness overcome her. David Gluckstein turned her gently to face the Reverend Stillwell as he indicated that he was about to commence the graveside formalities to despatch her baby. Slow censorious tones emerged from his thin, dry lips. The monotonous drone was broken only by the overstressed appeals to Our merciful Lady of all the Sorrows.

As she followed his exaggerated stares towards the hazy blue sky she heard him not. Far above, she caught sight of a small plane slowly making its way south.

Beneath it the beech tree nodded in the breeze. It shed a few of its reddened leaves into the grave and its upward facing boughs looked like strong arms to her, vowing to watch over and protect her baby while he lay beneath in the care of the tree.

Behind the tree, her eye found two young girls talking and laughing happily as they walked up the road on the other side of the railings, innocent noisy intruders from the living world, absorbed in comparing their new yo-yos.

She sprinkled the handful of earth over the tiny box. After a final look at the undersized gap in the ground that would forever be her son's resting place, she turned and looked back up the slight gradient to the rear of the double-ended chapel. It's twin windows became eyes that glowered pitilessly down on her, angrily reflecting the sun's flickering rays. Gently, David ushered her towards her tormentor.

The priest's heavy footfall echoed beneath the chapel's central archway as they passed beneath it, drowning the whispered conversations of the mourners waiting to enter the South chapel for the service denied to Winnie and her baby.

She almost tiptoed the rest of the journey back to the car. In the pale daylight David Gluckstein became sure that he had seen the mother's face before.

They returned to the hospital, no conversation having broken the silent circle of unspoken grief in the car. In the mirror, he again looked searchingly into the mother's face, with its fixed blank expression and tearless eyes. Where, and with who?

When he opened the car door again and helped her out, she looked deeply into his eyes and gripped his arm with such force that he was startled.

He suddenly saw the features of her face in a different way. The grief was breaking there now in the eyes, as her eyelids quivered in a vain attempt to stop the tears that were now rolling down her cheeks. But below that was as firm a mouth and chin as he had ever seen.

She might forget him, but he would never forget her.

David and Leon drove steadily back to the funeral parlour in silence. Outside on the forecourt was Leon's gleaming new touring car.

17

For the last time, the two women made their way back to Ladywood from the hospital.

Considering that Winnie had seen her future put together, and then buried in a pauper's grave, she surprised Dora by her apparent composure.

Dora realised that now that her baby was gone, Winnie might try and replace him with someone else. For almost the first time since her discharge from the Infirmary, she began to talk about van de Leure.

Dora listened with real pity as Winnie recited the events. How he seemed to gradually overcome his shyness. The enigma of the wedding. Their brief interlude of idyllic happiness. The letter. Fred's abortive visit to Wellington Street. The de Graafs.

When she began to talk about going looking herself, Dora had to remind her that she was still at great risk. One chance encounter and she would spend the rest of her life in the Asylum.

Her heart wrenched as she thought of the consequences if this still naive girl somehow found out the full truth about the man that she was now claiming she would follow to the ends of the earth.

She pitied any future suitor who had to compete with this flawed mortal whose mysterious disappearance had allowed him to join the Gods in Winnie's mind.

At tea time Winnie ate a little, for the first time for over a day, and tidied herself up a bit. Dora's daughter's dark dress, that Winnie had borrowed for the funeral, was replaced in the bedroom wardrobe. The pungent smell of mothballs, which Winnie had loudly complained about, was now free to resume its occupation.

Dora had decided to leave the announcement that she was planning until the next morning, but Winnie forced the issue by reminding her that Maria, or someone, would be coming up on Thursday. This journey would now be a waste of time. Shouldn't Dora send a telegram to Laurel Cottages and stop her. Perhaps they could even get a refund on the train fare.

Dora swallowed hard.

"Winnie, Maria will be coming on Thursday as planned."

"Why?"

"To collect your other son."

"Roy?"

Dora's eyes narrowed.

"Yes, Roy. I went to see him at Tennant Street on Sunday, and after seeing what it was like, I decided there and then that this was his one chance."

Winnie looked puzzled.

"But that woman's coming up for John."

"As far as she knows, she is coming up to collect a baby. Well, we'll give her one."

"But -"

Dora had no desire to test the depth of Winnie's composure. But she felt her temper rising at her guest's apparent lack of concern for Roy. Her eyes gleamed, and her face reddened.

"Winnie. You haven't seen what I saw on Sunday. *Roy is going to die if he is left where he is.*"

"Then there is your own position." Dora continued. "You cannot stay here. I'm leaving here myself next week."

"Where are you going?"

"I've got a small cottage down by the River Severn to go to. I've had enough of smoky old Brum."

"Can't I come with you?" Winnie asked plaintively.

The mild horror that the idea provoked in Dora's mind gave way to a sympathetic smile when she looked back at Winnie.

"No, I'm afraid not. Its only small, and I'm going to share it with my unmarried sister Gladys," she lied.

Winnie looked back at her with a slightly resentful look. Obviously, like her father, the Masons, Lorna, and the Poor Law Union, Dora was now going to arrange her life for her.

"Where will I go?" Winnie asked with a hint of indignation, as though this should have been Dora's primary concern, instead of her own selfish interests.

"I've written to my niece Agnes. She has just started a boarding house down in London. She needs a domestic. You won't be known there, and you can start a fresh life. I can't do any more for you."

"But I might not like it there. And John will never find me when he comes back."

Dora counted to five mentally.

"Winnie, when will you get this into your head. If you stay in Birmingham sooner or later the authorities will find you, and you will spend the rest of your life in the Asylum."

Winnie looked at her with a look of resignation as if to indicate that the predictability of life there might be a preferable alternative to the traumas of her present and future existence.

For the rest of the day Winnie retreated into her mood of self-pitying depression. Dora consoled her as the clouds turned to tears of grief and guilt. Occasionally she asked Dora questions about the riverside cottage.

Her reawakened interest in van de Leure surfaced as the evening progressed. Despite herself, Dora found herself gently prodding and prising. The most interesting remark that Winnie made was that she was cartain that she had seen the young undertaker before. She was sure that it was when she had been with van de Leure. Tantalisingly, she could not remember when or where.

Dora felt her investigative mind stirring, then reminded herself that she was about to retire gracefully and she could hardly press Winnie at this time.

By Thursday morning the flower cart had gone. Frances and her wheezing uncle had taken it the previous afternoon from the side of the house where it had been every night for so many years. She had offered to spend a couple of mornings with Frances, but they had decided that they knew all there was to learn. So she just passed the paperwork to Uncle Eli, took the money and left them to it. She hoped they didn't have second thoughts - she would be gone next time they called.

It felt strange not to have to go out early. She felt almost guilty.

She occupied her time getting things ready for her own move. Winnie was interested and proved a more than willing help with this. Dora realised that she was still sending her signals that she wanted to come with her, but Dora knew that this was only the appeal of security, and that it would disappear when her wings healed.

It kept her mind occupied, though. Whilst they worked, Dora encouraged Winnie to chat about van de Leure. What he had been like; their plans, the places they went, especially in the plane. Still nothing dropped out.

At twelve noon they sat down together to have a sandwich. Dora ignored Winnie's look of distaste at her unevenly cut slices of bread.

Winnie still maintained her implacable opposition to handing over her baby to Maria, even Roy, who she seemed to have had no maternal feelings for. Dora had tried reason, but now pointed out firmly that there was no real alternative. When Winnie persisted, she finally lost patience. She told Winnie bluntly that she would go to Snow Hill with or without her. Surely, in the name of pity, Winnie could see that her feelings must be put second to giving Roy a chance in life. Maria should certainly stand out amongst the other passengers from Winnie's description of her as a dirty old Welsh woman who stank of drink from ten feet.

Despite herself, Winnie's mouth spread into a thin smile.

They were talking quite normally as they waited on the platform as the 9.50 from Taunton pulled in at a minute to two. At first nobody seemed to be alighting, but out of the steam came a figure who was, and looked as though she was, from Winnie's past. Winnie felt her hostility rising, but Dora's presence prevented her making a scene. She just felt choked. Maria's appearance looked so bizarre in Birmingham. She was wearing the old pre-war suit and hat that served as her Sunday best. She looked like a character from a Christmas card or something. She started grinning nervously.

"I'm surprised that you think you've got much to laugh about," commented her visitor in her peculiarly Welsh west country lilt.

Dora ushered them away to a small tea room outside the station before any further unpleasant exchanges took place.

Maria showed a Devonian lack of urgency with time. By half past two Dora began to be concerned that they should get to Tennant Street. The ill-assorted trio walked through the autumn sunshine together.

Maria gazed in wonder as Dora pointed out the Council House and the Town Hall to her.

It was nearly three when they arrived at Sarah Wakelam's paint-flaked door. Dora knocked. For a heart-stopping, and seemingly endless, period of time there was no sound from within. Dora knocked again, louder. They heard a shuffling noise, and the door opened.

An elderly man in a cloth cap and muffler scarf peered out. He was chewing tobacco, and his discoloured bare gums showed as he called out that three visitors had arrived.

Dora knew who he was. She remembered Mrs Wakelam boasting that she had got her father out of the Workhouse to get his baccy allowance. He was listed as a childminders' assistant so that she could have more children to board.

Following a loud shout from behind him, he motioned them to enter. Sarah Wakelam was sitting in the chair between the front door and the fireplace. She was just as Winnie remembered her, except that she looked older and even more unkempt. Her clothes were ragged, her hair uncombed. Over her distended stomach a small, dirty child crawled. Its head was covered in the purple lotion used to control ringworm.

As she rose unsteadily to meet them they smelt a strong cocktail of drink and body odour penetrate the general acrid aroma of urine and stale tobacco.

On the floor of the front parlour, crawling around in rags, were three children. Two others were tied up in chairs.

Mrs Wakelam looked around her, like an animal seeking scent. She sensed the outrage radiating out from her visitors.

"It's no use being bloody critical." she whistled through her ill-fitting false teeth. "They pays me next to nothing. In any case, if stupid people didn't have them, they wouldn't be here, would they?"

Dora pushed herself between Mrs Wakelam and Winnie and Maria.

"This is the person I told you about Sunday, Sarah." She identified Maria.

"Oh! and look who else you've brought with you. Miss High and Bloody mighty Winnie Pow. If I'd known, I'd have dressed up for this."

"I've had the relieving officer here looking for you, you trollop." continued their host with aggressive indignation.

Sarah Wakelam swayed back as Winnie lunged forward with surprising agility.

She chortled triumphantly. "Maybe I should keep hold of her ladyship here and the young 'un until Mr Raymond calls. I'm expecting him later."

Dora was now getting thoroughly alarmed. She had not anticipated this.

"Now come on, Sarah, we go back a long way. Have I ever done you a bad turn?"

Sensing her position of power, Sarah Wakelam took her time.

"Well, no, but I can't afford to upset the powers that be, Dora."

Maria stepped in to try and change the unwelcome course of the exchanges.

"Can I see the baby? We're so looking forward to having him at home."

Whilst she considered the request, Sarah scratched her head, causing them all to flinch back. She then went into the back scullery and emerged with an almost naked child. He had plainly been playing in a fire hearth. His natural dark pigmentation was overlaid by the coaldust and ash over his hands and legs. She set him down on the floor. Winnie gasped as he crawled towards her using only his elbows. She shrank back as his arms sought her ankles. He grinned knowingly up at her. The trust in his eyes seared into her guilt.

"Rickets. Got it bad." Said Mrs Wakelam factually. "Ringworm too. Had it when he come here, mind. Proud of yourself are you now?"

Winnie began sobbing. Her whole body convulsed.

"Bit late for that now, my fine lady." Sarah intended to land every punch.

"We can see you've done your best with what they give you, Sarah" said Dora.

Mrs Wakelam studied Dora's face minutely for traces of sarcasm. "Miss Pow's family would like you to accept this to show their gratitude." Dora produced a small bottle of gin from her bag. She had hoped that this investment by the "Five pounds for Roy" fund could have been Winnie's unknowing show of gratitude to Maria, but the need to improve Sarah Wakelam's mood was now paramount.

"I hope you don't think I can be bribed," she said at length with grotesque coquettishness. Then she smiled, revealing again the tobacco stained false teeth.

"Cup of tea?"

Dora knew then that they were home and dry if they kept her sweet. She glanced forcefully at Winnie, and nodded assent.

"Charm, use your charm!" she hissed at Winnie, whilst their host was in the scullery assembling four chipped brown-stained cups.

"Nothing but the best for you, Dora." Sarah Wakelam joked, as she returned to the front parlour with a blackened metal teapot and the saucerless cups on a discoloured tray.

Winnie nervously laughed, trying to follow the run of the conversation and add charm as instructed. Dora and Sarah Wakelam both glared at her for different reasons.

Whilst the brown liquid was being poured, Maria asked Sarah if Roy had any clothes for the journey. Seeing her blank expression in reply, she told them that she would go to the corner shop and get him something.

"Well I never. What generous relatives you have, my dear." Sarah leered at Winnie.

"Cheer up now. Your child will soon be better with people like this nice lady to care for him," she mocked, with more effect than she could have known.

Feeling Winnie tense up, Dora gently laid a restraining hand on her arm.

When Maria returned, Sarah agreed to her request to let her wash and clothe the baby for his journey. Maria took Roy to the scullery. She almost retched at the smell, but persevered and warmed a saucepan of water on the grease-stained cooking range. Finding a small piece of discoloured hessian, she used this as an improvised flannel and began gently soaking the ingrained dirt from Roy's skin.

She froze as she heard a faint, but distinct, tap on a door, steeling herself to silence as two large black beetles advanced determinedly towards her across the brick floor of the scullery to investigate her activity.

The knock had plainly not been heard in the front room, and she could hear Sarah Wakelam's grating tones as she recounted again the idyllic period of Winnie's stay when her Mr. Austin was alive.

The sounds and smells of 154 Tennant Street invaded her senses. Through the crudely-taped broken window in the rear of the scullery, she could see the dilapidated wash house at the bottom of the blue-bricked yard. Adjacent to the scullery, the insistent dripping of water from an overflowing cistern indicated the position of the water closet, from which the stench was radiating out and gathering in the scullery.

Again she heard a knock on the door, louder this time. The noise in the front room died as Sarah shouted loudly to "Pop" who shambled obediently to the door. Winnie looked at Dora like a trapped animal. Dora put her finger to her lips, and tried to disguise her own pumping pulse rate.

"Why, hello Mr Raymond. I hope you bring a poor old lady some pennies."

The relieving officer started to enter, then seeing Winnie and Dora, stopped.

"Well, don't be shy. I'm sure my guests'd like to meet you. Come in." Sarah was enjoying this. Dora swore silent revenge.

"This is my old friend Dora Coote."

"Oh, I know Dora. Everyone in Ladywood knows Dora," he said cheerfully.

"I hear you're leaving us shortly," he said in an enquiring tone.

"Yes, I'm afraid the cart's got too heavy for me," she calmly replied.

Winnie felt the blood desert her face as George Raymond's deep piercing brown eyes turned to her.

"And how are you now, Celia?" he enquired sympathetically.

Dora looked hard at Sarah Wakelam, then at the gin bottle now exposed on the sideboard.

"Oh, much better, thank you."

"You know, I could swear that I know you from somewhere."

Winnie began to feel sick and faint.

"I've got it."

The room seemed to stand still.

"Its the family resemblance. You've got Dora's eyes."

Dora squeezed Winnie's hand. Men were such fools.

Rescue arrived from an unlikely source.

"I remember Aston Villa. Do you'm remember that fellah whom come on with an umbrella that time." Pop had decided to join the conversation, or, more precisely, to start his own.

"You'll have to forgive him, Mr Raymond. He can't hardly hear a bloody thing. Shut up, you old fool." Sarah shouted so loud that the veins stood out in her neck. The old man resumed his blank expressionless gaze. Conscious that he had been humiliated, he retaliated by chewing his tobacco with his mouth open.

"Would you like to join Dora and *Celia* here for some tea and cake, Mr Raymond?" Sarah Wakelam enquired demurely, brushing aside the deadly shaft from Dora's eyes.

George Raymond knew that peritonitis was quite a killer in Birmingham. This house was one very likely to add to the statistics.

"No, sorry my love, I must go on. Here's the packet for you to sign for. No problems?"

There was never any problems from Sarah Wakelam. That's why they liked her.

As the front door closed, Dora slipped through into the scullery. Maria was nursing Roy in her arms. He was now clean and clothed in the cheap cotton towels that Maria had purchased for him. Through the thin material Dora could see the blood beginning to seep through from his many sores and scratches.

The two women looked down at his smiling face. The tidemarks of dirt were still visible around his eyes, ears and hair, despite Maria's sterling efforts.

Maria was looking quizzically at Roy.

"Baby's hair must be awful dirty. Remarkable thing, I was told he was corn blonde."

Dora was used to the indirect speech of the Welsh. She looked into Maria's face. Bloated, unattractive, certainly. But she also read natural kindness, sympathy and affection. As Maria began to return Roy's smile she felt confident to continue the coded exchange.

"Yes, the air round here is very polluted, as I expect you've noticed."

"Most advanced for a baby a few months old, too."

Dora wondered whether to enlighten Maria, but decided to continue their oblique conversation.

"Yes, Sarah Wakelam's food must be more nourishing than it looks."

Maria looked at her with a firm gaze. She saw the plea in Dora's eyes.

"Oh, don't worry. I'm not leaving him here in this rathole. You can tell me the story one day. Maybe she will, who knows. Her father's going to have forty fits when he sees the state of him. What's his name?"

"He was christened Roy."

"Well, that's as good as any. We'll call him Roy Christopher, after St. Christopher, as he's a little traveller."

Roy's eyes closed contentedly as she gently rocked him.

Dora led Maria back into the front parlour. Winnie's eyes narrowed as she saw Maria nursing her child, but she was too racked with fear and nervous exhaustion to start a scene.

Pop was still chewing loudly on his baccy.

Sarah was nursing another grubby waif, and made no attempt to get up as Dora showed her the authority from the Birmingham Union for John Pow's discharge that she had obtained from Roger Wastlow at Selly Oak.

Sarah nodded sagely, then hesitated. Dora caught her breath and felt Winnie's bitten nails dig into her arm.

"Can't find me glasses. Same old trouble." Sarah's arms flailed in futile arcs on the floor by the chair. "Oh well, I suppose I don't need to read the small print. I can see it's from the Union."

Dora knew it was an act. She had noticed that Sarah had signed for her money with a barely legible signature. She could not read or write. She would not spot the change of christian name.

It was well past three o'clock and, Dora told her sadly, they must leave her excellent hospitality and go to the station. She could be as sarcastic as she liked now that the relieving officer had gone. An inadequate revenge, but the best that she was likely to achieve.

The experience had united the three women like travellers who have been involved in a disaster. After they emerged into the weak sunlight, and walked down Tennant Street and Broad Street, their brief unity of purpose was sustained. They felt almost light-headed with relief.

Dora listened as Winnie and Maria maintained their truce and talked to each other with cool politeness.

She noticed that Winnie made no attempt to ask Maria if she could carry her child.

After their ordeal at Tennant Street, they all felt dirty and clammy. The day was damply humid, and the heat brought out the dozing but persistent fly population for a last sunbathe. Dora decided that they would cut down Edmund Street to get back to the station. The tall, handsome buildings would throw shadows over them, and keep the frail child cool in his rags.

As they passed the offices of the Birmingham Union, from above them, in his office on the first floor, Ezra Keeley observed them curiously from the window. There was something odd about the group he saw below. They looked inconsistent. He hated inconsistent things. He frowned, and went back to his desk.

Soon the impressive facade of Snow Hill station came into view. They went down on to the platform together. After ten minutes the train arrived, and Winnie said an unemotional goodbye to the infant and the stepmother that she plainly wished had never entered her life.

Even as they left the station, she was talking to Dora about the fashions of other passengers.

Dora could hardly believe it. It was as though Roy had never existed to Winnie. He might have been buried in Lodge Hill Cemetery with her other baby for all the feelings that she seemed to have for him.

But one day he would return to her. One day, far from Birmingham, Roy would crawl back along the floor of her mind, and seek again in his mother's eyes the love that she had denied him.

Two days later Winnie was down at a station again, this time dark and cavernous New Street. She gave a wistful glance as they passed the nearby hotel with the red uniformed porters where she had lain in Room 112 with Roy's father that night so long ago.

This time she was at the station on her own behalf to catch the eleven-fifteen express to London, where she was to meet Agnes Petch at Euston. She had winkled the rest of Roy's £5 and a little more cash out of Dora for her fare to London and to go shopping. As always, she had decked herself out well for the amount she had spent.

The train was late, provoking Winnie to complain that this railway was not as good as the Great Western.

They began to run out of small talk. Dora wished the train would arrive. Suddenly, Winnie informed Dora that she had remembered where she had seen the young undertaker's assistant.

"He was at the undertakers once when John called there to deliver the special coffins - the babies' coffins," she excitedly told Dora.

"I remember because I got bored waiting and followed John into the chapel. John and that older brother were looking into an open coffin. I don't know what they were doing, but I startled them, and a lot of powder fell onto the floor. They were ever so cross, and John shouted at me to get out."

"White powder?" enquired Dora.

"White, yes, very white, white as snow," replied the girl simply.

"White as snow," repeated Dora to herself.

She smiled to herself. What an irony.

The girl had shared her home for four weeks and only now, whilst they waited for a train to take her to London, did it emerge that she held the keys to the information that so much fruitless time and effort had been put into finding out.

"Do you know where the special coffins came from?" she asked casually.

"Oh yes, of course. They came from abroad. John used to collect them from the place near Liverpool about once a month and fly them in. He said the local makers couldn't get the type of wood that these were made from. They were special orders. I often carried them on my lap during the flight home."

"Oh yes, they were certainly special orders," thought Dora. If Winnie's baby had not been buried as a pauper, he'd have stood a good chance of being buried in one of the "special orders" brought from Liverpool on his mother's lap.

She studied Winnie. Dressed in her new clothes, she looked sophisticated. She was unrecognisable as the waif who had stood at the graveside four days earlier. Her face was fleshier; her posture straighter. This was a survivor.

Had she any idea what John van de Leure was up to? Dora doubted it. Was it worth, even now, taking her to John Legg?

Whilst Dora agonised over this, the drab-looking train with its black engine thumped its angry way into the station.

Winnie smiled, a little sadly. The carriage door swung open.

There was a frantic exchange of flags and whistles, and then the train was on its way south.

Dora exchanged waves with Winnie, stopping only when Winnie's small white glove disappeared into the smoke-filled cutting.

She returned to Osler Terrace.

She would allow herself the luxury of a lie-in tomorrow, then she would give her neighbours and friends the bits and pieces that she was not taking to the cottage.

She looked into the fire and stroked Felix. He had never liked the intrusion of Winnie into his home, with her high-pitched voice. Now he knew that she had left, he had resumed his customary position on Dora's lap and he purred pleasurably. The correct order of things had been restored. He wondered why some of his furniture had been moved around.

"Life holds a few surprises yet, even for you, Felix," she told him as she stroked his chin. He continued purring. He trusted her.

Dora wondered how Winnie would get on in her new life. She did not feel unhappy now to see her go, and was confident that Winnie would soon be writing letters from Agnes's giving graphic accounts of her latest adventures.

She wondered how Winnie's poor weak little child would fare. The only certainty was that he would be better off with the despised Maria than left to the tender mercies of Sarah Wakelam.

She carefully took the framed photograph of her grand-daughter Fay from the drawer where it had lain since Winnie had been in the house. She could not have risked Winnie recognising the other figure in the picture. The blonde South African with the Prince of Wales smile, easily ecognisable, even in flying gear.

She felt her hatred rising again as she looked at his sickly grin.

She gently kissed Fay's likeness, taking care to avoid van de Leure, then packed the hotograph in her case of personal possessions.

She could not wait for Monday, when the van would come to take her to Bewdley. She felt uddenly younger.

Once she had lost sight of Dora in the smoke and shadow of New Street station, Winnie started er new life with fear and apprehension. She felt alone and exposed.

She was sure that all around were watching her, and checked her clothing. She sank further nto her comfortable seat.

She scrutinised her fellow passengers earnestly, carefully avoiding catching the eye of anyone who resembled her idea of a Poor Law relieving officer, official of the Asylum or plain clothes olice officer, any of whom would be certain to recognise her, stop the train and take her from it n handcuffs.

She even wondered whether to secrete herself in the toilet at the end of the corridor until the rain had left the Birmingham area, but found herself glued to her seat.

The train was nonstop, so she only briefly saw the place names. She caught a glimpse of Coventry, brooding and sinister, then they were out of the industrial Midlands.

Her spirits picked up. She looked out of the window more. The grass looked greener, the very air ten shades lighter. They passed damp-looking fields full of cattle or sheep. Not the rolling hills or red earth of Devon; a flat, featureless sort of countryside, but she was glad to see it. She had almost forgotten such places existed.

The lights came on and the train dived into a long tunnel. Then they were out into the sun again, hurrying along the chattering rails, as though the train itself wanted to get away from the grime and squalor behind them.

As they passed a great railway carriage works her mind went back to the very early days at Wilsons, when she had gone with samples to the railway works.

The rhythm of the train and the gradual release of tension relaxed her, and sent recent, more painful images into her daydream to interrupt the earlier innocent recollections. She felt her head jerk from its nodding. The young man with a handsome black moustache and immaculate wavy black hair was smiling at her from the end seat opposite her in the compartment. She had noticed him earlier.

"Bad dream?" he enquired, smiling, and revealing perfect white teeth.

"No, no, not all of it," she stammered enigmatically.

"Fancy a cuppa in the dining car?"

She considered for a moment, then graciously accepted.